"Every time I think about this story, I fall in love all over again. I adore everything about Liz, and I was rooting for both her and Tobin the entire time. I laughed, I cried (several times), I swooned and fell in love as they worked their way back to each other. These beautifully unique characters jump off the page and into your heart. The story is real, raw, fresh, and original. It brims with hope and fills my romance-loving soul."

—Helena Hunting, *New York Times* bestselling author

"If I loved this book less, I might be able to talk about it more. Maggie North's *Rules for Second Chances* is a beautiful marriage-in-trouble romance about seeing yourself reflected in someone's starry eyes but needing to find yourself first. *Yes, and* . . . It's also a novel about the power of improv to learn how to live in the moment and reconcile your past with your future. *Yes, and* . . . North's poignant sentences live in my body as a physical ache. When it comes to anything North writes, I will always be saying *Yes, yes, yes.*"

—Alicia Thompson, bestselling author of *Love in the Time of Serial Killers*

"*Rules for Second Chances* is a brilliant and unexpected debut. I was taken in by the writing, then the humor, and soon I was fully engrossed in this exploration of the subtle ways we hurt the people we love. I adored this book, and I know that I'll read it again."

—Annabel Monaghan, author of *Nora Goes Off Script*

"*Rules for Second Chances* is a breathtaking, deeply romantic story about the second chances we give to love, each other, and most important, ourselves. Maggie North has the singular ability to hit you with truths that are at once hilarious and aching, stark and soft, painful and necessary, and she writes Liz and Tobin's journey with an obliterating tenderness I felt in every corner of my heart. This book and its author land effortlessly among my all-time favorites."

—Jessica Joyce, *USA Today* bestselling author of *You, with a View*

"*Rules for Second Chances* is a wildly original take on the marriage-in-trouble trope, full of beautiful prose and visceral vulnerability. Maggie North is a capital 'T' talent."

—Rosie Danan, author of *The Roommate*

"Achingly tender, beautifully written, *Rules for Second Chances* is an unflinching marriage-in-crisis romance that hinges brilliantly on both humor and heart. An ode to neurodivergence; self-discovery; the work and wonder of a vulnerable, intimate long-term partnership; and the magic of making an authentic life with those we love."

—Chloe Liese, author of *Two Wrongs Make a Right*

"Delightful and sensual, Maggie North's *Rules for Second Chances* is a witty, one-of-a-kind romance, lush with tenderness and tension to make this a compulsive read. Maggie is one to watch!"

—Ruby Barrett, author of *The Romance Recipe*

"A witty, sparkling delight. Essential reading for fans of second-chance romance. Maggie North puts words together in the best way possible. *Rules for Second Chances* is slow-burn perfection!"

—Stephanie Archer, bestselling author of *Behind the Net*

Rules
—for—
Second
Chances

MAGGIE NORTH

ST. MARTIN'S
GRIFFIN
NEW YORK

First published in the United States by St. Martin's Griffin, an imprint of St. Martin's Publishing Group

RULES FOR SECOND CHANCES. Copyright © 2024 by Maggie North. All rights reserved. Printed in the United States of America. For information, address St. Martin's Publishing Group, 120 Broadway, New York, NY 10271.

www.stmartins.com

Designed by Omar Chapa

Library of Congress Cataloging-in-Publication Data

Names: North, Maggie, author.
Title: Rules for second chances / Maggie North.
Description: First edition. | New York : St. Martin's Griffin, 2024.
Identifiers: LCCN 2024000477 | ISBN 9781250910127 (trade
    paperback) | ISBN 9781250289629 (ebook)
Subjects: LCGFT: Romance fiction. | Novels.
Classification: LCC PR9199.4.N677 R85 2024 | DDC 813/.6—dc23/
    eng/20240111
LC record available at https://lccn.loc.gov/2024000477

Our books may be purchased in bulk for promotional, educational, or business use. Please contact your local bookseller or the Macmillan Corporate and Premium Sales Department at 1-800-221-7945, extension 5442, or by email at MacmillanSpecialMarkets@macmillan.com.

First Edition: 2024

1   3   5   7   9   10   8   6   4   2

For Jackson Thunderbolt and Mackenzie Thunderbolt-North, who successfully argued that since I got to choose my pseudonym, they should get to choose theirs, too.

And for the autistic authors and advocates who speak out about every part of autistic life—the struggle and the injustice, yes; and also the community, the connection, and the joy of it. I was so lucky to find your words exactly when I needed them.

Author's Note

Dear Readers,

This book features neurodiverse characters living in a world that, much like our own, was not designed for them. I hope I've shown the beauty and power of neurodiversity while also acknowledging the reality of life as a person who may not be accorded the same respect, opportunities, accessible self-knowledge, and ease of moving through the world as other people.

No single character can possibly represent the incredible variety and uniqueness of all neurodiverse people, but I've done my utmost to write Liz's journey with the authenticity, care, and heart we all deserve, drawing from my own lived experience as well as the insight of neurodiverse readers.

Please visit www.maggienorth.com for a complete list of content considerations.

Chapter One

Action begins with the disruption of a routine.

—Truth in Comedy

The first minute of my thirtieth birthday party is everything I want it to be.

My mother-in-law's house spills noise and warmth when I ease open the front door. Gusts of laughter cast an unexpected glow over the chic, pale (and frankly sort of sterile) decor, which has always given me the feeling of sharpened corners lurking everywhere. Tonight, bright GORE-TEX coats and trail shoes trashed by April mud soften the foyer's pointiness. Much nicer.

Though I'm late, I dawdle my way through the jumbled footwear, seeking a patch of floor to toe off my boots.

This is my favorite part: right before I join in. Before the classic introvert's fantasy of effortless conversations lit by the perfect tipsy buzz turns into the real thing: conversational faux pas that morph into awkward pauses that tumble me down bottomless crevasses of social death.

Before I remember how I'm always so lonely at these parties.

This time will be different, I tell myself, sliding into my black flats. I'm thirty, ugh; it's past time I sorted out my socializing phobias. Besides, I'm interesting. I have topics of conversation picked out. How hard can it be to hold a glass of champagne and say something sparkling?

I pull my shoulders out of their self-defensive hunch and practice a smile that goes up on both sides, like both halves of me are happy to be here. None of the right-side-up, left-side-down smile that makes people ask whether I'm joking or serious.

"Liz! I can't believe you're late to your own birthday." My sister, Amber, sweeps into the foyer to rummage through the outerwear. She looks beautiful with her streaky blond hair twisted into a pretty, puffy low bun. "Or maybe I can. Why did you let Tobin throw you a party, anyway? He should know you don't like them."

"I like parties," I lie. And then, more truthfully, "He asked if I wanted a party, and I said yes. And I'm late because I got stuck at work." Combing through my "ideas" folder in a sweat, pummeling myself into reaching for the brass ring one last time. "And then Mom called right as I got here to sing 'Happy Birthday,' and insisted on an encore when Dad got on the phone. Why are you leaving? It's barely six."

"Eleanor's babysitter bailed. I have to pick her up from aftercare and take her home for dinner."

"You could bring her here."

She raises an eyebrow. "Ha. The only person who hates parties more than you is my kid."

"I *don't* hate parties, Amber!"

"Sure. You plaster yourself to me and your husband all night because you're having so much *fun*. I wish you wouldn't do this to yourself, Liz. See you tomorrow night for auntie/niece time. Five thirty sharp," she adds, swirling out the door in a gust of April cold.

I'm sure she meant to wish me a happy birthday. She was stressed and distracted; it doesn't mean anything. Still, a chill wraps around my throat. Our parents are wintering in Arizona, and my best friend, Stellar, is away, so I was counting on Amber to smooth out any rough spots in my Very Successful Party. She's never much liked me following her around, but we're sisters, so she has to include me in the conversation when I materialize at her elbow.

But she's gone. I'm down to just my husband as a social haven, I guess.

I hear him before I see him: a golden voice drifting down the stairs, slightly ahead of the golden man himself. Tobin Renner-Lewis is the human version of a cloudless day on a coastal mountain: longish, dark whisky hair still tipped with last summer's sunshine, Viking cheekbones, rosy winter tan, eyes of glacier blue. His tall, lean-muscled frame speaks to a life spent paddling and mushing and lifting heavy things.

He looks unusually serious, a softcover textbook in one big, rough hand. Probably one of the business books he reads but won't talk about.

"I don't know if I'm in one place enough to get this going," he says, phone to his ear. "But I appreciate the offer. Can I have a couple days to think?" There's a tempered hope in Tobin's voice I haven't heard in a long time. I melt against the wall, eavesdropping harder.

Whatever he hears prompts a grin with a quirk that hooks my heart. I forgot he had that smile, rueful and real. For a second, I don't think about how far apart we've grown, and only remember the man I fell in love with underneath the summer stars.

Everything about Tobin changes when he sees me, morphing from something true into something perfect. A photograph of stars instead of the real thing.

"DIZZY LIZZIE!" He tucks the book under his elbow and vaults one-handed over the railing. A gentle breeze of knockout-level pheromones and cedarwood beard oil wafts across my body. I feel it right through my coat, which I'll have to return because this shit was supposed to be windproof.

"You got my note?" He knocks my toque from my head with his hug. I try to be soft in his arms. Happy the way he wants to feel we are, pretending our hearts have no doors we use to lock each other out.

"I thought this was going to be at our house." When he offered to throw me a party, I mostly said yes because people think you're weird if you don't want to celebrate milestone birthdays in the loudest possible way. Also, I may have imagined a magical fantasy glow-up party that would make me belong, like in *13 Going on 30*. Perhaps I secretly hoped he'd decorate with a "Central Park in spring" theme, after my beloved Nora Ephron rom-coms. Then I'd know he saw straight into my heart, and we'd be okay again.

"It was, but my mom thought it made more sense not to carry everything next door."

"Oh."

"Wait till you see the food! Mom outdid herself. I'll put in a day in her garden to pay her back."

I tamp down a hot flare underneath my ribs. He could've ordered food. And the party didn't have to be scheduled in the eighteen hours between him finishing one dogsledding trip and starting the next. But he wanted to celebrate on my actual birthday, even if it meant spending one of the few days we have together working for his mom.

"Let's go." He zips me out of my coat. "I invited a couple of the new guides. Couldn't leave them out, you know?"

"Sure. Wait. Do I look okay?"

"You look perfect." He admires me like I'm not the camouflage-colored mate to his bright-feathered goldfinch, my hair and eyes and freckles all the common copper brown of a tarnished penny.

"Are you sure?" I smooth damp palms over my black skirt. My blouse is builder beige, the ideal color for people to project themselves onto during the successful conversations I will be having tonight.

"You look *perfect,* Diz." He puts his arm back around me, hollering, *"Birthday babe's heeeeere!"*

The guests cheer for way less time than I anticipated; I wave half a second after everyone turns back to their conversations. Underneath my high collar, my neck itches. Stress hives already. It's fine. Amber's gone, but Tobin will stay with me, and people love—

"Tobin. I need you in the kitchen, *schatje.*" My mother-in-law, Marijke, is looking particularly tall, blond, and Euro-hot in a white ensemble trimmed with silvery faux fur that matches her current line of handmade children's wear.

It's hard to believe I once dreamed of having intimate, huggy relationships with my in-laws. Marijke bakes and sews and looks like Heidi Klum, but huggy, she's not. I'd say Tobin got his looks from her, if his dad, Tor, weren't also blessed with truly regrettable physical attractiveness.

"I can help, Mrs. Renner." I look forward to pronouncing her name correctly—Ma-RYE-ka, rhymes with "I like ya"—the second I'm permitted to use it. In the meantime, maybe I can sneak into the kitchen. I could pass a tray of hot appetizers using a trusty script: "Spring roll? Have a napkin." Later, I could ask how people liked the food. It's not exactly a conversational dream come true, but it's something to say.

"Nonsense. Enjoy your party." She sweeps her son away.

Now I'm truly alone. I catch myself rubbing my fingers to-gether and stuff my fists in my pockets in a way I hope looks ca-sual. Alone is *good*. I should stop relying on Tobin to grease the social wheels for me. I'm sure I can do this on my own. And if this is my year to enter—no, to *win*—the company's pitch competition, I *have* to do this on my own.

I activate a favorite party ploy: browsing the food table while I fake-casually scan for a conversational circle with a gap where I might fit. There's a tight cluster of guides (Tobin's underlings, since he became head guide at West by North, the wilderness adventure company where we both work), some neighbors discussing zon-ing ordinances, and a few of my colleagues from head office. Not promising.

Naheed, our head of marketing, wanders over to the sandwich station. "Hey, Liz. Tell Tobin he throws a great party."

Okay. It's happening. Conversation, take one. "I will! Thanks for coming."

"He's home for one night between trips, right? Better make it count. Lady in the streets, freak in the spreadsheets, am I right?" Naheed never runs out of pointed one-liners about popular, out-going Tobin being married to me, the operations coordinator—the human version of a calculator.

"Ha. I get it." I like my job, but not the way it gets pegged as boring work done by boring old me. But even if my laugh is fake, Naheed makes the dude bros in the C-suite chuckle for real. I should pay attention to his technique. "That reminds me. Can I ask you—"

"Happy birthday, Liz. You entering the pitch competition again this year?" Naheed's marketing minion David Headley has followed his boss here, as usual. He's one of the people who said he'd definitely come to my board game night. I organized it after our CEO, Craig, told me I was "hard to read" and "looked angry," before offering the immortal advice to "be more likeable."

In David's defense, no one else showed up either.

"I'm thinking about it. You?" I trace a finger over the skin above my collar. The hives haven't escaped. Yet.

"Oh yeah. This is my year. Naheed and I have been prepping my pitch since January. I've joined every project that ticks off a leadership skill and invested in a golf membership at White Oaks. If my boss here wasn't also my mentor, I'd almost think he wanted to get rid of me by winning me the competition and getting me that promotion."

A layer of crushed ice lands hard on my soul.

"Oh. Uh, I didn't know I should do all that." I don't have a mentor. Or even a boss, since mine left West by North last fall. Ernie was a good supervisor, but he was coasting into retirement, blissfully unconcerned with the future of the company. Or the future of me. Since he left, I've been covering his duties on top of mine, so I should be fine on the job skills front. Coaching, though—that's tough to find when you don't have a supervisor and the company has no senior women.

And pitch presentations are a whole different game. Like parties, and job interviews, and any other unscripted social situation, they're a field of garden rakes with the pointy side up: no matter which direction I step, a rake handle comes flying at my forehead.

"You're lucky to have a mentor like Naheed."

Naheed leans back. "I'm full up on mentees right now, Liz. Don't have room for another."

My neck burns. "Oh, no, I didn't mean—"

"Not to embarrass you, but the mentor usually chooses the mentee—"

"Please, I wasn't trying to suggest—" I wave my celery in a

slashing "no" motion, sending spinach dip sailing onto my right foot.

"—and really, it's about a good fit. Ask Craig to pair you with someone, maybe? Hey, I need a refill. David, come with." They walk away, chatting brightly.

I could use a stiff shot of something before my next attempt at small talk, but I don't think I'm supposed to follow them to the drinks station. Instead, I wipe dip off my shoe with a cocktail napkin. It's been—my phone says only twenty minutes?! God.

I shouldn't give up hope on the party of my dreams after one awful conversation, but the birthday present I most want after a terrifying day is to relax. Maybe watch a favorite movie. One where being hard to read and looking angry when you're not makes you a sexy Mr. Darcy type instead of the colleague everyone loves to overlook. Or one with a miscommunication mishap, which I've always found intensely relatable.

The lights dim, highlighting Marijke's candlelit figure in the kitchen doorway, Tobin and the guides assembled behind her. A white-frosted cake lit with a single silver taper makes a spectacular statement against her outfit.

Tobin hums a note; phones pop up in my peripheral vision. I put my mouth into the smile I practiced. No point looking like I just got told I'm not the kind of person people want to mentor. I should be able to brush it off by now. I know who I am.

"Happy birthday to youuuuuu," the guides croon, like the servers in one of those musical family restaurants, but with fewer jaded eye rolls. Tobin runs singing practice for the guides twice a year. Nothing makes the tips flow better than "Happy Birthday" in four-part harmony around the campfire.

Marijke sets the cake onto the table. As Tobin's troubadours hold the last note, I blow out the flame, then look up at the cameras.

They're trained on Tobin. Every last one of them. My two-sided smile slides off my face and smashes on the wide-plank oak floors.

He's more than earned everyone's love; I can't begrudge him that. It's not like he deliberately uses his magic to draw every eye his way and leave me unseen. It just happens, over and over. He's the likeable one, after all. My better half.

When the clapping dies down, I've already cut and plated four pieces of cake. Marijke gives an annoyed huff when she sees I've preempted the possibility of dramatic knife work, but I hand out slices as fast as I can, determined to wrap this party up in time to binge at least half a season of *Bridgerton* before I pass out.

"Excuse me. Are there any more of the sliders? They're amazing."

I look up from my robotic cake slinging. This must be one of Tobin's new guides: young, polite, with a physique my elderly neighbors would call "strapping." I'm about to point him in Marijke's direction when it hits me.

"You . . . think I'm working this party." It's not a question. I look around the room. Tobin's deep in conversation with the guides. Naheed's holding court with a half-dozen listeners while David watches and learns. Marijke is the coldly beautiful snow queen. Nobody would mistake them for staff, even if they were handing out birthday cake. Hell, Tobin could jump out of a cake wearing a bow tie and a smile and most of the guests would mistake him for the birthday boy.

This is my birthday. This is my party. This is my *life*. And I'm playing a supporting role. If I can't get noticed here, at *my own party,* what chance do I have anywhere else? How can I expect to win the pitch competition and get that promotion I've always been passed over for because nobody promotes dull, unlikeable Liz Lewis?

If I were a better person, I wouldn't be angry. I'd listen to the world when it says, *you don't deserve to be seen.* I'd accept that some people are born with that special magic, and I'm not one of them, and the best thing to do is stop wanting things I can't have.

But I *do* want them. I want people to see *me.* I want them to stop dismissing me because the quiet, awkward spreadsheet nerd can't possibly have ideas that don't have to do with columns of numbers. I want to be someone in my own right, not just Tobin's wife. And I want my husband to—well. Best not to go there. Not in public, anyway.

I realize with horror that I'm almost crying—something I swore at age seven I'd never again do at my birthday party. The best way not to cry at a party, always, is not to be at a party.

I push the knife at the startled kid.

"Do me a favor. Serve this cake."

"Did I say something—"

I'm already gone, breezing through the kitchen on my way to the front door. Marijke catches up as I grab my boots.

"Liz! Where are you going?" Her light Dutch accent turns shock and dismay into things of beauty.

My new jacket slips on in a whoosh of Tobin-scented air, and I almost stop. He doesn't like it when we don't do what his mom expects. And she'll expect an explanation, at the least.

But what excuse could I make? Not the truth. *Sorry, Marijke, I have to rest up for another big weekend at home, alone, as usual. I'd love to be out on the trail with someone—I'm not a fan of not hearing any footsteps but my own—but Tobin's always mushing or rafting. Everyone else has moved on with their lives and left me behind. All I have left are my Saturday rom-com marathons paired with a billion appetizers from the freezer section at the superstore. The mini quiches help the loneliness a lot, but I wouldn't underestimate the sausage rolls!*

After that, I'll head over to Amber's to babysit. Me and the six-

year-old will mainline ten episodes in a row of Barbie: Life in the Dreamhouse. *Not even ten different episodes! Maybe not even* two *different episodes! Very underrated show, by the way. Subversive as fuck. Ken's my favorite character.*

Ha. Honesty would go over as well with my mother-in-law as it does with my husband, who dodges the ugly truth of our faltering marriage as expertly as he steers his whitewater raft around strainers of fallen trees. Tobin's good at ignoring what he doesn't want to see, whether it's his parents' dysfunctional antics or his wife's slow, sad slide away from him.

"It was a great party, Mar"—No; can't do it—"Mrs. Renner. Spectacular. Sorry I can't stay."

Before she can answer, I dart outside, pulling the door shut behind me. For a minute, I stand there, damp wind pouring over me, just . . . breathing.

It's not yet dark—not at this time of year, this far north. The setting sun backlights the in-your-face magnificence of Grey Tusk, the mountain that gave its name to the glittering world-class ski resort twenty minutes away. Clouds rip off its distant, snaggle-toothed peak, like it's tearing a hole in the heart of the sky.

I didn't fail at this party because I'm uncaring, or uninteresting, or a bad listener. It's because I don't have Tobin's brand of magic—that *spark* that commands people's attention. For years, I told myself it didn't matter, that effort and loyalty and ideas would speak for themselves. But the truth is, magic is the *only* thing that matters. Without it, I'll always be a side character. I'll always be a voice that gets talked over. I'll always feel pinned by fear, poisoned with frustration and resentment.

I can't live like this anymore.

There must be a way to get what Tobin has. Buy it, borrow it. Steal it, if I have to.

I reach for my phone. It's predictably on-brand for me, but I can always count on a spreadsheet, schedule, or list.

I pull up a new note, stabbing my thumbs into the screen in all-caps fury.

GET MAGIC.

Chapter Two

Hearing and listening are two different things. When a player is given an initiation, they must let the words resonate, so they can decipher the underlying meaning. Listen with your emotions.

—*Truth in Comedy*

It doesn't take long for the "get magic" fever to cool off. A walk across two damp lawns in my now-clammy indoor shoes douses my righteous fire. An undignified amount of jiggling my key in the front door smothers the ashes.

I could oil the lock. It would take five minutes and only a little bravery to get the oil from the spider-infested basement storeroom. I'd save a locksmith visit and a hundred bucks on the (inevitably winter) day when I finally snap the key off in the lock.

But I have a stubborn, pointless wish not to be the only one who notices the broken things. Everyone glides by, not seeing the problems, not seeing the one who fixes them.

Like when Tobin and I started dating. He was the river guide who got all the tips, and I was the ex-guide demoted to camp chief and invisible work doer, keeping the guests comfortable so they were rested and ready to bask in his attention.

Like the guests, I knew being seen by Tobin was the greatest sensation on earth. He used to watch the breeze in my hair the same way he watched the wind toss centuries-old red cedars—and I knew how he loved those damn trees, because I loved them the same way. I'd do anything to have him look at me, *see* me, the way he did that first summer season.

All through river guide training camp, when most people gravitated to the loudest, boldest, drunkest personalities, he sought me out. He watched me so intently, like he was enjoying a particularly challenging puzzle. No one had ever listened to me the way he did as I unpacked my dreams from across the campfire.

You've got it all figured out, don't you, he said.

So do you. To save up for the day he started his own tour company, Tobin was guiding summers while working the winter high season at his mom's indie clothing business in Grey Tusk Village, which wasn't a village so much as an outdoor tourist shopping experience. Its winding streets and timber-and-stone chalets were a charming, shameless photocopy of the French Alps.

Not like you do. Tourism degree, two years in the field, five years in management with promotions at years three and five, then leadership with a specialization in niche ecotours, he quoted. Correctly, I noted. *What happens if it doesn't work out? The industry's pretty competitive in Grey Tusk.*

True. But I know what I'm up against. Most of Grey Tusk's twenty thousand locals made their living serving its one million annual visitors. Not many of those jobs were above entry level. Few expedition companies—besides local behemoth Keller Outdoor Epiphanies—could evolve fast enough to survive in alpine tourism. Take mountain biking, which wasn't even an Olympic

sport until 1996. A dozen years later, Grey Tusk Mountain was filling chairlifts with mountain bikers from May to October, and every
company without backcountry bike tours was feeling the heat.

I shrugged. *If I don't succeed, I revise the plan and try again.*

You'd never quit? Like . . . never? he repeated at my head
shaking "no."

Please don't say I don't know when to quit. It was my sister's
favorite phrase, often put together with words like "annoying" and
"weird."

I wouldn't say that, he murmured, the moment before he kissed
me under the shelter of ancient cedars.

Back then, every possibility hovered near, like I could pluck
them from among the stars. Now? I'm nothing like the partner he
thought he was getting when we made promises to each other. My
heart hurts thinking about it.

What would I have done then, if I could've seen the future? That
knowledge wouldn't have neutralized his kindness, his gentleness,
his gifts of tiny wild things only he would notice—the smallest
seashells, the most delicate flowers. A four-leaf clover tucked in the
zip of my tent almost every week we were on the river.

No, nothing could have saved my heart from falling.

But it might have hurt less when I hit the bottom if I'd seen it
coming.

Something warm blocks the evening breeze from biting my
ankles. I look down: Yeti, our geriatric ginger cat, twines around
my legs. "Hey, handsome," I tell him. He breaks out his broken old
purr, butting his head against my knee. He's a sucker for compliments.

"Don't give me that. Who were you with last night? The lady
with the salmon? Or the guys with the cream?"

Yeti is the biggest himbo in my hometown, Pendleton. Technically, he's mine, but he'll crash anywhere the snacks are popping.

At least four houses on our block think he's theirs, including my sister and niece three doors down.

The lock grinds open. Yeti zips between my legs, off to make sweet, sweet love with his food dish.

"Liz! Liz, wait. I got away as fast as I could. Are you okay?" Tobin jogs across Marijke's yard, shrugging into a fleece sweater flecked black with sparks from a million campfires. I've seen tourists beg to trade their brand-new gear for his battered stuff, hoping to take home his air of being the real thing. His guiding buddies have stealth-stenciled "LOST AND FOUND" on every tent he owns, on account of how many clients "accidentally" end up at his campsite after dark.

To be clear, the only nighttime visitor at *my* tent, in my short-lived expedition days, was a black bear.

"You didn't have to follow me."

"I couldn't stay. Not after you left like that."

"You should go back. Your mom will give me hell if you don't."

"She wouldn't be mad."

I let my head tilt.

"She wouldn't," he insists.

"Okay," I say, stepping over the threshold.

Inside, he pulls me close, lips in my hair. "Why didn't you come find me if you were ready to go?"

Why didn't I? Was it because this time I didn't want him to pick me up, tuck me under his arm, and act like his friends were my friends? Because I didn't want to pretend to have a good time while he pretended not to see how bad of a time I was really having?

I feel us falling into the circular grooves we've carved for ourselves, never closer, never further away. Apparently today is the day I try to scratch that record, because before I can think better of it, I blurt, "That was rude of me. To leave. I'm sure people were offended."

"No one was offended. I'm sure everyone understood."

I don't know why I do this to myself.

I always thought "for better or for worse" meant your spouse wasn't supposed to leave if you got sick. But maybe whoever wrote those words knew how painful a marriage is when it's only about the better parts of yourself, and the worse has nowhere to go.

All I want is for him to let me in, and let himself out. I want to crack him like a safe, my ear against his heart, listening for the softest, tiniest clicks to tell me my fingers are doing the right work. I'd spend years on it if I had to, getting closer to the combination every time. I'd only have to know I was making progress, and I'd never give up.

But he doesn't want to be cracked. He wants to believe his marriage is okay, even though I keep asking him to go to couples' counseling and our house is full of relationship self-help books that I read and he didn't. We're a couple worthy of a rom-com, trapped in a misunderstanding that could be solved by a single conversation. Okay, maybe not just one conversation. But it doesn't matter, because he won't talk.

"Think I'll head up to bed." I don't want him to swing from party mode into cheer-up-Liz mode. I want to cry myself to sleep against his chest, but tears make him hyperventilate. Except when it's his mom, crying about his dad.

"Bed?" He slides my coat off my shoulders.

He doesn't ask for sex with words, only with soft kisses and rough, strong hands to certain spots in a certain order with a certain rhythm. Yet, at some point, he almost always goes off script, finding an unexpected small part of me to lavish attention on. The crook of one elbow; the dimple in my lower back—I get delirious wondering when it will come, what it will be.

Lust murmurs promises in my ear. *Don't cut your last line of communication with him. Maybe sex is how we get through.*

Maybe this heat can melt the permafrost that grips the heart of our marriage. In the afterglow, I'll tell him I'm afraid my lack of magic means nobody will ever recognize me as a person who exists when Tobin's not in the room. And in return, he'll confess his tips were crap, and tell me his body aches from doing the things that used to be easy. And together, we'll find a way out of the mess we've made of our dreams.

I let him stroke behind my ears, run his thumbs over my collarbones, push up my skirt and hitch my legs around his waist. He lets me kiss him as hard as I want and breathe in the lingering sense of snowy pine on his skin as we climb the stairs.

"Your wrist's okay?"

I stroke the arm he broke last summer, rescuing a guest who fell overboard while taking photos in a rocky stretch of rapids. The guy sent him a framed print—magnificent; I want to burn it—to enjoy while he recovered from surgery. Tobin doesn't complain about his plate and screws, ever, but I see how he babies that arm after trips.

He grabs my ass with that hand, squeezing in time with his wicked smile. Okay, good.

Pushing aside a stack of his mysterious business texts, he lowers us to the bed, rocking me against him like he can't wait. It's still unbelievable sometimes, that this man who everybody wants—he wants *me*.

He takes my shuddering sigh as encouragement, loosing a sound of desperately sexy impatience at the difficulty of the tiny buttons on my top. He has the best voice, deep and windblown and a little rough from years of making sure people can hear him at the back.

That's what gets me: his voice, and all the things I imagine him saying. All the words whose shapes would fit perfectly into the spaces in my heart that ache to be filled with things like "I know" and "me too." It's not that my body doesn't feel good to be asked by his body. It's that the words are missing from this part of our marriage. And every other part.

I flick his hands aside and undo the shirt myself. He traces one finger down my breastbone, into my navel, lingering at the pink bow on my black underwear.

"Hot, Diz. Very hot," Tobin whispers, as if everything about me is a tiny treasure he's dying to collect. His clothes go away fast, pulled up and pushed down and tossed aside. His belly is winter white above his boxers, but even without his summer tan he's sexy in a way most people can only dream of, abs popping as he pushes closer, his eyes sleepy with an almost smile. He's never stopped looking grateful and a little surprised when the clothes come off, like he's woken up somewhere new yet familiar and wonderful. It's one of the things I loved most about him.

I mean, one of the things I *love* most about him. Love. Present tense.

I put his palm over my bra, where it'll push away my thoughts.

His face flickers as I lean up to kiss his neck. He pulls his hand away, not breaking rhythm. My nipple feels suddenly cold, and not in a sexy way.

"Tobe? You okay?"

He smiles, says nothing, and puts his other hand where it would've made me see stars ten seconds ago.

"Tobin." I reach for his bad wrist, but he leans on his elbows, putting it out of reach. "You can't go out tomorrow if it's this sore. You have to get someone to replace you."

"Last weekend of the season. Everyone's booked. I'm fine."

"You're not fine."

"I will be in a couple minutes," he breathes, planting his lips on mine.

Another day, I'd let it pass. Today, though.

Today, all the words we don't say gather in my chest. Today, I pick the word first in line.

"TMBNNNN," I shout into his mouth. "I don't want to hurt you. Can I do something different?"

"We're good." He bites my earlobe, my jaw, my lower lip.

He doesn't see me. Here, in bed, the one place we still communicate, he can't hear how it hurts me to hurt him.

My wanting sputters and fizzles. It's like I'm getting banged by the same hot stranger who's been showing up in my bedroom for the last three years straight. It might sound sexy, but the four hundredth time it happens, it's lost its shine.

I can't do this. Not with Tobin. I'm used to not being seen, but when it's his eyes with that thousand-yard stare? His ears, blocked by these cones of silence? It's unbearable.

Even so, nobody's more surprised than me when I blurt the second word in line.

"No."

He falters, coming to stillness.

That, he heard.

I pat his shoulder twice, one-two, like a wrestler at the end of the scripted entertainment.

"I'm done."

"What?" He looks confused, his brain still carried by the momentum of desire. But the part of him that's fading fast against my panties knows. He rolls away. "But I didn't think you . . . you're done, from that?"

"Not done like that. Done, like, *done.* I can't do this anymore." I'm through being invisible, here or anywhere.

His body stills, like a prey animal who's caught a whiff of wolf. "Is this, uh, a game?"

This is no game. I look right in his eyes and think the third word, the one that's been nibbling at my edges for a few months now.

Divorce.

I've been so afraid to say that word. It has a dark power that can't be undone once unleashed. I've held that word in my heart, in my throat, under my tongue.

I can't bring myself to say it. Not even now.

But I can't be this hurting, lonely, half a person I've become. I can't be the puzzle piece that looks like the right shape for his but has to be pounded into place by force. I *can't.*

"It's not a game. We have to stop playing, Tobin. Pretending we're close when we're just . . . near each other. We have to stop. *I* have to stop."

He doesn't recover his words until I'm dressed and rummaging through the closet for my weekend bag.

"What are you doing?" His voice is edged with panic.

"Taking a break. I need space."

"For the night?"

"For as long as it takes!" I say, unzipping the bag so hard I might break it. *Maybe forever,* I don't say. Looking at his face, though, I think he hears it, and I can't help caving a little. "Give me some time, Tobin. Please. Just let me think for a week. Alone. Okay?"

He nods, eyes pinched shut. The sound of his breathing, fast and harsh, cracks my courage with a shuddering splinter down the center of my body. I have to get out of here. Eyes everywhere but on my husband, I sweep underwear, tampons, charging cords into my bag. He wanted our marriage to be perfect, I know. He wanted *us* to be perfect. But we're not.

I don't fit at West by North because they *can't* see me. I don't fit with Tobin because he *won't*. One I can fix; one I can't. Not by myself.

Palming my phone, I open my List app. No more marriage where he turns away from my failures. And while I'm at it, no more failures. I want people's eyes to stop sliding over me because I'm not shiny or hilarious or loud. I want to be interesting, and welcomed, and valued. And not because I'm by Tobin's side. Because I'm *me*.

Whatever it is Tobin has that I don't, I'm going to get it. Whatever it is that makes the gatekeepers say no, I'll bury it in everything that makes them say yes.

GET MAGIC, I type a second time. Then I book it out of my house.

Chapter Three

Improvisers who are "determined to do their best" scan the "future" for "better" ideas, and cease to pay attention to each other.

—*Impro for Storytellers*

My new favorite time of day: the moment before I fall asleep, when logical ideas give way to comforting, dreamlike thoughts and I forget how much I want a take-back for Friday night.

My new least favorite: waking up in my childhood home on a Monday morning, one second before all the negative emotions resume their deafening parade through my brain.

I came so damn close to caving and going home this weekend. But then I imagined an empty house, Tobin on the trail delighting guests by showing them how to harvest spruce tips for a tea he'll serve that afternoon, all while lifting loaded dogsleds over bare patches in the snow. Tobin popping painkillers morning and night.

To know my words couldn't reach him . . . that would feel final in a way nothing else could.

Still, there's a strange sort of relief threaded through the agony. At least I can stop waiting for the worst to happen. At least I have Amber and Eleanor and their around-the-clock kid-and-pet chaos instead of the silence of a house with Tobin absent. Or Tobin present.

I've done countless weekday mornings with Eleanor, but they're a different flavor when my sister's here. For example, when Amber's wrapping up a night shift at the hospital, no one heaves the porridge pot into the sink with deliberate loudness, looking at me sideways.

My mom catches the clatter over the landline she insists on keeping so she can get a non-glitchy connection from Arizona to Grey Tusk. "Do you have to go, honey? Sounds like it's time for you to get washing so Amber can dry."

The Mothership is over the moon about Amber and me being roommates again, even though it means my marriage might be over. And although Mom was supportive when I sobbed out the story on Saturday, she couldn't help pointing out the importance of family in a crisis. I think she called this morning so she could hear me washing and Amber drying, Amber sweeping and me mopping.

It's easy that way. No fighting.

I didn't tell Mom I'm only here because Stellar's out of town. Her girlfriend, Jen, would let me crash, but I need someone to shove me into the shower every day or two, and for that I'd need Stellar's love. Or Amber's blunt frustration, which Mom calls love.

"Yeah, I'd better go. Love you, Mom."

"Love you, sweetie."

The second I hang up, Amber looks at me, looks at the pot, back to me. She's always beautiful, though I tend to get the severe, unsmiling side of her. Usually, a look like this one would make me fill with worry and hop to do her bidding.

Today, though, my emotional tank is full up with heartache and fear and a jumble of huge black letters spelling "WHAT NOW?!" There's no room for the drip-drip-drip of sisterly resentment.

"I want to dry," I declare.

"You're used to washing," Amber returns, slipping forbidden table scraps to Kris Kristofferson, her senselessly energetic rescue mutt. Kris is the smartest dog I know. She understands over fifty words and can find things on command, like her bowl, or her leash. Or the cat, whom she loves to pin down with one paw so she can hold his head inside her mouth. Gently. Just to show she *can*.

Yeti, too old for this game, vexes her by not trying to escape. Although it occurs to me I haven't seen the cat all morning.

Kris paws at Amber's lime-green scrubs, leaving a smear at the knee. My sister glances at it, shrugs, and moves on. She's a different person from the sister I knew before she married Mark and moved as far away from home as possible. Back then, Amber would have reacted to smudged pants with a whole new outfit, plus coordinating makeup.

Now her fashion sense matches the way my parents raised us. As dyed-in-the-wool outdoors enthusiasts, they were more concerned with function than fashion, as their constant hat hair and use of ski pants as leisure wear could attest. And as a single mom with a six-year-old and an ex who decided teaching English overseas was a better deal than marriage and parenting an autistic kid, my sister has to pick her battles.

Like me, she's picked this one.

"I could get used to drying, if anyone gave me a chance."

In the sink of my parents' place—where Amber lives and I'm crashing until they get home from Arizona—are two knives and a pot.

This is the hill I have chosen to die on.

"Drying isn't easier. And it's not like you got off the couch this weekend." She pushes a pair of rubber gloves at me with a movement I've seen her make a thousand times when we were teenagers. That impatient, abrupt motion meant she wanted to get the dinner dishes over with so she could retreat to our room, put her earbuds in, and ignore me.

"I never said drying was easier!" I'm regressing to our childhood so hard I can feel the pout pushing out my lip. I should get couch privileges for forty-eight hours, minimum, after leaving my husband. My heart is a black sun shining dark and heavy in my chest; I can only carry it around so much before I have to lie down.

Drying will make me feel better. I'm not sure how I know that; it just *will*. "Can I please dry? For once?"

"Can you not raise your voice around Eleanor? You know it upsets her."

"Eleanor's not—oh," I stammer, spying my niece lurking at the kitchen door.

Eleanor's the best. Adorably eldritch; a definite Ramona Quimby type. Wears socks only under duress. Refuses to stop cutting her own sandy-blond bangs no matter where her mother hides the scissors. Learned to read almost before she could talk—not unusual for autistic kids, although Amber had to recycle her parenting magazines in other people's bins after Eleanor started sharing facts about postpartum sex at kindergarten.

I bend down. "Eleanor, do you know where Yeti's hiding?"

She adores the kitty. Yeti accepts all cuddles (including overenthusiastic kid squishing) and is a three-time national purring champion. She vanishes in search of him.

"Sorry. Didn't see her."

Amber gives me a look I can't interpret. "I don't know why you're surprised. You loved to sneak around and eavesdrop."

She's got a running tally of every annoying thing I did as a kid, when our three-year age difference meant I wasn't capable of being anything but a pest, but Mom still made us share a room because, and I quote, "sisters need each other."

Amber's balance sheet includes things like the time she had to quit the curling team after her cringey little sister joined. Also, all the friend hangouts I ruined when Mom made her invite me along. It does *not* include all the times Tobin and I stepped up for last-minute sleepovers with Eleanor when Amber had to work. If I mention that, she whips out her Sword of Guilt: Eleanor needs her family; I'm the aunt who shares a special bond with her after three years of basically being an honorary parent. It isn't unusual for me to sleep over at my parents' place for a week of Amber's night shifts when Tobin's on his seven-day-on, seven-day-off dogsled guiding schedule and my parents are wintering down south, at the place they bought when they retired from teaching and Dad's arthritis got unmanageable in cold weather.

Eleanor's iPad alarm goes off—we're out of time to argue if my niece and I are going to get out the door on time for school.

Sigh. "I'll wash for today."

"You can dry whenever you want if you move back home. Some consistency and predictability would do you good. And you won't find anyone better than Tobin."

My black sun pulses with a heavy solar flare. That's not what she said about him at my wedding, but regardless of whether she believes it now, she doesn't have to remind me. Everyone knows he's way out of my league. Especially me. For years, I've been dreading the day when he finally figured that out, too.

"It's not about finding someone better."

"Everyone has limits, Liz. Accepting them isn't a bad thing. Blowing up your life is, though."

Amber isn't always like this. Friday night, when I showed up on my parents' doorstep with my overnight bag and my cat, she took us in without an argument.

Our family is all about closeness. Togetherness. Smoothing over our differences no matter what, the way we had to when we were kids and it was just the four of us hiking the West Coast Trail, or kayaking around Haida Gwaii, or skiing into remote backcountry huts. When you're twenty kilometers from the nearest road with only your companions and whatever you can carry, there's no room in your backpack for discord. On the trail, Amber and I secured each other's loose straps, smacked the horseflies off each other's shoulders, and swapped novels (back when she used to love romance). Dad always said she and I paddled a canoe like we shared the same brain.

The months after my wedding when Amber and I didn't speak drove Mom to the brink. Our relationship is still healing, but I want to believe Amber loves me. I don't call her Slamber anymore, even in my head. We're like Baby and Lisa in *Dirty Dancing*—family in the end.

I flip the dripping pot onto Amber's dish towel. "El and I will see you after work."

She stalks me to the front door, scooping scattered kid items into Eleanor's backpack on the way. "Think about what you're doing. This whole thing is about your unrealistic expectations—Tobin, work, all of it. Remember when you followed me into debate club and wouldn't give up even after you fainted during your rebuttal? You don't know when to quit, Liz."

Fair, but I would eat glass before conceding the point, because if Amber senses she's winning an argument, she fights even harder. Besides, persistence is one of my key strengths, even if it only works some of the time.

Take Amber: I spent years chasing her when we were kids, trying to catch her interest, piggybacking off her popularity. Back then, she only ever wanted to get away from her barnacle of a baby sister, and I ended up discovering how many after-school clubs I didn't fit into after she left. But now I'm a fixture in every part of her life, and the warm, loving sisterhood I've always wanted seems possible again, despite our differences. Would that have happened if I'd given up on her back then? No way.

I shove my feet into my shoes, hoping my nonanswer will trick her into backing off.

"Do you *want* to see Tobin with someone else?"

I fumble my jacket zipper, winded by her sucker punch.

Imagining Tobin alone and sad is bad enough. If he wordlessly handed the smallest sand dollar on the beach to a new love, with his special secret smile? If he quit being Tobin Renner-Lewis and hyphenated his last name with someone else's?

It burns. Especially because Amber predicted our divorce back at our wedding.

I give up on the zipper. "Eleanor! Put your socks on, it's time to go."

"I *don't* wear socks," she yells down the stairs.

Amber rolls her eyes and grabs Eleanor's favorite eye-melting neon-yellow socks from a basket near the door, tucking them into a mesh pocket where the teacher can see them. "The two of you should bottle stubborn and sell it. You'd still have more than enough left over to ignore good advice."

"I'm not six, Amber. I don't need your advice."

"Don't you? You walked out on a perfectly good husband. Everyone loves him, so you just *have* to be the one who doesn't. You should learn to recognize a good thing while you still have it."

She pushes Eleanor's backpack into my arms and walks away.

Primed by a school run spent singing surprisingly technical children's songs about weather (Eleanor knows all the words; I'm a disappointment to her in this regard), I gather my courage and knock on my boss's door as soon as he's had a chance to settle in after his standard 9:30 A.M. arrival.

Losing a marriage is one of the top five life stressors, and I need something to focus on to get me through. Between breakup-induced grief naps, I spent the weekend distracting myself with "get magic"–based research. I want to be seen as my own person, and the fastest way to break the spell of invisibility at West by North is a promotion.

And why enter an unwinnable promotion competition when all the online resources said women should just ask? This idea seemed like a slam dunk when I was reading the *Harvard Business Review* but feels a lot dodgier now that I'm hovering in the boss's doorway, disturbing his daily ritual of making a latte last half an hour while contemplating his stunning view of the Brookside gondola terminal, where Grey Tusk Village dissolves into the mountain itself. Outside his floor-to-ceiling windows, brightly dressed skiers and boarders swing into the sky in silver-and-red capsules that disappear one by one in swirls of low-lying cloud cover.

Craig's a self-described "creative type" who prefers not to "run on corporate time." This might be why he started his own company eight years ago, after his creative endeavors at Keller Outdoor Epiphanies—his former workplace—didn't pan out. Now his singular goal in life is besting them at everything. When he made "disruption" the theme of the pitch competition, what he meant was "disrupt Keller."

I give Craig finger guns, channeling our bro-heavy office culture. "Craig, uh, yo. Got a minute?"

"What's up, Lizzeroni?"

I smile at his nickname, the better to make myself into what he wants.

"Craig, I feel I have a lot to offer this company. My performance reviews are spotless, and I'm ready to take on more responsibility. Develop some unique tour ideas. Polish my leadership skills. In short, I'd like to get ready for promotion." I spent hours practicing my delivery, but somewhere in the second sentence, Liz the Leader goes unstable like a bucket of plutonium, morphing into an Old West character complete with an inexplicable drawl. "Promotion" gets seven syllables.

"Excellent initiative, Lizzeroni, but . . ." Craig does a head-waggling, hand-waving move. "No offense, but you're a numbers person. A behind-the-scenes genius," he pronounces, as if a statement starting with "no offense" could be a compliment. "Right?"

"I wouldn't say that." I'd say anxious introvert—potato, potahto—but I'm determined to quibble over anything that gets me closer to my goal.

Craig doesn't look convinced. "Wasn't it you who said spreadsheets 'talk' to you?"

My face burns. "Yes, but I meant that well-designed spreadsheets can illuminate both problems and solutions that aren't otherwise—" I catch his impatient sniff and stop talking.

"Exactly. You *love* spreadsheets. Which is why I wouldn't put you on"—he makes air quotes again, like he's speaking a language I wouldn't recognize—"*front-of-house* work. West by North needs you where you are to break out of our scrappy upstart phase."

I'm aware of my reputation around here, but I don't understand why being a spreadsheet person is a disqualification for every other job in a way that being, say, a marketing person isn't.

A week ago, I would've slunk out of his office, added an extra layer of feelings to the scream I'm building like a geode in the center of my soul, and spent my lunch hour huddled over Microsoft Excel.

Not anymore. "I would *love* front-of-house work!" Old West Liz exclaims, deciding to stir up the saloon with a slight compliment hitched to a devastating neg. "I tell everyone it isn't true you don't support women for the top levels of the org chart."

Something sharky winks from the teeth at the corner of Craig's mouth. "Love your enthusiasm. But my hesitation here would be fit."

This again. "Fit," the silver bullet that kills me every time. It means "we don't want you in our club."

"Tell me what I need to do to fit, and I'll learn it. Like I learned the rest of the job."

He shakes his head. "Leaders are born, not made. *Naturally* dynamic, supportive, positive. They're idea machines. The life of the office party. On the golf course Saturdays, networking. They're not spreadsheet types. Not that there's any shame in that."

His tone implies there *is* shame in that. But I didn't order a special sweat-proof undershirt (and pay double for overnight delivery on a weekend) to back down now.

"All I need is a chance to demonstrate my, uh, relevant skills. That I will learn. And that I already have. In this area of skills."

That isn't a *total* lie. Sure, I don't talk in meetings, but I've golfed. Okay, mini-golfed. And maybe I've skipped a lot of office happy hours, but I've never missed West by North's annual corporate retreats, where the pitch competition is held. Never mind that I glued myself to Tobin and relied on his sparkle.

Just the thought of my husband—my ex-husband? Oh no, that's not better—makes my eyelids tingle with a horrible threat of tears. My tear ducts are betrayers at the best of times, sometimes triggering when I'm not even sad. And today I'm so sad I bawled all the way from Eleanor's school to work, drowning out a song ironically titled "What Makes Rain."

Tears are a promotion killer at this company. There is no crying in wilderness tourism. I take a pretend sip from my empty mug, then fake a coughing fit to explain away my red eyelids.

Craig's eyes narrow, his gaze darting to my tissue-chapped nose. "Take the day if you're sick, Liz."

"I have allergies." I do, although these are not them.

He resumes breathing. "Why don't you throw your hat into the pitch competition if you want a promotion? But if you'd like to develop your leadership skills in the lead-up to the retreat, everything we just discussed should do it."

"Everything . . . ?" I ask, dismayed, before switching to a confident "I mean, yes. Everything. Very good." Networking, and positivity, and golf, all in the eight weeks before the pitch competition? And ideas, when Craig's always hated mine?

What have I done?

"And! This reminds me." He rummages through his desk. Oh, god, there's *more*?

He hands me a brochure titled *Grey Tusk Community Centre: Spring-Summer.* "Naheed pitched me a fantastic idea. He teaches improv comedy. He wants to add an improv segment to our leadership skills training at West by North to develop flexibility and quick thinking in our management team. His evening class starts next week. You should sign up."

"Oh." I scan the brochure. Our standard leadership training happens on company time. "Three hours a week for eight weeks? Would I clock this as overtime?"

"This is for your personal development, on your own time, Liz. Unless you'd rather not?"

"No," I say quickly, noticing my demotion from Lizzeroni to Liz. "I'm excited to take on any kind of leadership opportunity." Deep down, Craig's not a bad person. He's just single-minded in pursuing his goals. West by North is constantly outrunning our shaky bottom line, trying to find the breakout tour that puts us on a level with the likes of Keller.

He claps his hands together in satisfaction. "Excellent talk, Lizzeroni. Carry on. See you at the pre-pitching meeting."

Terror smacks me across the mouth. I forgot the pre-pitching meeting, where the field of hopefuls gets narrowed to three, is a month away. And *improv comedy*?! Fuck. I'm doomed.

But he's giving me a recipe for success, like Naheed did for David. If I wasn't sure before, I am now: magic has a formula, and I can replicate it.

I scuttle back to my desk to enact my plan B: plowing through leadership books and assembling the ingredients for a big batch of magic.

Chapter Four

There is no such thing as a "bad idea" in improv. Players take each other's ideas—no matter what they are—and make them work.

—Truth in Comedy

Somehow, I thought the Grey Tusk community center would smell different at night. In my imagination, its eternal scent of crafting supplies and little-kid sweat gave way to an erasers-and-coffee vibe that would permit people a smidge of dignity during Improv for Beginners, which might as well be called A Cry for Help.

"Your voice sounds like you're hitting turbulence over the Himalayas. You should try to get your pulse under a hundred. If possible." Stellar's calling me from her tiny clinic near a hard rock–mining town in Alberta. "That does not constitute medical advice, by the way, for the purposes of my malpractice insurance."

Stellar and I have been best friends since she fed me a pickup line at a university keg party. Something about every medical student having a fantasy of rumpling a hot, starchy librarian.

The next morning, post-hookup, she rolled over in my dorm room bed, scary-cute with her pixie undercut and chiseled arms, like a chipmunk with filed teeth.

"Look at you, Liz. You're smart, you're talented, you're even hotter when you're messy. I almost wish I did relationships. Just this once, I'm gonna be late to study group and buy you a coffee."

She mainlined a vat of Americano, black, and told me about the time she disastrously hennaed her pubes. I sipped chai and let her prod me into spilling the story of attempting to sexy-walk past a crush, tripping over a garbage can, and going down in a storm of trash.

And that was that. Every time we could have let circumstances pull us apart, Stellar simply refused. After her medical training, she packed her car and drove the two hours north to Grey Tusk—to be near her mom, yes, but also because I couldn't be anywhere else but the mountains. Getting my degree in Vancouver was necessary, but the coast and the city weren't for me; like a grizzly bear, I needed my own terrain.

I needed the bite of winter wind on top of the mountain and the perfume of awakening trees in spring. I was cold unless I could lie on a sun-warmed rock in a mountain stream in July. I needed to show people my beloved places so they would love them, too, because people don't fight for what they don't love, and people don't love what they don't know. The vulnerable wilderness needs friends as badly as I do.

Stellar fits in perfectly here. We bitch about how hard it is for younger women to get recognized in adventure tourism (me) and medicine (her). Or we did, until she left Grey Tusk General to take a three-month posting at a bare-bones clinic in the far North, and I got left behind.

"A pitch competition winner would arrive early to snag the best seat. Right?" I already told her about Monday morning in Craig's office.

I sneak a peek at the Elements of the Novel classroom. People have practically moved in, with laptops and notebooks arranged just so. Most of them look ludicrously young, photographing their artful setups, all the better to hashtag them later.

Something that's not quite FOMO zings uncomfortably over my skin. Look at these people, doing the thing. Getting it together in their twenties.

Thirty tolls like a bell at the beginning of every fact about me. Thirty and figuring it out. Thirty and getting wild at the community center on a Friday night.

Thirty, with a failed marriage.

I can't shake the fear that nothing will un-fuck my life. I'm not even splitting with my husband correctly. I should be cracking champagne and celebrating the dawn of my Era of Liz, where nobody says, "Oh, aren't you Tobin's wife?"

Instead, I'm remembering the backcountry ski trip we took to celebrate our engagement. Tobin led us to a 1920s mountain lodge, now a historic site and museum inside a national park. A favorite place of mine to visit in the summer, it was closed for the winter season, the red roofs poking out of the deep snow. The site was perfect, tucked into a cradle of peaks surrounding a cobalt-blue Rocky Mountain lake.

We fried our eggs before they froze, pitched our tent, and had sex winter camping style—going slow, to keep cold air out and compensate for the altitude, and ending up gently dying from the tenderness of it all. I died, anyway, when it was Tobin and me.

In the morning, cold air sparking off my skin, pink sky washing us in promise, he waved his bag of granola at the polished log walls peeking from the snowdrifts. "We could do something like

this. Not a lodge; those days are gone. But we could run tours together. Have our own company."

"You and me?" In that moment, my past, present, and future
felt seamlessly layered and blended, yellow into orange into fuchsia, like the sunrise. I didn't need to worry about West by North
and how my two promotions hadn't come. Not even one promotion. Everything felt so simple.

"You and me, Diz," Tobin said, picking me up and twirling me
in a hug, and I heard "forever," just like he meant me to.

"Trust your feelings," Stellar says, breaking me out of my rose-
colored memories. "You have a bad feeling about this. Me too."

"There's nothing wrong with improv."

"Hmph," she mutters, Yoda-like. "Beyond being an agonizing
activity that people inexplicably do on purpose, no, there's nothing wrong with improv. And there's nothing wrong with *you*."

"Maybe not. But I could be more *right*."

"Don't let those assholes at Waste by North tell you you're not
good enough."

"It's not just the assholes at my job," I point out. "It's also the
assholes at six other companies whose interviews I bombed. I
have to find a way to get seen, and this is it."

My own research shows that Craig was, unfortunately, correct
to send me here. People have written entire books describing how
improv crushed their social anxiety and forged them into invin-
cible public speakers. Naheed's class will lay the foundation for
networking, positivity, and not spontaneously combusting during
corporate "fun" events.

And pitch competitions. Improv is where I'll steal Naheed's
secrets for C-suite appeal.

"It sounds excruciating."

"That's how it works, Stellar. No social pain can touch me after
I've survived this level of nuclear humiliation."

I inch past Adult Tap, where a handful of unlikely dancers are inventing reasons to click around the classroom. It's as if putting on the shoes has transformed them into the performers they've always wanted to be.

Like magic.

"Fine," Stellar groans. "But let the record show this is not my favorite of all your ideas."

"I've had worse."

"Have you, though?" Background rustling makes me imagine Stellar adjusting her signature tank top where it's bunched against her blankets.

"How about when I was drunk and hungry and decided to make hot shortbread with jujube sauce?"

"Ugh, the kitchen smelled like melted plastic for weeks. But that was microwaving food, Liz. This . . . I think you're microwaving yourself. Your difference is your power. I want you to be happy the way you are."

"But what if I'm not happy? It's one thing to decide to be different. It's not the same when you don't have a choice. It's like . . . being alone versus being lonely. And, Stel, I'm lonely."

My throat tightens over "lonely." I've always felt like there was some memo everyone else got that I didn't. How to join conversations, find friends, make people like you and want to have you around. I'd like to make connections at work now that Ernie's gone. As the only member of Ops, I'm so isolated I miss seeing Ernie's one-word comments on the Ops Excel files, which is ludicrous.

And it's not just work. My whole life needs a renovation. I want to knock out a wall and build a room for a husband or wife who loves me. All of me. And I desperately want to bulldoze over this hollow, scraped-out place in my heart where Tobin used to fill so much space.

"If this is what you want, I'm behind you," Stellar says finally. "But your boss may die in an unlikely mishap is all I'm saying."

"He's not evil. He's trying to keep a small company going in a tough market."

She scoffs. "I'll bet a hundred bucks and a hot shower"—the local currency at her work site—"he raised his hand at diversity training to say *he* didn't have any unconscious bias."

A tall Black woman with a puffy ponytail brushes past me on her way into Improv for Beginners. Probably she's a good fit, getting in early. My stomach squeezes.

"I'd better get going."

"Talk tomorrow," she says. I can tell from the smooshed vowels that she's scrunched her face up in our code for "I love you."

My loneliness intensifies with the disconnection tone.

If I'd joined improv a year ago, Stellar might've come with me. Afterward, when I drove home, I wouldn't have realized I went to the wrong house by accident, like I've done every day this week after work. I would've been happy Tobin was waiting for me inside instead of guiltily wondering whether he saw me restart my car and drive away again.

But it's today, and I've got no one. I have to muster the courage to walk through the door on my own, even though my heart is thin and stretched out of shape from losing a presence as giant as Tobin's.

Inside the classroom, eight kid-sized chairs describe a loose semicircle in front of a six-inch-high plywood stage. A ceiling-mounted curtain in hospital green makes a sad backdrop for the non-hilarious comedy stylings to come.

Stellar wasn't wrong—improv is undignified. Only a desperate person would sign up, and now I'm surrounded by desperate people who don't know what to do with their arms and legs when they're perching on fourteen-inch-tall chairs.

I sit next to the woman who passed me in the hall, her mile-long legs scrunched, knees angled steeply toward her chin. I fold my very average five-foot-six body a bearable amount and pull my hair into a serviceable topknot in case things take a turn for the worse and I need to run away.

Two chairs down, a curvy fifty-something white woman in flattering knits pens a swirling "SHARON" on her name tag. Next to her, I recognize Jason Kim, sporting a BTS T-shirt captioned "I'm J-Hope's evil twin." Jason's one of those world-traveling Australians who pick up odd jobs in Grey Tusk between ski days. He was the instructor for the corporate first aid course I organized after an unlucky but treatable incident between an overconfident intern and a cranky printer. The Australians all know one another and are friendly exes with a dozen locals each; their gossip networks are legendary.

And oh, god. Off to the side stands David Headley from West by North, staring at an orange plastic chair like he's calculating the cost of dry-cleaning cooties off his pants.

Of course Naheed told him to take this class. He'll scout out every way to curry Craig's favor in the lead-up to the pitch competition.

My armpits prickle. I'd better be great at this, or between David and Jason, the embarrassing stories will take down my whole life.

As I take cleansing breaths and promise my stomach things won't get worse, in walks the biggest redheaded man I've ever seen outside of a Netflix fantasy series.

It could only be Tobin's best friend, McHuge.

And his badge says "INSTRUCTOR."

It's worse.

Everyone loves McHuge, an amiable ginger giant and part-time guide at West by North. He's the kind of person who inexplicably

does not look ridiculous with braids in his beard. Nobody but
Tobin calls him Lyle.

Everything hangs in the balance for five slow seconds as
McHuge strides to the front.

He must know. There's no way he doesn't.

"Peace and lov—urk!" McHuge chokes when he sees me.

My face is the approximate temperature of the sun. I would
leave, but the only thing worse than doing improv is not doing it.
Slinking back to my old life, defeated in minute one of trying to be
the new me. Watching junior people pass me by year after year,
pretending I can't hear the whispers of pity.

"Peace and love, everyone," McHuge manages, looking at Jason. "I'm Lyle McHugh. Everyone calls me McHuge, which is fine."

I raise my hand. "I thought, uh, we had a different instructor?"

"Bettina had a misunderstanding with a Canada goose, so I'm
teaching her classes until her cast comes off."

A flinching "ooohhh" ripples across the class. Canada geese
are twenty pounds of pure hatred in a deceptively attractive package, and springtime is their angriest season. Understandable—
they just spent five months in Arizona at peak tourist season and
they're about to have sextuplets.

I raise my hand again. "But wasn't Naheed supposed to be
here?"

"Naheed guides the Tuesday and Saturday groups."

Damn, I must've missed that on the antiquated registration
website. Saturdays I babysit Eleanor while Amber's at her single
moms' support group, but maybe I can transfer to Tuesday. Craig
specifically wanted me to register for Naheed's class.

"Moving on. Who thinks improv means making up jokes?"
McHuge's diesel-engine voice unlocks something in people. Four
hands go up.

The holdout is David Headley, who's flaunting his lowered

arms. I think his parents must've known he'd turn out this way, and that's why they gave him a name that tracks so easily to Dick Head.

"Common misconception. Punch lines aren't where the best laughs live. Improv is about uncovering what's universal and *real*. The truth. Is. Funny." McHuge locks eyes with everyone in turn.

Worry tugs at my gut. People hate it when I tell the truth. If I say meetings are inefficient or our processes can be improved, my coworkers ignore me for a week. Truth is how you lose a sister— you try to comfort her with something you think is reassuring, but actually, when you say *Maybe you two are better off apart,* it sets off the rant that breaks your relationship and grinds the pieces to dust.

I'm not here for truth. I'm here for the part where I learn to be a smooth talker. Not a liar, exactly. But I don't plan to reveal the parts of myself people don't like.

"Who knows the golden rule of improv?" McHuge rumbles.

"Yes, and!" Jason shouts.

"Yes! And!" McHuge makes big arm movements. He doesn't seem to notice what a sad ensemble we are, squished and sweating, with no idea what we're playing at.

"Take what your co-players give you, add to it, and give it back. Let's start by telling each other the truth and giving good 'yes, and.' Choose one true thing to share about yourself. Not something you're proud of. We grow closer by sharing our weaknesses, not our strengths. Who's opening their heart first?"

My tall seatmate whips out a pen, jots down a few words, then puts up her hand. She looks uncomfortable but game.

"Yes!" McHuge waves in her direction.

She reads with a trace of a French Canadian accent. "Hello, my name is Béa. I'm afraid of giving my wedding speech. I don't know if I can even talk to my guests without using notes. Or swearing when I get it wrong," she adds. Everyone laughs.

McHuge nods with his whole body. "Right on, Béa! Imagine a sketch with a bride flipping through her notes, trying to find the right thing to say. Tense, right? In improv, the audience wants to feel that tension with you. The truth is funny."

Béa crumples her note triumphantly. She's already getting what she came for. It looked easy.

When McHuge's finger points to me, I seize the moment.

"Hi. I'm Liz, and—"

I almost confess to being a millennial who's screwed up the moving-back-home stereotype by doing it when my parents aren't even here. But at the last second, I catch Dick Head's smirk. I hate that I'm fulfilling his low expectations by mumbling, ". . . and there's nothing funny about me."

Silence. Everybody absorbs my failure, the atmosphere growing wet and heavy.

In my hands, the truth isn't funny or interesting. Or magic.

"Okay!" McHuge claps his giant hands like thunder. "Liz gave us a fantastic learning point. Improv can get uncomfortable. When you feel uncomfortable, it's a great time to *not* change the subject. Stay in the moment, trust your partner. No one succeeds all the time, so when you fail, do it joyfully. If you're okay, the audience will be okay."

My ego shrivels and expires. I'm not okay, and everyone knows it.

Stupid crevasses, never there when I need to throw myself into one.

At the end of three hours, I've made zero jokes and zero friends. David Headley has now seen me pretend to be a calf getting born, which is even less flattering than it sounds. I died a little every time McHuge shouted encouragement about how tight the birth canal was and how amazing it felt to get out of there.

Everyone had a fantastic time but me.

The room tastes like other people's exhilaration as I grab my coat and shuffle toward the exit. I'm grateful to go back to Amber's-slash-my-parents' house. It's too late to watch a movie, but I downloaded a new romance novel today—Ivana Ryker's *Bone on the Fourth of July,* the highly anticipated sequel to *The Bone Identity* and *The Bone Supremacy.* Plus there's a Christmas novella—*Bone-Again Christian.* I password-protect them on my e-reader for Eleanor reasons, and also so Amber won't lecture me about reading something more "realistic." It wouldn't help our relationship if I told her the brain-bending sex might be unrealistic compared to *her* marriage, but it wasn't that far off for me and Tobin, once upon a time.

"Liz! Hey, scout. Stick around?"

"Yes, McHuge?" I glance at my phone, hinting I have an urgent appointment at ten o'clock on a Friday night.

He steps discreetly away from everyone, but he's six and a half feet tall and built like a brick wall. Points for trying, though.

"Liz. Sorry for the spit take; Tobin didn't warn me you'd be here. I wanna let you know, what happens at improv stays at improv. This is your safe space."

"Thanks," I say tightly, not believing him. He's Tobin's friend first, like everyone else.

"If you'd rather not have someone you know as an instructor, I'll make sure you get a full refund."

"Oh. Thanks. I might try to transfer—"

"Personally, I feel good energy between us. And some of the best people start slow."

"*Slow?* How bad was I?" Galactically terrible, if the teacher held me back after class. I thought improv would be the answer, but it's just another place I don't fit.

McHuge rumbles thoughtfully. "What brings you to improv?"

No reason. Just a million-to-one shot I decided to take when my whole life cratered a week ago.

"Craig sent me. For leadership development. I have to become excellent at improv in eight weeks."

"Oh. Okay, well, that's great and all, but I see the best results when there's a personal motivation to connect more deeply to the practice."

"I don't need to connect to anything. I just need to be very, very expert." I don't like how he nods, like I need to be humored.

"Let's put a pin in that. What were your scenes about tonight?"

Sigh. He won't find any hidden potential in this list. "Sharon and I did a long bit about dogs and teenagers. With Jason, K-pop and penetrating injuries, and we kind of took a detour into nail polish at one point? Béa and I talked muscle cars and indigenous art traditions. Dick Head—uh, sorry, David—"

McHuge coughs into one bearlike paw. Maybe the truth *is* funny.

"That's plenty. First, you remember everything your partners said."

I shrug. "Yeah, so?"

"So, remembering what's happened is huge. You have skills, my dude. Thing two: How much *Liz* was in your scenes?"

As little as possible is what I don't say. Until I figure out this magic thing, my two available personality modes are Weird Unlikeable Liz Lewis and Boring Beige Liz Lewis. I don't want to show either of those, so I agreed to every topic my partners suggested. Even Dick Head's.

"Exaaaactly," McHuge says. "You're giving your partners a lot of yes. Amazing." He whispers "amazing" like he's spotted a rare white spirit bear. "But they need yes, *and*. Bring *your* truth, Liz. Improv will only teach you as much as you let it."

McHuge lets this marinate as I look at the floor. Before, I categorized him as one of Tobin's charming brethren. This other side of him, where he knows a lot about comedy and is a generous, encouraging teacher—I didn't expect that.

I need another side to myself, like McHuge has. If I can find one, I can get this promotion. Prove to everyone that I can succeed even if I'm not naturally a McHuge.

Or a Tobin.

He chucks me on the shoulder. "Find a partner for extra practice once a week-ish. Focus on putting *Liz* in the games. Do the work, and you'll get what you're looking for."

"Thanks, McHuge."

"Peace, yo," he returns, stacking tiny chairs.

Outside, I make a note. **Practice improv once/week.** I can make up for my lack of talent by working hard and never giving up.

All I need is a partner, and in eight weeks, I'll be on my way to pitch competition victory.

Chapter Five

Making connections is as easy as listening, remembering, and recycling information. Nothing is ignored. Nothing is forgotten. Nothing is a mistake.

—*Truth in Comedy*

Eventually, I was going to have to go home.

After wearing my dove-gray pencil skirt in five different outfits this week, I need more of my work wardrobe. Amber's no help—she and I are different sizes, and besides, a rainbow assortment of nursing scrubs doesn't scream "promotion material."

I'd like to breeze in like I wasn't avoiding this moment, but as I learned in McHuge's class, playing pretend is not my game. I'm a reality person, and the reality is, I've been afraid I'd have to put my head between my knees from the blunt-force trauma of seeing Tobin and not having him belong to me. Even people who don't know when to quit get weak after days of not thinking about a certain angle of smiling lips, or an unintentionally artful splay of strong fingers. I used to feel that when we wrapped our arms around each other, both of our hearts recharged. Can I walk into a room full of his energy and not reach for it?

The cat trails me to the front door, Eleanor hot on his heels. "Yeti!" She reaches after him as he slips out from under her hand and through the front door. That kitty has a sixth sense for escape opportunities. So would I, if I could eat like a king at every house within meowing distance.

"He'll come back tomorrow, honey. See you soon."

It's a crisp spring evening in the neighborhood. Though it's less than thirty minutes from the wealth and glitter of Grey Tusk, Pendleton has a rough-hewn farming feel, its golden-green fields sternly flanked by gray-blue crags. Lots of Grey Tusk workers— including most West by North guides—live in the low-rise apartments that bracket Pendleton's block-long downtown, where you'll often see horses hitched to the false-fronted Old West buildings. The vibe is a little weird, a lot quirky, a ton of mind-your-own-business. That last part is especially noticeable on our street, on the free-spirited outskirts of town.

I grew up here, on the living edge of the wilderness, and this place is stitched into the deepest parts of my heart. The mountains feel so close you could breathe their breath. Sometimes I wake up and there's a bear in my apple tree.

Yeti's sunning himself on the front porch when I arrive. "Way to go, traitor," I tell him. "You're supposed to be on my side."

I don't mean it. My job is to pay the vet bills and be glad he's well loved. He does a great job of being a cat, considering he's half-blind and getting creaky. But I wouldn't have moved a cat his age to Amber's if he didn't already crash there twice a week.

Yeti's far from the days when Tobin and I, fresh off the high of moving in together, built him a haunted house out of an appliance box, dying of laughter when his paw snaked out from a spooky cardboard window to bat at us. Flat broke and stupid in love, we'd spent every dollar we had to buy the house from Mrs. Elias, the neighbor whose garden I used to weed in high school, who'd moved to Victoria to be closer to her grandkids.

Tobin wanted to wait to get a pet. He didn't want to miss the puppy stage while he was away every other week in the winter, and two weeks out of three in the summer. Besides, we couldn't afford puppy shots and neutering.

But I wheedled him into a trip to the shelter. Just to see. And there was Yeti, older, grumpy, camouflaged in the shadows at the back of his cage. My heart recognized him right away. *This one,* I begged Tobin.

After a week of hiding in the basement ductwork, Yeti blossomed into his himbo era, charming everyone on his way to ruling the neighborhood. For all of Tobin's reluctance to get a pet, he spent an awful lot of time crafting fluffy toys and refrigerator-box amusement parks to coax pounces out of Yeti and uncontrollable giggles out of me.

But Tobin and I are as far from those days as Yeti is. I don't remember the last time I laughed with him. Or the last time I wanted to tell him anything important—anything about my heart, instead of chores or schedules.

I let out an undignified *meep!* of fright when our front door abruptly squeaks open, scaring the cat off the porch.

Tobin stands there, looking so good, and so not good. His favorite gray T-shirt, thin from washing, outlines everything down to the tiniest muscle. He's barefoot despite the chill, too tall for the navy pajama pants that end above his finely turned ankles.

I haul my eyes up to his face. He looks exhausted, purple shadows underscoring those summer-blue eyes, his sexy smile lines transmogrified to wrinkles.

Our eyes meet for a long second. I'm hypnotized by his sadness the way I was once hypnotized by his joy, his passion, his implausible pleasure at being with plain old me.

He smiles. Tingles break over my body before I realize he's looking over my shoulder. "Hi, Eleanor. Be gentle with Yeti, okay?"

I *meep!* again, turning to catch Eleanor hauling an obliging Yeti off the stairs, his legs dangling to her knees. She must've tailed me the entire way here.

"Yeti lives with us now," she informs Tobin. Like him, she's wearing practically nothing: a too-short T-shirt, capri pants, no shoes. I want to wrap her in one of those silver thermal blankets, but she wouldn't allow it. She's the most weather-impervious kid I've ever met, wandering around in the dead of winter with her jacket unzipped, no hat, and maximum one mitten.

She marches homeward, sawn-off hair flipping unevenly away from her lifted chin, wearing Amber's stubborn expression. The cat wraps both arms around her neck and settles in, knowing that at the end of this journey, there will be cheese.

Tobin steps back after ensuring Eleanor's safely home. "You coming in?"

It wasn't smart to do this alone. Stellar obviously couldn't come; Amber's busy baking chickpea cookies for tonight's moms' group discussion on nutrition. I should have accepted Tobin's offer not to be at the house when I came by, but I couldn't bear to say yes to his devastatingly brief message—you want me gone?—right after texting him that I needed to get some of my stuff because I wasn't ready to come home yet. Even though I'm 99.99 percent convinced we're over for good, that fraction of a percentage point saying *But maybe we're not* makes me question myself. I hate it, but I can't make it stop.

I should have hired some lifties—chairlift attendants, strong from shoveling snow and swinging iron four-seaters under skiers' butts—to pose as my friends. They could've carried my bags while forming a protective barrier in front of my eyes so I wouldn't have to see what I'm giving up while actually giving it up.

I can't do this, I remind myself. I can't be the brakes in our marriage while Tobin gets to be the gas. I can't shine when I'm standing in his shadow.

Ignoring the pain in my chest, I cross the threshold.

His mom's been here. The house is aromatic with cinnamon and sweet plums from Marijke's signature cake. Where she got plums this time of year is anyone's guess, but they can't have been cheap.

It's self-absorbed to imagine she's happy I'm gone, but she might be, if she brought the damn cake. It's been my favorite since the moment I tasted its buttery, jammy, subtly vanilla perfection. She told me the recipe was reserved for family. I told her I'd be honored to receive it as a wedding gift.

She gave us towels.

It was me who antagonized her first, though. The day Tobin took me home to meet his parents, he should've warned me not to ask all those questions about his dad, Tor—had he called to say he'd be late? Where did he say he was coming from? Should we text him?

Marijke got chillier with each successive blunder. I apologized afterward, but it was too late. My dogged trying didn't carve one chip off her icy reserve.

Considering her feelings, I didn't expect what happened next. Sure, Marijke had been hinting that she was tired of commuting so far to the store. I thought that meant she wanted to move to Grey Tusk. I was ashamed of being a little bit glad. No more excuses for her to stop in Pendleton on the drive from Grey Tusk Village to her house in Linton, a sweet little town twenty minutes north of us. No more of her loving on Tobin while refusing to look at me on those evenings Tobin invited her to stay for dinner.

The universe bit me in the ass the day she bought the house next door.

The minute she moved in—barely a month after our wedding, just weeks before Amber and Eleanor arrived—felt like the final minute Tobin and I had to ourselves. Someone was always texting or calling, preempting our priorities with sales shifts at Marijke's pop-up events or appointments for Eleanor. If we didn't answer the phone, they'd peer in the windows. If I said we were busy, they did end runs around me to Tobin, who always said we weren't. Eventually, there didn't seem to be much point in defending our alone time.

I kick my shoes into a corner. "How do you want to do this?"

He hesitates for a moment, then turns away. "I'll stay on the couch." His bare feet whisper against the hardwood, a trail of mountain air wafting in his wake.

Christ, his ass in those pants. I force my gaze away for the second time, making for the stairs. The sooner I get out of here, the better.

The house is booby-trapped with memories. Along the staircase are the photos I painstakingly hung, measuring and sweating while Tobin nuzzled my neck and asked whether I was *sure* he couldn't help.

At the first step: a grainy, awkwardly posed shot from the trip where we first kissed, the sunset painting us in burnished gold.

Step by step, year by year, the photos march on: skiing, dog-sledding, our housewarming, our friends—well, Tobin's friends—and Yeti. The last one was taken as we walked back up the aisle at our wedding, me beaming shyly at Tobin while he turned a laughing face to our guests. I can still feel the echo of that moment, the sweet certainty of love spiked with the intoxicating thrill of possibility.

I stroke the frame, melancholy. There are no more photos after the wedding, because there were no memories happy enough to look at every day.

With a sigh, I climb the last few steps to the bedroom.

Pulling my suitcase from underneath a mountain of backpacks and gear, I knock over an unlabeled box, tumbling its contents across the dusty closet floor.

A poster tube with a curled-up print of my favorite Lawren Harris painting for when I get an office with walls. A copy of *The Seven Habits of Highly Effective People,* because the classics don't go out of date. Notebook upon notebook of ideas, inspiration, research, articles about successful eco-travel initiatives in places like Grey Tusk.

At first I kept the notebooks in my bedside drawer, ready for inspiration to strike. After a few years of pitching my ideas with no success, I moved them to the bookshelf. And then into a box at the back of the closet. When did I stop being the Liz whose ideas came from dreams, instead of desperation? Touching these books gives me a haunted feeling.

This stuff belongs to someone who died, and that someone was me.

I sweep the crap back into the box, but I can't get the lid closed. I reorganize and squish and retry, but the genie won't go back inside the bottle.

"Get in there," I mutter, shoving the lid. One corner pops back up. "Get *in* there, motherfucker."

Before I know it I've got the box in both hands and I'm throwing it down the stairs.

The lid flies off immediately, catapulting over the railing to flutter to the foyer below. *The Seven Habits* tumbles down the stairs, floppy like a dead body. Spiral-bound notebooks cramped from years of darkness sense their chance, unfurling their wings in a cascade of glitter-inked pages.

"Are you okay?!" I can hear Tobin tiptoeing through the disaster area.

"Throwing out some garbage while I'm here! I'll clean it up."

I heft the suitcase onto the bed, tossing clothes and gadgets in that general direction. It smells like him in here. Spring means snow and pine are giving way to clean earth and green sap, with a healthy, musky base note of Tobin.

Despite everything, my nipples pull tight, a flush gathering between my legs from just the *smell* of him rising from the bed.

But if sex were enough to keep us together, I wouldn't be dumping my jewelry into a zip pouch.

Whenever Tobin's around, I get . . . smaller. Quieter. Even less interesting. Without meaning to, he soaks up all the energy in the room, leaving none for me.

If I'm going to pick up my life and point it in a different direction, I have to crush the part of myself that relied on him to do the socializing and path smoothing.

And I need to find a formula to turn my base metal into his gold. Which reminds me to make a note.

Places to find improv partner: Online? At work?

I flinch while typing "work," but I'm desperate. No one wants to practice with me. Amber's slammed with work and parenting. Béa has a wedding to plan; Sharon doesn't want another evening commitment. Jason's busy the nights I'm free. Dick Head—forget it.

I close my bag. Time to go.

In the foyer, there's no sign of my box-throwing breakdown. I drop my suitcase to make a quick pantry run for soft cat food. Bribes might convince Yeti to sleep at Amber's more often.

When I come back, Tobin has the suitcase halfway out the front door.

"You said you'd stay on the couch."

He shoots me a look. "It's heavy." It's one of his only old-fashioned habits—carrying heavy things.

But I need to carry my own things.

I dart forward, yanking on the handle, ignoring how my hands spark against his. He's an annoying granite wall, repelling my efforts without even noticing. My feet tangle, I tilt, and the slow-motion disaster unfurls and unfurls like a thousand miles of scarves out of a clown's sleeve.

I face-plant into his chest, fingers still locked over his.

He brings his free arm around my shoulder. He did this with *one* arm. Infuriating.

"You okay?"

I'm not okay. My nose is at Tobin Ground Zero; my face is cradled against the softness of his shirt. I can't help closing my eyes and taking a big inhale.

Sadness pierces my chest.

This is the last time he'll hold me. I didn't know, when he was seducing me last week, that it wouldn't happen again. But now the knowledge is a countdown clock ticking away the seconds of my marriage.

"I'm fine. Let go."

He releases the bag, his hand flexing and opening at his side. "Let me put it in your car. Please."

"It's half a block. I walked."

He looks horrified. "You're staying with Amber? She—"

I give him the hand. "Don't. We're getting along fine."

"Are you, though? She isn't trying to make every single decision for you?" He has the audacity to look worried, this wreck of a man in his two-day-old pajama pants. He is not allowed to pity me. I will not have it.

"My sister loves me," I hiss. Defensively, because there was a time I was pretty sure she didn't. She was so *happy* those four years in Colorado, just her and Mark, no parents or sisters. They almost never visited Pendleton, which Amber brushed off with a breezy "Mark isn't into family." She posted pictures of the two of them hiking, skiing, climbing—all the things she hated doing with Mom and Dad. And me.

But then it turned out Mark actually wasn't into family. After he left, Amber got folded back into the Lewis family batter like a chocolate chip that fell on the floor for not quite five seconds— still good. And if scheduling me into Eleanor's life meant she loved me, then she really, really did.

"Oh? Then I assume Amber's being extra nice to you right now."

"I didn't feel like being babied."

"No, huh? You didn't feel like watching *The Big Sick* or *The Lovebirds,* with popcorn and wine, so the two of you could thirst over Kumail Nanjiani?"

Amber disapproves of my rom-com habit—according to her, they give people (me) unrealistic ideas about relationships. Tobin knows I wanted to comfort-watch and she didn't. He knows I know he knows she didn't. That's marriage: a hall of mirrors, where everyone can see everything, and no one can escape.

"Kumail Nanjiani is a *very* important comedian," I say, because Tobin hasn't been my sort-of ex long enough to make snarky comments about thirst. "And actually, it's *extra nice* to hang with Eleanor, who is an amazing human being, who I love spending time with. We made a lot of really good things with Legos."

He closes his eyes. "Fine. I can carry the bag to Amber's."

"You don't get to carry your ex's bags."

He blanches like I slapped him. "We're still married."

I muscle the suitcase down the stairs. It's really heavy. "Come on, Tobe. We should try to be realistic."

"So that's it?" His voice lowers, dark and wounded. "You

show up, you grab some stuff, you're out? I've spent hours on the phone trying to get us a therapy appointment sooner than July. I've stayed up nights reading every relationship book you can buy, and some you can't. And you won't even *try* to fix our problems?"

"Oh, *now* you admit we have problems. This would have been useful anytime in the past three years. Anytime I said we needed help before it was too late."

We're fighting. Actually fighting.

Tobin and I don't do this. It's terrifying and exhilarating, saying all the stuff I kept inside, afraid to give him the last push he needed to leave his boring, weird wife.

But the angrier I am, the more powerful I feel. I don't have to worry I'm not enough for him if I can decide he's not enough for me.

He can't leave me if I leave him first.

I roll off, keeping an eye out for Eleanor dropping down from a tree or popping out from behind a shrub.

"Liz!" It's the rawest sound I've ever heard him make. Raw enough to stop me in my tracks.

"Can we please talk." His head sags. "Please. I've given you space, like you asked. The whole week. Eight days. I'm losing it over here."

Unwilling to turn back, I peer over my shoulder. He's sweating. Clenched. Hyperventilating.

I'm leaving him, like his dad left him a dozen times as a kid and left his mom a dozen more since Tobin grew up. I'm impulsively walking out on someone whose psyche formed around the wounds from impulsive abandonment. I should dial 666 and make dinner reservations in hell, because I'm going to need them.

But also. Here's something he didn't mean to show me. Something not perfect. The opposite of pixie dust—plain old dirt.

Perfection is what Tobin manufactures for West by North tourists, who don't understand they're settling when they feast on Alberta prime rib after an easy float down the river. They've never tasted the glorious first bite of bannock—dough toasted on a stick—that you burned and ate anyway after a backcountry day when you felt like quitting dozens of times and didn't.

And Tobin—he's giving bannock vibes, charred edges hiding the steamy, tender insides. It's ugly and ordinary and *real*. It's my favorite, and I want it too much.

I should keep running, but that one click of a tumbler in his locked-down heart makes the whole world tremble under its impact.

I can't help but be shaken.

"All right," I say, wheeling around. "Start talking."

Chapter Six

Interest comes from connection, not conflict. Be true to the self that seeks to know and love others. YES, AND.

—*The Second Chances Handbook*

Seven minutes later, Tobin and I are posed stiffly on opposite sides of his truck, each of us an inflatable doll incapable of communication. My suitcase hovers next to my leg, the way people position it when they're waiting for their flight, ready to run.

Tobin's in the driver's seat.

Every little thing in our marriage carries meaning these days. There's nothing I won't overthink.

It was me who insisted we couldn't possibly conduct our business inside the house. And it's his truck. He retrieved the keys, unlocked his door, and reached across the cab to open my door because he knows I get flustered and clumsy when people open my car door from the outside.

But he's in the driver's seat, and I'm pissed off about what that says about us.

I'm also glancing around nervously because of what I'm reading.

"This." My voice squeaks, trying to weasel its way out of this conversation.

I pop the glove box and steal a piece of Tobin's gum from under the paper maps of northern BC and the Yukon (where the cell coverage is too patchy for Google Maps) and the roll of wrenches and other truck-fixing things I don't know the names of, which Tobin treats like the One Ring of Sauron.

This book in my lap looks almost like a real book. Evidence that it's not: on the front is a bright red sticker shouting, "ADVANCE READER COPY: UNCORRECTED PROOF." Also, first among the authors is Lyle McHuge.

McHugh. Whatever.

The book is enormous, like its so-called author, a textbook-sized softcover. Its background is the deep matte black of a box of Magnum-sized condoms.

"Thiiiiiiis," I try again, tapping the cover. "Is *a sex book*."

I haven't skimmed more than the first few pages, but I guarantee these chapters are crammed with soft-porn role-play and "creative" uses for chocolate sauce.

Tobin knows it. A few minutes ago, he gingerly handed me the book like an airport rando asking me to watch his bag for one minute as the sniffer dogs close in.

"It's a *relationship repair manual*." Tobin's wedged against the door, hands held awkwardly against his abs.

I can't remember ever sitting next to him without some kind of physical contact (unless seat belt laws were in effect). When we watch TV, he goes extravagant, arranging me on top of him in outrageously luxurious positions he's engineered for maximum contact and optimal ergonomics.

Now I catalog all the cracks I've never noticed in his aging vinyl bench seat, because I was hiding them with my ass as I cuddled up to him. We've done a lot more than cuddle in this car, quite frankly. Which brings me right back to the book.

"They want you to *think* it's a relationship book." I glance at the open window funneling my words to the neighborhood.

Tobin enjoys feeling like he's outside at all times. He's practically allergic to enclosed spaces. Now that I don't live with him, no one tells him indoors and outdoors should be different temperatures. The half-dozen open windows on the front of the house tell me he's enjoying his new climate control privileges. He's changed from PJs into shorts and a T-shirt, like he doesn't even feel the damp, foggy chill washing down from the glacier.

I turn back to the book. *The Second Chances Handbook,* it declares in a trendy, aspirational font. And below that: *Rules for Rebooting Your Relationship with Improv.* McHuge has added "Dr." before his name and "PhD" after.

The hell he is.

"Where did you get this?" I trace the raised letters. This is an expensive treatment. It looks . . . quite real.

"Lyle. We're lucky to have it. His agent made him send the rest of them to BookTokkers with huge follower counts. I had to promise to leave five-star reviews on all the bookseller websites."

McHuge the amiable slacker has an *agent*? I thought he mushed his dog team, steered his raft, and dominated Tinder in his peace-and-love downtime. Instead, he's written a book and gotten an agent and is allowed to call himself "Doctor."

I cross another name off the list of people who might make me feel better about myself by also being thirty and non-amazing.

And, chugging directly toward that first train of thought: McHuge, my improv instructor, whom I have to see every week, lent a "relationship" handbook to my husband.

The only life option left is to find a comfortable hole with Wi-Fi and a pipeline of chocolate-covered strawberries. I will commit the rest of my life to writing emo journal entries about how, if I were a superhero, my superpower would be opening up bottomless crevasses as a public service.

"McHuge . . . wrote this book?"

"Amazing, right? He doesn't brag about it, but his dissertation got a lot of press in the psychology world. His program gets better results than conventional marriage counseling. And, well. Book deal."

Tobin's twitching the way he does whenever he tries to sell something. He's terrible at asking people for things. He hates the end of his rafting and dogsledding trips, when he has to talk up prepayments for next year's trips.

He'd rather charm people into giving him things. Wait for clients to ask *him* about rebooking at a discount. Then he can say, *yes,* he'd love to see them again.

"Yes" is his favorite word. "No" is the word I get to say so he doesn't have to sully his shine in front of Girl Guides selling cookies or political candidates selling themselves.

Or his parents.

I google "Lyle McHugh," looking for a reason to say no to this, too. My screen floods with TikTok videos, some of them boasting view counts into the six figures. What the hell, McHuge? I click one. A gorgeous twentysomething waxes rhapsodic about the book, a thirsty slideshow of McHuge photos playing in the background— scraped from West by North's website, I note, with a preference for shots where his clothes are wet. Yup, sex book.

Switching strategies, I search for McHuge's original publication instead. Bingo. "It's not better than couples' therapy. They didn't reach statistical significance."

Tobin's mouth sets harder. The vulnerability of half an hour ago is lost. "We can't get an in-person therapy appointment before midsummer, unless we lose four hours driving down to Vancouver and back every week. And the science says the book works."

"You mean the book your best friend wrote, *which is a sex manual*." I tug the page so hard it rips a little. Sure, it's not *supposed* to be a sex book, but McHuge didn't factor in the impact of doing it with Tobin Renner-Lewis, which is approximately equivalent to the impact of a dinosaur-killing meteorite hitting ancient Mexico. Being near him, doing scenarios with him—I mean, McHuge spent half of last week's class telling us improv is all about intimacy.

"Can you please not damage it," Tobin snaps, glancing from the torn page to the open window, which happens to face his mom's house. I get a petty burst of pleasure from the window causing *him* discomfort, for once. "I promised Lyle I'd give it back."

"Oh my *god,* Tobin! Nobody wants your sex book back when you're done with it!" On purpose, I fail to keep my voice down.

It takes, like, fifty turns for him to hand-crank his window shut.

I face the man who looks like my husband, but feels like a stranger. My back is against the door, in a defensive position, but the fight in me has died.

He doesn't know me at all.

"I told you we've lost our connection, and your solution is *this*." The worst part is, I'm tempted. Breakups are fucking terrible and I'm so alone right now, with Stellar away and my parents in Arizona and Amber on my case. Yeti is very absorbent for my crying needs, but the only human who hugs me is Eleanor, and it's beyond inappropriate for me to pin my emotional support requirements on a six-year-old.

I'm able to recognize how unhealthy it is to want comfort from the person who's hurt me, who I'm hurting, too. I need to get as far away as possible from the Tobin he becomes when we're alone: quiet. Thoughtful. Charmingly almost shy; a secret that's all mine.

He listens so carefully, so closely, that for years I didn't notice the things he'd stopped talking about.

He gave me everything but himself.

I can't give in to the urge to burrow into his arms, stumble into his bed, smack into the same emotional walls, and start the cycle all over again.

"Sex wasn't our problem, Tobe," I say softly.

It sure wasn't. We took our time getting to home plate—practically unheard of, in the horny, monogamy-optional world of summer adventure tours—but once he fell into my sleeping bag, he never found his way out.

"For both our sakes, we need to make a clean break. And I have . . . a lot going on right now." No need to get into my "get magic" plan with Tobin. He wouldn't understand what it's like to have landed your only job through what you later realized was the sheer luck of having in-demand skills right when a struggling new company needed more people than it could hire. Or how it feels to get shuffled into a spreadsheet pigeonhole you can't break out of. All you can do is watch your hopes melt away year after year, like a glacier losing ground to summer.

I grab my suitcase again. This time, he doesn't reach for it.

"You need an improv partner," Tobin says suddenly. "This book is improv. I'll be your partner." He leans forward, resting his fingers across the open pages in my lap. His eyes are sharp as icicles, his mouth bracketed by brand-new creases. "*If* you do the book with me."

"How do you know that?" My voice shakes. "McHuge promised what happens at improv stays at improv."

"He didn't tell me anything that happened in class. We were hanging out and he asked whether you'd found a partner yet. It's not his fault; he doesn't . . ." He looks away.

"Jesus, Tobin. Haven't you told anybody?" But of course he

hasn't. He'd throw his best pair of broken-in boots in the fire before admitting things aren't as perfect as they seem.

He might be the only person lonelier than I am right now.

Still, this is suspicious. "Why did McHuge give you the book if
he doesn't know about . . ." I gesture at us.

Tobin looks away, catching his lips between his teeth. "He
asked me to read it. I'm interested in his new career."

I take back my thoughts about him being lonelier. He and
McHuge being all bromantic and reading each other's books and
DMing each other about the good parts . . . yeah. I'm the lonely
one. It's me.

"Do the book with me, Diz. We can still turn this ship around,"
he insists. "It's not too late."

"And if it is? What then?"

"Then I'll do whatever you want. Give you . . ." He swallows.
"Whatever you want." His callused hand is brown against the fresh
white page, fingernails stained from months of unknotting frozen
leather harnesses. It's shaking.

My eye catches on the word "Introduction" below his pinkie.
McHuge writes,

As a relationship counselor, I meet a lot of unhappily part-
nered people. Most of them are looking for a referee who
knows the rules of relationships and will blow the whistle
on foul play. They want accountability: Who broke which
Law of Love?

As a therapist and an improv comedy player, I believe
relationships aren't about the rule of **law**. Like improv, relationships operate by the rules of the **game**. Games mean
play, fun, imagination, and creativity. Games leave room
for unexpected things to happen. They bring teammates

together. Rules exist to make sure everyone has the most fun possible.

You might think joy, invention, and laughter have abandoned your relationship. You might have trouble seeing your partner(s) as anyone but the person or people who hurt you. Improv can turn that around.

As you progress through the guided, improv-based scenarios in this book, you'll rediscover fun, games, and each other. Your experiences, memories, and imagination will make the scenarios uniquely yours. And you'll uncover inner characters who can help you see your partner(s), and yourself, in a new light.

All you need is a rule book to get you started on your second chance.

Oh my god.

My party. My job. The pitch competition. I could never find the right person to be. But this book says I have inner characters who can help me be someone else. This book has a recipe for me to follow, like Craig's checklist for promotion.

I pull the next page out from under Tobin's fingers without ripping it.

The first rule for second chances is the simplest one. And the most difficult. As the improv greats say, finding ways to disagree is all too easy. Couples, threesomes, and more-somes can break the cycle of disagreement by saying YES, AND. When improvisers react honestly while seeking harmony, the relationships in their scenes come alive. When partners do the same, their relationship can come back to life, too.

"Liz?" Tobin's voice cracks, opening a matching fissure in my heart. He's stroking the hardware in his left wrist with his right index finger, a nervous habit he's picked up since his surgery.

This is too much pressure. I only want to say yes if I'm sure this will work. I can't bear to fail again; I can't put us through the blood and sweat and tears of trying unless we succeed.

And I don't know if we will. Neither of us does. Maybe I'm not brave enough to find out.

"I think I spoke too soon about this book," I say, stalling.

"It's not actually a sex book," he says, the tiniest hint of a smile playing at the corner of his lips. His eyes flick to where I'm rubbing the tips of my fingers together, something I do to soothe myself when I'm feeling uncertain. He knows I'm wavering.

"Some of it might be all right," I concede. "Parts of it look like improv, or at least role-playing."

Improv. I'd be practicing improv.

With Tobin, who's fantastic at saying the right thing, to the right person, at the right time. Tobin, whose supernatural charisma and uncomplicated devotion to sea-shanty TikTok can get an entire boat of soaking, freezing, wretched guests belting out a vaguely dirty chorus with hours left to go in a dark-skied day. Whose greatest talent is making people think it was their idea to do everything his way, without him even having to ask.

Tobin, the original magic man. I could watch him, learn from him, copy all his mannerisms and best lines. Use them to make myself into the kind of person who doesn't have to endure the sting of knowing she didn't get her retired ex-boss's job even though nobody else wanted it.

He thrusts the book into my hand. "Read it, okay? Take all the time you need." There's a light in those eyes as blue as an

August sky north of sixty. It's obvious hope has infected him, like a virus.

I need to get back to Amber's, if only to make sure Eleanor hasn't snapped Yeti into a Lego jail with a phalanx of Barbie prison guards, all of their hair shorn to match her own.

"I'll think about it," I say, shoving the book into the front pocket of my suitcase. It's a very convenient piece of baggage. Tobin laughed when I bought it at a Black Friday sale, saying he hoped we'd never take a trip that needed a suitcase.

I look up at him, hand on the door latch. "No promises."

"No promises," he echoes. He forgets I've known him for eight years, and I can hear the promise in his voice.

My phone pings with Amber's text tone.

> Guess you're not coming home, lol. Enjoy the makeup sex. Hate to say I told you so, but . . . I'm glad you decided to be happy with what you have.

Sisters are so complicated. I want us to be close. Yet there's this groundswell of fury inside me, as if I've failed to get promoted to adulthood with her the same way I've failed to get promoted at work. "What you want from marriage isn't important; be happy with what you can get." "You're not suited for leadership, Liz; you're happier with numbers, not people."

But what if I'm *not* happy? What if I don't agree that I shouldn't try for what I want?

Halfway out the door, I wheel around, riding an angry wave of impulse that washes away logic and reason.

I can *so* reach for something better. A job, a life, a partnership where I get to be more than background scenery. My only chance to save this marriage is to stop taking what I can get and start going after what I want. I don't think it's a big chance, but Tobin and I are going into this with our eyes open.

And even if the marriage thing doesn't work, I'll still be saving my job. After all, who better to learn improv from than the best?

"If we do this, I have conditions."

"Yes! Absolutely, name them." He blows out a long breath the way he does when the painkillers finally kick in.

"No sex."

"None."

"I won't move back in."

"But you and Amber—all right, whatever you want," Tobin amends hastily.

"We don't say 'I love you.'"

He flinches. "Okay."

"Deal," I say quickly, afraid of how his feelings can still grab my heart and yank.

"What if *I* have conditions?" His eyes are unaccountably dark. He's leaning in my direction, making me aware I'm leaning in his. I've never seen him so focused. Not asking—*demanding*.

It occurs to me that I wasn't the only unhappy one.

A chill breaks across my skin. "What do you want?"

"Ten weeks to finish the book. We commit to saving this marriage, for real, before I leave for the summer season."

"Ten weeks is too much," I whisper.

"I gave you everything you wanted," he counters. His sun-and-whisky hair falls over his eyebrows, framing a frowny V-shaped line I can't stop staring at. When did he get all those angry, pretty muscles in his neck?

Every second I'm in his orbit, I'm in danger of his gravity pulling me back in. I want his sunshiny power to win people over, but I can't ignore the risk of becoming his shadowy moon, with no light of my own.

"Eight weeks. As many as we get done." That'll take us to the annual retreat and the pitch competition.

"Deal. We start next week." He swings out of the truck fast before I can stare my fill at the rest of him.

I wrestle my suitcase out of the cab, not at all missing his help, and head back to Amber's. On the way, I stop to open my Notes app.

FIND IMPROV PARTNER.

Check.

Chapter Seven

Believe in what's happening in the scenario. Open your heart and your mind to the reality you make together. If you're only going through the motions, your scene will never come to life, and your chance to create a shared consciousness will pass you by.

—*The Second Chances Handbook*

There's something about the sight of six grown-ass adults filing reluctantly onto a baseball diamond—without any baseball equipment—that makes the part of my brain that says "funny" and the part that says "awful" start fighting over who gets to ride in the front seat.

There aren't a lot of flat spots for fields in Grey Tusk. It's a long, narrow town squished into the lowest part of a twisty, uneven dip between peaks, and the highway eats a four-lane stripe through the middle of everything. For this reason, the community center shares precious field space with the high school. Even then, the outfield is cut short by Grey Tusk's version of a Green Monster: thick-trunked cedars flanking the mountain's steep, sudden rise.

It must be fun to nail a home run into the trees and send the other team on a search mission for the ball.

Tonight, only McHuge looks like he's having fun. He's taking a chest-expanding lungful of April evening, ever the idealistic sitcom dad whose ideas are destined for disaster. I bet Naheed's classes aren't doing this. My efforts to get into Naheed's section failed—even the wait lists are full—but at least David couldn't transfer either, judging by the fact that he's still here.

McHuge pulls me aside. "Did you get a chance to practice this week?"

"I did a couple of hours of free association, some word games, some—"

"On your own? You need a partner, Liz."

"I might meet up with someone next week." Or I might not. I could still pull the rip cord and stay safely away from Tobin. My neck prickles at the thought of McHuge finding out my improv partner is Tobin and our textbook is his book. So awkward.

"See? You put the intention out into the universe, and voilà! Tonight, I want you to think about opening the creative flow with your classmates."

We look over at the pool of improv talent. Sharon's waving both arms at imaginary bugs. Jason frowns at the kids playing hide-and-seek in a giant hollow stump nearby.

At home plate, Béa kicks at the dry gravel with the toe of a trail shoe that's seen a lot of distance. To her left, Dick Head hops away from her dust, sending her an accusing look before leaning down to inspect the Italian leather situation on his feet.

"Will do," I say, earning myself a McHuge-brand shoulder squeeze.

I check my phone as he walks away. Stellar said she wanted to talk tonight, and I want to rant to her about the eternal spring drama at West by North, where it's goodbye, money season, hello, mud season and bug season. Off-peak visitors, too budget-conscious for our luxury tours, prefer free activities—like getting themselves marooned halfway to Hell, a hidden hot spring only reachable on foot.

More important, I want to bounce ideas off Stellar for the pre-pitching meeting. A couple of weeks from now, I'll be trying to snag one of three coveted slots for the final pitch competition. In an effort to prove to Craig that I'm a fountain of innovation (and to feel out which project he'd greenlight), I'm pitching him an idea a day.

So far he's shot down boardwalk tours of endangered wetlands (too boring and virtuous to be profitable), subarctic hiking safaris for photography enthusiasts (too much walking, not enough helicopters), and a mountaintop marriage proposal shuttle service (enough helicopters but only two paying customers).

Craig's always dismissed my ecotour pitches, but I'm freaking out a little over him not listening to my ideas for loud, flashy stuff, which usually gives everybody in the C-suite a good solid chub in their Armani. I was counting on that corporate half boner to help me get seen and promoted. Then they'd have to listen to me when I pointed out the literal self-sabotage (not to mention the environmental sabotage) of tours that destroy their destinations.

My parents constantly drilled me and Amber to respect and protect fragile alpine ecosystems. There's no reason West by North can't do the same, but Craig's eyes go unfocused when I talk about carbon. I spend a lot of time shutting down the storm brewing inside me from him ignoring me and brushing me aside.

Some days, I'm nothing but a primal scream in a beige blouse. Instead of screaming, I text Stellar.

> You want to remote-watch Romancing the Stone tomorrow?

Stellar doesn't love rom-coms, but she does love popcorn and alcoholic milkshakes and criticizing what passed for progressiveness in the nineties. We trade picks, so I get a chance to make fun of bad special effects in her classic sci-fi flicks.

> Sure. Can Jen drop some boxes of my stuff at your house? We broke up. Obviously.

Stellar's girlfriend said she was cool with short-term long distance. They were discussing marriage. Stellar hasn't even been gone a month. She must be devastated.

> Nnnooooooo!!! You and Jen broke up?!?! I'm so sorry, are you okay?

With supremely poor timing, McHuge calls, "Circle up."

Everybody takes half a step forward. Sharon's madly whiffing arms barely miss Jason's head.

"We're outside for two reasons. Number one: no point waiting until the showcase to feel the vibe of doing improv in public. It's a good energy, but it can feel like a lot in your body."

McHuge makes improv sound like a cardiac defibrillator. Based on my knowledge of *Grey's Anatomy* and this class, his description of big, painful electricity arcing through you sounds right on.

"Tonight, nobody's watching," he says, sweeping his arm unironically at the hide-and-seek kids, who stand riveted by his performance. "Even so, you won't have a room with a closed door to protect you. Make an open door in your heart to match the open door on this field. Lean into the vulnerability."

McHuge has a strange talent for making sense even when he makes no sense, but that advice is not for me. I am not here to be vulnerable. I'm here for an eight-week crash course in social skills that will turn me into a pitch-competition magician. I've had plenty of opportunities to explore vulnerability and failure, and they are not as great as people make them sound.

"Everybody pair up for warm-up. We're an odd number, so one person will work with me."

Everybody scrambles away from David. For his part, David steps directly over to McHuge to reserve the highest-quality partner for himself.

Béa and I commandeer the home-team bench, glossy from many seasons of ass polishing. She's a lot younger than me—twenty-four—but she seems cool and she's new in town. Maybe she needs friends, too.

"Baseball is such a weird game," I say, in my best friendly voice. "One person with a stick versus the entire other team. Gladiatorial combat could break out any moment."

Béa looks over my head. "I played varsity for Duke. Second base."

I love her accent. A Montreal lilt makes even a rejection sound almost delicious.

"Oh. Uh . . . oh. Right. I meant that I *love* weird sports. The weirder, the better."

Not an improvement, judging from her expression.

"Should we get started? Um, stars," I offer so I have an excuse to look away, up into the wash of sodium light.

"Celebrities," she answers.

"Scandal."

"Cheating."

"Athletes. Oops." I smack my forehead. "Sorry. That wasn't the right thing to say. I . . ."

McHuge claps his hands, waving us all to the infield. He's sketched two squarish shapes in the gravel with his heel.

"Second objective! Respect the environment! We're going to work with objects in space. Teams will decide what these shapes"—McHuge points at his dirt rectangles—"represent. The big one is something the size of a table or a car. The smaller one takes up as much floor space as a chair or a fence post. To you, they're real. No walking through the car. All good, my brethren? Okay, at the big station, Sharon, Dave, aaaaaand—"

Please not me, please not—

"—Liz. At the small one, Béa, Jason, and me."

I wish I could stop hating Dick Head, but there's a dark well of loathing in my soul that never runs dry. Today, he spent fifteen minutes in front of my desk telling Craig how his personal contributions have shaved 3 percent off our marketing budget. At least once a minute, he flashed his giant Rolex with a tiny diamond on its face.

I should start calling him David instead of Dick Head. I'll concentrate on his redeeming qualities. All humans have some of those, I feel sure.

David's eyes turn my way. His expression looks like he showed up for a casting call for "tall white guy, face like this party only has second-best caviar." If I were him, I wouldn't be able to resist punching my reflection in the bathroom mirror every morning.

He might be the exception to the redeeming qualities rule.

Sharon windmills over, neck cords popping. "I'm allergic to wasps. I get welts the size of a twelve-ounce steak. If I get bitten on my face, one of you has to give me my EpiPen." She indicates the zip pouch at her waist.

"I'm the first aid marshal at work; I know how. But really, it's all about prevention. Should you stay inside?" I eye her fanny pack. It's bright purple, hand-inked with "NOBODY ASKED YOU" in a trendy, loopy cursive. All right, Sharon. Way to dominate the quote game.

She gives a scornful harrumph. "Nah. Not afraid of needles. Or wasps. Mid-April's usually too early for them. But you never know where a queen might be laying her brood." Her eyes narrow at a nearby fieldhouse.

"Our shape could be a bug tent," I suggest. It has possibilities: low doorways, zip closures, tension between players inside and those left outside. And it's not a table or a car, which could involve pretend sitting. My thighs are in no way ready for chair-free imaginary family dinner.

"I say it's a gullwing McLaren." Di—David slides his wrist forward, checks his watch, scans to see who's caught the diamond twinkle. He smirks at me—fell for it, dammit—but his smile fades when his eyes slide to Sharon, whose mind is on wasps instead of douchey displays of wealth.

"A McLaren, Di—David?" Last time, I played along with all his self-important topics. In return, he's rejecting my very first suggestion. Although on second thought, a gullwing door could swing up, right into his face.

My inner scream thickens with another layer of shellac.

I didn't realize, before I lost it at my party and walked out on my husband, how much energy I was burning to make myself small. Managing people's emotions is hard work. Getting along and going along are *difficult.* I'm worn out.

I thought it would take so much courage to let out my scream. Turns out, the work is in keeping it in.

McHuge bustles over. I didn't think bustling was in the skill set of people who are six feet six, but he pulls it off.

"How are you three doing?" His tone says, *I can sense your negative vibes from across the field, my dudes.*

"Great!" I say, as Dick Head snarls, "Liz can't agree on what our object is."

"No problem." McHuge crosses his arms. "What was the first suggestion?"

"A bug tent," Sharon says, stepping inside its boundaries. Oddly enough, her waving settles down.

"Fantastic. Quick teachable moment: argument delays action. Listen to your co-players, give them a 'yes, and.' That keeps the scene moving."

Dick Head rolls his eyes as McHuge jogs away. Over at the small square, Jason makes shooing gestures at a growing gaggle of kids. Béa takes an imaginary microphone out of its stand and promptly freezes, mouth half-open, with what looks like non-improvised stage fright.

I feel so damn . . . vulnerable. God, I wish I didn't have to do this.

But that option isn't available. In this timeline, I have two choices: in the tent, or out of it.

I open the imaginary zipper and step inside.

"Shut the door, shut the door! The wasps will come in!" Sharon's waving starts up again.

I hustle to get the zip down. "Yes, and . . ." I turn to Sharon, struck with a wonderful, awful idea. ". . . They're zombie wasps! And, uh, they already bit David!"

"Bug spray! It's the only way to stop him," Sharon shouts, looking in all the corners as David unenthusiastically rattles the zipper.

"Grab the fire extinguisher!" I holler back.

Dick Head shoots me a dirty look. I immediately feel 3 percent happier. There's something to this lying business, after all.

"Oh, shit," Sharon says.

"I know! His Rolex pulled his hand right off! Most disgusting zombie I've ever seen."

"Worse than that one?" Dick Head points inside the tent. Sharon's on the ground, her left eye the size and color of a twelve-ounce steak.

"Zombie wasp!" I gasp, falling to my knees beside her. "*McHuge!*
I need help!" He sprints over.

"Effeefen! EFFEEFEN!" Sharon insists through puffy lips, both
eyes swelling shut.

I unclip the bag at her waist, zipping open all three com-
partments and shaking until the bright yellow box tumbles out.
McHuge squats on her other side, calling 911 with Jason's phone.

"Ready, Sharon?" I haven't done this before, but I review the
instructions every six months, the same way I read the emergency
card in the seat pocket every time I get on a plane. I jam the device
hard against her pants and smash the trigger.

David joins the group of concerned faces above us. "Classic
bee-sting allergy. I've dealt with it before. But you all were doing
a not-bad job, so I let you take the lead."

McHuge lets out an uncharacteristic grunt of frustration, then
has to reassure the 911 dispatcher everything's okay and he hasn't
started CPR.

I take Sharon's hand. "How you doing, friend?" Her face is a
horror show, but she gives me a shaky thumbs-up.

Both Sharon and McHuge are treating me like I'm supposed
to be in charge. They aren't talking over me or policing my facial
expressions. Is it because I was a different character a minute ago?
One who led our scene and brought ideas?

This is what I need: characters who aren't me, who convince
people I belong and I can lead. Survivors of the zombie waspoca-
lypse might not be the most useful types in the corporate world,
but hope still glimmers like a diamond on a Rolex. My scream
feels one layer smaller, after collaborating with Sharon and pushing back against David.

Maybe I have other characters, too. If I can find them, I might
have a chance at the pitch competition. I might have a chance for
a different *life*.

Painful as it is to admit, I can't do it by myself.

When Sharon's tucked into the ambulance and McHuge has canceled the rest of the class, I pull out my phone. I only hesitate a little before pressing *Send* on my text to Tobin.

> When should we get together to do the book?

Dots pop up so fast it's uncomfortable.

> Tomorrow morning? Scenario 1?

I pause a moment. Every second means something in the virtual world; I know, after committing all possible blunders. Replying too fast makes you look desperate. Waiting makes conversation agonizing, but I don't make the rules. Or break them.

> I need to read the scenarios first. But yes, tomorrow. You free at 10?

Immediate dots. Tobin has no regard for online rules. But there are always exceptions for people like Tobin.

> Send me pics of the instructions. 10 AM. See you then.

Chapter Eight

SCENARIO 1: THE MEET-CUTE

Just about everyone fears being judged. Sometimes it feels safer to hold back your thoughts, rejecting your own ideas rather than risking the pain of rejections from others. In improv, this is called **self-editing**.

In relationships, self-editing soothes your fear of being judged by people you love, whose rejections hurt more than anyone else's. The price: silencing your creativity and giving up your chance to be loved for who you truly are.

Sometimes it's easier to be yourself when the relationship stakes are low, like when you're talking to anonymous strangers online. For your first scenario, imagine your characters have never met. Using whatever text messaging app you prefer, create a scenario where your characters have logged onto an online messaging platform to join a conversation with the person (or people) they find there. Actually message each other, instead of talking—make it as "real" as you can! (Low-tech alternative: pass notes.)

Tip: Don't worry about how the conversation "should" go—focus on what your characters' unique personalities bring to the scene. What would they tell someone whose judgment they didn't fear in real life? What would make them fall for someone? Remember, there's nothing a *character* won't do, so make them do the unexpected!

—*The Second Chances Handbook*

A rendezvous with your ex to do an experimental marriage counseling session in public is a lot of pressure on a Saturday morning. A *lot.* Is it as much pressure as pitching your ecotour idea in front of sixty colleagues? No, but I have to start somewhere.

It took a fair amount of bickering to agree on a scenario, plus half a dozen illicit photos of the chapter, in direct violation of copyright law. I asked if McHuge could loan us a second copy of the book, but Tobin said no, which goes to show McHuge doesn't expect to get the first copy back.

Like I said, no one wants your used sex book. Tobin didn't appreciate it when I pointed this out a second time. He liked it better when I self-edited, I guess. Our conversation closed on a sour note.

It's funny, in a grim way, how I made him agree there'd be no sex. I was petrified that the night I walked out was a one-time perfect storm that sank my desire, and when a calm day came along, he'd float my boat in a hot second.

Now I'm in Second Chance Romance, a used-bookstore-slash-coffee-shop located in a renovated stable well off the beaten track. It's a compelling mix of old planks unevenly stained with decades of rain and new windows punctuating its long, low walls. It used to be one of Pendleton's hidden gems, but lately the weedy gravel parking lot is choked with cars—Grey Tusk tourists seeking a shot of local color in their Saturday morning brew.

Tobin insisted the scenario was meant to be done with the two of us in the same room, although it doesn't say that in the instructions. I refused to do it at the house, so we compromised on a café—very much a meet-cute type of place. I'm second-guessing this decision with my whole brain, but the point of improv is to learn not to die when you do something ridiculous in front of others, so. Here I am, clutching my phone so tightly I think my fingers might get stuck like this. Sex is unimaginable in this scenario, even if my memories of sexy, kind, generous Tobin weren't overwritten with how lonely I am whenever he's in the room.

Tobin gives me a tight wave from an alcove in the back of the odd-shaped room, where he's scored what looks like the last two seats. The place has a dim, old-fashioned-general-store vibe with its warped wooden floors, bursting shelves accented with crooked stacks of orange-covered Penguin Classics at the endcaps, and layered perfume of old paper and new coffee.

Up close, what looked like a generous windowed corner with two beat-up green corduroy chairs feels more like a fight-sized space already buzzing with the bad vibes from our texts.

"We don't have to sit at the same table," I whisper, in violation of the store's quirky, library-like policy of silence. To order, you have to point to one of six items on a laminated pictogram. I think the quiet rule moves product—if you can't talk, what else is there to do but sip and read?

"This was all there was." He pointedly picks up his chair and turns it to face the frosted window before settling into the balding cushions. "Better?" A touch of sarcasm leaks through his distant politeness.

"Yes. Thank you." It's still not big enough for Tobin, who's dressed like Ryan Reynolds circa *The Proposal,* his layered shirts and soft jeans smelling like they were sun-dried over pine branches.

He looked like this the day we met, at the West by North guides' orientation meetup. I walked into the restaurant fifteen minutes early, determined to show how keen I was by arriving first. When the server pointed me toward the table, Tobin looked up from his book, one hand propping the pages open, the other coming to the back of his neck as he stretched.

Words—usually reliable friends of mine—abandoned me when he stood up at my approach, his Guatemalan scarf falling from his shoulders as if even clothing fainted dead away in the presence of this man. This man and his thick golden eyelashes, and his generous smile for a complete stranger, and his body that unwound like a fern frond on the forest floor, from curled to open, with an unleashed energy that made it clear the indoors could never contain him.

He stuck his hand out. "Tobin Renner. Nice to meet you."

I twitched, somehow startled to be spoken to.

"Ah. Lynx," he said, grinning.

"I . . . What?"

"Rookies paint an animal on their paddle. When it wears off, you're a real guide. I don't get to choose, but I'll bet the head guide agrees on the lynx thing. You know, shy. Jumpy. Kinda brown, kinda tawny," he said, tilting his chin at my hair, which I'd washed and left loose, thinking it'd be dirty and tied back all summer. He waited a beat, then added, "Famously elusive. And you are . . . ?"

I realized I'd left him hanging. "Oh, god. Sorry. Liz Lewis.

Sorry," I repeated, fumbling his hand in mine. I didn't think I was meeting my future husband, obviously. No matter what fantasies my vagina was spinning, my brain figured he was in some kind of free love situation with several yoga instructors who were as physically stunning as they were genuinely kind, and whose fair trade scarves looked great on Tobin, too.

"I should be some other animal," I blurted. "I mean, lynx . . . People spend their lives wishing they could find one. They're . . ." Not like me. ". . . beautiful."

"Like I said," he replied, unruffled. "Lynx."

What I remember most about those fifteen minutes is how he made me feel: at ease, welcome, clever, funny in a way I hadn't felt since . . . well, ever. I hoped we'd be assigned together. Out on the river, my quieter, more cautious presence could be a good match for his confidence. I looked at my hands as he very kindly rebuffed a woman offering to buy him a drink, resolving never to embarrass myself by making a doomed, drunken pass at him.

Now I wonder how much of the warmth I felt that night was true, and how much was Tobin being Tobin. What parts of me did he like, and what parts did he silently judge?

I don't need this. I could go back to Amber's and practice improv with Kris Kristofferson. Despite being a dog, Kris is one of the most creative, persistent people I know. Yesterday, she managed to bite through the six-pack of beer I had picked up while she was torturing the pet-grooming team. She shotgunned one and a half craft IPAs in a six-minute drive. A dog who can get around underage drinking laws can navigate McHuge's imaginary objects, no problem.

Tobin waves me into the other chair before I can text Amber and ask her to offer Kris a deal she can't refuse.

My screen lights up.

Diz.

Ha. He cracked first.

> Don't call me Diz.

His body's turned away, but that frosted window sends his reflection straight to me, so the way his face tightens isn't a secret.

Not to me, anyway. After years together, our bodies speak a language no one else does. You don't forget how to interpret someone's sharp little exhale and rounded shoulders and thin-lipped, unhappy mouth, just because now you can put "soon-to-be-ex" in front of "husband."

I straighten up and slap on a neutral expression. For good measure, I turn my chair away from his, heads turning at the scrape of wooden legs on weathered boards. No way am I speaking any body language to Tobin, accidentally or on purpose. Magic is what I'm going for, and an illusionist only shows people what she wants them to see.

Even my text had too much truth in it. It doesn't just say, *I revoke your access to the nickname level of this relationship.* It says, *I'm angry and hurt. I care so much you can trigger me with one word. Three letters.*

I wish I'd self-edited before I pressed *Send.* That's what I thought people were supposed to do in their marriages, and their jobs, and their lives. Saying whatever you think is for dick heads and CEOs. The rest of us practice a little decency.

I'm spiraling. I need to forget about my marriage, forget about myself, be someone else for this scene. Someone not named Diz or Liz or Hey, Ops.

> My name is . . .

I immediately get stuck.

As a teenager, I wanted an interesting name so badly. Everything about me was awkward or odd; I was dying to be a boho Leta, or a stylish Lisbet, or a sporty-cool Loops.

I tried Lola at summer camp the year I was sixteen. For one glorious week, it worked. Until I got off the camp bus, and Amber was there to pick me up instead of Mom.

"*Lola Lewis?* That's what you told them?" she guffawed. Everyone looked at me like I was a total fake. I understood in that moment that I didn't get to choose who I was, because the person I'd always been would follow me everywhere.

I open my Camera app, flip to selfie mode, and train the phone over my shoulder.

Tobin's staring at his screen. His hair flops over his forehead, maple and rye mixed up with gold. My heart skips like it did when we were twenty-two, when he was still a guide and I was now the cook.

He left the campfire sing-along to help me with the dishes, which he didn't have to do. When he looked at me through that fall of sun-streaked hair, everything I'd told myself about not giving it up to a good-time guy who was king of the cool kids—all that vanished in a puff of woodsmoke.

My name is Lola. I should have a name that sounds good with "The Great" slapped on the end of it. I do a magic act for a traveling circus. I come to—where would circus performers congregate online? I can make up a place, it's not like it matters—BigTopChat to unwind on nights the show is dark. And you are . . . ?

> Ben. Elephant trainer. Wouldn't it be weird if we worked for the same circus? Maybe we've been barely missing each other for years.

I ignore the twinge in my chest that would like this to be the truth.

We're doing improv, I remind myself sternly. I've got to get this scenario going, and get it finished. This is how I make an identity for myself that isn't bound to his, or Amber's, or anyone else's, for that matter. This is not the time for me to take deep breaths, trying to find Tobin's smell under the wafts of dark roast and cinnamon rolls.

You smell nice. I type it to get that particular troublesome idea out of my head so I have room in there for Lola, then punch the *Delete* key.

Swoop! says my phone, the volume cranked down to minimum.

I stare at the checkmarks beside my message. Tiny keyboard sounds come from behind me. Crap, he's replying.

> I mean, your *coffee shop* smells nice. The one you recommended on the main channel. Haha, autocorrect.

> I'm glad you like it. Everything smells amazing there. My favorite is the lemon loaf.

I tell myself Tobin is not suggesting he can smell my lemon shampoo, and that the dip in my stomach is hunger.

> The people-watching is good too. There's a couple on a first date being all awkward and cute.

There isn't, not really. I hope he understands none of this is real.

> One of us should come back this day next year. See if they're celebrating their anniversary.

I let out a relieved breath. Tobin must be in character, because he and I don't mention anniversaries.

Sometimes screwups make a wedding memorable, and people laugh over the stories for years. Not ours. No one's spoken of it, much less laughed over it, in three years.

Amber dragged a reluctant Mark all the way from Colorado, hoping a wedding would remind him why they fell in love. They ended up in a drunken screaming match on the dance floor over who asked for the divorce first.

Meanwhile, Tobin's dad did his usual disappearing act an hour into the reception. This time, the excuse was that Tor hadn't raised his son to be the kind of (expletive) man who hyphenated his last name with his wife's. The real reason: Tor wanted to scamper off with the girlfriend of the best man, who quickly became the only friend Tobin's ever lost.

Tobin spent the reception consoling his distraught mother, while I scrambled for a last-minute fill-in to make the toast to the groom, then sat in a haunted forest of empty chairs at the head table.

But I'm not me, and Tobin's not Tobin. Lola can say anything. She's like everything I'm afraid of.

> I love anniversaries. But not the usual. No family party, ugh. Something wild, like a couples' skydiving trip and a night in the Undersea Expedition room of a sketchy themed motel. Better memories that way.

> I bet. I'm more the "every day is our anniversary" type. When I get married, I'll keep my wedding photo in a waterproof capsule so I can have it with me always.

The world lurches like a malfunctioning elevator, sending my heart into my throat.

Tobin has a waterproof capsule for matches and ID, in case the boat flips. But he wouldn't keep a photo of our wedding, with all the tense faces on my side and the obvious gaps on his. Would he?

> I'm not the wedding photo type.

My text looks stark, sitting there. I meant that Lola likes gritty candids, but it feels like she said "yes, but" instead of "yes, and."

From the length of time he's taking to reply, I'm guessing he feels the "yes, but," too. It's stopping our scene. I type a hasty addition.

> I can see someone's smile just by thinking about it.

Three dots pop up, disappear, come back. I catch myself leaning around the side of my chair, trying to read his screen.

> What else do you think about?

He doesn't see me watching his cheeks pinken. He looks better than last week. Stronger. Like he's been getting some sleep. The side of his mouth quirks up the tiniest bit, showing off the tight trim of his beard.

I'm afraid to find out what my own face looks like right now.

But Lola would not blush in public, especially not at this text, which no one would call sexting. She's a magician. A carnie. She's seen it all during her twice-nightly shows, working her sequins and top hat while she incinerates hecklers with flamethrower wit.

She sells sex appeal, so what she wants from love is . . . safety, I think. Comfort. The ability to drop the illusion.

> I think about someone special meeting me backstage with a dozen donuts and a brand-new tube of . . .

I send it, then wait a beat. . . . foot massage cream.

His soft snort practically kisses my ear. His chair has somehow rotated in unnoticeable increments toward mine.

If we both reached out, we could touch.

> I bet you have beautiful feet. Hardworking ones.

> That's the circus life. Hard on the feet.

My fingers fly. It's amazing how easy this is.

> Yeah. One time I broke my toe. The doctor said, looks like an elephant stepped on it. I was like, got it in one.

I laugh out loud.

Tobin grins, one elbow propped on the armrest, feet crossed. His shoulders unwind, pulling his faded T-shirt tight across his chest. He leans like a mountain-town James Dean, carabiner of keys clipped to one belt loop, waiting for me to come along and find him cocking that eyebrow full of bad-boy suggestion.

Although he's the furthest thing from bad. He's more the strong, silent type. Emphasis on *silent*. I don't know when we last had a conversation like this, flirty and knowing.

Except Tobin and I aren't having this conversation. Lola and Ben are.

Our history comes back in a painful rush. Lola starts to pull out of my grasp.

Did you take enough time to heal from that? I turn my chair to look pointedly at his bad wrist.

He clocks my stare and stops leaning.

> If the elephants don't go through the ring of fire, I don't get paid. I can handle work.

"You can. But at what price? You spend all of yourself out there, and pretend you're fine when you get home, but you're not. We stopped saving the best parts of ourselves for each other, Tobin." My voice breaks everything: the silence, the trust, the whole scene.

Forget the best parts of him. I wonder whether I had *any* of him.

"Excuse me," comes a whisper from above. "Perhaps you're not aware of our quiet policy."

On a delightful vintage book ladder perches Béa, one arm laden with antique volumes, wearing a name tag with the letters *B-E-A* pictured in American Sign Language. She dips her chin a little: yes, she recognizes me; no, she won't blow my cover.

Did she hear what I said? It's like every cringeworthy part of my life is bleeding into every other part, making it all exponentially worse.

Sorry, I gesture, hand to heart, then point to my chest and wave: *We're going.*

Lola wouldn't ask Ben to leave. Lola would rely on herself.

I silence my phone. Shut it off. Shove it to the bottom of my bag as I make for the door.

"Hey!" Tobin bursts into the spring sunshine a second after I do. "Where are you going?"

"I think we've done enough," I toss back at him. Is it the truth? Is it a lie? I don't know anymore.

"But we haven't picked the next scenario. We haven't set a date for—"

"Pick whatever you want! Pick all the scenarios forever," I shout at him, walking backward. "Text me the details! It doesn't matter, okay?"

I can get Kris Kristofferson up to speed in seven days, and then I'll cancel this cursed deal and file a restraining order against myself, so I can't get within a hundred meters of this man.

I'm going on Goodreads and writing a one-star review for McHuge's book. "Unrealistic. Did not finish."

And then I'm going to wipe from my memory the way Tobin looks when he's watching me walk away.

Chapter Nine

Scenarios can be funny, silly, outrageous—enjoy your-selves! But I don't recommend **trying** to make them funny. Avoid punch lines; they hurt the scene and the trust be-tween players. When you reveal your deep emotional truth, that's when you'll get laughs that last a lifetime.

—*The Second Chances Handbook*

The Kraken is the kind of fishnet-draped bar you'll find a hundred kilometers from the nearest ocean. It's definitely not a Village bar, where drinks are marked up a couple hundred percent and the theme is either quiet extreme wealth, or loud extreme wealth.

My improv classmates and I are far from the touristy parts of Grey Tusk tonight. The buildings are low and unpretentious, hidden from the road by a thin, scrubby belt of brush and trees. There are no cobblestones or vintage-style streetlamps or upbeat piped-in music, and the window displays have pictures of mani-cure art and shawarma platters instead of frosted lettering and carbon-gray mannequins wearing great sweaters. The highway turnoff to this little retail strip doesn't even have a traffic light.

The Kraken is striving to be the kind of over-the-top destination deemed "authentic" by travel websites. But on a Friday night in the shoulder season, they're officially off the clock as far as trying is concerned. It's karaoke night, according to a tired banner behind the stage, but nobody's brave or reckless enough to sing under these conditions. A projector plays wavery background effects behind a microphone stand that lists sadly to one side. It's offensively well lit. And quiet.

So quiet.

McHuge claps his giant paws. "Improv shows often end with music. It's a crowd-pleaser. Performers need to get comfortable being uncomfortable, whether they're singing or talking. So! We're flowing our energy to karaoke," he announces brightly. Everyone turns pale, even David.

"You won't always get to pick the song, but they're usually familiar. . . ." He considers. "Ish. So I'll assign you a Top Forty hit."

McHuge pulls two tables into a single long surface with as little effort as Eleanor making her Barbies kiss. Then he's off to the DJ booth with his set list of doom.

Béa hurls herself despairingly into the chunky slat-backed chair next to Jason. "*Tabarnak*," she whispers, the French Canadian swear layered with elemental fear. This is bad for us all, but it's probably worse for someone who hates talking so much she got a job at a silent bookstore. I already cornered her to tell her I was doing extra improv practice at her coffee shop last weekend and not to worry about anything she overheard. If she believed me, I couldn't tell.

David drifts away, phone to his ear. I have my suspicions about how real his "call" is.

Sharon plops down, patting the neighboring chair. "When somebody saves your life, you have to save them a seat. Maritime law," she says with a pursed-lip smile.

"McHuge and his field trips," I mutter, settling in.

Sharon shrugs, tapping her fanny pack. I'm amazed she's back. I mean, improv feels like a near-death experience for most of us, but Sharon literally almost crossed over last week. Her right eyelid is still a bit puffy and purple around the sting. Underneath those mom jeans is a real badass.

Sharon's motivations are a mystery. Béa said that thing about her wedding; Jason hoped he'd meet a cute, funny guy. Even David didn't come as that much of a surprise, given what I read about improv sometimes attracting creeps. But Sharon seems so competent—not someone who needs to risk death for a community comedy course.

Unfortunately, emotional overwhelm—like the kind you get while contemplating your imminent death onstage—makes me even more unfiltered than usual. "Sharon, what are *you* doing in this class?"

Sharon smirks. "You mean, why am I the only person over fifty? Over forty, even?"

"Oh, no! That's not what I meant. At all. I would never imply, uh," I fumble.

"It's all right. I know how old I am." She squints, purposely emphasizing her crow's-feet. "Also, I lost the ability to be embarrassed when my kid came out ass first. When a gorgeous ob-gyn is up to the elbows in your hoo-ha, and another is hauling the baby out of a place that didn't used to have an exit sign, something changes in your brain."

She laughs at whatever she sees on my face, some combination of backpedaling and horror. "You're still so young, you don't even know how young you are," she says, popping a mint from a tin of Altoids she produces from her bottomless purse. She waves the container at me.

I shake my head, muttering, "I'm thirty." I'm not thrilled to be seen as a kid, even though the big three-oh makes me feel ancient.

Sharon laughs at me some more. "When I was your age, I thought I'd be settled and comfortable at fifty. But, Liz, I am bored. *Bored.* I'm tired of everything fun and new being reserved for twentysomethings. I don't want to paint, or quilt, or sign up for a new social media platform every year from now till I die.

"I need to feel *alive,* and this is really doing it for me. And it's easier on the joints than training for a marathon," she adds sagely. "Enough about me. What brings you here? Beyond having a socially acceptable reason to stare at *that* for three hours a week." She nods at McHuge's ass with a look of deepest appreciation.

Looks like we're trading prying questions. One of the leadership books I read recommended unusual questions as icebreakers. I thought that was overly optimistic, but Sharon's bald honesty is a tall glass of ice water right in the face: a hell of a wake-up, but also kind of refreshing. I've never had a friend her age, but . . . maybe I could?

I push past the instinct to hide my unpretty parts. "I, uh. Hit a bit of a breaking point at work, and my husband . . . he's sort of my ex, I guess, although we're doing this thing . . . never mind, TMI. But it's as if nobody sees *me.* No one looks beyond a first impression, and those are not my strength. As we saw at the first class."

"It wasn't so bad."

"It was, though."

"Yeah, it was. But you don't give people much else to work with, do you? The first time I saw you peek out of your shell was when you stuck a needle in my thigh. I was impressed. You should show your strengths."

Sharon's observation prompts a weird rush of defensiveness mixed with uncertainty. If I don't show myself, it's because I have to guard against rejection from people who only see the label they slap on me after knowing me for five minutes.

"It's not a big deal. My job involves a lot of emergency problem-solving. But I'm looking to move into leadership. I'm here to practice being innovative and social so I can pitch tour ideas my boss doesn't hate."

"Oh? Like what ideas has he hated?"

"God, so many. My favorite was Quiet Rafts. River rafting crossed with a vow of silence, for people who want to hear the sounds of the wilderness instead of that one guy who won't stop telling dad jokes."

Sharon frowns. "That's . . . quite good. It could attract a demographic we don't usually get in adventure tours. Who do you work for?"

"Craig West, at West by—"

She holds up a hand. "Never mind, I know Craig. Did you ever think of switching companies?" Sharon says as if it's as easy as deciding to go.

"I tried. But job interviews turn me into a semi-sentient blob of goo. Along with every other social situation. Anyway. People don't see me, so I decided to be someone they *could* see, and I have to be positive and have ideas and *network*," I say tragically. "And learn to golf."

Sharon's headshake is such a mom headshake, right down to the disapproving nasal breath.

"Oh, honey. There's a difference between *doing* something new and *being* someone new. But I remember how it felt to get unsolicited advice when I was thirty, so I won't do that. The golf, though. That I can help with. I'll book us a tee time at my club. Hit the driving range a couple of times first and you won't do too badly."

"You have a club?"

"White Oaks. Keller comps executive memberships. What?"

she asks, taking in my dropped jaw. "You think we shouldn't fraternize because we're competitors in the industry?" She waves a hand airily. "Forget that."

Something about Sharon tickles my memory, but I can't quite pin it down.

McHuge drifts back to the table. Sometimes I forget how gigantic he is until he's up close and making the furniture look like we're in the kids' display area at IKEA.

Kinda like that big guy at the corner table who's doing a hell of a job making the chairs seem short. His longish, mid-tone hair is pulled back in a stubby ponytail. Waterproof patches dot his dark red puffer coat, like—

Dismay bursts like static behind my eyes.

Tobin's here.

He sees me and pauses, a mini donut halfway to his mouth. He has a terrible weakness for deep-fried dough, despite his quasi-religious commitment to fresh, simple food.

And he's sitting next to a woman who's looking at him like he's warm and covered with cinnamon sugar.

He wouldn't be on a date. I hate my brain for going there. He's just Tobin; people naturally gravitate to him. Pulling groups together is his favorite thing. He has special radar for clients who aren't natural joiners, hyping them until everyone loves them, giving them nicknames and made-up backstories and even theme songs.

I wonder if I was one of those people to him.

He puts down the donut and pushes out of his chair as the last of the rookie guides troop in, shedding layers and shoving each other good-naturedly.

I meet him halfway, not wanting to do this in front of the improv crew. Or the guides. I hadn't envisioned my work life and my improv life untidily crossing over, beyond the regrettable fact of Dick Head. And McHuge. Already, improv makes me feel like a different version of myself—so who should I be now that my worlds are colliding?

"Hi." Tobin's smile is an eight out of ten instead of the usual eleven out of ten. "I didn't know your class would be here." He scans my table, a confused line popping up between his brows. He doesn't know these people, and I do. This is a new dynamic for us.

"Me either."

"I can move the guides' orientation meeting. It wouldn't be a big deal." Behind him, a server brings a giant tray of drinks to his table. It's already too late.

"It's fine, Tobin. We can coexist at the same bar."

I shouldn't have said that. McHuge's karaoke-based desensitization therapy is bad enough without my mostly ex-husband watching me go down in flames.

There's a burst of feedback from the sound system. "I'd better go. We're, uh, doing a thing."

The DJ comes on. "Good evening, folks, and welcome to karaoke night at the Kraken," he shouts, fight-night style. His peppy tone is all wrong for those of us currently shivering in fear, clinging to the table like we've been shipwrecked. Although Sharon looks pretty chill. She's survived worse, literally.

"First up! Please welcome! The amazing! LIZ! Performing 'I Will Always Love You'!!!" Every one of his many! exclamation! marks! stabs me right in my quivering soul.

"Which version?" I whimper at McHuge.

It doesn't matter; both of them violate the First Law of Karaoke. Namely: one does not attempt to match the greatest voices of our time without a) a flawless voice of one's own and/or b) a highly original take on the song.

I have neither. My voice isn't great, or terrible. It's easy to ignore, like the rest of me, which is fine until I'm onstage trying to hit the high notes like Dolly Parton or Whitney frickin' Houston.

I'm going to poison McHuge in his sleep.

McHuge shrugs off my glare. "I know you like romance. I thought you'd appreciate this choice. *The Bodyguard* and all." To his credit, he said "romance" in a normal way, without that dismissive flick in his voice that some people use while discussing media that has the audacity to end with happiness and love.

"It's a love story, not a romance," I snap, even though arguing with McHuge is pointless. I don't think he knows how.

The DJ waves at us, then points at the screen. The video's starting.

"Shine on, Liz," McHuge says, giving me a playful bump. He's not the kind of big guy who doesn't know how strong he is, so his nudge isn't a believable excuse to keel over and fake my death.

I don't remember climbing onstage, unholstering the mic, and sending the stand to the wings (good decision; if there's a chance to trip over something, I'll make the most of it).

According to the monitor, my blackout ends at the thirty-five-second mark of the Amazing! Liz! silently white-knuckling the microphone. The bar is frozen in the spectacular badness of this moment.

I wish my eyes wouldn't swing to Tobin, but they do. He's tense, mouth flat, muscles bunched. He looks this close to sweeping me into his arms and carrying me away from this peril.

I've spent years trying to get Tobin to see our failures, both separately and together. To see *me*—not the perfect me he wants, not the all-wrong me I am at work, but the real me. And now that I don't want that anymore, here he is. Watching me fail in real time, when he can't even bear to hear about it secondhand.

In a horrible haze of panic, I turn to the improv table. Jason looks like he ate a bug; Béa shields her eyes. I manage a faint smile when Sharon throws double horns of the devil, like this is Norwegian death metal instead of eighties power pop.

Over at the bar, David swirls amber liquid in a highball glass, wearing the mean smile I know too well. He sported that smirk the day he happened to be standing at my desk when Craig scoffed, "*Cat* earrings, Liz?" I loved those earrings, with their sparkling peridot eyes. They felt like *me*. But after that, they were always tainted by Craig's judgment and David's pleasure in my embarrassment.

I could step down from this stage. But if I go, I'll have yet another painful memory to tuck away next to my lucky earrings, among the crowd of thin-edged moments that pop up whenever I get the urge to give myself a mental paper cut.

I have to sing.

AND I—I—I, prompts the screen as the softly plucked guitar notes swell.

I reach far, far inside, looking for Lola.

There's no one down there but a pair of black cats with green eyes, sealed in a plastic bag and forgotten.

When I open my mouth, what comes out is a weak, sad "Meowwwwww," to the rhythm of "And I . . ."

My voice dies fast and the song is slow. A century passes in plinking arpeggios over a blank screen.

Someone lets out a high, nervous laugh. My non-performance has them on the edge of their seats, squirming, desperate for this to stop.

Comedy is about tension, McHuge said. So much the audience almost can't bear to look.

But they also can't look away.

I have the audience. I *have* them.

I let in a breath I didn't realize I was keeping out. Everyone inhales with me. David's smile gets 3 percent smaller.

Pure green spite flows straight to my heart. This is the worst possible motivation to succeed, and I don't care. That's a problem for future me. Current me needs anything that will get her going. If that's spite, so be it.

"Meow meow meow meow meowwww," I trill to "Will always love youuuuu."

Liz Lewis is in no way fit to sing Whitney Houston. But a lynx sings whatever she wants.

I stalk around the stage—no, I *prowl*. The bar goes bananas, as much as a bar with eighteen patrons (I counted) can. The more I meow, the more everyone dies laughing. And the more they laugh, the more I ham it up.

When I trip over the microphone cord, I yowl angrily, and people have to mop their eyes. With thirty seconds to go, everyone starts screaming and pointing at the screen, where the DJ has switched the video feed to a YouTube supercut of cats miscalculating ambitious jumps.

As I purr the last note, everyone's on their feet—even David, who didn't sit down in time. I take a sloppy victory leap off the stage into the arms of my classmates.

I'm alive. I'm alive, and I killed. I fall into the empty chair next to Sharon, ears ringing with adrenaline.

I can't help myself; I look over at Tobin's table. The shock of finding it empty buzzes through my body, scrambling my heartbeat.

I didn't want him to see me. Guess I got my wish. All the same, my winning smile weebles a bit.

The DJ, keen to keep the energy going, calls Jason's name. I fade into my seat, grateful to be out of the spotlight. And also . . . a little envious?

Jason head-bangs convincingly through "Crazy Train," hair flying. Sharon goes extremely torchy for a Lana Del Rey number whose melody and rhythm she obviously does not know in the slightest. I hate to see it, but David's good, too, even though McHuge made him sing a BTS song made for an ensemble all by himself.

But the star of the night is Béa. And it's not because she's good. The song is a softball: "Islands in the Stream."

From the very first note, she ruins it. She sings her off-key heart out, and she's gorgeous, and she's grinning. She sticks the landing 100 percent.

And the crowd loves her for it. There are fifty people in here by now, all going goddamn wild for her.

I succeeded. I showed myself; I told the truth. Yet I'd give anything to go up there and fail like she's failing, with that kind of joy lighting me up.

I hang back on the way out to the parking lot.

McHuge waits for me. "You made a real breakthrough tonight. I hope you feel good."

"It was fun." I don't sound like I had fun.

McHuge looks down at me from Mount Olympus, or whatever altitude his head resides at. "You're judging yourself."

Self-judging is one of the many improv sins. That was in my scenario with Tobin. "It's rude to read people's thoughts, McHuge."

He snorts, amused. "Every beginner fixates on what went wrong. Don't forget what went right. You took a risk. You got some real laughs. You warmed up the audience for everyone else," he says, ticking things off on his fingers. "It looked like you were living your truth up there. Whatever you're doing, keep it up, because it's paying off."

I thought my scenario with Tobin hadn't helped anything—not improv, not our marriage—but here's McHuge saying it did.

Does it feel good because I'm a sucker for praise? Because it gives me hope I'm on the right track? Or is it because I have a reason to make another improv date with Tobin?

I thought our love had died, a fire doused by days of unexpected, unending rain.

But under the ashes, something still glows. And Tobin's the

stubborn one trying to feed it, while I'm torn between missing its heat and fearing its warmth is keeping me from discovering my own inner flame.

Tobin texted me earlier with a bunch of possible dates and times for our next scenario. Very businesslike. Flat. Not like him at all. I didn't expect bland courtesy to be the rogue wave that swamped my heart with regret, but . . . yeah.

I pull out my phone.

> Hope you didn't leave the bar because I was there.
> Does Tuesday at 8 work for you?

I hesitate, then open my Calendar app. **The Second Chances Handbook. Tuesday, 8 PM.**

Chapter Ten

SCENARIO 2: SAY SOMETHING

The act of talking to a sympathetic listener can clarify feelings you've kept inside. Listening and responding to a partner's words brings energy to a scene and opens connections.

In troubled relationships, breaking a habit of silence can be very difficult. Talking is harder than texting. It pushes us to think fast, and it doesn't have a backspace key. You may be tempted to self-edit so completely you end up saying nothing at all.

For your second scenario, ease the transition from text to talk with some distance. Instead of talking face-to-face, phone each other (try not to be in a shared space, if

possible—be far enough away not to run into each other).
Invent a situation where your characters have to talk.
What would a character in a marriage like yours say, if
they knew someone would listen? What have your characters been holding inside, and why?

—*The Second Chances Handbook*

It's snowing.

It was supposed to rain, but spring in Grey Tusk always has
one last "fuck you" tucked into her bra. Tobin can usually predict
snow, but an unexpected north wind defied his weather sense,
bringing wet flakes that melt on contact with the ground.

I yank off my stupid nylons (tolerance for uncomfortable corporate clothing choices being a prime leadership skill) and throw
them on the floor of my parents' bedroom.

The after-work team-building hour was "optional," ha. I don't
love events organized around informal conversations I don't
know how to join. Or leave. Usually I lurk in a corner, giving off
a high-pitched sound that tells front-of-house people to stay far,
far away.

But today, I was on a mission: show I belong at West by North,
and get the promotion to prove it. Emboldened by my questioning
success with Sharon, I nursed a non-alcoholic gimlet and barged
around, spewing inquiries in all directions.

Right away, I failed. My mistake was picking someone I knew
as my first target, thinking Dick Head would like to debrief our
karaoke victories. Barely a minute later, he said, "Oh, look, there's
Naheed. *I'm* going to go talk to him."

After a mini breakdown in the bathroom, caused by non-joyful
failing, I was able to rally with a new mandate: random questions
for randomly chosen people.

The good thing about random questions is nobody sees them

coming. People are too shocked to do anything but answer. It's a networking sneak attack.

That's how I discovered the weirdest thing Bethany from accounting ever saw was a round aircraft with a lot of different colored lights. I also learned she's not the type to call it a UFO, even when it's technically an object, and it's flying, and she doesn't know what it is.

It must have looked like a good conversation, because Jingjing from innovation joined us when we'd moved on to first-date mistakes. She advised waiting to try charcoal ice cream until after sleeping with a new flame, instead of eating it on the first date and ending up with a ghoulish black smile. Solid tip.

Team building was tiring, but with the few skills I've learned so far, it was a good 25 percent easier than before. It was not-terrible enough that I didn't come home early to plug in my car, like I planned.

My battery is teeth-clenchingly low, and Amber needs the minivan for carpooling to gymnastics. If I'm going to have enough juice for this whole scenario, something's gotta give, and it's going to be the heater.

I tear through the living area, drop a quick kiss on Eleanor, and think better of stealing any of Amber's grated cheese. There's no time to bite the hook she's baiting with that arched eyebrow and side-going mouth. She knows I'm seeing Tobin; she doesn't need any more excuses to tell me I should take him back already. Obviously, I didn't tell her about the scenarios. I'm spending tonight driving all over hell's half acre while impersonating my own imaginary friend; I can well imagine the lectures that would inspire.

Flinging myself back into my car, I crank up some John Cena. I decide the song is now "Bad, Bad Cat" instead of "Bad, Bad Man" so I can meow along.

The snow isn't sticking; it's safe to head north, up the valley, instead of hitting the better-plowed but more crowded highway between Pendleton and Grey Tusk.

It makes me sound like a granddad, but I love this drive. The mountains aren't as high or fierce as the Rockies, but from across the valley, the misty tint of distance gives the bare rock above the tree line a soft, dreamy filter. Behind the white caps of lesser peaks, Grey Tusk's sharp pinnacle hides in ash-colored clouds, keeping its opinions to itself. The highway swings sharply around soft-sloped gullies, its continuity broken every so often by iron bridges painted orange to hide the rust.

My tires sizzle past the milky teal waters of the river, its shores lined with black cottonwood trees, bare branches filled with the secret leaves of spring. In a couple of weeks, Tobin will carry the sharp, dusty scent of their sap under his shirt. This used to be my favorite time of year to tuck my nose inside his collar and imagine that he might be part tree.

I send him a hands-free text.

Okay, I'm ready.

My phone rings.

I crank up the volume over the roar of the defrost, which is only somewhat succeeding in keeping the windshield clear. "Hello?"

"This is Dr. Redfern's radio hour, you're on the air." Tobin suggested we do a radio call-in show from our cars, and since I told him he could pick the scenario, I had to go along.

"Uh. Hello."

"What's your name, caller?" Tobin asks, low and growly.

I distrust how soothing it feels to let his mellow, raspy tones wrap around me, warm in the chilly car. This must be why people confess everything to strangers on the radio at night, seduced by moonlight and the illusion of anonymity. Earlier, I unlocked alien encounters and blind date disasters, just by asking. Put a question together with a voice like his . . .

I'm in danger of telling him way too much.

"You can call me Elsa," I say, a flurry swirling around the car. Tonight, I want a name that's chaotic and a bit bad.

"The topic of tonight's episode is Your Hopes and Dreams. What's your dream, Elsa?"

Oof. I revise my opinion of surprise questions.

Tobin used to ask about my dreams all the time. He was my biggest cheerleader, helping me put together presentations for the annual pre-pitching meetings, telling me Craig was an idiot for not seeing the genius in my path-less-traveled tour ideas.

Making me say "no" a million times with his questions about whether my promised promotion was coming, or if I'd had any new ideas Craig was sure to love, or whether I was applying (yet again) for openings in other companies, to then flame out in yet more interviews.

Eventually, I told him I didn't want to talk about it. He stopped asking, but I could see the words in his eyes. When he hugged me, I felt the questions in the tension of his biceps around my shoulders.

I'm glad I didn't tell him I'm gunning for the pitch competition again this year. I won't have to dodge questions he doesn't know he should ask.

I grab the last tissue from my glove compartment and scrub at the frost on my windshield. "I don't have dreams." Elsa sounds like me. I'm not doing a great job at being someone else right now.

There's a huff of breath. I picture him pulling his lips between his teeth, thumbs lifting off the steering wheel in frustration. It's a pretty emotional display for Tobin.

"Everyone has dreams. That's the topic of the show, and you called in. You must at least hope for something."

I do. But not the way I used to. I was so excited to join West by North—I'd never doubted wilderness tourism was where I was meant to be. Pretty much all Grey Tusk locals are devoted to climbing, skiing, and trekking. There really isn't another reason to live somewhere this expensive and remote.

Spending childhood summers as far from civilization as possible meant everyone we met on the trail, from expert to tenderfoot, loved the wilderness like my parents taught Amber and me to. Out there, I was part of a family and a community that cared how fast I could start a fire, how well I could use a compass, and what wild food I was willing to eat. There were no fashion mistakes, no conversations with hidden meanings. In the bush, you said what you meant because everyone's safety depended on it. The rules were simple; I knew I belonged.

But when I went to university in Vancouver, I realized a lot of people avoided the wilderness because they felt uncertain and unwelcome there. And if anyone knew about feeling uncertain and unwelcome, it was me. It was like a light bulb went off. I was sure the right tours—*my* tours—could help them see how they fit. I was sure the ideas my profs had praised would have no trouble getting seen.

What happened, of course, was that my dreams got eaten like a wool sweater munched by moths. Every time my proposals got torpedoed or ignored or, worst of all, laughed at, another hole appeared. Every time I emerged from a job interview sweaty and near tears, a chunk fell off. Bite by painful bite, they turned from sturdy fabric to fragile lace, barely there.

"Dreams aren't practical at my age. I have . . . targets," I say. *GET MAGIC*, an interior voice pipes up, perhaps one notch quieter than a couple of weeks ago.

"Targets . . . ?"

"That's what I said. You set a target, then after the measurement interval, you look back at market conditions, analyze what prevented you from reaching your target, set new targets, repeat."

When you don't reach a target, you lose money.

But you keep your heart.

There's a long silence. In the background, Tobin's truck rumbles as he accelerates along some road somewhere. We're both out here, in the twilight, maybe driving toward each other. Maybe getting farther apart.

Then, finally, "When you had a dream, how did it make you feel?"

The man on my radio both is and isn't Tobin. It's his voice, but somehow not the person I've been afraid to trust.

The same way I'm myself, and also I could be someone brave, who's willing to try again. Like both versions of me could be true at the same time.

McHuge is clever with the scenarios, damn him.

"It made me feel—" I stop, torn.

At first it felt wonderful, like a treasure I could hold in my hand. But years of "no" turned me uncertain, then frightened, then sick over it, all the time. Failure whispered in my ear: I wasn't good enough, and everyone knew it but me.

This is my worst, most corrosive fear. Whenever I've tried to tell him before, Tobin glossed over it. "I believe in you," he'd say, and order me a new textbook so I could make a better business case next time. We planned my victories together, but I cried over my failures by myself. We stopped talking about starting our own tour company.

Tonight feels different. But is it? I want to tell and not tell, take a risk and be safe at the same time. I can't give myself to him anymore. Not until he gives himself to me.

"If you want to talk dreams, we could discuss yours."

"That's not the way the show works, Elsa." He's back to the radio personality voice that sounds like a smooth stretch of golden skin with no tender spots to accidentally poke.

It's all too familiar. I shouldn't have told him he could pick the scenarios when I was glitching in the bookstore last week. No surprise, he made himself the host, an overproduced personality who reveals none of his own secrets. Same schtick, different day.

"I hate this," I say, bleeding into Elsa the way I bled into Lola. "I hate it when hosts make it all about the caller, like it's a good thing. I don't want to be the only person in this conversation."

McHuge's ludicrous improv truisms are killing me right now— when you're uncomfortable, stay in the scene. Go for the hard truth. Listen to the other person; bring yourself.

This is the hardest thing in the world. Maybe too hard for Tobin and me. I breathe in, hold it, hold it, waiting for him to say something.

My breath comes out short and shallow as I reach for the phone.

"Don't hang up," he blurts.

Some things about me, he knows so well. Wherever he is, he can tell from one breath that I'm about to end the call.

"I could tell you what my other callers dream about."

Great. Now we're talking about neither one of us.

"If that's what you can do." I swing into a roadside rest stop to make a U-turn. The flood of memories distracted me from my battery, and now it's so damn low I'm barely going to make it home.

"I—uh, *they* tend to dream about pretty basic stuff. Wife. Family. Like, three, four kids, so it's not just one kid carrying their parents' expectations all alone."

Goddammit, Tobin. How dare he bring to mind pictures of him as a kid in old-fashioned short pants, hands at his side but fingers curled into claws, waiting to tear the tie from around his neck.

"What else?" My voice is not 100 percent steady.

"Most people want to contribute to the family. I—they want to do their share. And that's hard because some of them don't have great jobs that'll last forever. Their job might break them down, physically. And if they're working on something new, they might not want to get anyone's hopes up before it's a sure thing."

"They're keeping secrets, is what you're saying." I'm a hypocrite—I haven't exactly told him about the pitch competition. But he's the one who closed off first. Who dug out my old business books, then deflected questions about what he was doing.

Just like Amber said he would, in the hotel bathroom on my wedding day. As her marriage had filled with secrets and silence, so would mine, losing a little closeness and tenderness every day until it was all gone.

"I'm not keeping secrets."

"God, Tobin, yes you are! What *isn't* a secret between us? Name a hope or dream you *do* talk to me about."

"We tell each other—" His automatic denial buckles under the weight of truth.

"Yeah, we—holy crap!" I swerve hard to avoid a pair of shadowy gray-brown goats loitering in the road.

"I'm okay," I say, before he can ask. "Goats. I'm pulling over for a bit."

The sign for the local mountain biking area looms ahead. I can park here for a few minutes, save battery, not sacrifice any innocent animals with my car.

"I'm parked. Where were we?"

"I never meant to keep secrets from you," he says. The radio fiction is broken; his voice is a bruise. "You could ask me anything you want to know."

I didn't expect that. He set the roles in advance; I didn't prepare any questions.

"Liz? Are you there?"

"I'm here," I say slowly. Another huge *thunk* of tumblers slides into place. But unlike last time, I'm not so sure it's a good idea to try to crack him open.

I might like what I find.

This conversation feels so dangerous. I need something to put distance between us, for safety, like the first scenario said. Something he'd never admit to.

My mind flashes back to the night I left, when the last good thing about us crumbled. "Okay. What do you wish I would have done differently in bed?"

I'm being a jerk. It's not a comfortable sensation, especially when he's being sincere, but then again, none of the things I've done lately have been comfortable. I have to ignore my instincts, which have gotten me nowhere in life.

He makes a startled noise. "Um, I don't know. What we did— what we do—is good for me. I wouldn't, uh, change anything. Necessarily."

It's déjà vu all over again. Tobin won't tell me what I'm doing wrong, just like Craig wouldn't explain or clarify "people think you don't like them," just like all my interviewers wouldn't reply to my follow-up emails asking for feedback. I shiver, probably because the heater's even weaker when the car isn't moving.

"I hurt you last time. It sucks, knowing I've done that. And not knowing what to do better, because you won't talk to me." This would be easier if I were angry, but instead, someone's hooked a hundred-pound weight onto my heart, sinking it to the bottom of Lake Sad.

He sighs long and slow, a trail of silver bubbles rising through troubled waters. "I wish we'd never gotten married."

There's a lag on the line, a poor connection that's been cutting off the beginning of his sentences. So maybe he didn't pick up the painful way I gasped.

"Not like that," he says hastily, confirming he caught my little "oh!" of hurt and surprise.

"Everything changed after our wedding. When you laughed, it didn't sound right anymore. You used to look at me with, uh." The connection perfectly delivers the dry sound of his swallow. "It sounds stupid, but you used to look at me with stars in your eyes. And then sometimes they weren't there anymore. And now I haven't seen them in so long. I felt you . . . pulling back. Maybe I, uh. Maybe I drove you away."

I'm flooded with memories of our wedding day. Tobin, conspicuously absent from the head table until I recruited a groomsman to go get him before every toast. Amber sending me a bitter, knowing look in the bathroom mirror. *Spare me the pity, Liz—I might be getting divorced, but you always follow in my footsteps. I mean, you're marrying a guy with family issues, you're plowing through a field of red flags to do it, and your reception is even at the same damn venue! In a few years, you'll be where I am now. So what if Mark doesn't love me anymore? It's not like* you're *so easy to love.*

Obviously, I knew how few friends I had, and how I didn't seem to fit in anywhere but the remote backcountry places most other people didn't go to. But I hadn't thought it was because I was hard to love. To hear it like that, from the person who'd known me longer than anyone . . .

"Tobin. That's not what happened."

"But *something* happened. And you didn't tell me what, so how was I supposed to react? You fell in love with me when things were easy and fun. I wanted you to fall in love with me again, so I tried to give you more of that."

My fight is ruined. My tears water the shores of Lake Sad.

I'm out of tissues, because I used the last one on the windshield and the ninety-nine before that on school runs with Eleanor. The only thing that can muffle my sobs is my hat, even though I'm freezing. My battery indicator flashes a single grim, red digit.

A pickup truck rolls to a stop beside me, its profile blurred through my frosty window. I don't bother to scrape the ice; I know the voice of that grumbly old junker as well as I know its driver.

"Why are you wearing mittens?" Tobin asks, jerking me back into reality.

I take my face out of my hat. "How did you find me?"

"You come here whenever something's on your mind. You hike to the old shack and poke around. There's always dust smudged on your face when you come back."

He knows me better than I like to think.

The mountain bike reserve used to be private property. There's a one-room shack a ways down the trail, with a sign on the door in shaky, old-timey handwriting:

*Please do not
damage this cabin.
There is nothing
of any value
inside.
We love this place.*

Someone's broken the padlock and left it dangling from the door. Inside, a rusted-out woodstove hunches in the corner; a dish rack sits in the cupboard underneath the sink, still full of plates. In the corner near the door, a huge axe leans, the head loose.

Not one teen has tagged the place. No one's smashed a single glass. It's uninhabitable and about to fall down, yet everyone has decided, for some reason, to defend it.

It gives me hope, that place. It's nothing like the rest of the houses around here, not pretty or new or even possessed of indoor plumbing. Not easy to love. Yet someone loved it once; cherished it for what it was, not what they wished it could be. And that love cast a spell of protection over it and made everyone else love it, too.

I brought Tobin there years ago, half afraid he wouldn't understand what I liked about this dim, crumbling cabin. Maybe he'd think it was creepy and I was weird; it was the kind of thing I had to be careful introducing to my partners. But he ran his fingers over the candle drippings on the dark tabletop and said, "They liked it cozy, didn't they?" It was dusty and musty and probably full of pack rats, their nests glinting with shiny stolen buttons. For health and safety reasons, we should have gone back outside. Instead, I stayed in the circle of his arms a long time, until I could be sure I wouldn't cry with relief.

"It looks cold over there," Tobin observes. "Battery low?"

I jam my hat back on. "I layered. I'll be okay."

"It's nice and warm over here. I could drive you back to Amber's. You can call for a tow tomorrow."

Curse him for knowing why I pulled over. My dignity has a quick scuffle with my desire not to run out of juice on a dark, frozen highway.

I use the last of the battery to lock my doors.

God, it's warm in his truck. It's pathologically clean and smells like cinnamon donuts and Tobin.

I press my bare fingers against the vents. It's impossible to meet his eyes. I feel naked, like he can see through layers upon layers of gear right down to my broken-open soul.

He picks up my hand, cradling it between his big hot palms. They're rough from his work, but the feeling coming from them is so . . . soft. So loaded with years of tenderness.

There must be something that can make me forget we've kissed in this truck, young and laughing and swatting giant northern mosquitoes so that when the clothes came off, we'd be the only ones feasting on each other's bodies.

"Hey! We agreed, none of that!" I pull my hand against my chest like he's burned it.

"It's just hand warming," he argues.

"No, it's not."

"Why can't you let me take care of you?"

"Why are you arguing? Argument delays the action. It says so in the book. The *sex* book." It isn't a sex book, but saying it will make him back off.

"Okay. All right," he says, holding up his hands. He throws the truck into reverse with a snap.

For some time, there's only the sound of windshield wipers, tamping the sleet into an icicle at the bottom of the glass.

"It's true," Tobin says, out of nowhere. "I held things back from you. But you held things back from me, too."

I did hold back, but not for the reasons he thinks. I *wanted* to tell him when I broke a fingernail and when I got more likes than usual on my social media and when I thought the football commentator looked like an egg with a face painted on.

But that's the stuff that's hard to love. Nobody wants to hear that.

"You didn't miss anything good," I say.

"Didn't I, though?"

The way he says that. Like it's the boring stuff that makes a marriage. It can't be all his fault that he didn't know me, if I didn't let him in. Not twenty minutes ago, I didn't have the courage to tell him how scared I am about that damn pitch competition, even though I wanted to. I wanted to, so much.

We're almost to Amber's when he speaks again.

"It's because I'm trying not to . . . you know."

"I'm sorry . . . ?"

"You said I don't talk in bed. It's because I'm trying not to, uh, not to finish."

The air inside the cab turns heavy and slow, like a summer night. Every part of me is burning. What the hell kind of nuclear-powered heater has he put in this old piece of junk?

His eyes are deep navy under the streetlamp as we glide to a stop in front of my parents' house, his face thrown into sharp relief, cheekbones and jaw and generous mouth.

"You're so, uh. You smell so good, and your skin feels, um. Really soft. And the way you move, it's . . ." He scrubs one hand across his beard. "Anyway. I have to try not to. I have to work on making it good for you."

Jesus, that's hot. But heat alone can't sustain us.

"I'm lonely, Tobe. When I talk and you don't answer, I feel like I'm the only one there."

"I'm there, Diz." He turns to me, one arm resting on the wheel, the other slung across the back of the bench seat. In the dim light, he shines. "I'm here. I'm talking."

Air. I need air. I have to tear off my clothes and lie in a slushy puddle until this fire under my skin is good and drowned. But somehow, I'm not leaving. He's leaning toward me, and I'm leaning toward him, and we're not stopping.

The deep, brassy honk hits like a horror movie jump scare, sending us reeling backward. Tobin belatedly pulls his elbow off the horn, while I scrape my soul off the ceiling.

"Wait," he says, but I'm out the door and halfway to the house.

"Bye, Tobin!" I shout, too forcefully. "Thanks for the ride!"

He's laughing, the big jerk. Sexy lines pop up next to his eyes. His head is thrown back (a lot like when he . . . nope, not going there), and his hands look like they want to grab me and hold me and do all the things to me.

I can't slam the front door because it's Eleanor's bedtime. But

I can close it and lean against it, and get my breathing under control, and feel the deep warmth of his laugh like a shot of scotch burning its way from my mouth to my heart.

Maybe true love only happens once in a lifetime.

But what if it happened again with the same person?

Chapter Eleven

Support and trust are as important in improv as they are in partnerships. It's much easier to jump fearlessly into a scene when you trust someone to catch you.

—*The Second Chances Handbook*

There's nothing like the out-of-body feeling I get when Amber acts like I'm twelve and she's the boss of me. Since her divorce, she's all in on Mom and Dad's doctrine of family closeness. Once the oracle who predicted my split from Tobin, now she's his biggest fan, constantly pointing out the ways I can't get along without him. Instead of sloughing me off, she micromanages my every move, picking at my mistakes past, present, and future, telling me to take what I get and be happy.

"Eight thirty sharp. If you let her stay up, she'll be a mess tomorrow."

"Yes, Amber." I grit my teeth to keep from saying more. I've been Eleanor's go-to caregiver since she was three. I've done diapers and fevers and nosebleeds right alongside the Legos and storybooks and trips to the bunny hill. Amber *must* trust me, after all that. So why treat me like a summer intern on day one?

My sister gives her daughter a long, tender squeeze. Eleanor dissolves into delighted giggles when Amber counts individual hugs, insisting she needs a hundred before she goes.

My ovaries flip.

I always thought I'd be a mother by the time I hit thirty. For a long time, I dreamed of a baby with Tobin's easy laugh and startling ice-chip eyes. And then there's Eleanor, bright and funny, hilariously stubborn, with a bananas imagination. I'd love to have a kid like her.

But if I were a mother, Tobin would be the father.

Every year at Pap smear time, when my doctor asks if I'm thinking about babies, I imagine myself at Disneyland, hot and irritated from the press of too many bodies, arguing with my husband on a stretch of baking tarmac. *No more cotton candy,* I snap. *They've already had too much.* Later, I see myself cleaning up after upset tummies, because he's sneaked the kids treats anyway.

And I ask for another year's worth of pills.

Because he'd be the Fun Dad who only says yes, I'd become the Mean Mom who says no. On top of that, nobody would listen to my no. I'd get all the punishment, without even a taste of the crime.

And it's not like I don't want to say yes. But by the time I get there, Tobin's already used it all up. So many times, he's said yes even when it hurt him.

Even when it hurt us.

He's spent weekends hardscaping his mom's yard while I pulled weeds in *his* vegetable garden. He's said yes to every passing acquaintance who asked him to help them move because he's big and friendly and has a truck. He agreed to rotate someone's tires when he was still in his wrist cast, and I had to be the Mean Wife who shut that down.

"You had ice cream with dinner, so none with the movie. Aunt Liz won't eat any in front of you, because that wouldn't be fair."

Even Amber wants to make me take all the no. Forget that—if Amber wants an obedient babysitter, she can pay for one. Free babysitters only say yes. And technically, nobody forbade movie popcorn with extra butter.

"Aren't you going to be late?"

She shoots me a narrow-eyed look. "Have fun, you two peas in a pod." Her nursing scrubs are printed with rainbow unicorns. If she met a unicorn in real life, she'd snap off its horn and tell it to be happy being a horse.

"Should we call Grammie and Gramps while we make popcorn?" I ask when the minivan is out of sight. Eleanor sprints for the popcorn maker while I call my parents twice. They always need two chances to figure out how to answer a video call.

My mom's face appears with the cheery connection sound. "Eleanor! Hi, precious! What are my three girls doing tonight?"

"Mama's at work. Me and Aunt Liz are having a movie. And popcorn. I have to concentrate while I pour." Eleanor frowns, carefully tilting the jar of kernels over the microwaveable popper.

"Too bad your mom's not there. She and your aunt used to love watching movies together. There were these awful vampire films. . . ."

"*Twilight* was a global sensation, Mom. And it was also about werewolves." Ever one to root for the underdog, I was Team Jacob. Amber was Team Edward, but at least we agreed on what to watch. The Christmas I completed my *Twilight* DVD collection—necessary in Pendleton, where the broadband used to be too sketchy for streaming—Amber and I watched all five movies. We cried our eyes out; it was glorious. We didn't have many moments like that, but the ones we did were pretty great. I'm 90 percent convinced that one Christmas is the reason my parents got me and Tobin a DVD player for our wedding.

Even my wedding gift was about being close with my sister.

"You're not watching those with my granddaughter, are you? Weren't they very sexy?" Mom looks worried, as if Eleanor isn't the kid who knows where episiotomies come from.

"Stellar's not getting here till eight, and you know El passes out ten minutes into a movie. Besides, we're watching *Legally Blonde*. Where's Dad?"

"He's picking up Thai. We're too tired to cook." Mom relates their hiking adventures in Sedona while I take back half the enormous chunk of butter Eleanor's hacked into a tiny ramekin and squish it back onto the stick.

"Too much, El, the popcorn will be all wet." Food texture matters a lot to Eleanor, and in the case of popcorn, she's correct: dampness would be a problem for both of us.

"Gotta go, Mom, the situation here is going nonlinear." My parents got us into the habit of using backcountry terms like "nonlinear"—the moment when the edges of a snow slide turn outward, triggering an avalanche—as ordinary speech. I love how it feels like code, math, and mountains all at once. I'd teach people that kind of insider secret language on my tours. If I had tours.

Clenching my teeth, I correct myself: *when* I have tours.

"Bye, Eleanor! You're still my favorite granddaughter!"

"Grammie, I'm your *only* granddaughter," Eleanor points out seriously.

"Hug your sister for me," Mom commands, delusional as ever.

"Um, sure."

Eleanor installs herself on the anti-popcorn towel I've spread over the couch, Yeti click-purring at her side. He's better at remembering this is where he lives now. He still hates it when Kris

Kristofferson stirs the pot by pretending to gnaw him, but he puts up with it in return for Eleanor's devotion to finding all his favorite scratching spots.

"Hel-loooooooo," comes a yodel from the front door. "Who wants to see the cool rocks I brought?"

"Stellar!" I forget I meant to be chill and rush to squeeze her. She's tiny, so I can pick her up and jiggle her until we're both laughing uncontrollably. She's here for a couple of days, then back out to her clinic for another seven weeks, so I have to go hard on the hugs. Especially because she's acting so casual about her breakup. She only does that when she's hurting badly. I've learned not to push her; she'll open up in her own time. Unlike Tobin, who opens up never.

Except he did, in the truck.

"Auntie Stellar!" Eleanor yells.

"El's Bells!" Stellar shouts back. "Did you build me a Lego Millennium Falcon?"

"I ran out of gray."

Eleanor and Stellar open negotiations on what colors the Millennium Falcon can be and still remain canon. I bring over the grown-ups' bowl of popcorn for our sacred movie ritual, which consists of Stellar and me talking over, through, and around the action onscreen.

If it's a rom-com, she's criticizing the unlikely coincidences while I'm squeeing over the near-misses and delicious tension.

If it's sci-fi, I'm pointing out romance subplots, and Stellar's telling me to pay closer attention whenever an important character is about to be killed.

And regardless of genre, both of us are doing a comparative gender analysis, because as a pair of thirsty bisexuals we don't hate it when Uhura wears a miniskirt, we just want Kirk and Spock to wear a bit less also.

True to form, Eleanor's asleep before Elle Woods gets dumped by her boneheaded boyfriend. "Emmett," I moan when Luke Wilson smiles. "I'm trash for a soft boy. Trash. Did Jen get in touch about the money?" Maybe a sneaky question will trick her into opening up.

"Jen's being an ass." Stellar idly twists her platinum hair into a swooping topknot over undercut sides. She's gorgeous—a tiny, gritty millennial Marilyn Monroe. "I shouldn't have trusted someone who wanted me to take her name after marriage, when that name is Keller. What was it you said about rhyming names?"

"I said it was very Julia Gulia. Like *The Wedding Singer*." Stellar deflected me all too easily with that last-name gambit. Just like I deflected Tobin when he changed his last name to Renner-Lewis, like we agreed, and I didn't change mine. He doesn't even know why—I knew if I didn't bring it up, he wouldn't either, and I'd never have to explain.

"I should've known not to get myself into any situation with a rom-com equivalent. You know, the queer rep in this movie is not ideal. I wish the lesbian character had a girlfriend. And some dialogue. Speaking of dialogue, how's that . . . marriage counseling thing? It's going well?"

"It's going. We're doing our third session this Saturday." Less than a week after our last one. I intended to space out our scenarios, run out the clock. But lately I feel so *tender*, like there's a spot of exquisite pain I want to check over and over again. Like I want him to kiss it better.

This inexplicable kissing impulse goes against everything I'm trying to accomplish: be my own person; succeed on my own merit; *get magic*, for fuck's sake. It doesn't have to be the biggest or best or loudest magic. It just has to be enough. It just has to be *mine*.

"And Amber's supportive?" Stellar doesn't criticize my sister to my face, but she does ask careful questions about what I'm willing to put up with.

The answer is: a lot, because of Eleanor.

I'd do anything for Eleanor, and Amber knows it. She's a terrific mom—she's built a real community around her daughter, with family and friends and autism supports. And me.

Our relationship broke once already. If I push back, it could happen again.

"Amber's still Amber," I say, glancing at Eleanor even though she sleeps like the dead. "She's not exactly inviting me to go running or join her book club. But who needs her, when I have you?"

We make scrunchy faces at each other.

Onscreen, two women mock Elle's dorky, awkward study buddy.

I cringe. "I hate this part. They make it seem like this guy should *want* to date people who were mean until Reese Witherspoon pretended she slept with him. Sorry, but no."

It's like the times people made fun of my spreadsheets or my finger tapping, but changed their tune when they saw me with Tobin or Stellar. And then they acted insulted when, unlike in the movie, I didn't forgive and forget. *People think you don't like them, Liz.* Well, for some people, that was true.

"They did a better job with the autistic-coded character than the queer character, though," Stellar says. "At least he gets laid."

Popcorn falls out of my mouth. "The what?"

"The autistic-coded character," she repeats. "A lot of books and movies have characters who aren't labeled autistic *per se,* but we get hints they are from their mannerisms, clothes, speech, whatever. This guy I worked with pointed it out when we watched *Don't Look Up.* Funny dude; he joked that he disclosed his autism up front because *his* communication was fine, but non-autistic people needed help learning to say what they meant." She laughs.

I stop paying attention to the movie. The character whose life reminds me so much of mine . . . is autistic-coded? Does that mean . . . ?

No. Somebody would have picked it up, like with Eleanor. My teachers, or my parents, or my doctor. A decades-old movie is not a diagnostic test. I'm just exhausted from getting magic, and emotional from everything else, and that line of thinking needs to go away right now.

In the background, Elle Woods prepares to destroy everyone who's ever underestimated her because of the way she presents herself. Although even Elle had to change herself to get taken seriously.

Stellar's phone bursts into Darth Vader's theme music. "Work, ugh," she says, though her tight shoulders tell me it's probably Jen. "Babe, I'm so sorry, but this will take a while. I'd better go." She sets the popcorn bowl on the floor and shakes crumbs into it from her shirt.

"Ahhh, noooo. You just got here!"

"I know. Can we finish the movie tomorrow? I'll make time for your presentation thingy, too."

"Tomorrow I'm going to the driving range, then straight to improv. Saturday?"

Stellar's face flattens in a blink. "The driving range? You hate golf. You said it's an environmental disaster combined with a tax avoidance nightmare."

"Yes, but I have to learn how. People won't listen to my pitch unless I have the right business skills."

And I have four weeks left. One week till the pre-pitch. Between improv, the driving range, extra practice with Tobin, and after-hours work events, I'm burning all my free time before even opening my pitch materials. The last two nights I've woken up sweating from Q&A session nightmares where I fail to answer the same basic question over and over.

"Liz . . ." Stellar's mouth looks like she put bad milk on her cereal. "Are you sure you're doing this for the right reasons? It's fine if that's what *you* want to do," she adds quickly. "I'm just worried you're losing sight of what you believe in. And I love you the way you are."

"Yeah," I say, bitter. "You and exactly no one else."

She makes a frustrated sound. "Why don't you leave Waste by North? There are so many jobs where you'd shine—"

"Jobs where I couldn't get past the interview, remember?"

"—without having to give yourself a creepy personality makeover so your square peg fits into a round corporate hole."

"I *want* a personality makeover, Stellar! You've never been the square peg. You don't know what it's like not to get things because you're the wrong shape." I blink away tears. "I'm thirty. My career's going nowhere. My marriage is in the toilet. I can't waste this chance, Stel. I need some doors to open, even if I have to pick the lock."

I think of what Sharon said at the Kraken. "I can do things differently and still be myself. Like when people who are afraid of spiders touch a bunch of spiders and then they get much better at, uh . . . touching spiders. I'm aware that doesn't sound like a good prize, but you know what I mean."

"Okay," Stellar grumbles. "But I hope you're all right, babe. I'm here if you need me."

The house has a hollow quiet once Stellar's gone. Eleanor's asleep, contorted into one of those anatomically improbable kid positions, drooling into Yeti's fur.

The cat complains when I extract him from his bestie's embrace to lift Eleanor into my arms. He limps to the edge of the couch, readies himself to jump, and launches crookedly at Stellar's bowl of buttery popcorn shrapnel.

Everything flips—the cat, the metal bowl that clashes across the hardwood, the greasy kernels flying in slow motion toward my parents' dry-clean-only decor. Yeti leaps sideways in confusion and fear, scrambling up the back of the entertainment console.

"Yeti, no!" I whisper, as he bumps the DVD player out of its slot. It tilts, sliding off the shelf at first slowly, then all at once.

The level of noise is astounding: the cat yowling, expensive things smashing, and me hissing "fuck" on a loop.

Eleanor doesn't twitch an eyelid.

I stand in the wreckage for a while before I'm able to make a list.

1. *Put Eleanor to bed.*

2. *Make it so Amber can't lecture me for breaking the machine that plays Eleanor's shows.*

I need another DVD player by morning, when Eleanor will mainline her episode of *Barbie: Life in the Dreamhouse* while eating raisin bran.

Which means I have to text Tobin.

If he's even home. He was a partier when we first got together, one of the rare straight guys I knew who loved to dance. After a few years, he turned into a homebody because that's what I am. I'd encourage him to go to the bar without me, he'd demur, and I'd feel bad.

I'm torn between hoping he's out living the life he gave up for me, or hoping he's at home because he's the only one who can help me.

> Are you at the house? So sorry but I need a favor.

> Everything okay?

I can almost hear the concern in Tobin's voice.

> Nothing serious. Can I borrow our DVD player?

My parents bought themselves the same machine they gave me and Tobin. I can swap them out with nobody the wiser.

> Sure. You coming over now?

Is there an internal organ that manufactures guilt? His immediate yes pokes me right where it lives. I both love and hate that I knew he'd never say no, no matter what I asked.

> Babysitting E. Put it on the back porch? I'll come by first thing.

> I'll take care of it.

Five minutes later, I'm on hands and knees scanning for popcorn kernels under the couch when a soft rap sounds at the front door.

Tobin stands there, clutching our DVD player.

"What are you doing here?" I ask, though it's obvious. "Agh, Yeti." I scoop up the cat before he can escape.

When I straighten up, Tobin's eyes are popping.

I forgot I'm wearing my new, very pretty, very V-necked sleep romper, bought in a spiral of feeling like I'd never get laid ever again. It was stupid expensive, but it helps me imagine I'm one step closer to being my new self.

We stand there staring for far too long. He looks rumpled, like he's been lying on the couch, too. He smells like Ben & Jerry's New York Super Fudge Chunk, which he only eats when he's sad. I'd bet my organic cotton romper he's been on the seed websites, buying a million kinds of zucchini we don't have room to plant.

His face rests in an easy, neutral expression, but his eyes are working to stay above my neck. I'm all too aware of how little clothing I'm wearing, and how easily he could take it off. It's the kind of thing you can't help but know when you've been with someone as long as he and I have been together. Or maybe as long as he and I *were* together?

I don't know anymore.

"Can I come in?"

No, he may not. I'm having too many gigantic feelings; there isn't room in the house for Tobin, too.

Someone outside says, "Tobin? Did I get the time wrong?"

McHuge stands in the middle of the road, looking bemused. Bizarrely, he's carrying a nylon mesh laptop bag. Was the real McHuge abducted by aliens? The one I know doesn't have a phone, much less a computer.

"Hi, McHuge." I wave with one hand, gesturing frantically with the other for Tobin to get inside. "One second."

"No, that's fine, I can see you're, uh. Busy. With, uh. *Repairs,*" McHuge calls, loud enough to notify the entire neighborhood.

He makes it sound like Tobin and I are role-playing a low-budget porno. I clock Tobin's low-slung jeans and thigh-weakening T-shirt. Also my adorably detailed romper, worn with no bra.

This does look pretty porny.

I yank Tobin across the threshold. "He'll be home in a minute," I sing, through the closing door.

"Hey, buddy," he croons, reaching for Yeti. "What's this?" His callused finger drifts to where three stitches peek through a shaved spot on the cat's chest.

"The vet says he's okay. He was probably squeezing into a tight space." I leave out how he was gone for almost two days. I wish I could've thanked his rescuers, but the Humane Society couldn't tell me who they were or how he got hurt. Or where he picked up that unbelievable smell, like a barnyard died in his fur.

He needs to become an indoor cat, for his own safety. And for

mine, because Amber almost killed me over how upset Eleanor
was when he was missing.

"I bet it was expensive. How much do I owe you?"

I gesture to the machine. "It's fine, Tobin. We're even."

"Do you want me to hook it up, or—"

"I can connect it, you've already done—"

"Let me do it, Liz. You've got the cat, anyway."

In the family room, his head swivels from the fractured face of
my parents' machine to the stray kernel of popcorn I only now see
nestled against the earth-colored area rug.

"It wasn't my fault."

"I know." He sets the DVD player on the couch. "You're too
careful for that."

He can't be kind to me like this.

I want kindness too badly right now. If I took what he's offering, I wouldn't know whether I wanted him or whether I just
wanted one person in this world to tell me everything will be okay,
and I'm not an irredeemable screwup getting ready to throw my
thirties down the same hole as my twenties.

Turning away, I manage to put my heel right on the damn kernel. I pinwheel wildly, knowing it was my destiny to end this night
on my ass.

Tobin's hand in the small of my back saves me.

How five fingers can do so much is a mystery. I can feel every
whorl of his fingerprints inking a tattoo into my skin. His palm
burns hot through my outfit, which promised to be substantial,
but is clearly as flimsy as my willpower right now. His eyes are a
thin rim of spun crystal around a well of deepest black.

Against my very specific instructions, my nipples tighten trai-
torously. If Tobin didn't know I was braless before, he does now.

"You okay?"

I have a lot of questions about why my body is tuned to the

specific frequency of his voice. Why none of my parts are listening to my brain's frantic pleas to ignore him. Whether I am in fact okay, or maybe not okay at all.

"Amber will be back any minute," I lie, not ready for the answers. "And McHuge is waiting."

"Right," he says, carefully. "So our choices are, risk Amber finding out that everything's fine, or I take the evidence and rappel off the roof to avoid getting caught."

I can't stop the smile from popping one side of my mouth up, the other side down.

"Ah," Tobin says, biting his lip. "I missed your dimple." He indicates the down side of my mouth.

My hand flies to my face. "My smile is weird. It looks like half of me is frowning."

"No," he says. "It looks like you have a secret. Something hilarious you're keeping inside. I wish I knew what that was anymore." His hand hovers, then strokes my smile, featherlight, up and across and up.

I can't speak.

Not when he settles me firmly on my feet.

Not when he lets go.

Not when he picks up the busted black box and walks out the door, leaving nothing but silence behind.

Chapter Twelve

SCENARIO 3: STUCK WITH YOU

Agreement—**yes, and**—is the one improv rule that should never be broken, and the most difficult rule for partners in crisis. Nothing is too small to fight about; I've seen spouses spend fifty minutes arguing over the most efficient route for the five-minute drive home. Partners who can't agree on little things often worry they won't know how to work together when big things happen, like illness and loss.

Now that you've established new pathways of **communication**, Scenario 3 is about **collaboration**. At this point in your relationship journey, we're ready to raise the stakes, to keep everyone engaged. Invent a situation where your characters get into big trouble, then work together to find your way to safety. Make the problem something nobody could solve alone. How about a perilous journey, a time-sensitive crisis, or a delicate diplomatic situation?

Tip: Don't get sucked into disagreements—remember, conflict makes bad improv. Arguments keep the scene small, when the point of this scenario is to go big!

—*The Second Chances Handbook*

McHuge's book is like a backcountry trip with no ops support: unnecessarily rough.

After our breakthrough last week, I expected Tobin and me to be on a stable, linear path, either toward reconciliation, or toward breaking up. It should be predictable, moving from ten to one, or the other way around, one number at a time.

The Highway to Hell trail is the perfect metaphor for the path we're actually on: a rocky, muddy mountain trail made of upward scrambles sandwiched by steep downhill switchbacks.

Today is not a majestic day on the way to Hell. It's a beautiful route in summer, starting from the cool, evergreen-scented shade of the forest, breaking through the tree line into purple-flowered alpine meadows framed by majestic peaks and soaring, narrow waterfalls, ending in the crumbly, swirling black rock formations of the hot springs. You might spot a grizzly lumbering across a neighboring slope, heading home after a morning spent fishing in a lake bluer than the sky.

In summer, the mountains will take your heart and not give it back.

But at the beginning of May, the conditions are at peak sloppiness. The no-see-ums—half the size of mosquitoes and twice as thirsty—come with the thawing ground. Disappointed tourists slump back down the trail at 10 A.M., too early to have gotten more than halfway to the hot springs. Bloodied by bites, they look ready to snatch the bug netting right off my hat.

Tobin sends me a brazen grin, black paisley bandanna tied low over his nose, crude eyeholes snipped slightly too close together. It's all very Dread Pirate Roberts. He did specify a shipboard theme, but when he said he'd be dressing appropriately, I thought he meant what I'm wearing: full-body coverage against every hazard.

"There are no costumes in improv," I point out acidly.

"I thought you'd like this. You could join me next time. They have lots of five-dollar dresses at Thrift Town." He smooths his puffy black shirt, inviting me to admire.

Unlike me, Tobin can wear a costume on a public trail without getting mercilessly mocked. He's not afraid of judgment, so somehow nobody judges him. Quite the opposite, in fact; a couple of dudes have tried to high-five him.

I make a mental note: *McHuge correct. If you're okay, audience okay.*

One hand on the wheel of our imaginary ship, Tobin strides across the marsh where we're seeking hidden treasure, in complete control of himself and the scenario.

"One of us should watch for swamp fire. The last thing we need is a hole in our hull. All we have to do is steer around it, and we're home free." He looks supremely piratical in his tight black pants and swashbuckling smile. I feel like a sullen stowaway in my jeans and boots and bug hat. And bad attitude.

"You mean, all *you* have to do is steer around it."

He looks at me askance.

Two days ago, when he touched my crooked smile, he *saw* me in a way nobody else does. But he doesn't see who I *could* be. He's comfortably in charge; I'm supposed to go along, I guess.

When he and I were both river guides, I thought we made a good team. Some of my clients inevitably wanted to switch to the "fun" boat. But some of his passengers were happy to come with me and listen to the wind and the water, instead of another twenty verses of "Barrett's Privateers." That's where I had the idea for the quiet tours I semi-pitched to Sharon.

By chance, a family reunion got canceled at the same time a camp chief—the expedition manager, chef, and concierge rolled into one—quit. West by North needed one less river guide, and one more cook. Me.

Looking back, that was the turning point in my career. I still had a job, but I couldn't help noticing how uniform the guides were without me. All men, all cast in the same extroverted mold. There was one right way to be a guide, and my way wasn't it.

After that, Tobin got a zillion opportunities to sharpen the leadership skills he already had, rising from guide to expedition leader to head guide. I got shunted in the opposite direction: cook, paper pusher, second banana in a one-person ops department. Our reputation for loud, nonstop good times drew more and more loud, nonstop clients. Even if I'd gotten my raft back the next summer, there would've been no one who wanted to ride with me.

Who would I be, if the company had chosen leaders with diverse skill sets instead of the same kind of person over and over? If I'd insisted on being the front person in our marriage sometimes, instead of relegating myself to a supporting role?

They're hard to break, these routines we've made. I hate my part in creating this one, where I point out the places we shouldn't go, and he gets to decide where we should.

"I fear there may be creatures in the depths," he prompts. "Alligators. Snakes."

"You could go look."

"I'm steering. I need you in the crow's nest." He braces his legs against the iron-gray waves, wiping salt spray from his face. Wet and cold are nothing to him. A pirate captain doesn't feel such things, much as he doesn't notice pain or sadness.

I know he's playing a character, but it's one that comes from inside himself. How different from Tobin can this pirate be?

We must have hit some swamp fire, because every stick of emotional dynamite lights up all at once.

"I already took a turn in the crow's nest. I came down because it's *my* turn to steer."

"I've captained this ship for nigh on eight years. Your keen eyes can spot trouble miles away. That's how we'll survive the marsh, which none have traversed alive since—"

"I know about the *marsh*," I snap.

"Apologies." He sweeps a sarcastic bow, annoyed I'm not giving him a "yes, and."

One part of me thinks, *Good. At least when I'm angry, he feels something.* But there's a little sparkle of fear at the bottom of my treasure chest of fury, a memory of our one fight before this year. Not even a fight.

We'd just taken ownership of the house we could barely afford. He thought we wouldn't need movers, but only one of the people who'd owed him favors showed up to help us move. By 10 P.M., the house was still chaos and we were so, so over each other. I wanted us to go crash at my parents' house, which I thought was a normal thing to do when everybody was furious and nobody knew where the mattress was. He said he'd stay and keep unpacking, but at midnight he climbed in the window of my childhood bedroom, eyes red, begging me not to leave him over one bad day.

We kissed each other's tears away, and I came home. We found the mattress in the living room, collapsed behind the couch. We didn't even have the energy to put sheets on; we just found a blanket and folded into each other like exhausted origami. I thought we'd done okay, for our first fight.

Except there was never a second fight. Tobin made himself the peacemaker in our relationship, just like when he was a kid refereeing his parents' marriage. But what if breaking our old patterns breaks that one, too? If I'm angry, and he's angry right back, what then?

I pile justification on top of the fear to cover up its cold brilliance. "Let me ask you something, Captain Crunch. How come you're in charge?"

He looks at me like I'm beautiful, but slightly touched. Can I not see what a fine figure he cuts in his buckskins and boots? Does not his shirt gape open at the front, revealing his manly chest? Who else could be captain?

A tourist squats on the next rise, gigantic camera pointed our way.

"I rose through the ranks, like any captain."

I know. I watched him get chosen. "No. Not *how* you became captain. *Why*. Why you, and not me? Name one reason I couldn't lead."

His eyebrows bunch so hard the bandanna gathers at the middle of his forehead. "I don't . . . this is what I always do. Why would you want me to do something else?" Fair point. In an uncomfortable situation, Tobin defaults to what he does best: leading the expedition, filling silences with games and songs and adventure and himself. He's fantastic at it. Clients love it. Everyone loves it, if I'm being honest.

But I don't want to be his client. Or the stage crew for his performance.

"I don't *want* you to do something else, Tobin. I *need* you to. I don't want to play the same roles forever, where you ride in on your white horse and save the day and, oh yeah, I'm there, too. I want to *grow*. And I want you to value the invisible work I do, because you do that work, too."

We break off as a pair of defeated hikers trudges past. They look inexperienced, but they could get to Hell if they had opportunities and support. If their first failure wasn't taken as a permanent judgment on what they could do.

Enough. "I want a turn being captain. And if you won't share, I'm getting my own boat." I march to the stern, looking for a plank to walk.

"Li—sailor! Stop!" Tobin yells. "The marsh is too dangerous. We won't survive if we split up."

I'm cracking him. Breaking through his character, peeling it off him strip by strip. Ignoring McHuge's commandments. Tobin's trying to preserve the fiction, but the fear in his voice feels real, sawing across my heartstrings in a jagged screech.

He doesn't want me to go. But if the power of "no" is the only power I have, then that's what I'll use.

I look over my shoulder. "You're right. I don't know what's out there. Maybe a sparkly merman with washboard abs. Could be a kraken who'll eat me alive." I shrug. "But I need to find out."

His hand drifts to his stomach, checking the architecture of his own abs. Is he jealous of an imaginary merman? The lower half of his face looks . . . insecure. Unhappy.

"This is a problem in our marriage, Tobin," I say gently. "You don't see me as someone who can lead. Neither of us did, if I'm being honest. And you didn't see yourself the other way. You didn't picture needing help. Or standing there while someone else says yes to everything on your behalf. Oh, and you'd be in an absurd dress where you can't move or breathe."

"You're wearing jeans, Liz," he points out curtly. "I mean, pantaloons."

I thought he'd figured things out after the rawness of the radio scenario, where we made progress by doing things differently. Instead, he's wrapped up in the role, determined to rescue me.

But in real life, no one rescues you. No one offers you opportunities if you're different from the people who've always gotten those chances.

In real life, you have to rescue yourself. You have to GET MAGIC, as my phone reminds me every time I open my Notes app. It doesn't say ask people to let me have magic or wait for magic to find me.

It says, GET MAGIC.

I can't keep waiting for Tobin to give me the roles he's gotten comfortable taking, probably without noticing how lopsided our marriage has become.

I have to take the lead. Tell him what I need, and make sure I get it.

It's terrifying. And it's my only choice.

"You know what? You're right," I say, stowing the phone in my pantaloons. For the last half hour, I haven't been able to forget we're two non-pirates on a rainforest trail. The most wavelike things I've seen are breakers of moss foaming across the pale gray rocks. Those tall straight things all around us have never transformed from lodgepole pines into the mainmast and the . . . I don't know, the other masts.

Now I only see the helm as I storm up to it. "You're absolutely right," I repeat.

"I am?"

With one hand, I grab the wildly spinning wheel. I have to stretch an undignified distance to swipe his mask, but I manage. I doff my hat and pull the black cloth down my nose. Too loose, it droops over my chin.

Magic fits me poorly. But I'll make it fit better.

"Hold this," I instruct Tobin, nodding at the wheel. Surprised, he takes it. "Don't get used to it. That's my helm."

I spit out the bandanna and remake the knot while adjusting

my mouth into a crooked smirking scowl, one side up, one side down.

"Like you said, this is a pirate ship. But you're not the captain. *I* am."

A shiver vibrates through his silver-buckled boots, up the sinews of his legs, all the way to his chest. Maybe to his heart.

"You can be captain next time."

I scoff. "Who says I can't be captain every time?"

His face is a mirror for an internal struggle so mighty I can't help but laugh.

"Fine," he grits out. "I can be first mate."

"Don't need one!" I sing. "You can swab the decks."

"The decks don't need swabbing. I want to help you."

I outright giggle. "If you're bored, sailor, why don't you ask me about my adventures? Hold on, we're tacking around another swamp fire!"

We're deep in the improv red zone, fighting for our separate versions of what should happen. Too bad this scenario is falling apart; it's been a long time since I've had this much fun. I spin the wheel merrily, wracking my brain for a sea shanty whose words I know at least 50 percent of.

"I can navigate." He strides to the gunwale, one hand shading his eyes.

Giving up on the words, I whistle a jolly pirate tune and slap at the beasts biting my neck.

"Alligator! Must be thirty feet long!" Tobin shouts, pointing.

"Hard to starboard," I holler. Ha. He's playing *my* game now.

He staggers with a deep impact, sending me an evil glance. "It rammed us, Captain!"

Oh, that jerk. This whole time, he was scheming. No one wins a game this vindictive, but this ship left port a long time ago.

"We're taking on water! Deckhand! To the pumps!" I point to a mud puddle. "You can do it, put your back into it," I call after him, whistling the bass line from Ice Cube's iconic contribution to the *Save the Last Dance* soundtrack. Classic.

"You have to help bail." He scoops water from the deck. He has to bend and flex a lot. The neckline of that black shirt is all over the place.

"It's no use. Save yourself. I'll see you in Davy Jones's locker." I salute, prepared to go down with my ship.

"We're in a marsh. It's six feet deep."

"Then I guess we'll be six feet under."

If either of us gave one inch, everything would change. But I can't, because I'm so enraged with him, and with myself. We got here together. Both of us built this uneven boat that drifts in painful circles.

And I think . . . I think I might be angry with him *because* I love him and I want better from him. If I didn't, I'd have walked away a long time ago.

He's at my side, radiating frustration. Good. Mr. Happy Guy should get upset once in a while. It gives the little people hope.

"I'll save you." He grabs me around the waist with delicious roughness, delivering a shock of awareness that burns all the way up and all the way down my right side.

"No, you will *not* save me. I'll save *you*." I put my arm around his waist right back, yanking hard to show him my impressive saving powers.

His pupils spin wide, a rim of unreadable ice around a black pirate soul. "The water's up to my knees," he says, getting down in the mud. "The gators will breach us any second."

He doesn't pull me down with him. There's no reason for me to end up on my knees, too, unable to look away from his face, my arms around his waist. I seem to be breathing hard. So does he, which I guess is what happens when your ship's going down.

"I'm afraid," he says, so softly. "For this ship. And the crew."

Oh. *Oh.*

How did I lose control? I *had* this scene, and it slipped away.

"We may die today. But you've . . ." I pause to clear my throat, unaccountably hoarse. "You've performed your duties with honor, sailor."

I should salute him. I should not slide my hands up his back and notice this tugging heat inside my pantaloons.

"I've never," Tobin says, with the same sea-roughened voice I've got, "never served under a better captain." His butt touches earth, and I understand how fast the water's rising.

His hand comes to my sinking hips. "I'm taller. I can hold you above water." He tugs me toward him. Protecting me is what he's always done, but even if he's doing it for the best reasons, his magic isn't enough anymore.

I need my own.

"I know you want to save me. But I have to save myself," I whisper.

I can't let him rescue me here, because he can't rescue me anywhere else—work, family, any of the million ways I'm on my own.

But how I want to slide into his lap. How it would feel to settle onto those thighs, fit my chest to his, and *take* everything I want.

"Okay," he says, his lips closer every second. "If that's what you need to do." He looks in my eyes like he's drowning in them. Like he *wants* to drown.

I've heard it's normal to be turned on by a near-death experience. Which is definitely the only reason I pull off the mask to put my cheek against his, closing my eyes. I don't intend to go any further, even if my heart is pounding and my skin is tightening and I'm squeezing my thighs together to fight the urge to let them fall open.

Tobin's tiny sigh is what does it. It's a brokenhearted little thing, clinging to a passing chunk of hope to stay afloat. His fingers flex against my jeans, like they, too, are so close to what they want, yet hold back for reasons of their own.

I'm not smart, so I snort black cottonwood straight off his skin, watching him watch me do it.

Fuck it.

The second I move, he moves with me, a fast yet slow turning of heads, a softest meeting of lips.

There are a lot of kinds of kisses in this world. This one is the kind that tricks me with its easy give, with an unspooling that starts slack, then tightens with a snap.

A stunning shot of pure longing fire lights me up everywhere. And I want.

I *want*.

Sweetness dives out of the way of the oncoming blaze, leaving only ungentle greed. Harsh breaths and fistfuls of hair and Tobin hauling me into his lap by my knees and hips, tight, tighter. His piratical outfit hides nothing. Not the way his chest swells, not the way anything else is swelling, either. He can surely feel me gasp, see the flush that makes my skin so hot.

"Oh, Diz. Oh, yeah," he's chanting, between kisses, face pressed to mine. "I missed you, I missed you."

It's too easy to fall back into his arms, to move the way we've learned to move together. The familiarity of his body, his smell, everything about him promises I don't have to be scared anymore.

If I just fall back into this pattern.

"Stop, Tobe. No sex. I have to not do this."

My vagina is furious at me right now.

We're silent and stock-still in each other's arms. I need this moment with my body against his. It's reckless and risky; the flex of his thighs, that extra pressure where it counts, douses my parched libido in gasoline and throws a match at it.

We were always hot together, patching the cracks in our relationship with orgasms and optimism. Sometimes a patch absorbs the shock of a rough spot, getting you through. And sometimes it lets the cracks grow into chasms that might be uncrossable.

He takes a shaky breath, forehead against my collarbone, then exhales with purpose as he lifts me up and away, high enough to get my feet under me. His strength is infuriatingly hot. Does he *have* to show me how easy it would be for him to put me right where I'm dying to be?

Tobin rolls to his feet, covered in mud. "As you wish."

I *cannot* with this man. "I knew it. I knew you were the Dread Pirate Roberts."

He shrugs. "Like I said. I thought you'd like it."

"That's . . . that's . . ." Cheating is what it is. Now that I think about it, the other two scenarios looked suspiciously like scenes from *You've Got Mail* and *Sleepless in Seattle*. He's using romantic comedies against me, like insider information.

"That's it. From now on, *I* choose the scenes."

"Fine," he says, the dangerous spark in his eyes flying right at me.

"I assign the roles."

"Fine." The repetition deepens the rumble in his voice.

"I'll . . . I'll see you next week!" I shout, backing away, shaking my finger so he doesn't follow.

His satisfied laugh is not at all like my safe and gentle husband. I know I'll replay the husky, knowing sound tonight—alone, and wishing I weren't.

Chapter Thirteen

Don't be afraid of your scenes. Fear and discomfort can
stop you from discovering the truth your scenes will reveal, if you let them.

—*The Second Chances Handbook*

Stellar's texting from work again. Rural medicine—her *dream*
job, yay me for thinking those words without needing a blood
transfusion—was supposed to be challenging, but she's finding a
lot of time to send memes, somehow.

Sneaked onto the supply plane to Calgary. Got a new lipstick. Vicious
Pink. WAY too expensive. Stellar sends a picture of her gorgeous lips,
which aren't a pop of color so much as a punch.

LOVE IT. SO PINK. AM JEALOUS. I press my own neutral-shaded
lips together, imagining.

Feels AMAZING. It's got peptides, or whatever.

What do those do? I add scientist and laugh emojis, but I'm worried. That's a hell of a trip for a tube of lipstick.

> They can reinvent your lips. VERY powerful.

Stellar is my person. We've shared every milestone, every heartbreak. And we're talking about lipstick, when there's clearly something deeper going on.

> How's the clinic?

Long pause. No dots.

I glance at the time. I want to hit the boardroom well in advance of my pre-pitch time slot.

> Love you, gotta run. Update later.

I dash into the bathroom for a last-minute check. Mistake. When I look in the mirror, I suddenly hate everything I'm wearing. What made me pick out this gray suit, when I'd feel much more like myself in a fuchsia blouse and Vicious Pink lipstick? Obviously, I own neither of those things. Right now, I can't remember why not.

On the way to the boardroom, I practice positive self-talk under my breath. "I am powerful. I am valuable. I am . . . I'm a *peptide*. I am a Powerful Pink Peptide."

"You're what?" David cuts in front of me at the boardroom door.

"Oh! Hi D—uh, David, don't mind me." I give an unconvincing laugh. By now, I know better than to look for a crevasse.

He walks in, not needing any more encouragement to pay no attention to me.

In the large boardroom, where the thermostat is permanently cranked down to "three-piece wool suit in July," my sweaty skin turns cold and clammy.

It feels strange to take a seat at the table. When I attend

company meetings here, I wait out West by North's Darwinian shout-fests in my safe spot in the corner. Craig feels a competitive environment breeds excellence. I feel it amplifies the loud voices, and silences the quiet ones. Like mine.

But that's corporate culture everywhere, I'm sure. It's not my style, but I don't get to choose. I have to learn to yell, or die from the bitterness of never being heard.

I wish I'd spent the last seven years practicing speaking up, instead of shutting up. Until now, it made no sense to burn my finite lifetime number of fucks screaming into the chaos, only to have my ideas rejected—or worse, taken from me, like my boat. The only times I surfaced were to point out when Craig's wilder proposals were cost-prohibitive or logistically impossible.

Across the table, David flips through full-color handouts. I'm guessing he has the slot before mine. At least he doesn't seem to be paying attention to me nodding my head as I rehearse the beats of my presentation. Or the way I'm trying to unobtrusively fan my armpits with my handouts.

Three ideas will get the green light for the final competition, and I counted fifteen time slots for pitches. I've never gotten past this barrier to entry before, and my track record of pitching failure does not feel like it's been adequately addressed by three whole improv classes. There's a five-to-one chance I'll get nowhere with this pitch, and if that happens . . .

I push back against a wave of anticipatory despair. What will I do if I'm finally forced to admit I'll never get anywhere in this company?

It would sting to apply for an entry-level job somewhere else, but I might have to. If I did, say, fifty interviews, surely one of them would accidentally go well.

The door to the adjoining small boardroom opens, and Craig motions David in.

"Good luck," I say, because it seems called for. David smirks, grunting in acknowledgment. I strive to be polite to everyone—I offend enough people as it is, and we *are* Canadian—but no one makes me regret being courteous as quickly and sharply as Dick Head.

Five minutes pass like I'm waiting for the verdict in my murder trial. No one arrives in advance of the last time slot. I distract myself by calculating my odds of making the final round with thirteen competitors instead of fourteen (still terrible).

The door opens and David and Craig reappear, laughing over some closing joke.

"Liz? You're up." After thirteen five-minute presentations, Craig looks restless.

The five panelists take their seats—Craig, Jingjing, Bethany, our head of legal, and a guy from IT. I launch my PowerPoint.

Craig cocks his head. "How's that improv thing going, by the way?"

"Um, good."

"Just 'good'?" He raps his pen against the table, frowning.

He wants to talk about improv *now*? My eyes sneak to the countdown timer in the corner of the big screen. A scratchy new bump appears under my shirt with every lost second.

"It was, um, an inspired recommendation. A lot of the skills are generalizable to leadership qualities like, uhhh, establishing trust, performing under pressure—"

"You know what, Liz, save it for when the clock's not ticking."

My inner scream pushes hard against my ribs. Too short, too long: my answers are never just right.

"Thanks, Craig. After a deep dive into our online reviews as well as our competitors', I propose disrupting"—I've bludgeoned the word "disrupt" into my presentation five times in five minutes—"the low season by capitalizing on underdeveloped opportunities. Specifically, launching guided hikes to attractions like Hell Hot Springs."

"There's no profit in guided hikes," Craig interjects.

"Oh. Uh . . . oh." I can't remember my next line. I've only practiced with people who gave me a "yes, and." One "ha, ha, no" from Craig was all it took to drop-kick my pitch down a bottomless crevasse. My precious three hundred seconds slip away, grain by grain.

"Actually." Jingjing from innovation leans forward. "I like it." This is the woman who ate charcoal ice cream on a first date. She called it a mistake, but they're engaged.

"I agree. Can you elaborate on the deliverables?" Bethany from accounting gives me a big wink, showing off the courage she got from surviving a UFO.

It takes a second for my brain to translate Bethany's corporate speak into "yes, and." Craig's not playing by improv rules, but Jingjing and Bethany are.

"Craig's correct—it would be revenue-neutral. But seventy-seven percent of online reviews mention guides. Negative reviews most often mention trips without enough experienced guides. Our guide turnover rate is twenty-five percent per year."

I click to a picture of Grey Tusk's newest neighborhood. "We're losing guides to year-round work like construction. We could disrupt the tour market *and* other companies by attracting their best guides while keeping our own. Earnings would go up, turnover would go down, and less experienced hikers could complete challenging routes with expert support. Tourists want to connect with the mountains. To love them without feeling excluded from places that seem like they're for insiders only. West by North wants a niche in a market crowded with big, established players like Keller. We can stand out by building a one-of-a-kind reputation."

Jingjing nods. "Highly original pitch, Liz."

"Agreed," Bethany chimes in. "I appreciate Liz's unique perspective on tourists seeking a sense of belonging."

They're doing that thing women invented to prevent men from taking credit for their work, where they say my name and reinforce my idea. Yes, and, corporate style.

Craig looks around, gauging the nods. "Interesting. Could work. What if we took it one step further and launched a luxury pickup service? Put guides together with dog teams and wagons. Rent satellite phones, so hikers could call us from anywhere. People could give their all to reaching the hot springs, and West by North will go to Hell to pick them up. With champagne and appetizers. Now, *that* would be disruptive. And much more profitable."

Everyone stares at Craig, then at me. The panelists are supposed to give feedback so we can refine our pitches before the final competition. Surely someone will point out Craig's proposed a logistical and legal nightmare. Encouraging hikers to get themselves into trouble so we can get them out of it—the search and rescue folks will have opinions about that.

The head of legal jots a note on an otherwise untouched yellow pad, catching my eyes like he's waiting for me to do what I do in meetings, which is shoot Craig down.

But I'm supposed to be positive and supportive. And this is the closest to a "yes, and" I've ever gotten from Craig. Is this why he nixes all my ideas—because I nix his first? Am I the sucker who does the dirty work of disagreeing, while everyone else keeps their hands clean?

"I'll definitely look into it. I'm excited to incorporate your feedback into my final pitch."

Craig smiles; I exult in the thrill of unlocking a secret level of his game. "If there are no further comments . . . ? Great pitch, Liz. Your eye for ideas is coming along well."

The head of legal escorts me out. "Nice job," he says, then mutters, "By the way, I recommend you drop the rescue bit. We could never get insured."

I whisper back, "Great point. I think that message should come from the legal department." He gives me a dirty look, but I'm done taking all the "no" around here.

Outside, McHuge waits in the large boardroom, his suit not doing much to make him look tamed. He must be my final opponent. Well, good for him. I'm so pumped, I doubt there's any competitor who could shake the certainty that I've locked down a spot in the top three.

"McHuge! I didn't know you were pitching today. Good luck, my dude."

His eyes fly from half-mast to wide open. "Liz?! What the—" He looks left at me, then swivels his head all the way to the right.

A tall form unfolds like a sleight-of-hand illusion from behind McHuge's broad shoulders. Slim suit, no tie, top button undone.

I know that body, its movements as familiar as my own. I know what comes next: he'll rebutton his jacket, straighten his collar, shoot his cuffs. If there's something he knows how to do, it's look perfect.

My eyes lock with Tobin's like I'm iron and he's a magnet. Our jaws drop in twin expressions of shock.

You.

Chapter Fourteen

Instead of dragging your partner(s) where you want them to go, invite them to go with you. Honesty and sincerity draw audiences to improv players, and they will draw your partner(s) to you, too.

—*The Second Chances Handbook*

Amber sighs as we pull up at the community center, way early for improv. "Are you sure you can't skip tonight?"

"I can't miss class now. There's only four weeks until the pitch competition."

The first time I read this afternoon's pitch competition email, all I could do was scan for my name. When I saw it, I punched my wrist rest, overflowing with so much emotion I had to run outside to scream, "ME!," like Elle Woods.

On the second read, overthinking mode kicked in. I knew I'd see Tobin and McHuge, and there they were, in the first slot. Next was David Headley. In the bottom position, me. Not alphabetical, not chronological—why were our names in this order?

I think this means I'm on the bubble. In the next few weeks, I have to pour it on even harder. And I have to do it without Tobin, because now he's the competition.

Amber heaves another long-suffering sisterly exhalation. "It's not too late to change your mind about improv. Or the work thing. You're pushing yourself too hard. Like, burnout hard. Not to mention you could save the family forty bucks for the babysitter."

Thirty is a cursed age. It feels like everyone younger than me has discovered the cure for cancer and everyone who's older can't resist bossing me around. Case in point: Amber invoking The Family when I'm in the passenger seat of my own car, because she's driving it to work while the minivan's in for repairs.

A wrenching twist of younger-sibling frustration wrings pure unfairness all over me. How *dare* I have a life beyond the duties she's scheduled me for? "Taking a cab to work would've cost you forty bucks, too. How about we call it even."

Whoa. Which inner character did *that* come from?

Amber's mouth puckers. "You could call it a favor, since you're living in my house. With your gross old cat."

She did *not* just insult Yeti. Granted, he smells like day-old soft food and bumps into a lot of walls, but he's a good cat. Anyone can see he and Eleanor are in love.

"Yes, and I'm splitting the bills *and* the school runs *and* the dog walks. And I've babysat Eleanor for free for three years. And actually, it's Mom and Dad's house."

I wait for Amber's comeback, but she only stares, mouth opening and closing. Conflict might not make good improv, but "yes, and" sure packs a punch during a fight.

Having never won an argument with her, I don't know what to do now. My first instinct is to back down. Edit myself for The Family. Forgiveness above all.

"I don't want to fight, Amber. I want you to support me, like I've

supported you since your divorce." How much more gently can I
hint that she can't treat me like a kid while asking me to contribute
like a grown-up?

"Those aren't the same thing. Besides, Eleanor doesn't need
some teenager. She needs someone who understands her."

Amber's eyebrows do a wiggling sort of lift. She does this when
there's some connection she wants me to make without being told.
She loved to play "if you don't know, I'm not going to tell you" when
we were kids, the stuff designed to drive a little sib to tears. I'm
ashamed to admit I didn't learn to stop playing until after my wedding.

"Amber, is there something you want to say?"

"It's really not my place. You need to figure this out on your
own."

There it is: the thin edge of the wedge she insists on driving
between us so we can never quite be close. Amber and I would've
been so much better off if our parents had let us find our own
relationship with each other. Them smashing us together drove
Amber wild when we were younger; now that we're grown, I'm getting a taste of her aggravation during our summer treks, stuck in
a tent a hundred kilometers from nowhere, every choice imposed
on her from what she ate to who shared her sleeping space (me).

I'm convinced she took up distance running as an excuse to
leave the family behind and make her own path for an hour a day.
She was born to run, with her willowy frame and effortless gait
that made her seem to float like dandelion fluff. I was the better
skier—lower center of gravity, with a natural talent at sensing the
fall line—but I always waited for her to catch up. Whenever she
ran, whether it was a backcountry trail or a move to a whole different country, she did it to put distance between us.

Maybe distance is what we need right now.

I grab my bag as I open the door. "Have a good shift. Plug the car in if you want to use the heater on the way home."

I want to catch McHuge alone, to make sure he's okay with me as a student now that we're both in the pitch competition. I'd prefer him to Naheed—god, this town is too small—but if he'd rather I transfer, I'll see what I can do.

And sooner or later, I'll have to deal with Tobin, too.

As if I summoned him with that thought, I'm confronted with Tobin's uncompromising profile the moment I turn into the shadowy cloakroom. He's sitting with McHuge at a table spread with papers and devices.

It's wrong to linger, but once I start eaveslooking I can't stop. The ordinary intimacy Tobin and I used to have was one of my favorite things about us. I loved watching him turn a page, as he does now, penciling a quick note. Sometimes I'd imagine us older, streaks of snow in his sunny hair, him a little sensitive about his reading glasses no matter how many times I told him he was a silver fox.

When was the last time we lounged on the couch, foot to foot, tossing a bag of chips back and forth as we read for pleasure? I'm shocked to realize it's been years. He was on a trip, or I was working, or our families needed us. Our life together broke under the flood of demands from everyone around us.

McHuge leans back, swiping a hand through the air like he's making love to a rainbow. Tobin picks up a spreadsheet—I can spot printed boxes through paper anywhere, anytime—and taps it with his pencil. McHuge, the ideas person; Tobin, the business-minded one. There was a time I imagined sitting where McHuge is now, and I can't say it's not painful to see someone else in that seat.

McHuge leans over and crosses out something Tobin's written. Quick as a hummingbird, Tobin goes for McHuge's strikeout with his eraser. He's outclassed, as practically all humans are against McHuge, but they're laughing and tussling like brothers, books hitting the linoleum left and right. Tobin leans down to pick one up, making as if to launch it at McHuge's head, when he spots me and freezes.

His unforced, unfiltered laughter cuts off like I'm a human *Pause* button. I feel the absence of its brightness all over my skin.

"Sorry. I just got here." When, oh when, will we cover how to lie in this class? "I'm super early. *So* early. I'll go hang in the lobby."

"No, I'll go." Tobin sweeps papers into his weather-beaten backpack, exchanging some last murmurs with McHuge, who tactfully wanders away.

On his way past me, Tobin stops. "I looked for you after the pre-pitch meeting."

"Sorry. I was working remotely until the shortlist went out." Translation: I hid in the dimmest corner of the phở place a block away, because I needed to eat noodles and think. If Tobin's name hadn't been on the list, that would have been the easiest thing. But it was.

"Why didn't you tell me you were doing the pitch competition?"

Oh, he is *not* blaming me for this mess. "Why didn't *you* tell *me*?"

His mouth goes tight. "I wish I'd known is all I'm saying. We could have figured something out."

"Yeah, well. What's done is done. Our deal is off, obviously."

"What?! No. The deal's still on."

"That's not realistic. This is a good/fast/cheap situation."

"A *what*?"

"Like when you're sourcing supplies for an expedition—you can't have all three of good, fast, and cheap. You competing, me competing, us doing improv together. Pick any two."

"We can have it all. There's room in this company for both of us, Liz."

Tobin would think that. "Look, we both know I'm no genius at public speaking and improv is my chance to get better. You're supposed to be my practice partner, but it's to your advantage if I don't make progress."

"Why would I want to win unfairly? Do you really think I'm such an asshole?" He crosses his arms, staring at me.

I drop my gaze.

Sigh. "You're not an asshole, Tobe. And maybe David will win, and we'll feel silly for making a fuss. But what if it's one of us? I see a lot of complicated feelings coming from that."

"But that doesn't mean the winner takes it all. If you or I drop out, and David wins, we get nothing. But if one of us wins, we can make things happen for whoever didn't. We can be a team even when we're competing against each other. This is how both of us get where we're going."

I hesitate, because his logic is impeccable and it would be juvenile to stamp my foot and tell him I don't want him to win for me. I want *me* to win for me, no matter what the math says.

"Lyle and I have worked hard on this. I'm excited, Diz. We can keep our pitches secret. Cones of silence. All we have to do is improv." His eyes plead with me. "We've come so far. We don't have to let this stop us."

I feel the badness of this idea like grit between my fingers as I rub them together. But when I'm next to him, all I feel is *want*. He's right; the scenarios have been good for us. Better than I could've imagined.

We have a real chance to fix our problems. I don't care that it's a small chance; after all, he's the master of saving all the tiny things.

Still. "There's no way someone doesn't get hurt, Tobe."

Whatever he sees on my face, it makes him smile. "I'll take that chance, if you will."

It aches, the careful way he reaches for me, his big, soft eyes tangling me up in blue silk. An arm sliding at my waist, another across my back. A slow lean in, a sigh when his forehead touches mine. It's a prayer, almost, the way we stand together, my hands light around his shoulders, his hands light on my heart.

Goddammit, Tobin. How does he always do this—set out a net, and coax me to swim right into it?

After not enough time, he steps away. "I'll see you tomorrow, for our scenario. I've got a surprise."

When I can't hear his footsteps anymore, I turn to find McHuge watching me. Surely Tobin told him what's going on in our marriage. But McHuge doesn't say anything except "We'll talk after. Help me set up?"

McHuge opens class with, "Welcome, kindred spirits! Reminder to all, three more classes between now and the showcase, the greatest night of your lives."

We giggle uncomfortably, none of us fooled by McHuge's hype.

We warm up with an old favorite: animals getting born. It's almost disappointing when no one watches me. By the end, we're raucous and full of ourselves.

"Freeze!" Béa roars as Sharon and I skip down the Yellow Brick Road. Sharon leaves the scene, and Béa and I link arms against a category-four hurricane. I'd like to get to know her better, but I hate feeling like I'm galloping up to someone shouting, "HEY, WOULD YOU LIKE TO BE MY FRIEND? . . . Oh. No, huh."

But I'm trying to be different, which means I need a weird question for her before she gets her coat on.

I'm gathering the courage to ask how many words there are

for rain boots in French when Sharon walks up, shouldering a designer bag that seems incongruous against her stretchy, low-key clothes. Although now that I look closer, I recognize the high-end tailoring I've seen in Marijke's handmade knitwear. Huh.

"We're going to the Kraken for beer, calamari, and baseless speculation about which celebrities would be *down*"—Sharon clears her throat meaningfully—"with which kinds of sexy times. You coming?"

I'm tired after three hours of emoting. I'd intended to go home after The Great Rainboot Translation.

But Sharon has a point. Sexy baseless speculation played an important part in Stellar and me becoming besties. Well, also we hooked up that one time, which broke down the shyness barriers. But I can rainboot Béa as easily in the bar as I can here.

"You in, McHuge?" Sharon asks.

"Not tonight. Work to do. Gotta conserve my life-force. Liz? A minute, before you go."

"I'll be there in five, Sharon," I say impulsively.

Once Sharon's gone, McHuge turns to me. "I have to say, my astrologer did not see this situation coming. I take it you came to class to build up your confidence for the pitch competition."

"I'm sorry, McHuge. I can try to transfer, if you'd rather."

He shakes his big ginger head. "You're welcome here, Liz. David's in this section anyway; if both of you left, we wouldn't have enough people. Besides, I learn stuff from my students all the time. You should be refusing to teach me, little bud."

"Ha. Good one. And thanks, McHuge. I . . . like your class. A lot more than I thought I would."

He rumbles appreciatively. "You did fantastic work today. One tip: let go. Let yourself *exist* in the scene, reacting to what's happening. Trust yourself; trust your co-players to take care of you. Let them know *you*."

I draw back. That feels like a lot. It's the opposite of why I got into this game, which was to learn to *not* be me.

McHuge pats my shoulder. "It's just a scene, Liz. It doesn't have to have such high stakes."

Doesn't it? "Yeah, sure. Thanks."

After the evening chill, the warmth of the bar hits like a wall, damp and filled with aromas both delicious and dirty. The improv group is crammed into a corner booth, caught up in a story Béa's telling.

"Up his shorts?!" Jason shouts.

"Well, not all the way up, but I knew something terrible was happening. Liz!"

Everyone cheers and raises their glasses. We're not yet friends, but it feels like we will be, and I'm so damn grateful for this moment.

I haven't gone out with friends since I left Tobin.

I miss him in a sudden rush. He brings out the best in everybody. Especially me. He'd take the wheel socially when I flamed out, so I could enjoy being in company without feeling I always had to sparkle. He's adorable the rare times he lets himself get a little tipsy—handsy as hell, bugging me to slow dance to the sappy songs he's bribed the DJ to play, framing my face with his hands as he comes in for smooches.

I sidle across the sticky maroon pleather next to Sharon instead of touching my lips where they're tingling from the memory of last weekend.

"So what happened?" Jason prompts Béa.

She shrugs her elegant shoulders. "Stéphane and the squirrel agreed: he didn't want her in his shorts; she didn't want that either. But for a second there, he had the biggest . . . I don't know the word in English." She drapes her jacket over her arm, making the fabric twitch like it's restraining an agonized boner, or a very confused squirrel. Our table erupts in scandalized screams of laughter. Sharon's almost crying in her calamari; Jason's Aperol spritz is now a spritz-take.

"Not too shabby, if you could mistake the squirrel for Stéphane's . . . something else," Sharon comments, when we're able to catch our breath. "You're not doing too badly either, Liz, judging by that guy you were talking to last time we were here. Who's he?"

"He's, uh." What level of detail is correct for new, delicate friendships? "That's my husband, Tobin."

Sharon gives me a keen look. Too late, I remember my overshare at karaoke. Time to change the subject.

"So, Béa. How are you liking Grey Tusk?"

"Oh, I love it! We're here for Stéphane's job—his company wants to get established on the West Coast, so he is posted here for six months. My job cannot move—I work at the Montréal Museum of Art—so we thought, why not get married while I'm on leave? And next time we have to choose between his job and mine, he'll step back."

Sharon nods. "I envy how your generation refuses to take shit for prioritizing work-life balance. Kareem and I struggled with that twenty years ago. Our parents taught us to value outward success. No problem, until we had our kid and realized we were going to end up divorced unless we struck a better balance between work and home. Not to say we totally de-prioritized work, but our careers had to take turns growing. Right, Liz?"

My smile feels more like a grimace. My marriage was all work, no life; perfectly fine until it wasn't. And we never confronted what his absence and my endless striving did to our relationship, or discussed making sacrifices so we could have a different kind of life.

"Some people my age are still committed to—" With supremely ironic timing, my work ringtone cuts through the conversation.

"That better be your hot-ass husband, Liz." Sharon takes a deep swig of her pint.

"Uh, nope. Guide team. Excuse me a second."

I hurry outside, to the relative quiet of the street. The satellite phone signal is patchy, but the important words get through: "Clients . . . forest stream . . . unpurified . . . six more days! . . . Fuck."

We're running a custom river trip right now, at the wrong time of year, for a VIP client who wanted to replicate the conditions on a popular Pacific Northwest survival show. Ultra-wealthy clients are the most dangerous kind; they've gotten used to money making their problems disappear. They forget beaver fever doesn't care about your bank account.

Fifteen minutes later, I've found a bush pilot who's flying in that general direction tomorrow. She'll make an extra supply drop: a gross of supersoft toilet paper, multipacks of underwear, plus an assortment of medications, salt tablets, and broth packets. My supplier promised to package and deliver everything to the Pendleton airfield by 6 A.M., latest. In the morning, I'll arrange a new extraction point at twice the price of the original, shredding our margin. Good thing I suggested padding the trip price.

And Craig says guided hikes aren't profitable. Ha.

Back at the table, Sharon grins. "Béa's coming on our golf date!"

"Jason called us 'predictably corporate,'" Béa chimes in.

"Make sure it's not your turn to cover the emergency phone that day, Liz."

"My turn . . . ?"

Sharon gets this *look*, sharp and blunt at once. "You aren't telling me you always cover?"

"I'm the entire ops department. It has to be me."

"No, it doesn't. Put together an after-hours manual with your ten most common emergencies and make a call rota. My god," she exclaims. "What if you're sick? What if you leave? Do they not have backups?"

"We've never needed a backup."

"Seriously?" Sharon doesn't look like she thinks this is an accomplishment. "Okay, well, trust me when I say you've got some room to set boundaries."

I shrug. It seems boastful to say I've always come through, and pathetic to admit I hoped going above and beyond would make people notice me.

Also, problem-solving is my favorite part. Patching together solutions reassures me of my deep connections with the industry, the area, and its people. I always wanted to feel embedded in West by North in the same way—like Tobin is with the guides—instead of being a barnacle clinging to the outside.

And my chance is finally coming. A week from today, I'll check off another one of Craig's boxes on the golf course with Sharon and Béa. In less than a month, I'll be competing for the promotion that puts me right where I want to be, in the center of my own tour.

And yet everything seems to spiral further out of control all the time.

Getting magic is so much harder than I imagined. It's not just about changing what I do, but how I do it, and why. The countdown clock to the pitch presentation keeps eating the time I need to try new things, fail at them, learn something, and try again. I have to get everything right, right now. No second chances.

And I don't know if I can achieve that anywhere in my hot mess of a life. Especially with Tobin and our unwise plan to be both allies and competitors.

Yet deep down I was hoping he'd want to keep going with the book, because *I* want to keep going. No matter whether someone gets hurt, no matter that there's a 95 percent chance the hurting person will be me—in my heart of hearts, I don't want to say no anymore.

What would it mean if I said yes to him and whatever he's got up his sleeve for our scenario tomorrow? Or said yes to myself?

I don't know.

But I have no choice except to show up and find out.

Chapter Fifteen

SCENARIO 4: HAPPY ENDINGS

Humans are wired for stories. We cling to familiar beginnings, middles, and ends. Partners in crisis often feel they've reached the unhappy conclusion of their story, and have trouble imagining an alternative ending.

What if you rewrote your story? What if this wasn't the end of your tale, but a place in the middle where the tide could turn?

Your assignment: pick a classic story with a tragic end, and improvise a retelling with a happily-ever-after. What new middle will lead to a happy ending?

Tip: you aren't your character, but you share the

same brain. If you get stuck, reveal a secret or try something unexpected. Remember, in improv, nothing is a mistake!

—*The Second Chances Handbook*

I give my black satin vest one final tug, then force my reluctant fingers to reach for the doorbell.

"Push it, you coward," I mutter. "What are you afraid of? It's just Tobin. Probably nude. Maybe wet. Fuck my life."

Picking the scenario is harder than I thought. There are plenty to choose from, but they all have names like "Forbidden Lovers" or "Close Quarters"—way too dangerous sounding, after what happened last time. I feel I should be forgiven for assuming a book with a chapter titled "Happy Endings" was a sex book, although I was relieved to discover this scenario is about stories.

When I told Tobin I wanted to rewrite *The Little Mermaid*—the bloodthirsty 1800s version, complete with knives and death—I imagined being safely in charge. No more driving scenarios where I need a lift. No more hikes where I catch him smiling all the way back to the parking lot.

Granted, Disney rewrote it first, but I've made some improvements on their version, too, in that I made Tobin be the mermaid. Who can't speak. Nothing's safer than that. Or so I thought.

I'm only now remembering how good he is at body language. He's a toucher, forever looking to make contact. Talented with the single eyebrow raise from across the room that promises he's planning to break the bedframe later.

Before I met Tobin, I was half convinced body language was fake, like people bending spoons with their minds. I often can't guess what people are thinking, beyond obvious smiling and frowning. And for all their supposed nonverbal communication skills, other people can't read me either. They bug me about my face, telling me I look sad when I feel calm, or scary when I'm bored. They can't tell when I'm joking.

But Tobin can read me, when he looks. And sometime in the past four weeks, he started looking again. And he started letting me see him, too.

Now, on this porch, is a bad time to be admitting my vulnerability. I try to swallow the heart that creeps into my mouth— probably to yell at my brain at close range.

Heart: *It cracks me right in half, how hard he's trying.*

Brain: *Go ahead and put your key in the door, if you want to crack in half. I bet he hasn't even noticed the sticky lock. If he has, he's waiting for you to oil it, because you're operations. Back of house.*

Heart: *Why are you* like *this?*

I'm terrified of what's on the other side of this door and what it will do to me. I wouldn't put it past Tobin to be reclining in a giant clamshell.

I swallow and recheck my costume: sturdy boots over dark leggings, loose white shirt under a black vest, all topped with a feathered hat. It's an outfit for a princess who walks the beaches alone, searching for someone she doesn't even know she's missing.

In the pocket of my vest, my phone buzzes.

> Knock and enter. Lock door behind you.

Argh. He knows I'm here. Knows I'm standing on the stoop, arguing with myself. And whatever he's set up in there requires a locked door.

Double argh.

The heir to the realm wouldn't hesitate. She'd go anywhere she wanted. She owns this place.

Knocking twice, I push the door open. Its squeak has disappeared. The dead bolt turns smoothly, too, sliding home with a firm *thunk* that feels . . . *lubricated.*

But I won't think about sex words, or well-oiled dead bolts sliding home. Or anything besides the scene. Our problems are by no means fixed, and sex isn't the way we'll make progress.

It's warm in here, with a tropical caress of coconut and saltwater in the air.

Already too hot, I unbutton my vest. "Tobin?"

There's an odd swishing sound from the direction of the living room, but no reply.

"Where are y—"

I forget what I was going to say at the extraordinary sight of my husband framed against the wide-open window, nude from the waist up. He perches high on the back of the couch, which he's swathed in gray blankets to resemble a giant rock.

His jaw-length hair ruffles in the breeze, glittery blue streaks matching the highlights he's added to his beard. His oiled chest gleams golden under a triangular dusting of light brown hair that leads straight down to his . . .

Tail.

He's wearing. A tail.

From the waist down—a generous description, because the tail hardly covers anything—Tobin's bedecked in the tightest, stretchiest, sparkliest tube of fabric possible, capped with a wide, ribbed tail fin. He flips it at me, sending me a saucy wink when my gaze bounces from his fin to his eyes, skidding over lines of scale-shaped glitter tattoos on the way up his arms.

"Ah," I choke.

He is . . . beautiful. Breathtaking, really, bending his raw sexuality into a bold new shape that is everything sexy and strong and pretty, everything powerful yet vulnerable, barely contained in a single package.

A flare of incandescent heat down low sends a warning shot of fire to my cheeks. "Jesus Christ. What have you . . . How did you even . . ."

He grins and flutters his outrageous fake eyelashes, accentuating the crystals that nestle along his eyelids. My mouth goes dry; my breath abandons me. He's some kind of fantasy come true, looking at me like he wants to eat me whole and hold me forever.

I've never wanted him this badly. Never. And judging from the way his sparkly scales bulge in the front, he's in the same boat. I watched a lot of bisexual pirate TikTok to get into character for this scene. Or I watched it because I like sexy birates. But *this*? I hope the birates are taking notes.

I trawl through my silent brain for remnants of the storyline, but they're all gone, sunk by a rogue wave.

I have to improvise.

"Ahoy there," I begin. Mistake. He's no sailor, unless the navy has changed a whole lot since I last checked.

Gritting my teeth, I try to reset. Normally another player would jump in to help, but Tobin can't say anything. I'm sucked down into a whirlpool of awkwardness.

Will I ever master joyful failing? Not today, clearly.

"Hello there, fair . . . person. What brings you to our shores?"

If he thinks I'm inept, he doesn't show it. He hoists himself up to the windowsill, scales rippling in time with the flex and release of his sparkly washboard abs, drawn over his real abs. The fabric of his tail tugs against the gray blanket, pulling the spangles down far enough that a new shadow emerges at the waistline, where the first few millimeters of dick print are now just plain dick.

Coconut and salt cascade off him in an undertow that promises to pull me far out to sea.

He grabs a fork he's stashed on the sill, running its tines through his sparkling waves of hair. I don't think he realized the extent that glitter gel would mess up this stunt. The fork stalls halfway through his hair, firmly trapped in his eighties wet look. He tugs at the handle, panicky eyes meeting mine.

Mr. Magic Man screwed it up. Interesting.

I blink as something occurs to me: he's got the power of surprise, and the sucker punch of his beauty. But I have words. I have the power of "yes, and"; the luxury of making mistakes and letting them go.

"Might I offer my aid?" My courage is bolstered by the way the words come out all smooth and shiny, with no stammering or hesitation. I saunter across the room, swinging my hips, my footfalls heavy and deliberate in the low-heeled boots. His nostrils flare as I approach, his tail fluttering apprehensively.

I'm myself, and I'm also the princess. And Tobin—this is a version of himself I haven't seen him play. He usually feeds the conversation, accommodating others before himself. He doesn't sit back and *take* like this. By the glitter in his eye I can tell it's as strange and exciting for him as it is for me.

I could help him get the fork out of his hair and we could call it a day.

Or I can lean all the way into this and see where it goes.

"You've come a long way, merman. Looking for someone?" I shuck my vest and kick off my boots. Barefoot, I scale the couch-rock, one slow step at a time. Seduction is a hell of a drug; no wonder people risk rejection to try to get a hit of it. I'm high on his flushed cheeks and wide eyes as he nods yes.

Framed in the windowsill, summer sun outlining his gold-and-glitter angles, he's half Norse god, half sea siren, all edible. And dammit, I'm hungry. I've been starving for years.

Something big swells inside me, smashing through every flimsy barrier I've put up against him.

I'm the princess of the realm. Lovesick subjects throw themselves at my feet on the daily. I'm the queen of scoundrels and no one man can hold my heart.

Although this one—I'd like to see him try.

I prop one knee against the rock as I take the fork, easing strands from the tangle. Goose bumps rise along his neck. I can almost taste that gleaming skin, feel the sharp buds of his nipples against my tongue. I force my breath out when I want to gather a lungful and hold it in, savoring the scent that rises from him, deep and secret as the ocean.

"This might take a while. Shall we pass the time with a story?"

He nods, mindful of the fork.

"Once upon a time, there was a sad princess. She tried so hard, yet she wasn't the princess people wanted. Year after year, she asked the king, 'Am I now fit to rule?' And the answer was always 'no.'"

I'm untangling slower than I need to. Stealth-tugging his hair, watching it mess up his breathing.

Lifting his hands from the rocks, the merman sketches a wide circle with his fingers, then mimes putting it on my head. A crown.

"Yes, I'm a princess, but not the one in the story." My nipples tug and tingle, so sensitized that the slightest brush of the shirt against my thin, lacy bra sets them aching. My skin is alive. I can have him right here on this beach. Or I can coax his legs out of that tail and bring him up to the castle.

"One day, she realized all her joy had died. Stricken with grief, she threw her crown in the sea. A beautiful merman emerged from the waves and handed it back to her. They fell in love. But he could no more live on land than she could live under the sea."

The last of the tangles dissolves. I set the fork aside.

"So she went on a quest to find the magic that would bring them together for good. Some say she's still searching. Some say she found it. Some say they've seen the lovers on the beach at dawn."

Our eyes meet. A bolt of energy shocks my heart to life, pain and pleasure mixed. He bites his lip, and somehow puts the better part of a decade into one small movement. Our history, our love, closeness and distance, triumphs and failures, everything.

Everything.

Of course I fall in love with him again. Of course I do.

Braced against the rock, I hover one finger over his belly. When he nods, I trail my shaking hand down ridge after ridge. He gasps, stomach muscles jumping in time.

One hand comes to my chest as he leans back a little. Then a little more.

Then way too far, way too fast, out of my reach in what feels like no time at all, arms grasping at nothing.

He goes down without a sound, scales sparkling, tail giving one last flip as he tumbles ass first out the window. In character, right to the end.

"Tobin!" I shriek, shoving my head and shoulders through the window. "Oh my god! Are you okay?"

Six feet below, he lies in the soft, raised earth of his herb garden, chest heaving.

"'S okay," he pants. "Wind . . . knocked out . . ."

"Don't move!" I race for the back door, shirt flapping like a sail. What if he's hurt? What if he landed on one of his cute copper garden markers (whose lethality I only now appreciate), and there's a spike labeled "cilantro" in his chest?

Out of my mind with fear, I wrench the door open with a bang. It ricochets closed as I leap over the railing and stumble to my knees beside his inert form.

"Oh, shit. Oh, Tobe. Lie still." I try to remember my most recent first aid training, which was meant for fingers that crossed paths with staplers, not vital organs turned into kebabs.

Sparkle-encrusted eyes wide, he follows the movement of my hands over the slick, square planes of his chest, his muscles jumping under the touch I try to make gentle, clinical.

His eyes flutter closed as I skim a hand underneath his head and torso, checking for bleeding. My face grows hotter the lower my fingers go, from nape to back to ass cheeks.

He makes a tight sound when I move to the other side.

I freeze. "Does it hurt?"

"No." A stripe of hectic pink paints his cheekbones.

My hands come up dry, if dirty.

He cracks one eyelid. "Can I get up now?"

Deflated, I sit on my heels, brushing my hands on my pants. I abruptly feel the ridiculousness of rummaging through a lumpy patch of dirt crusted with last year's leaves while barefoot and sporting an almost-new white shirt. "Why'd you lean back so far?"

"Just following the rules."

"The rules?"

"Your rules. No sex. Look away." Diving one hand beneath his costume, which blazes like a disco ball under the direct sun, he readjusts himself with a sigh. "Ah. Better. The third-leg look is damn uncomfortable anywhere beyond a semi."

I can't help sneaking a peek as he rolls to his feet. His third leg is going strong, by the looks of it.

And his tail is ripped from ass to ankle, showing a heart-stopping length of heavily muscled leg leading to a devastating curve of cheek.

A cheek that is completely exposed, because he's gone commando.

I slap a hand over my eyes. "We should go in. Get you washed off. Find you something . . . less comfortable." I wave in the general direction of his assets.

"That sucks," Tobin remarks, like he's pulled a thread instead of tearing open an interdimensional space portal. "I was hoping to get more wear out of this." One at a time, he slides his feet out of the fin, then swishes past me, footsteps reassuringly limp-free.

I follow him up the back stairs, eyes on the ground and only the ground.

"We can start over. Hang on while I . . ." The back doorknob rattles under his hand, at first softly, then much harder. "Um. Did you happen to leave the front door unlocked? By chance?"

I pull my hand away from where it's massaging my forehead. "You said lock it."

"I did. Thing is, we're locked out. Can you handle it if I boost you through the window?"

His mom has a key. We gave her a copy last December, when we visited my parents in Arizona. But to get it, somebody has to knock on her door in full costume. Or, in Tobin's case, what remains of half a costume.

It's nothing but bad luck that I'm the one with intact clothing. Still, it feels like another back-of-house chore that naturally falls to me.

"I'll go over to your mom's," I snap, stomping down the stairs. "Just . . . stand with your wardrobe malfunction against the house."

"You might not want to go, considering." He nods at my top.

A huge chunk of my shirt is gone. Right over my left boob. I follow Tobin's gaze to where the missing fabric dangles from the locked door.

I tug the ragged edges; they're nowhere close to meeting. My bra is the sexy kind that doesn't hide anything, and why did I choose that one again?

This feeling inside me isn't good. I like things to run smoothly. I don't like having to explain myself when screwups happen, so I don't let them happen.

And maybe that's part of why Tobin hasn't stepped up around here—because I don't step down. I haven't left any room for him, like he didn't leave room for me in the magic department. I remember pushing him out of the kitchen at our parties, saying, "This is my thing. You go do your thing." Our guests needed someone captivating, and if I couldn't be that, then I'd better take care of everything else.

But now that I'm gone, the door doesn't squeak and the lock doesn't stick and he single-handedly turned the living room into a fantasy suite.

We can solve this together. We *need* to solve this together. The scene, this disaster, our house, our marriage. All of it, together.

Climbing down from my high horse, I say, "How do we do the boost?"

The window didn't look this high from inside.

Tobin follows me to the lawn. "Well, we—"

"Tobin? *Liz?!*"

I swivel my head in slow-motion horror.

Marijke peers over the diagonal wooden latticework adorning the top of our good-neighbor fence. "I heard a strange sound."

"Mrs. Renner!" I croak. Tobin leaps to shield me with his body, his coconut-scented chest an inch from my face.

"What on earth are you wearing?" Marijke exclaims, inspecting his rip.

"Turn *around,*" I hiss, spinning him by his arms.

"And who made it? I hope you didn't let them charge you full price for last year's novelty knit. It's on sale at Fabric World," she says, raising a blond brow at the front view. "I can see why; it's none too durable. You should have asked my advice."

I dart in front of Tobin, my back to his mom, my cheek against his pectorals. "Good tip," I squeak, voice artificially chipper. "Mrs. Renner, do you have our spare key?"

Her snort is legendary. "Oh, you're embarrassed. North Americans are so prudish about sex."

"Mom. We really need our key." I've never heard Tobin use such a firm tone with her. Seeing him stand up for our marriage is extremely sexy, even if his seriousness is undermined by him hitching up his tail in the front, causing an unsubtle ripping sound from the back.

"I'm sure I have it somewhere." Marijke makes no move to leave.

"You know what? I remembered we have a spare key around the side." I telegraph Tobin a look that says "help."

For a second, he doesn't get it. We've leaned on each other lots of times to cover for our respective weaknesses. But we haven't tried to solve our real problems together, in strength.

Now, with our bodies and souls on display, we need each other. Neither of us can make it out alone.

A light comes into his dawn-sky eyes. It shines right into my chest, where something pale and undernourished turns toward his sun.

Taking my hand, he guides it behind him, closing my fingers over one edge of his tail. Ah, I get it. I grab for the other edge. We both twitch when I brush high across his bare leg on the way.

Gripping a handful of tail, I shuffle forward, pushing him backward. All my senses, already on high alert after the last ten minutes of misadventure, snap to attention.

I could bury my nose in his skin for a hundred years and still not get enough of his smell, like clean earth and tropical nights and some elemental note of Tobin. The flex of his thighs against mine, the shadowed ripple of muscle in his shoulders, the bass vibration of his chest as he bids goodbye to Marijke: all of it shakes a primal relic deep down inside me that awakens, stretches, and says one word.

More.

We hobble around the corner, welded into a single unit like we've invented a whole new three-legged race.

As soon as we're out of sight, Tobin sags back against the brick, pulling me with him. "Did my mom just invite us to order cosplay gear from her?" His mouth twitches.

I snicker, only a little manically. "I knew when she moved next door we were gonna be close, but not *that* close."

He waggles his eyebrows. "Your parents are only three doors down. Why stop at just one set of in-laws?"

"We should move to Linton. No, to Alaska. They can't spy on us from there."

He laughs openly. "Negative. They can drive to Alaska. We need something stronger between us, like an ocean. Hawaii!"

"Tobin!" I moan, seized with giggles. "Stop, I'm begging you. She'll hear us." I clamp my hand over his mouth.

And then I'm looking up at him, our faces too close, our gazes locking together so firmly I can almost hear a snap. Our hilarity dissolves and wafts away, leaving weightless, hovering anticipation. Every breath softens my belly against the pulse between his legs, brushes my nipples a fraction of an inch up his rib cage, then down. Fullness blossoms in my core, unfurling its petals one by one.

He blinks, eyelashes glittering, lowering his head until my fingers, still across his mouth, meet my own lips. Carefully, he draws my hand away, letting my thumb linger on his full lower lip, dragging it down with friction that flares into heat.

"What are we doing?" There's a thrum in his words, longing mixed with throttled power. I'm the one pinning him in place; I can step away anytime I want to.

But I'm staying.

His sigh whispers across my lips. "Diz. I don't want to . . . I won't break your rules. I'm gonna assume it's no—"

"Yes," I say, too breathy, too helpless and soft. "Just this once." We're not ready to be together again. Not all the way; not yet. But we can have this.

He closes his eyes, throat working. His lower lip trembles like a glass of water in *Jurassic Park*.

"You know what we need?" Tobin's voice is low, rough, a little scratchy. "A new back door."

Bending down, he grabs my thighs and hoists, settling my hips against the hard length of him. The bright burst of sensation goes straight to my head, weighing it down until it drops to his shoulder.

He strides briskly back into the yard and up the stairs. I can't help a moan of protest when he sets me down on the porch, taking away his miles of lovely skin and all the hard places I will die if I can't touch.

He shoots me a look so hot I want to tear off what remains of my shirt. "It's gonna be loud," he warns, setting his feet. One medium-strength impact of his shoulder against the door pops it open with hardly a splinter.

Through my fog of lust I think that, sometimes, closed doors can open again.

"That wasn't very loud." My voice crackles in my ears, jagged with lust.

He reaches back to tear off what's left of his tail, letting it fall where he stands.

"It will be."

Chapter Sixteen

When a player discovers what his co-performer wants, he
should give it to her!

—*Truth in Comedy*

We're a whole mess. Dirt rains from Tobin's back in damp clumps
as we kiss our way across the kitchen. Stray bits of rainbow glitter
waft from my clothes like pixie dust. We're all over each other,
hands and lips and incoherent sounds of relief, stopping every few
steps to take as much skin as we can get.

"Shower," I mumble, licking his neck.

"Shower," he agrees, squeezing my ass through my pants. I'm
getting off on the power of being clothed while he's not.

In the bathroom, he turns on the water, our old pipes *tha-
thunking* as they warm. We hit that moment of delay when frantic
hunger turns suddenly bashful, afraid to ask for what it wants.

The scene stalls, players fumbling for the next move.

He turns slowly, eyes on the fluffy bath mat. Oh my god, he's feeling *shy*. Easygoing Tobin, gregarious Tobin, the human version of social lubricant himself, doesn't know what to say.

Neither do I. But that's okay. We can make it up as we go along.

"Here," I tell him, capturing one big, rough hand and bringing it to the buttons on my shirt.

His touch is light, lighter, lightest, butterfly kisses at my collarbone. Desire is a galaxy of stars and fire inside me, burning for all time.

One button slides free, then the next. His hand whispers along the torn edge of my blouse.

I bought this shirt for an event I didn't want to go to. It looked right on the hanger, but on me it wouldn't sit straight. It was never good—only good enough. Now it's not even that. It can't ever go back to the way it used to be.

"Rip it," I order, my raw voice making us both shiver.

He winds a strip around each hand, laying his fists against my chest.

"One." He's looking right at me, and I at him.

"Two." We're about to tear more than this shirt, and we both know it.

"Three," we count together.

The rip sounds soft and dusty, like the shirt's hardly trying. It flies apart in his hands, the front tearing most of the way off the sleeves.

Ripping seemed hard but turned out to be nothing at all. The truth is so, so funny.

He's laughing, too, and we're kissing again, his mouth ravenous against my lips, my face, my ears. I haven't laughed during sex in a long time. I forgot how hot it is. The awkwardness of the rest of my clothes coming off has its own beauty, of limbs amusingly in the wrong places, of soft parts daring to show themselves.

He steps under the spray long enough to rinse off half a garden of dirt, then turns us in the narrow stall, backing me under the soft, soft water until my hair is streaming and I'm warm from the steam at my back and his body at my front and his hands everywhere, everywhere.

He ends a long, hot tangle of lips and tongues with a soft nip and a wicked smile. "Don't let me drown, Diz."

Before I can parse his meaning, he's on his knees. We never got around to removing the grab bars in the shower when we bought this house. Now, as Tobin hikes my thigh across his broad shoulder, I swipe unseeingly for a bar and wonder if Mrs. Elias installed these because she was eighty, or because she was a genius.

Oh, his mouth. "Slower," I tell him. I really want it faster, but what I want even more is to be in charge of the magic we're making. Although "magic" isn't the right word for this power between us, with his face between my legs and my sounds bouncing off the tile. Anyone could see how he enjoys doing this, but he can't possibly take as much pleasure in it as I do, so it's my spell and I'm going to speak it.

"S-slower," I gasp, and it works again. My body arches, and wrenches; I can't stop it and his eyes are fire, blue like the hottest kind of flame.

The next long, long, exquisitely leisurely move—I love him, I hate him—pulls me to the top and holds me there, suspended, until I tip into color and sound and light.

And Tobin.

Tobin with me, dragging brilliance from me one epoch at a time, a thousand years of pleasure with the slow violence of stars colliding.

"Okay," I whisper, when it's over.

I've forgotten there's such a thing as quick and that he can be that, too. He's on his feet with my legs around his waist and my back against the wall so fast. So fast.

But when he nudges me where I'm soft and he's hard, what he says is "Slow." The word sounds like it hurts him, but he says it and he does it and he never takes his eyes from mine. His neck is corded with the effort of holding back, but he doesn't let himself go even when I cling to him and shake all over again, lost.

The laugh bubbles up from some deep well that was dry, and now it's in flood. "Tobin," I hum, wrecked with the aftermath, my hands nudging grit from his back.

"What?" he asks, muscles motionless.

"Rip it."

"Rip it." He makes a sound, half laugh, half gasp. There's nothing he doesn't do gracefully, so it's a miracle of motion how he pins me and holds me and keeps us tight, tight together, his body wrapped around mine as much as mine is around his. When he cries out, my name is dark and rough in his mouth.

After a time, he lifts me down. We hold each other, new and weak like baby animals, water cascading from one body to the other, until the spray goes cold.

Waking up in our bed is an odd homecoming, everything the same yet different.

The sheets smell like wind and sunshine and the morning version of Tobin, a healthy, outdoorsy man with the sweetness of sleep still on him.

My absence left a bigger mark here than my presence did. Five weeks was enough to erase the layered notes of my peach deodorant (nonnegotiable; all the others smell like bug spray) and volumizing styling products (totally negotiable; I adore pretty packaging and improbable hair promises). My pillow was undented before Tobin wrapped me in a thick towel and led me, trembly kneed, to bed.

Early evening sun puts a soft touch on this still life: the afternoon-delight wreckage of the bed, the half-open door showing the empty side of the closet. The strangeness I felt last time I was in this bed is back, but this time the stranger isn't Tobin. It's me.

Tobin didn't feel it, judging by the way he passed out hard with my head on his chest. The laws of nature clearly state, "Thou shalt not remain awake while entangled after sex," so I didn't have time to ponder, either.

But now, waking up alone among the familiar/unfamiliar humps of bedding, feeling the smug soreness of some truly gymnastic sex nestling against the uncertainty of having broken my no-sex rule. . . .

Not sleeping with him was a good rule, actually. We were making real progress, and I might have unraveled it all by listening to my vagina instead of my brain. And I know I *said* it was just this once, but that's not the way Tobin's gears turn. Especially after everything that went on with his dad. He'd rob a bank before he'd have sex outside a serious relationship, much to the dismay of West by North's clients. When he and I got together, we slept in the same tent for weeks before he produced a strip of condoms, whispering my name like a question.

I just fell into bed with a man who considers sex more or less the equivalent of a blood oath. I didn't think I was the kind of person who slept with someone, knowing they were in "yes, and" love with me, and I was in "yes, but" love with them.

He wanted this. I wanted this. We're consenting adults. The part of my brain that's telling me I'm an asshole can yeet itself into the sun, thank you very much.

Downstairs, Tobin's moving around the kitchen the way he

does when he's trying to be quiet. A drawer opens and closes with meticulous slowness; a chopping board lands softly on the counter. The cooking music is just loud enough for me to catch snippets of Bruno Mars. He's making dinner for two; I'd bet my life on it.

It's almost like I still live here.

But I don't.

Discomfort launches me out of bed. You can't not rock out to "Uptown Funk"—another law of nature—so I boogie while rummaging for clean clothes. This evening's look will be me going commando under out-of-season workout gear, right on the heels of The Great Commando Merman Incident.

It's funny, but my laugh feels forced.

Olivia Rodrigo is how I figure it out. Tobin doesn't like sad or angry songs, blaming his mom's emo music binges whenever his parents split up.

But he doesn't skip "good 4 u," even though he always flinched at the way I sang it in the shower (not well, while also not knowing all the lyrics). And he doesn't skip JP Saxe and Julia Michaels's "If the World Was Ending," the world's certifiably saddest song.

It's a playlist of my favorite songs. I didn't know he had this. I didn't know he *knew* this.

He thinks we're back together and everything's okay. He's saying yes—to himself; to me. And I'm just starting to figure myself out—what I want, who I am on my own, who I want to be when I'm with others. I need us to figure out how to take care of ourselves first, so we understand how to take care of each other. It's like the closet: sometimes we stop seeing the spaces people fill, until we see the spaces their absence leaves empty. Seeing me gone forced Tobin to *see me,* and I'm not ready to be less visible.

I'm so afraid this was a mistake.

Deep breath. Steady. Get down there and be fair to him and yourself.

"Diz." Tobin meets me at the kitchen door with a kiss and a half hug, holding his wet hands away from my back. "Hope you're in the mood for barbecue."

He's taking care of me again.

"You don't have to cook." I make it as gentle as I can.

"I want to."

"Tobin . . ."

"Don't," he says softly, sliding away from me. "I know you're not staying."

"How?" His lack of surprise doesn't make things any better. I still feel like I let him down.

"I know you. You're worried about what this means. But it's only dinner."

My hands twitch at my sides. "How can I help?"

He gives me a look. "You can stop acting like I'm making you sign away your soul when all I'm doing is chopping vegetables. I know you can take care of yourself, Liz. I know you don't need me. But just because you won't crumble on your own doesn't mean it's not nice to be cared for."

Tobin should know. He was expected to look after himself and not crumble at a shockingly young age, when his mom was a single parent hustling to make ends meet and his dad was god knows where.

I suddenly see his million friendships in a new light: a lonely kid, looking for connection. If Marijke had moved to our street twenty years ago, I can picture eleven-year-old Tobin discovering my family's enforced togetherness, charming his way in, and blossoming in the same soil where Amber and I had failed to thrive.

"And caring isn't all I want. I want a role here. I don't like it when you shut me out of stuff like vet bills, as if Yeti's not my cat, too. I hate having to beg you to take what I'm offering. I want us to make it *good* for each other." The muscles in his bare forearms tense as he speaks.

All this time, I've been so angry about the ways he didn't know me, and ignored the ways he did. Glossed over the way I didn't know him as well as I thought, either.

The truth hurts sometimes, too.

But that wasn't the whole truth. "You're right. We need to be good to each other. And we need the hard stuff too, Tobe. We have to trust each other with our failures. Our secrets. We can't be intimate without them."

He looks at me, wary. "We agreed not to discuss our pitches."

"I didn't mean the pitches. I meant us. The scenarios are fine—"

"—oh, they're *way* better than fine—"

"—but I'm talking about us. Our lives. Our *real* lives, our real marriage. We've theoretically been learning how to communicate, but we haven't talked outside of the scenarios."

"We could talk anytime, Liz. If you still don't want to come home, we could go out." He rips into a head of lettuce.

"Like . . . out? On a date? A *date* date?"

"Yeah. *Date* date. We've got a month till rafting season starts. After that, we can keep doing the book, or not. Schedule sessions with a real counselor for the fall, if you like. Just let's . . . hang in. If we can."

He's working hard at this, voice not as even as he'd probably like it to be. For the guy who had "lost and found" stenciled on his tent, he seems pretty lost right now.

"Okay. I . . . Okay."

"Cards on the table, I don't regret anything we did today." His throat bobs. "If you'd rather go back to no sex, that's fine. You won't hear about it from me until I hear about it from you."

"I . . . I don't know if we'll do that again," I fumble. "Is that okay?" My vagina is calling me the worst names. The confidence in his smile—it slips along my skin, cool like a razor blade the moment before you know whether it's cut you.

"Whatever you need. We'll do it however you want."

It's not fair to let him think he's got me back. "We still have a long way to go, Tobe. The book, counseling, all of that. I'm trying to . . ." I grope for words. "I'm trying to change my life. Change *myself*. And I think it's working. But it feels like I shouldn't promise too much when the pitch competition's hanging over our heads. You know?"

He sighs. "I wish you could see yourself the way I see you. Nothing about you needs changing, as far as I'm concerned."

He gives me a look so hot, for a second I swear I smell smoke. But it's just the barbecue.

I can't let him hypnotize me with smolder, or I'll forget everything I'm trying to do, and spend all my days and nights in his bed.

"That's nice of you to say. But I need to do this for me."

"Okay. Then I'll go on a date with the new you. You pick the time and place."

"Okay," I whisper. I shouldn't legally be allowed to watch his bare forearms while I make decisions. "You could, um. Come to my improv showcase. It's the same night as the pitch competition, so maybe you'd rather not. But you could. If you wanted to."

He looks delighted by the prospect of watching me flail around onstage with several of the area's least professional comedians. "Yes! I didn't think I was getting an invite—I mean, I'd love to. Really. I would love to see that. I know it means a lot to you."

I nod, imagining an audience that's silent except for Tobin going wild. It's tense, so McHuge would call it funny.

"And," he says, going back to his tomato, "now that we're dating, I want you to meet my parents. So to speak."

This can only mean one thing. One terrible, horrible thing.

"Your dad's coming to town?"

He nods, eyes on the salad. He's playing it so light, maybe only I could see something moving underneath the surface.

"When?" I ask, not liking how ungenerous I sound.

"First week of June. Mom says he's got a special surprise." He's going to amputate a finger if he doesn't stop talking about his parents while operating a sharp object.

An emotional land mine of a reunion dinner. Right next door, where we can't get away from it. We'll have to pretend our marriage is fine. I give it a 50 percent chance of ending in flames. Like, actual fire. I want to do very few things less than I want to do this.

But I'm in, or I'm out. No half moves.

"All right. I'll come."

I know I've done the right thing when he sets down his knife and draws me back into his embrace. Breathing him in should be illegal. *He* should be illegal, with his warm chest and strong arms and sexy smell that is literally the smell of sex. I'm high in one second flat. I want to climb him. I want him to wear me underneath his clothes.

This is why I can't let my guard down around him.

"Thank you," he says into my hair. His clean breath tickles the sensitive spot behind my ear. My vagina asks to approach the bench. Denied.

"It'll be fine," he says, lifting me onto the counter to lean into the hug in a disappointingly nonsexual way.

"Yes. Totally fine," I agree. If the truth is funny, then that's the least funny thing I've said in a while.

Chapter Seventeen

Snappy banter is fun, but not necessary. The point of interacting is to discover the **relationships** between characters. In your scenarios, everything you say should serve the relationships you're creating.

—*The Second Chances Handbook*

Morning in the mountains is shadowy and cold. The sun's struggling over the ridge when Béa's car pulls up next to mine.

The sliver of sunlight makes the green-on-steroids of the fairways pop against the flat water of Emerald Lake. This morning, the lake looks more black than bejeweled, its surface slipcovered with reflections of the shaded evergreens on the opposite shore.

Nestled in a low channel between mountains, Grey Tusk naturally has a handful of lakes. Emerald is the biggest. It used to have a wetland at the east end; now it has a golf course.

Stellar wasn't quite right when she said I hated golf; what I hate is that there's a golf course *here*. In a town where space is so precious the community center has to split field time with the high school, this course sprawls over thirty acres. In a place famous for mountains, people spent millions bulldozing a place to play flat sports. Tourists travel hours or even days to reach our unique eco-system, just to play a game they could access anywhere.

Even when you're a world-class resort destination, there's no room to be different.

Béa rubs her hands together as we walk toward White Oaks. "It is the bum of dawn," she mutters, her French Canadian accent twanging. "Golf. Who enjoys playing at this hour?"

"It's 'ass crack of dawn.' And probably no one. It's like waxing—the opposite of fun, and you talk about it more than you actually do it. But you still sort of feel like you have to, uh, keep up."

"Ass crack. Thank you," Béa says.

Around the corner of the snooty clubhouse—a modern, airy echo of the Village's cedar beams and slate-gray roofs—Sharon's chatting with a white-haired foursome. She looks crisp in pristine white golf shoes, a tailored polo, and a single glove. Her visor—white with a clear green shade—is one I've never seen worn unironically.

I'm envious for a hot second. Like Tobin, Sharon is 100 percent okay with herself, so nobody blinks at her choice of headgear. What's it like, to jam whatever you want on your head and dare people to judge?

Spotting us, Sharon waves. "I know it's early, but there are fewer assholes on the course first thing in the morning. We'll get played through a few times. Don't let it bother you."

"Sure." I nod like I understood anything other than "assholes." My expeditions to the driving range didn't come with vocabulary lessons.

Béa practices her swing, following through with an easy grace that leaves me gaping.

"Nice form. Did you say you've played before?" Sharon hefts

a driver that's almost as big as my head. It's got its own name, inscribed in fancy golden lettering: "Heavy Betty."

"Varsity softball." Béa flashes a grin. "You swing one stick . . ."

"I haven't swung *any* sticks," I admit, as cheerfully as I can muster, which is not very. I didn't know if there would be bathrooms on the course, so I only drank half a cup of coffee and my brain is smarting.

"It's fine," Sharon says, waving my fears away. "Golf isn't about that."

"It isn't?"

"Nope," she says, waving us forward. "You have to hit the ball. Straight, if possible. But the most important thing in golf is—pay attention—*not caring.*"

"The men at the museum talk only about golf. I think they care too much." Béa does a fancy spinning trick with her club.

I try a twirl with mine, dropping it halfway through one tangled-up rotation. It hammers a divot into the perfect uniformity of the fairway.

I've been here five minutes, and already golf has made me its bitch.

The white-haired foursome glares as I attempt to reshape the lawn with my shoe. Their matching pink shirts look sweet, until you see the logo on the back that says "Senior Hitizens." There's a bloodthirsty drawing of a stick figure giving a golf club beatdown to another stick figure, whose legs bend in too many places.

"Have fun, if you can. But caring is a luxury you don't have, especially if you're bad." Sharon shakes Betty at me. Béa preens.

"Even if you're good," Sharon says, rounding on Béa. "You *will* have bad days out here. You don't get angry. You don't cry. You don't forget to network. Winning, on the golf course, has nothing to do with the game."

"Jesus, Sharon," I blurt, brushing soil off the handle of my stick. "What is this, *Fight Club*?"

Sharon considers. "Close enough. Let's go."

I am terrible at golf. No, horrible. I hit three shots to every two of Béa's and one of Sharon's.

Sharon is a fountain of tips: searching for your ball in the weeds takes time and pisses people off; grab a new ball (from a bucket of cheap scavenged ones) and take the penalty. Don't cheat, because some dick wad's counting your shots, waiting for his chance to put you down in front of the boss. Whatever score you get, you love that score. You're not embarrassed; you don't apologize. You're having *fun*.

I think golf is about failing joyfully. It seems implausible that the score doesn't matter, but then again, I also thought work was about work, when actually a lot of it is about who your friends are. In retrospect, I think Bethany and Jingjing got me into the pitch competition with their sneaky support. I make a mental note to ask them to critique my presentation before the big day.

By the fourth tee, I might be having fun. Béa's hit a rough patch, so I'm only the worst by a kilometer, instead of a mile. I step past the pro tee, past the respectable tee, all the way to the kiddie tee on the edge of a steep drop-off.

"Hey, Liz. What's wrong with your life that made you sign up for improv?" Béa says, just as I wind up.

"What?" I whirl around, legs twining together like rope.

"Watch your feet! Golf is about your feet!" Sharon shouts.

My calves untangle. For a moment, I think I'm safe, until my right foot meets air, air, more air.

I pitch off the side of the fourth tee in a cartoon cloud of flying limbs and gear.

When I come to a stop, two concerned faces are peering over the cliff.

"Are you all right?" Béa's gorgeous features pull down with chagrin.

"Good lesson, good lesson," Sharon lectures. "Don't talk when someone else is taking their shot. Any injuries, Liz?"

I brush off grass and dirt, flushing with remembrance. Everything I do reminds me of Tobin. Tobin dirty, Tobin naked, but also him being tender. Caring for me. Talking to me.

The last thing I need at golf is another distraction. Sharon could've told us this was an extreme sport, damn.

"Nothing hurt but my dignity," I mutter, picking my way up the slope.

"And your ass crack." Béa angles her chin at the gigantic stain on the seat of my pants.

"Wrong." Sharon's eyes narrow like a coach whose bone-headed rookie just made a move that'll play on every sportball lowlight reel for a week. "You're either hemorrhaging or you're feeling fantastic and ready for another fourteen holes. Do or do not."

Thanks to Stellar, I can identify a Yoda quote at a hundred yards. "There is no try. Got it. Do I count falling off the tee as a shot?"

"Never seen it before," Sharon says, which doesn't make me feel better. "Probably not. Hold up, Liz. They want to play through."

The Senior Hitizens march onto the fourth tee, murder in their eyes. Silence reigns as, one by one, they whack astounding shots from the pro tee, then leap in their cart and drive straight off the precipice like Vin Diesel. I don't bother checking whether they've crashed; an accident knows better than to happen to those four.

"So?" Béa prompts me. "You never told the class why you signed up for improv. But now we're golf buddies, so you have to tell."

"Network later! Tee off now," Sharon barks from the ridge,

where she's watching to make sure the Hitizens are out of striking range.

I regret giving this tee another shot at humiliating me, but here goes. I wiggle my ass and wind up. Eyes on the ball, elbows locked, fun fun fun.

The ball sails down the middle of the fairway in a beautiful arc. It's kind of cheating, because the tee is so high, but I'm not above feeling a thrill of undeserved victory.

"I did it! Did you see that?" I hop around, brandishing my stick. Béa jumps into my arms, squealing.

I stiffen in surprise before realizing I have to keep jumping or Béa's bouncy hug is going to dislocate my shoulder.

A sharp whistle from Coach Sharon stops us. "Break it up. Béa, you're up. And good shot, Liz. What? I'm not a monster," she adds defensively.

By the eighteenth hole, I have golf figured out. Not the sport; I'm still murdering the lawn with every swing. But the networking part is like a romance novel: you force people into close contact for a good amount of time and by the end, they love each other. I started with an honest answer to Béa's question about my messed-up life; we discovered we both read the same article on improv comedy for people with social anxiety; three hours later she's as invested in my pitch competition as I am. Sharon's offered to find us some decent secondhand clubs at White Oaks's annual gear swap, which I take to mean she would accept being seen with us on the course at some future time, and we've all texted our families to tell them we're going for lunch at the nineteenth hole.

I've just shanked another ball into the rough when Béa says, "I would love it if the two of you could come to my wedding."

"Really?" I say, delighted. "When?"

"Next weekend," she says, lining up her shot.

I bobble my stick. "Next *weekend*?"

"I know it's late, but seven guests backed out this week and Stéphane and I can't get a refund from the caterer, so . . . why not?"

"I'm in!" Sharon crows. "Do I get a plus-one? And where are you registered?"

"*Ben oui,* you get a plus-one! And the gift I want is for you to dance at the beginning of the night, when the party needs help getting started."

"I can dance. It's mom dancing, though. Not good." Sharon experimentally shakes her butt.

Béa's left eye twitches. "No, that's helpful. The worse you are, the more people will join. What about you, Liz?"

"Are you sure? What if you look back in ten years and there's this random Liz Lewis person in your pictures?"

"You won't be the most random thing at my wedding. It's very possible my aunt Jacqueline will kidnap the officiant so she can perform our ceremony herself. And she can't remember Stéphane's name for more than five minutes. Sylvain, Simon, Serge, everything but Stéphane. Nightmare." She grabs my hands. "Please come. Bring your husband with the cool name. I'll invite McHuge and Jason, too; it can be a reunion! We can bond, to get ready for the improv showcase."

A front-of-house person would say yes.

And for once, I *want* to do the thing I'm supposed to do. Suddenly, I'm someone who gets spur-of-the-moment invitations to my brand-new friends' weddings.

"I'd love to come."

"Ahhhh, this is making me so happy! And your husband?"

Sharon watches me, her eyes altogether too knowing. Now isn't the time to unload my marital troubles—not when Béa's inviting us to her wedding—but I bet Sharon could advise me whether to bring my almost-husband.

Pro: it's a date we could go on, before we walk into the mouth of the beast at his mom's house.

Con: it's a *wedding*. In our twenties, people didn't ask someone to be their wedding date unless they were serious or desperate. Everyone knew the dangers: huge hooking-up energy, the pressure to make a commitment.

Weddings were evenings where Tobin interrupted his fun to take me home early after I flamed out on unfamiliar faces, stilted conversation, and too many drinks drunk too fast so I'd have something to keep my hands busy.

This time, I promise myself, it *will* be different. Not like my birthday. I'm a front-of-house person now.

"I'll see if he's free."

Béa claps her hands. "It's beachy semiformal dress."

"Oh god. I don't know what that is."

"I can raid my daughter's closet if you're stuck," Sharon offers. "So. Many. Dresses."

"Perfect! Bring a layer in case you're feeling romantic and decide to enjoy the gardens." Béa winks.

There was a time when Tobin and I sneaked off to make out at weddings, before we were married. At a winter wedding a few months before ours, we held hands during the ceremony, squeezing each other's fingers with the unsullied confidence of people who have no idea what the hell they're getting into. *That'll be us soon,* I squeezed at him, when the couple cried at the sight of each other in their wedding clothes even though they'd lived together for half a decade. *I can't wait,* he telepathed back.

What made me tear up wasn't the couple, though. It was the tenderness of a community coming together, everybody in the room united in love and hope.

Some weddings aren't like that. Sometimes the groom's side

leaves him impossibly torn between chastising his unrepentant father, comforting his inconsolable mother, or paying attention to his new bride. Sometimes the bride's side overshadows her wedding with somebody else's divorce, and then makes a prediction for the marriage that might as well be a curse.

I want to feel hope at a wedding again. I want to run out of tissues and have Tobin pass me one of his. I want to embarrass myself on Béa's dance floor.

I want to dance with somebody who loves me.

"I can't wait," I say, realizing it's true.

Béa does that infectious Gen Z squeal with jazz hands, all three of us hopping with excitement. Well, not Sharon, but she goes so far as to give a little shimmy as we reach the green.

A familiar voice interrupts our fun. "Sharon. Hey, Sharon!"

Craig, Naheed, and David walk up, a teenaged copy of Craig trailing behind. There's no way they haven't seen the grass stain. I smooth my ponytail nervously, coming away with a dry leaf.

Come *on*.

Sharon's face morphs from a girls'-day-out expression to something I've never seen before. Business Sharon. Barracuda Sharon. She looks like she should be on a website or a brochure. I have that uncomfortable feeling south of my sternum, of realizing too late there's another memo I've missed.

"Craig." Sharon has a way with a clipped greeting that lays out precisely what she will tolerate from this interaction: twenty seconds of pleasantries, a few insincere smiles; now get out of my sight. She could improv a heck of a business character, although I suppose the point of improv is to take a break from being yourself.

"The course is good for mid-May. A little soft on . . . Liz?"

"Morning, Craig. Great day out there. Set a new personal best," I chirp. It's true, from a certain point of view.

Craig's smile grows fractionally tighter. "Keller wouldn't be poaching from West by North, Sharon? Because Liz is one of our most valued employees."

That's news to me, but I can't process it because I've just realized Sharon from improv is Sharon Keller-Yakub, vice president of Keller Outdoor Epiphanies.

It's not a total fail on my part—she's known for hating photo ops. At least Béa looks surprised, too. As does David.

"That's wonderful," Sharon agrees, smooth but deadly. "Keller has the same policy of rewarding talent and hard work. We know the best ones have choices."

Craig's eyes narrow. "Liz, I hope you can join the West by North foursome next Saturday afternoon. David can't make it."

David's jaw drops. He glares at the teenager, clearly outraged that the Craiglet made the first string when he didn't.

"Oh, thanks! But I have a function that day." I try not to smile too big.

For years, I've given Craig what he supposedly wanted: a well-run department, strong relationships with suppliers, contributions to the team. I didn't demand answers to questions like: If I'm good at my job, why hasn't he promoted me? And: If I'm not good enough to promote, why am I still the only member of ops?

But Sharon sussed out his motivation in sixty seconds. He wants someone he has to compete for. He wants to fend off a Keller takeover attempt for me, just like he's done for West by North. What I'm doing today means more to Craig than any real work he's ever seen me do.

Sometimes I don't understand people at all.

"Excuse us; we have a lunch reservation," Sharon says.

Craig's mouth pinches. "Nice to see you, Sharon. Liz." David's urgent whispers carry back to us as we head for the clubhouse.

Sharon laughs like a warrior wiping blood off her sword. "I

hope you don't mind. As your unofficial mentor, I think Craig could stand to feel a little less sure of you, my dear."

"A lot of men should be less sure of themselves," Béa adds. "Your boss seems like a real ass crack."

"Sometimes he really is." I kind of can't believe this is happening. I'm invited to my new friend's wedding. I'm asking my husband on a date. My mentor, Sharon Keller-Yakub, is making me look wildly promotable in front of my boss. For the first time, I feel like I don't have to worry about who I'm competing against. I can focus on my presentation and let go of the doubts about myself.

It feels almost too good to be true.

Chapter Eighteen

Improv and partnership demand the courage to share ideas **and** the flexibility to let them go. Don't ignore what **is** happening in favor of the idea you **wanted** to happen. Change your ideas to fit the scene that's happening now— not the other way around.

—*The Second Chances Handbook*

I blame Pinterest for the blasphemy that is beachy semiformal dress. This isn't September in SoCal, it's the May long weekend in the mountains, and I'm a mountain person whose wardrobe is 40 percent work-ready separates and 60 percent all-weather technical gear. I have nothing that says "Malibu," or even "Coachella."

Amber appears next to my parents' bedroom mirror. "Your husband's here. And you have a huge rip."

"Argh." A shoulder check reveals a torn seam in my only sundress, right over my ass. I'd call it epic, but I've seen Tobin's merman malfunction and my standards have been reset.

I dive back into the closet. There's no time to repair my dress; I spent too much of the afternoon pitching my proposal to Eleanor and her panel of Barbie judges (who asked penetrating questions about what snacks would be available on my tours), then burned forty minutes failing to achieve beachy waves in my stick-straight hair.

And I gave Amber ammunition to boss me when I should've been safely on the front porch, waiting for Tobin to roll up.

"You need to make up your mind about him."

I can't see Amber from inside the closet, but I *feel* her in the doorway, arms crossed, frowning.

"I'll think about it!" My newest sister tactic: not engaging. I don't have to choose between fighting or getting steamrolled. I can deflect her arrows, much like Wonder Woman. *Kapwinnnggggggg!*

Steeling myself, I reach for the dress Sharon dropped off this morning. She swore her daughter didn't want it back, but one look at the label told me this was not a piece of clothing I could wear anywhere near food or alcohol. Or my armpits.

Tiny embroidered bluebirds pretend they're dots on a deliciously fine lawn whose pale yellow shade somehow makes my hair look lit from within. The smooth cotton caresses my torso before widening into a skirt that swirls dreamily with the slightest movement. It's an outfit to slay a rom-com hero when he sees his love interest laugh from across the dance floor. Not an outfit for a scene where the main character argues with her overbearing sister-mom.

Amber's sigh means nonengagement didn't work. "I wasn't going to tell you, but Mom and Dad want to come home early from Arizona. I told them not yet, but you've been here six weeks, Liz. Eleanor needs to get back to her normal routine with her grandparents. And I could use the extra hands at home."

I burst out of the closet, furious. So much for not letting her push my buttons.

"I just talked to Mom yesterday. She didn't mention wanting to come home." She said they'd decided to hike the Grand Canyon, then she cut the conversation short to indulge Dad's obsession with the early-bird special at their regular restaurant.

"I asked her not to. I know you can only deal with a limited number of things at once. I was giving you a chance to figure it out without my help."

My temper notches higher. She thinks she's scored the winning point. She hid the truth from me, yet failing to guess is my fault.

"I can't believe you all are secretly discussing me like I'm a problem child. I'm *thirty,* Amber. If you wanted me to move out, you could—just spitballing here—tell me."

She's right, though. It doesn't matter if Mom and Dad said I could stay as long as I needed.

I have to get out of this house.

I slip into the dress. "How does two weeks' notice sound? You can cut me a check for the rest of the prepaid bills. I can put it toward first month's rent." Two weeks isn't enough for me and Tobin to finish the book, so I can't move back in yet. I'll need a short-term place if I don't want to break any more of my rules.

I emerge from floaty layers of fabric to find my sister's mouth slack with surprise. I'm not a fan of how spitefully good it feels to score points on her for a change. Would it be so hard for her to rally with me, for once?

I have to turn this scene and hope she'll give me a "yes, and."

"Zip me?" I look over my shoulder, lifting my hair off my neck.

"You *know* I meant you should move back in with Tobin. This kind of impulsive decision is why I didn't tell you. Don't get stuck in a crappy apartment with a dozen Australian lifties just to make a point."

"We're both living with our parents, Amber! How come you get to treat me like a child, when I'm moving out and you're not?" I grab a long cardigan, shove my feet into weathered, flaking gold sandals I hope no one will look at too closely, and run out of the house before she can say anything else.

Tobin's at the curb, leaning against his freshly washed truck.

"Sorry I'm late. Let's go." I throw the sweater over my exposed back.

"Do you want to—"

"Please, Tobin. Please, let's just go."

"Whoa," he says, scrambling to scoop my dress in behind me as I storm into the passenger side. Half a minute later, he has the truck rumbling down the street.

We don't talk until he pulls into the parking lot of Grey Tusk's Mountainside Conference Center. It's the old community hall with a fancy name slapped on so they could charge 50 percent more to host all the same banquets.

The blue-and-white building has the generic, vaguely refrigerated look of a hockey arena, with its low-pitched roof and corrugated metal accents. McHuge stands at the entrance, dressed in full kilt and sporran. He's playing the bagpipes, because of course he is. He's a one-man Scottish spirit squad.

"You want to tell me what happened?"

Tobin hands me a tissue, and I realize I'm crying. In front of him. And he's acknowledging it instead of running for the men's room.

"God. Sorry. We're so late; I'll tell you after." I check my face in the rearview mirror.

"It's not so bad."

He's right. I didn't have time to apply makeup, besides a little sparkly bronzer. There's not much to fix. I shoulder my door open, coming around to where Tobin's leaning against the tailgate.

"Ready?" He's wearing a loose Henley in a natural linen color, his blue pants rolled at the bottom. Golden light caresses the vee of skin at his neck. No shadow dares to touch him, except the one in his eyes.

"I, uh. Need a zip."

There's the barest flicker at the corner of his eye; then he follows me between two trucks, where no one can see my bra.

His slow hands ease up the tail of my cardigan, thumb nudging the base of my spine as he grabs the zipper. Maybe I shiver, or maybe he trembles, or both.

My sweater tumbles back down, sending a puff of air across my hot-and-cold skin. I can't erase the tingling from the little stroke he left as the zipper reached my nape.

When I turn, there's an angry flush across his cheekbones, clouds darkening in his gaze. "Let me guess. You fought with Amber. But you don't want to make a big deal of it, and you won't—" He presses his lips together, pushing an angry breath through his nose.

"Can we drop it, Tobe? Please. We can just be us, just for tonight. No family, no pitch contest." Neither of us can suppress a twitch at "pitch contest," like I could summon an evil ghost if I said it twice more.

"Okay. Just us. Just for tonight." He fits his hand to the small of my back, sending a ripple all the way up to my scalp. "Is that the bride?" He points at Béa with a flock of colorful bridesmaids. It looks like the ceremony's starting any second.

"Dammit. Run." I pick up my delicate skirts so I don't tear them with my un-delicate knees and revise my dry-cleaning estimate upward by a lot.

Béa turns as we skid across the parking lot, giving us the hand. Damn, we're too late. We'll have to sneak in once she's walked down the aisle.

"Liz!" Her deep brown eyes careen from me to the building. "You're from here. You know people. Do you know anyone who can officiate a wedding? In the next half hour? Our guy called.

His kid put a whole package of raisins in his other kid's nose and they're all in the emergency department."

"What about your aunt? Didn't you say she's an officiant?"

"Who cannot remember Stéphane's name!" Béa's eyes threaten to spill, and unlike me, she's got a couple hundred bucks of professional wedding-day makeup on the line.

"Okay. Don't panic."

"Please say you know someone."

"I don't. But Sharon's here."

Béa nods, hopefully, desperately.

Inside the hall, people rustle and murmur, checking watches and phones to confirm that, yes, the ceremony should've started by now.

"What's Sharon look like?" Tobin scans the crowd.

"About fifty. Blond. Curvy. Great tailoring."

"That description is not as helpful as it could be."

He's got a bee up his butt today. I google Sharon, then pass him my phone.

"Your friend Sharon is *Sharon Keller-Yakub*?"

"There she is." Her upswept hair and high-collared forest-green dress make me want to swear fealty to her as my queen. I scoot up the side aisle to where she sits next to a gorgeous brown-skinned man and a couple of empty chairs.

"Liz! I saved you a—"

"No time. Sharon, you remember Tobin. He can save our seats while I borrow you for one little second."

Sharon's eyes narrow. She could eat a stack of minor emergencies for breakfast, with a fruit plate on the side for proper nutrition. Between my logistical power and her actual power, we've got this covered. I fill her in, sotto voce, on our way to the bride.

"Wait, what? There's no such thing as an available officiant at the last minute on a long weekend. It has to be the aunt." Sharon pauses at the exit.

"But if she screws up Stéphane's name, Béa will cry."

Sharon does barracuda eyes at me. "I know I promised not to give you advice, Liz, but apparently I can't help myself. Don't focus on the problems you can't solve. Find the ones you can."

"What does that mean?"

"It means our problem isn't the officiant. We're here to help Béa embrace chaos on her wedding day. I'll do the talking. You back me up," she orders, leaving me scrambling to catch her long stride.

Sharon might be the most frighteningly versatile person I've ever met, pivoting seamlessly from telling me to straighten up and fly right to unleashing incredible mom energy on Béa. Hugs, reassurance, brushing imaginary fluff from Béa's simple, gorgeous satin gown. I should take notes.

When Sharon gets to the part about the forgetful aunt, though, Béa balks.

"*Non. Absolument non.* How can Stéphane feel welcome in my family after that?"

"It's funny in *Four Weddings and a Funeral,* though," I whisper to the nearest bridesmaid.

"I don't know that show," she whispers back. "Is it new?"

God, I'm old.

"It's the surprises that make weddings beautiful, honey." Sharon takes Béa by the shoulders. "At my Christian ceremony, the priest reeked of whisky and rambled about dragons for a full ten minutes. Then I made an accidental dick joke during my speech. People still tell me and Kareem what a great time they had."

"Dragons?" Béa asks, just as I say, "Dick joke?!"

"All true," Sharon says. "Back me up, Liz. What do people remember about your wedding?"

Oh no.

"Um . . . my wedding was not the kind with funny mistakes, ha ha," I say weakly.

Béa blanches.

"I said, back me *up,* Liz." Sharon gives me a look like she and her kind have dominated the oceans for fifty million years and I'm about to discover where I stand in the food chain.

"It was . . . wild," I hedge, thinking fast. *Breathe in. Breathe out. Improvise.* "Tobin's mom cried more than I've ever seen a human cry." True. Béa doesn't need to know the reason why.

"My sister and her husband got, uh, crazy on the dance floor in a way that no one wanted to see." I'm implying they were dancing rather than announcing their divorce, but who's counting.

"And Tobin's best man, Phil, got super messy"—when Tobin's father picked up Phil's girlfriend—"and we had to find someone else to give the groom's toast at the last minute."

"And everything turned out okay? You two are happily married? With happy families?"

My neck itches like wildfire. "Uhhh, family is complicated. You know?"

"*Tabarnak!*" Béa wails, mouth crumpling. "*My* family is complicated!"

Sharon sends a furious elbow to my ribs.

"Whoops. That's not what I meant!" I almost yell. "I meant to say no one can ruin your wedding if you don't let them." Amber's tearstained voice floats to the surface of my consciousness like rotten seaweed. *Don't look at me like your husband's better than mine. So what if family isn't Mark's top priority? At least he's not like Tobin, who can't pry himself away from his mother even on the day you become his wife. You think you've finally found someone you can follow around. But who's Tobin following?*

Her opinions on Tobin did an inexplicable one-eighty after she came back to Grey Tusk—or did they? She's never said she likes him or respects him. She only said I should stay with him. I don't know what's true anymore when it comes to her.

What I do know: Amber's lashing out changed the course of my marriage. She wasn't wrong about the unhealthy patterns Tobin and I were already tumbling into, but it was me who put my faith in the opinions of someone who clearly didn't wish me well. If I hadn't given her words such weight, or if I'd ever mustered the courage to demand an apology, things might have happened very differently.

"How do you know?" Béa whispers, looking faint. I maneuver myself into position to catch her if she goes down.

"Full disclosure?"

Sharon's waving her hands and mouthing *no no no no no,* but it's too late.

"My sister ruined my wedding. She was splitting up with her husband; he embarrassed her in front of everyone. She'd had a few too many, I think." I don't know that I've ever said that out loud: she was drunk, she was humiliated, she'd had such high hopes. "She said some pretty awful stuff. Like, my-marriage-was-doomed kind of stuff."

Silence. Terrible, terrible silence. Even Sharon's mouth is hanging open (only one set of teeth, I can't help noticing). The inescapable smell of truth hangs in the air, its acidity stinging my eyes. Improv gods, help me now.

"That, plus his family's shenanigans, wrecked my wedding. Pretty much forever. We don't even celebrate our anniversary. The thing is, though." There goes my voice, squeaky and tight. But I'm still bringing myself to the scene. Letting my fellow players see me. And I think it's helping.

"The thing is. *She* said horrible things, but *I* decided to make them the most important thing to happen that day."

And Tobin, too. We gave our families that power, and, no surprise, they used it.

"I could've let it roll off my back. Chalked it up to an unhappy person on their worst day and moved on. I didn't do that. But you could."

Béa takes a long, shaky breath. I belatedly notice her bridesmaids gathered around, drinking from the fountain of drama.

Now feels like a good time to sink into a crevasse.

"Your sister did that on your *wedding day*? Liz, I will murder a bitch." Béa's voice regains its power.

A shocked laugh pushes past my lips. "No murder while you're wearing white, okay?"

"Nothing that happens today will be as bad as *that*. I'm sorry, but that's the truth," Béa says, slashing the air with one manicured hand. The bridesmaids nod, adding words of agreement like "impossible" and "I would die." Sharon whips her phone from her bottomless purse, possibly to google emergency therapy services.

Wait. Sharon's purse. Her lettering.

"Sharon, do you have a pen in there? Like a waterproof marker, maybe?"

"I have an anti-forgery pen with non-dissolvable ink," she says, reaching for a pocket without looking.

"I knew you would. Béa, hold out your hand. What style of lettering do you like?"

Béa clenches her hand against her bodice. "What's this?"

"Insurance."

Chapter Nineteen

Improvisers should learn to be "obvious," because then
things will happen. . . . Being "obvious" means being your
own person, not somebody else's.

—*Impro for Storytellers*

This is the best wedding I've ever been to.

Pictures of Béa's hand with *Stéphane* inked down her palm and
onto her ring finger are already hitting social media, along with
stories of how her aunt nailed the groom's name (with the help
of Béa's cheat note), then flopped spectacularly with, "Brigitte . . .
Bernadette . . . Bijou . . . *Tabarnak!*"

The entire hall did a collective intake of breath, letting it out
on a peal of laughter from the glowing bride.

It's been a sweet blur of quite reasonable house white—though
I switched to club soda after two glasses; I won't be nervously
overdoing it tonight—emotional speeches, and most surprising of
all, great conversations. And not even with anyone I know. Béa's

busy with her guests; Sharon and McHuge are deep in conversation, passing McHuge's phone back and forth.

I haven't talked to Tobin since dinner, but I don't need to worry about him. We stuck together at parties because I needed him, not the other way around. He can have fun mingling for once; I can give him that gift.

Meanwhile, I'm working this wedding like a walking question machine, asking everybody every deep, intimate, strange thing that pops into my head.

I didn't realize how much energy I've been using for worry. Fretting about whether I talked too little, or too much. Overthinking what to say and when to say it, then realizing the moment to speak had passed me by.

But this wedding is like the best of improv. I'm in the moment, connected to other players, in a McHuge-like flow state. Maybe it was a matter of finding the people who'd give me a "yes, and," instead of finding a different person inside myself.

Béa's aunt Jacqueline, a sixty-ish white woman, tells me about the weirdest trip she ever took, which involved stealing the wrong goat and waiting out a thunderstorm in an abandoned barn with Béa's uncle (owner of said goat).

"Everyone thinks it's romantic," Jacqueline booms, the apples in her cheeks expanding with the warmth of the room and the wine. She has the most infectious laugh, which must come in handy after blaspheming in the middle of a wedding ceremony. I should get myself a laugh like that, all loose and inviting, to deploy when I make mistakes.

"Take it from me, getting naked in a hayloft was a terrible idea, all three times. But young love. You and your man would do the same." She nods at our table, where Tobin's chilling on his own.

Funny. That's not like him.

The tinkling of knives on glassware announces the bride's

speech. Béa's aunt winks, pops the last piece of someone else's torte in her mouth, and vanishes back to her seat before I can agree.

The bride stands. *"Ma famille. Mes amis."* The room hushes; Béa beams.

She continues in French, "Thank you for being here on this special day. Please excuse me for using notes. I guess forgetfulness runs in the family, *tabarnak.*" She grins at the ripple of laughter as she pulls index cards from a hidden pocket in her dress.

"All jokes aside. Stéphane and I have been together for six years. Not all in a row." She glances mischievously at her husband, who looks at her like she's the slice of raspberry torte he's been waiting for his whole life, the sweetness he can have and eat, too.

"But hard times leave unexpected gifts. They move us in directions we might not otherwise have had the courage to explore. That's why we took vows for all the times, good and bad. And I know everyone here will support our brand-new family."

Béa's so much younger than me—how can she be wiser, too? How did it take me all these years to grab hold of my own life? Why did I make myself into what I thought other people wanted, instead of what *I* wanted?

Turning thirty was an event I loaded with meaning, making up all kinds of dark deadlines that, once missed, were gone forever. But *being* thirty made me think about who I am, and who I want to be. I have my birthday to thank for everything good that's happened to me this year—Béa and Sharon and McHuge and improv and truth.

And myself.

And hopefully my marriage. We just have to get through one more hard thing. Less than two weeks, and the annual retreat will have come and gone. Tobin and I could be on our way to better times. I have to believe he's right, and we can have it all: a winner, a loser, and a marriage all at once.

"Tout le monde—on danse!" Béa tosses her notes in the air to the opening notes of Pharrell's "Happy."

"I promised I'd dance!" I shout over the music. Tobin takes my hands as we stand, spinning us so my face meets his back and my arms wrap around his waist. Entwined, we head to the dance floor, Tobin clearing the way with his big body.

Béa didn't need to worry; half the guests are crammed onto this square of hardwood. The tight crowd shoves us together until we give up trying to leave room for Jesus.

And then it's just us.

It's the first time since April that we've been together, on purpose, as ourselves. Every other time, we've been trying to do something or be something or create something.

Tonight, I have Tobin, his body moving with mine, the cologne he wears on fancy occasions sneaking memories into my heart with every breath: nights of loving him, wanting him, making promises to him that felt as unbreakably pure as a gold ring. Tonight I have his eyes, deepened to indigo by dim lighting and desire. His hands on my hips, thumbs curving into my waist.

A chill-wave version of "Harvest Moon" comes on, dreamy with a soft, fragmented beat. I haven't heard the words this way before—a beckoning, from one knowing lover to another.

Because I'm still in love with you.

Tobin's left hand slides down and back; his right rises to trace the delicate neckline of my dress. Easing the fabric away from my skin, letting it fall. Slipping down to the dip between my breasts, sliding up the other side.

Every muscle I supposedly control turns slack; every other fiber twists tight, belly pulling toward my spine. My hands twine around his neck; I let one thumbnail climb his nape, push through his hair until his eyes fall closed, his eyebrows a little lifted in that expression of pain and pleasure that means he wishes he didn't have to hold back. He's hot under my hands, as I must be under his, the dance floor creating a place perfectly private and shockingly public all at once.

He gathers me close on a long exhale and an arch of neck that travels down his spine in one long wave, opening his chest to mine so we can feel each other, body and soul. There should be better words for how I can't get close enough to him, for this desire that makes me want to press my heart to his forever.

We're nothing but two bodies and a pair of promises, and he's mine, he's mine.

The magic of the song dissolves into echoing beats, then into Earth, Wind & Fire. It's impossible to stay fused in the bumping crowd, but the promise lingers where our palms meet. *Water,* Tobin mouths. He walks backward off the floor, a wicked look in his eye saying he's thirsty for other things, too.

We're almost free when a hand snakes out to grab mine—Sharon, twirling me away from Tobin and into the bridesmaids' dance circle.

Everyone in the wedding party screams when they see me. It's so unexpected and amazing, I can't help but scream back.

It's wild that this is how magic works. I told half a dozen strangers one of the most painful stories of my life. I didn't solve Béa's officiant problem in the slightest. Everyone here has gotten a question from me that was straight out of left field. Yet somehow, I'm the life of this party.

And I can't pretend I don't love it.

I look back at Tobin, biting my lip. Something changes on his face, a pinch at the edge of his mouth so subtle I can talk myself into believing it's nothing.

If anyone would understand how special it is for me to be included this way, it's Tobin. We've had each other for years; it's okay if I take a few songs with my friends. He'll wait for me.

And besides, Tobin's at home anywhere, anytime, with anyone. He's landed in countries where he knew no one, had no money, and didn't speak the language, and come home a few weeks later with an allover tan and a brand-new appreciation for the importance of wearing shorts when surfing.

Soon, I mouth at him.

And we go our separate ways.

Long after I've forgotten I'm not supposed to work up a sweat in this dress, one of the bridesmaids leans over. "Your date. Hot," she yells.

Tobin stands in a circle of tall, older Black men—Béa's uncles, I think. He's smiling and nodding instead of talking and laughing. That's *really* not like him.

He needs to go home. I think he's needed to leave for a while, and I didn't notice. *Or,* my conscience pipes up, *you chose not to see.*

I hug everyone goodbye and make my way through the uncles to Tobin. "Are you done?"

His smile doesn't reach his eyes. "Stay as long as you want."

"No, let's go. Usually you love parties, so I thought . . ."

When it becomes clear neither of us is going to say more, I grab my purse and we sneak out. We've learned to do an Irish goodbye, or people will find any excuse to keep Tobin from leaving.

He waits until we're in the truck to speak. "I don't love parties, Liz."

I frown, scooping my dress into the passenger side. "Yes, you do."

Tobin's his most animated self at gatherings, working the biggest conversational circle, replenishing people's food and drinks whether he's hosting or not. He has to shake off flirts like a dog shakes off unruly puppies, even when I'm stapled to his side. All my sense memories of parties have a soundtrack of Tobin's open-throated laughter.

The truck rumbles to life. "They're a lot of work for me, if you haven't noticed."

"Oh. Because you have to babysit me. But you didn't have to do that tonight."

His sigh is long and sad, a wave retreating from a shadowed beach. "Standing beside you was what I *liked* about going out. The effort was for everyone else. People assume I'll get the party going. Sometimes the hosts expect me to perform, almost. It's like the price of admission for me."

His thumbs tap the steering wheel, restless. As the truck puts distance between us and the lights of Grey Tusk, the valley opens up, a rim of velvet-dark mountains cradled by the radiance of a clear mountain sky, stars so bright you can almost watch the world turning through the night.

"I thought we were going to this wedding together. Nobody knew me, so I could hang with just you. Talk. Hold hands. I guess I shouldn't have let you think leaving early was your idea all this time, because I promise you all I ever wanted was to take my wife home to bed."

His eyes glitter in the dark. "But you were off doing your own thing, with everyone but me. And I'm happy for you! You always wanted a million friends. And I'm not so oblivious that I can't see you're happy, too. Happier than I've ever seen you at a party where I had my arm around you."

I didn't think he knew that, about me wanting a ton of friends. It was less painful to pretend the only friends I needed were Stellar and Amber.

"I love being by your side, Tobin. But I felt like . . . sometimes you had to hold my head above water, socially. You couldn't even go to the bathroom, or I'd sink. And I want to be able to swim on my own. It doesn't mean I don't want to be with you. Please don't be jealous."

"It's not jealousy, Diz." He sounds tired. Discouraged. "I'll cheerfully share you with the world. I know you're making changes, and you love how different you feel. But the person you were tonight is the person you've always been, to me. You don't have to be popular at a party for me to know you're funny, and smart, and kind, and deserving and sexy and good. If you want this, then I want it for you. The question is, do you want it with *me*?"

"I do want it with you. Always with you, Tobe."

He swings the truck into our neighborhood, rolling down the quiet midnight streets lined with alpine evergreens.

"I don't want to be the asshole here, pushing you when you're not ready. But I have to know. Do you still want me? Are you, uh." He grips the wheel convulsively. "Are you ever coming home?"

Oh, god.

"I can't. Not yet. I'm sorry, Tobin." I've already hurt him, and myself, by sleeping with him and walking it back. I shouldn't break a rule like that again.

The sound he makes is no less animal for being barely audible.

"How did it get this bad? How is living with me worse than living with Amber? Sometimes I think it hurts me more than it hurts you, to see her push you around. It kills me that you'd rather stay with her than come home."

"It's not that I don't want to come home! I need to figure out who I am on my own, before I can be the partner you deserve. I've made so many mistakes. We both have.

"I can't do that anymore, Tobe," I whisper. "I need to clear out the space in my heart that I've given to people who want to throw their garbage into it. I want room to say *yes*, to you and to myself.

I want to celebrate our real anniversary, because that's the day I married you! If we're going to be together, Tobin, it has to be as the people we are now."

He pulls up in front of my parents' house, throwing the engine in park.

"Look, I shouldn't have said anything. I'm fine waiting for you to make the next move. Just . . . not too long, okay? It's the not knowing. You know."

"I know." He's done enough waiting for a lifetime—waiting for his dad to come home; waiting for Tor's grand promises to come true. And when the promises broke, doing it all again, and again.

I've asked a lot from him. The day might come when he can't hang on, and I'm not ready.

My brain would say Tobin and I still have real problems. This week, we attempted Scenario 5 (Crafternoon Delight—honestly, McHuge) in my parents' backyard. Like all our scenarios, it bombed, ending with a broken birdhouse kit, a near escape for Yeti, and a related meltdown for Eleanor. We're acting like our agreement to ignore the pitch competition is the same as making it not matter, when one or both of us will have a lot of rethinking to do when we lose.

But my heart says there's no competition here tonight. There's only him and me, and mistakes we've made, and mistakes we're going to make, and our will to get through it, together. If I've learned anything from our wedding, it's that we don't have to hand the microphone to our worst moments.

The truck smells like warm pine and clean skin and longing. Tobin looks young and end-of-the-night rumpled. We could be in a time warp, four or six or eight years ago, racing home from a wedding so we could tear off each other's fancy outfits before we got in the door.

"Can we go on a date on our anniversary?" I whisper.

His shoulders freeze, like he's afraid to turn. "Yes," he says. "Sure, let's do that."

I search through my hair, slipping out the special ornament I made for Béa's beach theme.

A tiny sand dollar, glued to a hairpin.

Tobin gave me this shell four years ago. We were camping on Vancouver Island in the shoulder season, at a beach that stretched forever at low tide. *How far out do you want to go?* he asked. *All the way,* I said. *The tide will come in fast on the flats,* he warned. I shrugged. *So we'll get wet.*

We took off our shoes and walked straight out to sea, clams squirting us as we passed. I'd never seen so many sand dollars, a confetti of fuzzy black living ones mixed with bleached white shells thrown across the rippling sea floor. Tobin stooped, fingers diving into a puddle. *Whatcha got,* I asked, and in answer, he took my hand and pressed a tiny, sandy disc into my palm. When he didn't let go, I glanced up, and there was this . . . look on his face. *This isn't a capital-Q Question,* his eyes said. *But it will be.*

A few weeks later, he proposed in an extravagant Grey Tusk restaurant, on bended knee, and it was beautiful. But I've always felt this sand dollar was my engagement ring. I wrapped it up and put it in a box, because I love it and it's fragile. Tonight, I wanted him to see me wearing it and know how long I've kept it safe.

Tonight, we can judge ourselves by our best moments. I can be the Liz who wanted to chase the tide all the way out, and he can be the Tobin who impulsively dropped a promise into my hand when we got there. We can be the people who cared more about the joy of adventure than we cared about getting our only clothes soaking wet.

Gently, trying not to pull or pinch, I slide my treasure into his hair. "Two weeks."

Understanding breaks across his face like stars coming out.

"It's going to be stupid busy with last-minute pitch stuff, but we'll do as many chapters of the book as we can before then. You pick the scenarios, I pick the roles."

"Two weeks," he repeats, voice crackling. "What if we don't finish?"

"Then we wrap up after I move back in." I'd be breaking the rule about not living together while we're doing the book. But moving back in doesn't mean we have to stop working on our relationship. We'll figure out what we need to do afterward.

After the competition changes everything.

He closes his eyes, hand over his mouth. "You don't have to, Diz. Not if you don't want to."

"I want to. It's all right."

I reach for his hair, tracing the outline of the sea creature that was. Touching Tobin the pirate, Tobin the prince, Tobin my merman, my husband, my love.

"I can't invite you to Amber's. But you could invite me to stay with you."

He knows what I'm asking. I'm not moving back in tonight. But I'm coming closer.

He makes a sound, a breath of disbelief and pleasure, like he's found something he'd given up looking for, and it was right there all the time.

He throws the truck into reverse and practically Tokyo drifts into our driveway, tires squealing through the quiet street.

"Tobin! You'll wake the neighbors!"

In answer, he jumps out, throws his door shut, and leaps across the hood of the truck like Luke Duke. He yanks open my door and hauls me into his arms, crushing my mouth against his, tasting of raspberries and coffee and himself.

My heart bursts into flame.

Almost before the front door closes, his fingers are at my back, searching for ways in.

"Careful, this dress isn't mine," I say, going for his pants.

"I know." He's breathing hard, and I don't think it's from running up the steps. "I'd recognize it. But can you please buy it off whoever owns it? You look so good I had to stay under the tablecloth or advertise the goods to the entire wedding. Ahh, watch it when you unzip my fly, I'm . . . thank you, you always were good at that."

He holds the dress while I step out.

And suddenly it's not four or six or eight years ago. It's now, and we know each other more deeply than we ever could have imagined as twenty-two-year-olds.

I don't want to hear the little voice that says knowing someone is not the same as knowing how to make a life with him.

I only want the voice that fills me with smug, hot certainty that he can't choose between fucking me up against the wall or doing it in bed so he can fall asleep inside me afterward.

That voice pushes me to take his hand and pull him to the stairs. I'm sure he's got his own voice that tells him I want it to last forever, and also that I'll change my mind about that sometime after the third orgasm, when I've had my fill of his hands, and his mouth, and his body.

And I know he'll always, always try to give me everything I want.

And he does.

Chapter Twenty

SCENARIO 6: FUN AND GAMES

Partnership is a continuous discovery of the familiar and unexpected. A successful relationship depends on partners finding common ground while enjoying the ways each is different.

Discovering your partner(s) anew means releasing your old ideas about love and remaking the rules of the relationship. It's harder than it sounds! Familiar environments and routines nudge you back to your old rules, which feel comforting even if they're unhealthy.

In Scenario 6, you'll help your characters overcome their outdated relationship habits. Create a scenario set somewhere the usual rules don't apply: on vacation.

> Where would your characters go to leave their comfort
> zone? What will they dare to do together? What rules
> would **you** break with your partner(s), if you could?
>
> Tip: for legal reasons we must advise you not to break
> any laws in effect in your territory.
>
> —*The Second Chances Handbook*

It's much nicer on the North Pacific than at the office. The sun's
not warm, but it's brilliant, with the novelty of wide-open sky in
every direction—although I do prefer the security of mountains
at my back.

The ferry rumbles serenely through the surf, rolling with
occasional rough patches of tide. Deep cobalt waves fizz with
whitecaps, the air fresh with salt spray and possibility. Under my
feet, iron decking hums along with the engine. Small islands slide
by, ochre-trunked arbutus trees twisting over rocky, log-strewn
coves. Offshore, the mermaid-hair blades of bull kelp stream in
the sharp tidal current.

Tobin suggested we drive the ninety minutes to the coast.
Maybe so we could get properly out of our environment and into
the romance of the open ocean (such as it is, on an island-hopper
ferry). Maybe so I couldn't make an unscheduled departure from
the ship this time. Fair, given what happened before.

But I'm optimistic that being trapped onboard for hours
means we'll finally finish a scenario.

I took the afternoon off work to avoid the weekend sightsee-
ing traffic on the famous Ocean-to-Peak highway, a spectacular
winding track carved into the coastal mountainside, with a flimsy-
looking guardrail separating the road from a hundred-meter dive
into the waves below.

I wasn't being productive at work anyway, just messing with my
presentation—adding a slide catering to Craig's useless feedback,

afraid he won't pick my pitch without it; deleting it again because it's ridiculous and I'll end up fielding silly questions.

Craig got wind of my last-minute personal time and dropped by my desk to ask where I was going. I could've corrected his impression that I had a job interview at Keller. Instead, I improvised a cagey conversation using my inner Sharon, who refused to answer questions Craig didn't ask. He loved it, getting so energized he almost ran back to his office afterward.

"Hey," I complain, as Tobin takes advantage of my distraction to shrug his hoodie over his bare chest. "I was drawing that."

From a respectful distance comes a chorus of groans. I kind of love his growing crowd of fans for not even trying to be discreet, but I'm also tempted to pretend I've spotted a pod of orcas off the bow, so everyone will rush to the front and leave this corner of the observation deck to us.

"This stateroom is breezy. And not very private," he adds over his shoulder. A fifty-something man blows Tobin a kiss, getting an outraged arm smack from his partner; a trio of teenagers dies of embarrassment as a parent hauls them away.

"I'm a serious artist." I lick my thumb to smudge the lines. I succeed in putting a big wet thumbprint right between his legs. It could be a fig leaf, if I squint.

"You must be finished by now." He peels himself off the life-jacket locker he's been using as a makeshift fainting couch and comes to peer over my shoulder. "I asked you to draw me like one of your Paris boys. I didn't mean draw me like the ones who only have one nipple."

I cradle my lumpy, crooked stick drawing to my chest. "It's *Impressionist*," I huff.

"I'll show you Impressionist." He leans down to kiss the sweet spot at the corner of my jaw, then laughs when I shiver. "See? Made an *impression*."

I wish we hadn't walked on the ferry just to save a few bucks. If we'd had his truck . . .

I press a soft, courtly kiss to the inside of his wrist. "Oh, we've been making a big impression all over this ship."

This is pure fact. You wouldn't think there's much novelty to be had on your hundredth ferry ride, but I underestimated how many rules I was following without even thinking about it.

We started our sail in the dining room, feeding each other everything that caught our eye—hot chocolate with whipped cream, fries, donuts, even the eerie fruit cup. Everyone stared—wistful, disapproving, horrified. All the staring subtypes.

"People's opinions of us are none of our business," Tobin announced, dipping the cherry from his fruit cup into the rapidly melting cream, then holding it to my lips.

"Nothing to see here," I agreed, dunking a donut, fastening it between my teeth, and leaning forward for him to take a bite.

After lunch, Tobin pulled a huge bag of change from his pocket, laughed when I was disappointed the lump in his pants was only money, and bought me all the overpriced vending machine treats I wasn't allowed to have as a kid.

It was when we ended up scampering all over the ship to escape one particularly judgmental passenger (who followed us around arms akimbo, demonstrating her distaste for our antics by continuing to watch them) that we realized we were more or less Jack and Rose in *Titanic*. Or, since I get to pick the roles now, Jackie and Ross.

We caused a serious traffic jam on the observation deck—half-naked Ross did, anyway. Ferry employees slow-walk past us, certain we're about to pull another senseless stunt.

They're not wrong.

For our last mission, Tobin and I join hands and sneak off to press against the curved section of railing at the bow.

"I want to show you something, Ross," I murmur, cuddling up

behind him to slide my arms under his, my wedding ring chiming against the metal railing. "Close your eyes."

"Do you know all the lines by heart, Jackie?" His voice has the indulgent curl of a lover who's only pretending to tease.

"Of course not. That movie is like seven hours long. Three and a half, if you fast-forward through the tragic parts." My comparatively short arms squish him against the railing. I can't see a thing with my face smushed between his shoulder blades, but I feel his silent laughter.

Warmth blooms down low. It is a true, true shame this ship has no privacy. Although I bet people have found a way. What do you call the seafaring version of the mile-high club? Whatever it is, Jackie's halfway to daring Ross to join it with her.

I slide my hands up his sides and over his shoulders, caressing down to his hands to lift them into a flying position. I'm rewarded with goose bumps that pop up on the slices of his wrists visible below his sleeves.

"Jackie." His voice is a wish and a warning, filled with the same ripples that cover his skin.

"Okay. Open your—"

Someone clears their throat right in my ear.

"Excuse me. Ma'am. Sir. Come with me, please."

The ferry employee is straight out of *The Simpsons*—complete with logoed polo shirt, shock of upstanding hair, and wavering voice.

Tobin and I spring apart guiltily. Or rather, I jump away and he stays plastered against the railing, for reasons I'm pretty sure aren't a sack of quarters.

"We weren't doing anything wrong." It's true; the only rules we're breaking are our own. I have no desire to do actual crimes and get banned from the ferry system.

He beckons me and Tobin with a friendly two-fingered motion

that is still quite angry when deployed correctly. "I'd appreciate a moment of your time," he says. He's very stern for someone who looks like the world's oldest awkward teen. His name tag says "Pauly." He is totally a Pauly, never a Paul.

I can't be confrontational with someone named Pauly, even if I'm right. I doubt he'd accept my explanation that we're in the middle of something important, and we've got to get it done this time.

Pauly ushers us down two flights of stairs and through a door marked "CREW ONLY." His radio crackles. "I'll be with you in a moment."

The door is not quite closed when Tobin remarks, "So this is third class." He looks around like we've arrived at the belowdecks shindig and he's a sheltered scion of the upper class.

"Stop it," I whisper, smacking his arm.

"If we get thrown off the ship—I mean *literally* thrown off, I'll share my flotsam with you."

I haven't seen him this happy in forever. He wraps his arms around me from behind, tucking his chin into my neck, the flutter of lashes behind my ear telling me he's closed his eyes to breathe me in.

"That was a very sad moment and you should not be laughing," I inform him.

"Agreed," Pauly says, coming back in.

The two of us shut our mouths and straighten up like school-children caught eating chalk.

Pauly heaves a beleaguered sigh. "Look. Sir. Ma'am. You've had your fun being the king of the world, and I'm sure you'll agree we've been very accommodating. But the ferry company has no desire to repeat the years 1997 through 2010. Misguided romance fans—"

"—*Titanic* is *not* a romance—"

"—singing Céline Dion all over the decks. One person climbs the railing; the next one jumps down to the foredeck. Before you know it, someone's got a broken leg from falling fifteen feet onto inch-thick steel, and I've got eight pounds of paperwork. I'm respectfully asking you to cut it out."

"Absolutely," I say, smashing my smile into a serious line. "We'll be on our way. I promise you won't hear from us again."

The second we're out the door, we burst into furious giggles.

"At least he didn't throw us off the ship. Literally," I snort.

"We better count the lifeboats. Just in case," Tobin wheezes.

He pulls me into an alcove off the stairwell and claims my mouth with his. It's a kiss and a laugh and a secret all at once, warm and sweet on its way down to my heart. It speaks a kind of light, easy promise I forgot we could give each other.

We used to be good at that. On the last two-week rafting trip of that first summer, I heard Tobin's familiar post-campfire scratch at my tent flap. Instead of coming in, he crooked a finger: *Follow me.*

"We're not supposed to leave camp," I whispered, pulling on an extra sweater. "What if someone comes looking for you?" Two trips ago, company brass had lectured us about "discretion." Our relationship wasn't against the rules, but clients liked it better when Tobin appeared available, like a K-pop star performing singlehood. And ever since I'd become camp chief, I'd fearfully followed every possible regulation, hoping that would undo my demotion.

"Five minutes," he whispered back. "I'll take the heat if we get caught." We tiptoed down to the round rocks of the beach and stashed our clothes behind a boulder.

"Ahhhhh, it's freezing!"

"Five minutes." He waded to a shallow eddy, then stretched out on his back, beckoning me to float beside him. "Look up."

We bobbed together, watching the August meteor shower decorate the sky, my skin zinging with the beauty, and the cold, and the thrill of disobedience. We didn't last long, but the memory of that stolen moment is so bright.

I wish I hadn't cared so much about doing what I was told. I was careful and rule-bound, yet I lost my raft, and a boisterous but reckless guide kept his—what was left of it, after his countless expensive whoopsie-daisies that put entire expeditions at risk.

Sometimes it seems like the people at the top of West by North's strange social hierarchy are the players who figured out which rules to break. Like today—I'm flouting the rules that say I'm supposed to be a hard worker and a loyal employee, and Craig likes me better.

McHuge is on to something with this scenario. Love is about making your own rules, and so is life.

I gasp, my mouth popping off Tobin's.

"You okay?" He's looking at me with equal parts concern and *we'll finish this later, at home* in his eyes.

"Yeah, sorry. I, uh, realized something surprising."

"Really. I was kissing you, and you had bandwidth left over. Guess I'll have to do better."

Wow. Tobin's "better" is . . . it's . . . ah. I can't brain with his tongue doing that thing, and with the hands, beard soft, *unf.* Am dizzy; can't feel the ground; need more.

I'm so kiss-drunk when he sets me back on my feet, I have to take a fistful of his hoodie to stay upright. I swear he sparkles, or maybe I'm not used to having all these stars in my eyes.

"I have a huge favor to ask."

"Uh-huh." I'm ready to say yes to anything he wants. He doesn't have to act so twitchy, like he has to sell me something.

"Can we push our anniversary date back a couple of hours? Do a midnight movie instead of an early show?"

"Why?" I scan his unstable smile, apprehensive all of a sudden.

"Dad's coming to town early, so Mom rescheduled our get-together for Tuesday. She's baking up a storm. All your favorite pressed cookies."

Above us, someone opens the door to the windblown observation deck, sending a blast of cold air between our bodies. This time, the goose bumps aren't from passion.

So many times, I've tried to talk to him about his parents. I can understand him defending Marijke. For all her flaws, she loves her son and had to make compromises to provide for him. I can't begin to comprehend when it's Tor, his father in name only.

But we're supposed to communicate when it's easy *and* when it's hard. And today, we're practicing letting go of the old rules, and making new ones. Ones about us, and our love.

I wrap both hands in his faded, fraying, beloved sweatshirt. "Oh, Tobe. I was hoping we'd spend our anniversary together, alone. Can we tell them we're busy that night? See your dad Wednesday, maybe?"

His expression is heartbreakingly certain. "You know Dad—his social calendar's always full. We'll still have time for the movie. Mom's so excited. Dad says he's got a surprise that will bring us together."

Tobin's dad loves having secrets bubbling on the back burner—one to give him an excuse to come home, and another to "force" him to leave. Tor is clever, never triggering a full-fledged fight, never hanging around long enough for Marijke and Tobin to figure him out.

"Okay, but this is *your dad*. You know, Tor Renner, whose all-time parenting high score was three continuous months with you and your mom before taking off again? Who's stopped mentioning the eight grand he owes us? It wouldn't be bad to shake up that relationship a little." *Break the rules with me,* I silently beg. *Break the rules for* me. *For us.*

"Come on, Diz. We all need second chances. I'll turn it down if you say no, but . . . I want to go."

Curse those big blue puppy-dog eyes that grab my heart and pull.

This is exactly what Tobin and I don't need. Tor will execute his familiar routine: parachute in, hug and kiss for a day or six, flit away with everything his light fingers can lift. Marijke's high hopes will tumble and smash. Caught in the middle, Tobin will make promises to keep the peace, and I'll get roped into fulfilling them.

But I can either break the rules or say yes to Tobin. And I've made such a big goddamn deal about saying yes. I have to give him this, even though I can't count how many second chances his dad has doused in gasoline and lit on fire.

"Okay. We'll go. I'll eat cookies and play nice. But you have to promise not to give your dad money for whatever pyramid scheme 'surprise' he springs on you."

"I promise. And it'll be a good surprise."

I'm imagining a lot of things Tor Renner would call a "good surprise," and they're less "I bought you a puppy!" and more "I forged your signature on my mortgage!" Whatever Tor's brewing up in his good old Cauldron of Disappointment, money will only be the first way we'll end up paying.

"Hey." Tobin lifts my chin with one rough, strong finger. "It'll be fine. And guess what, we finished a scenario! Just in time, too," he says, as the prerecorded docking announcement instructs people to return to their vehicles.

"Yay, us. We did it," I say, because I've said all the words I can about our anniversary, and his dad, and the patterns we can't seem to break. Saying them again won't make him hear me.

This stairwell feels like the bottom of a crevasse all of a sudden.

"Come on." Tobin grabs my hand. "We'll have the deck to ourselves. You can ask permission to kiss me."

"What if I don't?"

"You will," he says.

And he's right. When I remember this afternoon, I want memories of how we triumphed over the damn scenarios. I want golden images of us entwined in each other, not this donut-shaped sense of dread in my stomach.

So I ask him to kiss me. And then I pretend everything's all better.

Chapter Twenty-One

The more of yourself you put into improv, the more you get out of it. Commit to the scenario. Nothing destroys unity faster than one person deliberately holding back.

—*The Second Chances Handbook*

"You didn't have to wear a tie." I fiddle with Tobin's double Windsor knot as we hover on his mom's walkway. "Seems like overkill for the backyard."

"Mom wants it to be perfect." He grimaces, visibly trying to control his fidgeting.

Tobin will wear a stifling lifejacket for hours. He refuses to complain when a client's overstuffed backpack blisters the tender skin of his shoulders. But ties are where he draws the line for everybody but his mom. Under my fingers, his muscles tense with the confinement of silk around his collar.

Silk, at an afternoon cookout. I mean, it's not a *good* sign about his level of investment.

I ease the knot looser, wanting to spare him; his impatient hands come up and tighten it again.

I hate this for him. Hate this for us. I want to leave right this second and skip the way tonight is going to end in tears.

But I promised. *Yes, and.*

Stellar signed off our text conversation an hour ago with the perfect sentiment.

> Good luck. Die well.

"About that. I'm worried we're getting into a prom night situation, what with the intense buildup and the repeated use of the word 'perfect.' And the tie. How 'bout we lower our expectations ten points on a scale of ten."

He passes a hand across his eyes. How he's able to convince himself this is excitement, instead of terror, is beyond me.

"Warm-up time. Practice something to tell your dad. Get the nerves out."

A muscle in his jaw twitches, a wild look in his eye. "I'm developing a business plan with my friend Lyle. It was shortlisted for the company's annual pitch competition. We're going to—" He breaks off, eyes on mine.

I blink. "Are you . . . telling your parents about your pitch?" I venture oh so carefully.

He runs a finger across his collar. He looks the way I feel when I'm checking for stress hives, hope and misery leaking from his very pores. "I know we said we wouldn't. But tonight's my chance to impress Dad."

That news goes down like an unchewed baseball: hard. Painful. Tobin's planning to break our agreement, and he didn't tell me, and he's doing it all for the person who hurts him, instead of the one who loves him. The presentation isn't for another three days and already it's toying with us, threatening to knock us down like so many Lego figurines.

"I wish we'd discussed this first, Tobe. I can skip tonight, if you want? Or maybe leave early when you start talking about it?"

"No, stay. Please," he blurts. "You don't have to tell me yours. I know you wouldn't sandbag my pitch, and this close to the competition it doesn't matter anyway. But Dad won't understand why I can't explain."

True. Tor absolutely would not understand anything that wasn't about himself.

I clasp Tobin's sweaty palms in mine.

"So let him misunderstand. Or we can bail! You could say we're coming down with something."

"Please, Diz. I gotta tell him. That stuff is what he cares about. What makes him happy."

He doesn't want to hear that Tor won't care. He just needs me to say yes, the way he'd say yes to me if I asked him to come to dinner with Amber.

I wrap my arms around him. His heart kicks hard, right through his suit. "Okay. I'll try to go to the bathroom at strategic times, or something. But tell your dad because it makes *you* happy, Tobe. Okay?"

He nods into my hair. "Right. You're right."

Tobin's mom bursts out the front door, dressed to the nines in a slinky hot pink wrap number. Even her apron is sexy—a fitted, frilly thing in coordinating shades of peach and petal.

I picture Marijke at her professional-grade sewing machine late last night, sweating over layers of ruffles while dreaming of the perfect outfit for the perfect dinner that leads to the perfect reunion with her perfectly rotten husband.

Nausea swirls, green and black, deep in my soul.

"Tobin! Liz!" Marijke calls, waving from the porch. "Come and help set up!" Her accent gets stronger when she's stressed out. The tighter she winds herself, the more Tobin will knock himself out trying to make everything okay, and the harder they'll both fall when Tor predictably bounces.

Tabarnak.

I want to lock them both in therapy jail. They can apply for parole when they've completed their Narcissists 101 course.

Marijke dispatches Tobin to wipe down the patio furniture and sweep the deck. I pull kitchen duty, loading trays while she arranges bursting plates of smoked salmon and crudités.

Asking her a weird question will make me feel less sick with dread. It might even put a crack in this in-law ice big enough not to freeze over by the next time I see her.

"Can I ask you something?"

"Sure," she says, trying a radish rosette this way and that, balancing it in a shape that might catch a straying husband's heart.

"What's your secret for a long marriage?" Of the many, many weird questions I've asked, this is the riskiest. I banned myself from asking Marijke anything about Tor, ever, after that first awful time. Trying my hardest to erase that mistake hasn't improved our relationship, though. I've been afraid to enter the no-fly zone I've created around Tor, but maybe that empty, poisoned space is what's standing between me and Marijke.

"Still thinking of leaving my son, then?" The look she gives me slices and dices my hopes for conversation. It's freaky seeing Tobin's eyes looking out of Marijke's face, her expression light-years from her son's soft love.

When I thought about my marriage ending, I didn't picture how Tobin's eyes would look if he stopped loving me, like the stars had gone out. Like this.

"We're working things out." Given that Marijke's forgiven Tor's walkouts eleventy-five times, I guess irony isn't a country she visits very often.

"I see." She shoves the rosette into place with a movement as clipped as her words. Glossy grape tomatoes and spotless mushrooms go flying; the radish bounces to the floor and rolls cheerfully under the fridge.

Marijke slams her hands against the counter, fatally traumatizing a stray tomato. Its innards spray the front of my jade-green top, chunky and red like a Christmas murder scene.

"I will not accept criticism from someone whose own marriage has lasted less than a tenth as long as mine," she growls, head down, back hunched.

I seriously think she wants to fight me. I'm younger, and I likely outweigh her, so I've got a chance if I can pin her early. But she's taller and faster and I hurt her only child, so I don't want to be unrealistic about my chances of winning.

"Marij—uh, Mrs. Renner, I honestly wasn't criticizing—"

"I am quite aware of how my relationship with Tor appears. From the *outside*. I have no illusions about what certain people say behind my back. But my marriage is no one's business but my own," she says, straightening up to look down at me from ten thousand feet. "It's not so easy to set aside thirty years, no matter what has happened. All the love and memories will leave you if you don't care for them, and then what's left?"

She sweeps out of the kitchen, leaving it dimmer and shabbier, like my conscience.

I think of Stellar, how we've had each other to take the memories down from their shelves, cherish them, and keep them shining. And Amber, our worst moments winking blackly at me from my Wall of Shame.

Tobin and I have been together almost a third of our lives. What would I forget, if he and I split?

Bad things, yes.

Good things, also yes.

But I don't have to think about what the last eight years of my life would mean if Tobin and I decided not to love each other anymore. We're going to be okay. Him breaking our rules doesn't have to be an international emergency, even if a little alarm bell has been going off inside me for the last half hour.

I'll get through this dinner, like I promised. I'll laugh off Tor's infuriating comments, right along with his hints that he needs to borrow a few bucks. If that bastard goes after his son, I'll tell him I have cramps and heavy flow right to his sexist face, and take my husband home for our anniversary.

I slink outside with the biggest tray, Marijke on my heels with a double handful of cut-crystal champagne flutes.

The backyard is full-on twinkle overkill, fairy lights overhead, merry flames in the firepit, upbeat music playing on Tobin's portable speaker.

Dread, dread, and more dread.

"What happened to your shirt? It's stained." Tobin's on me immediately, picking at a tomato seed I missed.

"Let's not call it a stain. How about *garnish*."

Marijke pours plastic tumblers of sparkling water—no crystal till Tor gets here. Tobin's gaze cuts to the copper tub filled with ice, eyes jumping from bottle to bottle, lips silently counting *seven, eight, nine, shit*.

Under the bug covers, Marijke's food goes limp and loses its shine as Tobin's dad doesn't show up, and doesn't show up, and doesn't show up.

The small talk is dragging along, mostly dead, when Tor's cheery Norwegian "Hi-hi" floats down the driveway.

Tor Renner is an old-world marauder, with a big broad chest and a big booming laugh and a fondness for overdone Viking-style gestures—nonnegotiable crushing hugs, bone-breaking back slaps.

In twenty-five years, Tobin will have Tor's ageless Kurt Russell look—full head of hair, worn longish to let the ladies know how thick it is. Solid body, a little blurred with time, still respectable in a set of surf trunks. Eyes like a dark crystal, fanned with sunny smile lines.

But where Tobin's eyes are gentle, Tor's are harsh. They constantly compute a person's value, his silver tongue ready to deploy any of a dozen quick-release platitudes to get himself out of an underperforming conversation. His smile is a command: *You like me.*

The worst thing about Tor is how much of him I see in Tobin. His wide grin. His easy chatter. The greetings designed to make you feel special and welcome.

Especially now that I know what it costs Tobin to act like his dad.

Tobin's so on he's almost manic. His mom has an identical weird light in her eyes. Tor has to be catered to, fed, and coddled. His crude jokes must land in a goose-down pillow of appreciative chuckles.

I don't think Tobin could stop if he wanted to. The magic act might be all he knows how to do during tough times.

Black and green ribbons cinch tight above my heart, choking it with fear that nothing will ever change. Not between Marijke and Tor, not between Tobin and me. Everyone will do the same painful dance, year after year.

"Marijke, you're looking *very* well. And Liz! My favorite girl!" Tor strides toward me, arms wide. I skip back a step, point to my uterus, and mouth, *cramps.*

Tor coughs, readjusting quickly. He thumps Tobin on the arm hard enough to mess up his hair. "And Tobin! Have you gotten tired of this one yet, Liz?"

Marijke, Tobin, and I flinch in unison.

"Let's eat," Marijke says, fake bright. Tobin whips covers off entrées. Tor hunts through the platters for the choicest bits.

He loads a piece of homemade crostini with an obscene pile of smoked salmon. "Great fish. I'll give you the name of my seafood guy in Vancouver. Same-day delivery. Even fresher than this." He open-mouth chews—one of Tobin's rare, rare pet peeves—as he dispenses this priceless, pricey advice. Reaching for the copper tub, he snags two beers, uncaps them both.

I'm sure Tobin didn't intend to make that small, hurt sound.

I can't work with this. I can't "yes, and" this guy, unless it's "yes, and now you start paying attention to your son."

For a few minutes, things don't get worse. Tor asks about Tobin's summer schedule (up in the air), my job (no, I haven't gotten a raise; yes, they should appreciate me more), and Marijke's company (doing great, which she shouldn't have told him).

"Son. Have you given any thought to your future? Beyond carrying luggage for tourists."

My *oof* is audible.

"Actually, Dad, I have great news."

I squeeze Tobin's hand as I wiggle out of the picnic table seating, making *excuse me* faces. He manages an eight-out-of-ten smile.

"There's an annual pitch competition at work. Very prestigious, comes with a promotion and a raise. Anyway, this project I put together with my friend Lyle, it's one of three shortlisted. . . ."

Tobin falls silent. Halfway up the steps, I turn to see Tor holding up a hand, not noticing how Tobin's smile has turned frail.

"You're putting in all this work with a two-in-three chance of getting no money and no title? You're getting conned." Tor pulls out his wallet, flashing a sizeable chunk of fresh red fifties as he hunts for a business card to pass to Tobin. "If you want real money, so your wife can take time off for babies, I have a wiser opportunity. One that pays for sure."

The crostini hardens to glass in my stomach. I will kill this man. I will kill him whether he's pressing this button knowingly or unknowingly.

I march back to the table. "We don't need the money. And fathers can take parental leave, too," I butt in.

"Oh? He is planning to be a stay-at-home dad? That's why his name is Renner-Lewis, and yours is just Lewis?"

I wonder, a little wildly, whether Tor realizes he's the only one laughing.

Tobin would give a lot to be a stay-at-home dad, which is a miracle considering how he grew up. I've caught him hanging around our spare room more than once, a thoughtful look in his eye, like he's imagining a yellow paint job and a crib to replace the pullout sofa.

And he's married to me, who's only ever said "no" or "not now" or "maybe next year."

Tobin's back takes on a terrible straightness. "We're not looking for investment opportunities, thank you."

Shrugging, Tor polishes off the carpaccio. "You'll regret missing this one. Junk in Your Trunks. Catchy name. Will totally disrupt the decluttering industry. Guaranteed twenty percent return. Minimum buy-in is ten K; I can get you onboard for five, tonight only."

"Dad! I said we're not looking."

"You should. Marijke, you and I can talk profits later. Right now, I'm thinking you must have an amazing dessert hidden somewhere."

Marijke floats away, buoyed by the power of Tor's meaningful "later."

Tor turns back to us. "I could negotiate an extension until to-morrow morning. Noon, at the outside. This could—"

"Hello? Tor?" A very beautiful, extremely pregnant white woman hovers at the edge of the backyard, nervous hands clutching her purse strap.

Tor's halfway across the yard before my brain can think, *Surprise!*

"Renata! What are you doing here?" He puts a comforting arm around her, sweeping her away from us. It would look unintentional if I didn't know Tor, the king of premeditated actions.

Tobin's head swivels between our new guest and Marijke's kitchen. He caught on fast, like he, too, suspected this day would come.

"I'm sorry to disturb your meeting, *liebchen,* but I couldn't check in to the hotel. The credit card . . ." She tries to smile, lips trembling. "They wouldn't hold the room, and your phone must be on silent. Oh, horrible pregnancy hormones, it's not worth crying. . . ." She flaps a hand at her flooding eyes, leaning into Tor's chest.

Oh no.

"What. Is. This." Marijke stands at the kitchen door.

Tor's got his hands on the woman's shoulders, ready to spin her out of his arms, but it's too late. She looks up at Marijke, all apology. "Excuse me, so sorry to intrude. I'm Renata. Tor's fiancée. Please carry on, I just need to borrow Tor for one minute." I hope she's not as young as she looks—twenty-five, maybe?

Tobin comes to stand behind me, his breathing quick and sharp, fingers trembling as they sneak around my shoulders.

"How can *she* be your fiancée, when *I* am your wife?" Marijke storms to the table, carrying a cake frosted to resemble breasts in a frilly bikini. The icing matches her outfit.

"Common-law," Tor points out.

"Common. Law. *Wife*," Marijke shoots back. "We never agreed to separate. You never even asked!" She slams the cake down on an ill-placed serving spoon.

The platter cracks cleanly across the spoon. The boobs lift and separate, flying to opposite sides of the patio.

Marijke's baking was my reward for enduring this supposedly joyful event. Now the boobs have paid the ultimate price, and I have nothing left to lose.

Renata's game smile wobbles. "Tor, darling. You aren't married?"

"Of course not, *liebchen*," he says, stroking her belly, buffed nails glowing under the fairy lights. "A misunderstanding only."

Marijke seizes the fish platter, hurling the contents at Tor with a Valkyrie battle scream. This scene is awful, but that scream is excellent. I want to bookmark it.

"Misunderstanding, huh? Every time you promised to come home!"

She wings a handful of tomatoes. Her aim is terrifying; Tor takes a cluster bomb of deliciousness across his Hawaiian shirt.

"Every time you begged me for money."

Eesh, there goes the hummus.

"Every time you promised to be a father to your only child!"

The pitcher of margaritas with ice. Lots and lots of ice.

"I should have listened to Liz when she said I was stupid and deluded."

Tobin's body jerks like he's been shot.

"I never said that!"

"Didn't you?" Marijke shouts. "Didn't everybody?" Panting, beet-red, she looks from Tobin, clutching me like I'm a piece of flotsam in the North Atlantic, to Renata, hands curled protectively around her belly. "How many children, Tor? Not just these two, I imagine."

Silence.

"Well." Marijke props her fists on her hips, surveying the damage. "Not one more minute. Not one more minute of my life, or my son's life. You may get off my property. You'll hear from my lawyers."

A slice of salmon peels off Tor's shoulder, landing with a splat on the driveway.

Tor turns to Tobin. "I apologize for your mother. She isn't herself tonight. Would you mind putting up your old dad? Renata needs a supportive mattress, but you two could camp out on the sofa bed. For family's sake."

Marijke pauses her grand exodus at the kitchen door.

Tobin's intake of breath whistles in my ear.

No, I chant silently. *No no no no. Say NO, this one time, for the love of innocent boob cakes.*

He doesn't say it.

Tobin's whole upbringing was about pleasing this awful man. His mom better not be pissed that, after a lifetime of grooming her son to make himself irresistible, Tobin doesn't know how to resist.

The back door slams furiously behind Marijke. Barbra Streisand—the perennial soundtrack when Tobin failed yet again to be the thing that kept his father around—blasts through the open window.

I add her name to my murder list.

"That's settled, then. Renata and I will—"

"*NO.*" It's a crime to shout down Barbra, but one does what one must.

Tor's brow wrinkles with the beginnings of confusion. "Son! I am very surprised at Liz. What kind of person would ask Renata to sleep in her car, in her condition?"

"Of course—"

"NO!" I interrupt before Tobin blunders into Tor's extremely obvious web.

It stings to have to say it. I already agreed to push back our anniversary celebration—the first one we've ever planned, thanks in no small part to this man, who unsurprisingly hasn't remembered the date or wished us any happiness. We should already be drinking champagne and losing interest in a candlelit screening of *Pride and Prejudice* because we can't keep our hands to ourselves. I refuse to give this moment away for Tor, again. It's *ours*.

I turn in Tobin's arms. Someone has to say no. If it's me, he has to back me up. He has to be with me, or he has to do this without me.

His golden skin is ashen. His lips tremble. But I know when my husband's giving me the green light. We don't need words or movements or even a blink-once-for-yes code.

"That won't work for us, I'm afraid. No need to sleep in the car; I'm sure there are thousands of hotel rooms in Grey Tusk available for cash. Come on, Tobin."

I pull him the first few steps, then we're both running down the narrow driveway. By silent agreement, we head to my car (charged this afternoon; almost like I saw this coming).

It's been fifteen minutes of some of my best angry driving when the first low, animal sob comes from beside me.

It's not too late to slam on the brakes and cut hard into the mountain bike park entrance. I hug him awkwardly across the console, but it's not enough for the huge, tearing grief that pours out of him.

I get out, pulling him from the passenger side. We stand together, holding tight, the pain in his voice mixing with the wind in the trees and the rush of glacial melt down the sheer mountainside.

"None of it mattered. Nothing. All these years," he says, the words dull and dead.

I hug him tighter, his breath shuddering under my hands. "I'm sorry, Tobe. You didn't deserve any of it."

"Thank you," he whispers into my dampened hair.

He's so good, and so broken, and I'm an asshole for thinking about myself. For wanting to tell him how the wind is banging an unlatched door inside my chest, howling through the rooms of my heart.

Saying no can't be only my job. I can't be the bad cop to his good cop.

That's not fair. That ends with vomit on the sidewalk at Disneyland.

If it doesn't end long before that.

Tobin lets go, wiping his nose on his tie before tearing it off and throwing it in the bear-proof trash bin on the way back to the car.

"Why didn't you take my name?"

My hand jerks on my seat belt latch. "Don't, Tobe. Don't let him do this to us."

His throat bobs. "Why didn't you *want* to?"

I hate Tor Renner. He isn't even here, yet he's *here,* the way our families have always managed to wedge themselves between us. We've been fighting about who gets to wear what costume in made-up dramas, when we should've been paying attention to our own villain origin stories.

"I wanted to. I was going to. But then after the wedding . . ." Ah, my breath is shaking. I don't want to cry, but a lot of things happen the way you don't want them to, and you just have to keep going. "Our wedding day . . . we didn't do a good job for each other that day. It seemed like . . . like neither of us could break away from our families to put *us* first. And I already felt so small, like nobody saw me. I don't know. I didn't want to disappear completely, and if my name was Renner-Lewis . . . yeah."

A mountain biker rolling past does a double take at the car filled with crying people.

"There's no privacy here. Let's go home." Electric cars are unsatisfying at times when you want to stomp on the accelerator and make a lot of noise, but I do my best. Tobin opens his window, drifting his fingers through the slipstream. Across the chalk-blue river, Grey Tusk broods, too.

"I'm sorry I hurt you, Tobe."

"It's all right."

"It isn't." It is bonkers that I want him to be angry and not forgive me right away. I don't want him to please me in the creepy way he's been taught. And I don't want him to think pleasing me counts as an apology. I'm not the only one in the wrong here.

Maybe that realization is why I decide to push it. "I need you to say *no* sometimes, Tobin. It's hurting me, having to defend us against everything. I know it's hard with your parents, but someone who loved you wouldn't want you to hurt yourself to please them."

He sets his hand over mine on the steering wheel, caressing my fingers, all intimacy and no sex. Emotions smash inside me, love and fear and anger doing their best to mess each other up.

"Okay. Whatever you want, Diz, I can do that."

I asked him for what I needed, and he said yes.

I couldn't have played myself better if I'd planned it. If he refuses, I lose. If he agrees, I can't know whether he wants to, or thinks he has to. And I lose. But I can't ask him a question with no right answers and then be angry he got it wrong.

All I can do is keep driving, and hoping, and trying. Change doesn't happen overnight.

But one thing could change right now. Me. I could take him at his word, believe he wants to do this for us. For love. And I can give him a commitment in return. Yes, and.

"I'll file the name-change paperwork tomorrow."

He stares at me, blank-faced and puffy-eyed. "You will?"

"It'll take a couple of weeks to get processed, but if I go to the office in person, it'll be faster."

"You don't have to." In the curve of his lips, I see a boy torn between asking for love and pretending he's fine.

"I want to. I want us to put each other first. I want us to be there for each other, and I—" I almost slip right into the word "love." "I think that means we don't pretend bad things didn't happen. We ask for the things we need. And we need this. *I* need this."

Something in him loosens, letting his body fall into its proper shape. "Yes. Me too."

It's lucky we've made it back to the house, and we can stagger inside and give up on this night together. Something in me still vibrates to the feeling of *coming home,* to this place, with this man. Tobin's as much my home as any physical place I've ever been.

I wait for him to walk around the car so I can take his hand and climb the stairs of the house we bought together, into the life we made together, into a future we could have together if we can just keep trying. It doesn't matter if the steps we take are small, as long as they're toward each other.

And in the morning, when we wake up in the same bed, it feels right to turn toward his body. To go slow not because I asked him to, but because we both understand we're reaching for each other's hearts.

Chapter Twenty-two

Time behaves differently in improv. A second chance doesn't mean rehearsing the scene until you get it right, or repeating the same joke at the next performance. In improv, there is only this moment, which means your second chance is neither in the past, nor in the future. It's **right now**.

—*The Second Chances Handbook*

It's day one of the West by North corporate retreat, and like all the employees jostling each other in the parking lot, I'd rather do a week in detention than get on this school bus.

For everyone else, it's basic survival instinct: don't be the first penguin to get pushed off the ice floe and into the grim orange vehicle disguised as a forty-minute team-bonding exercise.

For me, it's the feeling that no matter what I do today and tomorrow, I can't avoid collateral damage. Anxiety rubs like a burr under my skin, its hooks sinking deeper with every move. To stop the fidgets, I pull out my phone and review the schedule for the hundredth time.

If I'd planned this retreat, I would've provided useful activity choices, like "Option 1: The Competitor. Barricade yourself in a private room with your slide deck for twenty-five straight hours. Option 2: The Emotional Wreck. Unwind by crying under the luxe rainfall shower and making playlists of angry power songs on the complimentary Wi-Fi."

Instead, today's one option is: a Lighthearted Sports Day (plus Challenging Obstacle Relay with Accessible Stations!). Tomorrow, after a "restful" night in a four-person green glamping yurt, everyone will attend the pitch presentation.

My stomach squeezes into a terrified accordion at the thought. I tell it to chill, kicking my suitcase a little to show I mean business. The past eight weeks have been a fever dream of preparation. I have to believe I'm ready. Ready as I'll ever be, anyway.

On the horizon squats a bank of dense, low clouds. I smell weather. Should've packed more socks.

Tobin wanders over from the Team West bus, jaunty in his strappy backcountry rucksack and classic tan leather boots with red laces.

"You want to sign up for the three-legged race with me?" Another genius idea from the organizers: split the office into two teams to promote "healthy" competition, but make an event where one member of Team West and one from Team North are literally tied together and call that "bilateral collaboration."

"Don't you think it would look . . . weird, if we were partners?"

"Weird how? Everyone's doing it." He drops a saucy wink to remind me of the three-legged race he and I were doing just hours ago. I slipped out of our bed at dawn to shower and dress at my parents' house, keeping up the fiction that I've respected my rule about not moving back in even though I've slept over every night since the fracas with his parents.

"It might be good to pair up with other people. You know. Make new connections." Every other year at this event, I never left his side. From the moment we got together, my identity at this company has always been stacked underneath his.

This year needs to be the opposite. We drove in together because McHuge needed to borrow Tobin's truck for a meeting this morning, but our partnership ends there. In a crowd of people who believe in nonverbal messages, my outgoing message has to be that I'm with him by choice, not necessity.

The rising wind fans a whisky-hued lock of hair across Tobin's face; he frowns, tucking it behind his ear. "It's just one race. And you and I are an amazing team. When we're working together, no one can beat us."

"What's this? You two aren't conspiring to rig the pitch competition, are you?" Craig's hearty laugh cuts short when I jump away from Tobin.

"Craig! I didn't see you there. I assure you Tobin and I have taken steps to avoid actual or potential conflict of interest around the pitch competition." I glance around. At least a dozen people nearby have mysteriously discovered a need to fiddle with their suitcase zipper while staring anywhere but at our little group.

Craig looks between me and Tobin like each of us has the number two tattooed on our forehead and he's just done the math. "So when you said no one can beat the two of you together, you meant . . . ?"

Tobin's sunny "Just the three-legged race" gets rained out by my guilty "Just the three-legged race!"

Craig lowers his voice, looking pointedly at our height difference. "No offense, but you two aren't the obvious choice for the three-legged race. Are you sure Keller hasn't sweetened the deal by offering for the pair of you?"

"Keller did what?" Tobin asks, looking at me sideways.

"Keller didn't do anything! And we're not racing together," I add. Nothing sounds shadier than the truth, but improv didn't teach me how to lie. I only learned how to work with "yes, and"—but Craig's favorite things are conflict and competition.

Eleanor would call Craig's laugh "angry-happy." "Lewis, you're a player. I respect that. When the two of you are ready, let's talk." He strides away.

Cool, wet terror eddies around my feet like mist in a graveyard.

"What was that?" Tobin wraps his arms over his ribs.

It was a mistake, I don't say. I overplayed the hand Sharon dealt me with her headhunting hints on the golf course. At the precise moment when I need Craig to see me as a distinct person, he's lumped me and Tobin together. Because why would Keller offer for just me, right?

I can't make any more unforced errors on this retreat. Real life isn't improv. You can make mistakes. Big ones. You can lose years of your life to them.

My whole life feels like a giant knot of mistakes, work tangled with marriage tangled with who I want to be. I said I didn't want sex to confuse things, but I've been sleeping with Tobin for weeks. I'm supposed to be moving back in tomorrow night, even though Tobin and I will be trying to deny each other a promotion in the morning. And I bet it all on improv, but Craig doesn't follow McHuge's rules. Improv taught me how to survive social situations on my own, but I want to do better than not dying.

I want to *win.*

I have to show Craig what I've got to offer. Give everything to this retreat as myself—just me, and nobody else.

"It's nothing," I tell Tobin. "Look, I'm spiraling over my pitch and I'm not fit for human consumption. And it seems like Craig has some weird ideas about us racing together. We should find different partners for this one."

Just like we took a break from reality on Béa's wedding weekend, we need to take a break from being married until after the presentation.

He looks at me sharply, maybe sensing what I've left unsaid. "Okay," he says after a moment. He reaches toward me, but I step back.

"Not here, Tobe. It . . . doesn't feel right."

"Yeah. I can see that," he says, his arms recrossing between me and his heart. "See you on the other side."

Onboard the bus, I breathe its undead perfume of week-old lunch box cheese and try to prepare myself for what's about to go down.

There are times when even the most die-hard wilderness enthu-siasts lose the ability to put the word "great" in front of "outdoors."

That time is now.

This resort must be nice in summer. An hour south of Grey Tusk, the property is nestled in a patch of coastal rainforest near sea level. Its artful, upcycled design is all about recovered planks and old doors with layers of distressed paint. I'm sure the hand-split cedar shingles cost the earth, but they boast unmatched longevity in the year-round creeping damp of the Pacific Northwest. The secondhand furniture is perfectly mismatched, as are all the dishes. I hate to think how many garage sales the designers had to go to in order to find hundreds of jokey mugs to pair with random rose-patterned saucers. Around the two-story lodge, a boardwalk connects geodesic yurts. A path of round river stones leads to the obstacle course.

Today might be my worst day ever at West by North, and that's saying a lot. Corporate morale is at an all-time low after a rain-drenched Team West versus Team North showdown with more cheating than the Russian Olympic team.

Tempers flared after Team West got caught sneaking hard-boiled equipment into the egg-and-spoon race. This was uncovered by a Team North member who "accidentally" tripped a competitor, then "happened" to cross into their lane to finish off their egg. Neither team was penalized; both West and North are giving each other the silent treatment. And no one's speaking to Ryan from accounts, who turned up with an ankle cast he's not allowed to get wet. Nothing can be proven, but his girlfriend is an orthopedic surgeon and his story about a "possible sprain" is wispy enough to evaporate by Monday. Meanwhile, Ryan's in the lodge, harvesting three uninterrupted hours with Craig while the rest of us rack up bug bites and hypothermia.

I scrape mud out of my face and reach cold-stiffened fingers toward Bethany, seven feet below. David and I are on top of The Wall, the next-to-last obstacle in the resort's reality TV–style obstacle course. From up here, I can pick out Craig's navy-suit/orange-tie combo through the windows of the lodge's glassed-in patio.

The Wall is very corporate in that your ability to climb it is highly related to how tall you are, yet we're expected to pretend getting to the top is about individual merit. Also in that it's a random barrier you could just go around, but the powers that be have decreed that We Must Defeat Obstacles Only in the Expected Way.

Bethany grits her teeth and leaps again. Her hands touch ours long enough to give me hope, but it's a slippery emotion that slides through my grip, like Bethany's fingers.

The ever-expanding puddle at the base of The Wall splashes grandly as she lands. "I should've mentioned," she puffs, tugging her soaked, sagging T-shirt back up over her bra. "I got cut from the basketball team in eighth grade. Can't jump."

From the sidelines, our Team North allies who suffered through the blindfolded maze, the ropes course, the sand pit, and the bean-bag toss cheer us on weakly, shivering. At the last station—the puzzle—our remaining teammates scream at us to hurry as Team West sinks their last beanbag and tags in Tobin's threesome, who race toward The Wall.

Right now, Craig's watching my team—watching *me*—squander a huge lead. We have to pull out of the dive right frickin' now.

"This isn't working. David, you have to get back down and boost Bethany."

David scoffs. "No way. She got The Wall all muddy; I won't be able to get back up."

Of all the things I hate about Dick Head, him being right is the worst. The Wall's too slippery for that parkour thing he did before, where he ran up the side for a step or two. I bet he visited the resort in advance to practice the course. Smart.

Evil. But smart.

"Bethany and I can pull you up."

"Then it'll look like *I* slowed us down." Dick Head glances toward the lodge, putting his hands on his hips like he's king of the castle.

On the West side of The Wall, Tobin uses his clasped hands as a stirrup to launch his smallest team member to the top. He's watching Team North fall apart, a concerned V building between his eyebrows.

I look away. The last thing I need is to catch his eye and have him interpret that as a cry for help.

"Fine," I snap to David. "Stay where Craig can see you, then."

I'm no better at jumping than Bethany, but something has to be done. I back my butt over the edge, dangle a little, then close my eyes and let go.

The bottom of the wall is as slippery as a road paved with good intentions. I truly believe, until the second I face-plant into the puddle, that frantic flailing will save me. Spoiler: it does not.

"Oh shit," Bethany says as I lever my face out of the water.

Wet, clean-ish fabric moves across my eyes. When it feels safe to open them, she's staring down at me, the hem of her shirt bunched in her hand. "That had to hurt."

Though I'd rather stay down and reconsider my life choices, I haul myself to my feet before Tobin can come charging in. The entire front of my body is slicked in icy mud. When I spit, it's black. But I didn't hit my head and nothing's broken.

"I'm fine! Soft landing." I project my voice, so everyone can hear.

Tobin's a careful, conscientious guide, so although his body is tensed with the need to look over, he stays focused on his lift.

From the corner of my eye, I see him release his second teammate's foot and turn my way.

"I can—"

"Not *here*, Tobe," I plead in a low voice, shaking my head. "Please." I know I said we should help each other, but I absolutely cannot let him help me. It would be better to lose the whole thing than have everyone credit the win to Tobin's one second of heroism instead of my willingness to go face down in the mud for my team.

The entirety of Team West sees him hesitate and screams at him to go, go, *go already we're winning what are you doing.*

"Liz."

"Go, Tobin. This isn't *The Great Canadian Baking Show.* There's no aiding the enemy. Come on, Bethany." I go down on one knee. "Use my leg as a stool and Dick Head can pull you up."

"Dick Head," she repeats wonderingly, the treads of her hiking boots cutting into my thigh. "Yes. That's always been his name."

David grabs Bethany and hauls her up, feet scrabbling. A second later, both of them reach back down.

I need this jump. I need this win so badly. David's a dick, but he's right: it's better not to show weakness out here. *Please please please please please.*

"One. Two. Three—"

I've never jumped like this before—high, easy, right on target. The only word to describe it is "magical." Our hands lock, clasped at the wrist, and I'm floating up The Wall.

At the top, I glance at the lodge. Craig's leaning forward to watch, elbows on his knees.

"See?" David says. "I was right to stay up here."

"Shut up, Dick Head," Bethany and I chorus as we race to tag in our puzzle team.

After the open-air awards ceremony, everybody sprints for their yurts. I want no part of the inevitable death match at the lodge over the four shower stalls. My plan is to sacrifice a set of dry clothes, spend an hour running through my slide deck, then shower once the fifteen-deep lineup is gone.

It's a disgusting strategy, and I'm blitzed with fatigue, but if I miss this opportunity to practice I'll regret it in the morning. Every intensely planned paragraph needs to feel fresh; each sentence has a word I painstakingly selected for extra emphasis. Every spontaneous mistake I could make can be polished away, until I shine too brightly to overlook.

Engrossed in mental rehearsal, I bump into Tobin in the corral-like exit to the obstacle course. I overcorrect, tripping over my feet; he reaches out.

Then stops himself, pulls back, and waits.

My body regains balance, but my brain is thrown off by the weirdly *closed* look on his face. It's pleasant, but off-limits in a way that gives me an uncomfortable vibe.

"Congratulations," he says, nodding at my Most Valuable Player ribbon. We're getting left behind in the stampede toward the main compound.

"Thanks," I say, embarrassed for no reason. "Too bad your

puzzle team misplaced that piece after you made up so much ground on The Wall."

"Yeah. At least Team West lost by a lot. So no one can say a couple seconds' delay helped the North side too much." The cords in his neck don't stand out when he's merely angry. His jerky, mechanical steps propel him up the grassy hill with furious efficiency, forcing me to speed-walk after him.

"What do you want me to say?" I ask, catching up on the pebbled path to the yurts. "Our teams spent all day low-key sabotaging each other. If the woman in the company's only couple flames out on the physical challenge, and her husband throws the game for her, how do you think that looks for me?"

"It doesn't look like anything, if you turn around and help me up after you."

I throw my hands in the air. "You got up that wall in two seconds! You didn't need my help."

Even under the dark, lowering sky, the strain around his eyes shows. "Not physically. But we could have showed them how a real team works. So what if it wasn't a baking show—we could've made it into one!"

His starry-eyed optimism is laudable, but not especially realistic when applied to anyone but himself.

"That's fine when we're alone, Tobin. But we're in the middle of a company event with sixty witnesses watching our every move. Where, like every workplace, bias still exists. You can get away with stuff I can't."

"Okay. You're right. I'm sorry," he says, eyes closed, chin sunk to his chest. "If privacy is what you want, Lyle left my truck in the parking lot. Let's take some time to ourselves after dinner."

The thing is, I want to say yes. There would be no sex—my body's been sending me increasingly dire damage reports now that the adrenaline rush of victory is fading—but I would die to be able to abandon all muscle control while clinging to his chest like a baby koala.

But it's too risky. "People will find out."

"We're married, Liz. I think everyone here knows what happens when two people love each other very much," he snaps.

I understand what people would think. Maybe better than he does. If I slip back into my yurt after a nighttime visit to Tobin's "lost and found" truck, I'll never be my own person—only his girl.

"It's better if we don't do personal stuff on company time. Just until tomorrow afternoon, okay? The second Craig names the winner, we can act like a couple again. I promise."

"Sure." His smile is so pinched, my heart can't take it.

"It's not for long, Tobe. I'm still moving back in tomorrow. C'mere." I grab his hand, tugging him behind a thick copse of cedars. "We can hide here for a second. Nobody's thinking about anything but hot water and antibacterial soap anyway. This can hold us till tomorrow," I murmur, tucking myself into his arms.

We're cold, and wet, and the rain keeps falling. But eventually, in the places where we're touching, I imagine there is warmth.

Chapter Twenty-three

With luck, partners will discover that improv is a way to
tell a story. A good story isn't about uninterrupted good
times. Every scene has moments of fear, contradiction,
and struggle. But in the end, individual wins and losses
matter far less than the choice to keep telling your story,
together.

—*The Second Chances Handbook*

I paid forty-five dollars for this sweat-proof T-shirt, complete with
built-in bra. I wore it once before, in the office, but I should've taken
it for a test drive somewhere extreme—CrossFit, maybe?—before
trusting it with the biggest day of my professional life.

I'm not just hot. I'm *humid*. There is *weather* underneath my
shirt.

When I imagined this day, I pictured myself acting smooth on
the outside because I felt smooth on the inside. It was a pretty fantasy. I should've visualized myself filled with a giant ball of burrs,
pointy on all sides.

All I can do is wait. And try not to check if my neck is as bumpy
as it feels above this unwise low-necked pirate shirt I've paired

with bright pink pants and my cat earrings. If Sharon were here, I'd google "can EpiPens clear up stress hives" and, depending on the answer, I might have tried to steal her life-saving medication.

I miss Craig's opening remarks, my ears blocked with pressurized bubbles of pure fear. David launches his pitch, flashing his watch to a soundtrack of *mwah mwah mwah mwah*. His slides for a destination wedding tour look great. There's a spectacular artist's rendition of a wedding party in a river raft, with the bride in a skirted white wetsuit, the bridal attendants in pink neoprene, and the groom's side in dove gray.

It's solid—the right amount of familiar blended with new. Still, David's not who I'm worried about.

Tobin's up next, then a coffee break. Then me.

Presuming I survive.

Tobin and McHuge take the stage, looking supremely snacky in their charcoal suits. They're wearing matching oxford ankle boots, like brothers who bought their school clothes together. It's cute. Kinda hot, really.

I'm sure it's not a coincidence that 75 percent of the kitchen staff are managing to loiter at the back of the room.

McHuge clasps his hands, straining the shoulders of his suit; a sigh flutters up from the back. Tobin steps to the microphone and powers up a megawatt smile.

Magic sparkles in the air like they've applied an Instagram filter to the entire room.

"Ladies and gentlemen, I'd like to introduce Dr. Lyle McHugh, PhD." Tobin pauses to let that sink in. "Author of the highly anticipated upcoming release *The Second Chances Handbook*. And together, we'll marry—so to speak—the eleven-billion-dollar North American self-help industry with Grey Tusk wilderness tourism."

I read an essay once about "room tone"—a particular sound of silence created by people paying close attention. I've never heard it at West by North. Our meetings have soundtracks of muffled message alert tones, gum snapping, and whispers.

I hear it now.

It's the sound of Craig's spine straightening. The sound of a truly disruptive pitch. It's not even based on McHuge's book; this is a second totally unique idea. Anybody could see its potential— luxury wilderness relationship therapy as a spin-off from a brand-new pop-culture phenom. The two of them are magic onstage, playing off each other, landing laugh after laugh.

Tobin doesn't look at me when he describes how they would need a dedicated ops support position. Which is fine. He shouldn't. I don't want him to. I don't want anyone to look at me right now, because they'd see I'm sold on the idea, too.

I'd love to do ops for this project. I'm picturing myself at the table with Tobin and McHuge, bouncing ideas around, having fun at work the way they were having fun at the community center. It wouldn't be like working for Craig at all.

I check David's reaction. He's pale minty green, with a shine of sweat on his forehead. It's not just me whose stomach is flipping harder than Simone Biles, then.

This is the winning presentation.

The second the moderator cuts off their lively Q&A, I bolt to the farthest stall in the bathroom, climb onto the toilet, and hold my phone up to the window, where I can get two bars. I add Sharon and Stellar to a group chat titled "PRESENTATION EMER-GENCY."

ME

Sharon, meet Stellar. Stellar, Sharon. I know you're at work but
🚨 I need help

STELLAR B

. . . Aunt Sharon? Although I guess I should just call you Sharon now that Jen and I broke up

ME

The two of you know each other???? What

SHARON K-Y

Stellar! You're still family, even if you're not with my niece anymore

My signal craps out, the refresh icon spinning hopelessly. Someone comes into the bathroom, so I step on the flush lever to cover my swearing. When the chat finally loads, Stellar and Sharon are twenty messages deep. No time for backscroll; I have to focus on the present.

ME

Can I interrupt because it's an emergency

STELLAR B

Yes, speak

ME

I have to present in 10 minutes and Tobin just blew everyone out of the water. My idea is too quiet ☹ His has a future best-selling book, and mine doesn't have a single helicopter

SHARON K-Y

what is a helicopter? Is this code? Please remember I am an Old and translate accordingly

My shoe keeps wanting to slide off the toilet seat, my arm is cramping from holding up the phone like I'm trying to contact extraterrestrial life, and I am explaining regular words to Sharon. But my presentation is on the line. I'll stand *in* the toilet if I have to.

ME

> Sharon it's a helicopter. I just mean mine isn't fancy. What can I do????

STELLAR B

> BE YOURSELF

SHARON K-Y

> Can't believe it. A younger person has *asked* for my advice. My moment has come

<Sharon K-Y is typing . . . >

STELLAR B

> I LOVE YOU

ME

> My plan was senseless. Eight weeks of improv? HA. I should've pitched Craig's idea no matter how absurd and illegal

STELLAR B

> Quit! Quit already, aaaahhhhhhh! Let them have their bro company all to their bro selves, you can do better. I can do better! WE CAN ALL DO BETTER

I've just about given up on Sharon when she hits the chat with a wall of text two screens long.

SHARON K-Y

As per my previous advice. 1. Only focus on things you can fix. Therefore, 2. Don't waste time worrying about their presentation. 3. They have a high-concept pitch, but not everything that pitches well is the right move for the company, right now. 4. You're pitching your idea PLUS the added value of *you* as someone who generates a particular type of idea that is powerful in its unique approach, not its flash. And 5. Stellar please call me, you know my thumb joints can't take all this texting

STELLAR B

WHAT SHE SAID

ME

I just. What if it doesn't work

What if this was all for nothing

SHARON K-Y

Then throw a match over your shoulder and film yourself walking away

STELLAR B

AUNT SHARON 😭

SHARON K-Y

You said 10 minutes. It's been 9. You have to go

Oh, shit.

STELLAR B

> DO IT LIZ. LIGHT IT UP. BURN IT DOWN

I jump down and speed-walk back to the dining hall. The moderator waves me to the front, impatient.

The white noise in my brain feels like karaoke cranked up to a million, except I can't meow my way out of this one. *Come on, magic.*

"Good morning, everyone. I'm excited to be here today." My voice cracks over "excited." "As you can tell, ha ha."

Polite laughter. Not as good as the real laughter Tobin got, but it's something.

"Today is a special day. Today, the spreadsheet nerd talks about branding." Smile, raise my eyebrows, next slide. "West by North's brand is high-end tours in a world-class mountain destination. Our ideal customer wants to buy an upsold version of the wilderness—stunning vistas, effortless luxury, and uninterrupted fun. Like Grey Tusk, our most profitable season is winter, with summer a decent second and spring and fall far behind."

Here's where I diverge from Craig's vision. I'm short of breath, gasping between sentences. There's a quaver in my voice that just won't go away.

I don't feel magic. Fuck.

"I propose that we disrupt *our own brand.* Our luxury offerings don't fit spring and fall consumers. They're here for inexpensive events like leaf season or the craft beer festival. For this market segment, we need a different brand."

Craig's face is expressionless. I think I'm having a heart attack, like my heart is actually attacking me. I swallow the major organs that have collected in my mouth and look elsewhere. At Tobin. Right as I put up the slide about guides' income.

It couldn't be more obvious that I was thinking of him when

I came up with this idea. Day hikes to local attractions would be perfect for a guide with a sore wrist. He wouldn't have to sell big trips on commission. He'd be home every night with salary and tips. Maybe then he'd stop tracking the gap between his income and mine, and I wouldn't catch him pretending he loves patching gear he really should replace just because he won't spend more than he brings in.

He's got that closed expression again. Like I'm here, but he doesn't see me.

I've had almost every emotion you can have during this presentation, but I didn't feel lonely until this moment.

I push through slides of smiling hikers and graphs with reassuring upward curves. My last second runs out as I finish saying, "Thank you. I'm happy to take your questions."

Perfect. I did as perfect a job as I could. I quell the urge to check whether my sweat-proof armor is controlling the deluge.

The moderator turns on her microphone. "Are there any ques—"

"Yes," Craig interrupts. "Surely there's *some* market for high-end tours in the offseason. What if we offered luxury dog-wagon service to these destinations instead?" He looks deeply annoyed to be repeating his comments from several weeks ago.

Oh, god. I have to decide who to be, right here, right now. Am I the Liz who gives a truthful, risky "no"? Or the Liz who goes with a canny, self-preserving "yes"? *Be yourself,* Stellar said. Well, *BE YOURSELF,* but same thing.

"Good question, Craig. Unfortunately, huskies overheat in warmer weather, particularly on hilly terrain like the Highway to Hell." I skip the part about getting sued. Even I have my limits on how much "no" I can deliver at once.

The moderator moves in. "Any other—"

"Be that as it may, luxury customers want exclusivity," Craig interrupts. "Is this true disruption, or brand dilution?"

He's pushing back *hard*. He didn't do this with Tobin and McHuge. "We can preserve our luxury brand with a separate website or even a different company name. Like Lexus and Toyota."

Craig glances at Naheed, who nods.

I can do this. *You are the added value,* said Sharon.

"And," I continue, "as much as I hate to argue with the boss, in order for West by North to become truly innovative and disruptive, we need ideas that go beyond our brand. To get those ideas, we need people who think differently."

Me, I think, looking at Craig. *See me.*

"When we say 'no' to the status quo, and challenge our perception of who we are, we become a better company."

The moderator breaks in. "That's time. I'm sure our speakers would love to answer more questions over lunch."

Bethany and Jingjing wait offstage; everyone else heads toward the buffet the resort laid out during my presentation.

"You did well!" Bethany exclaims at the same time Jingjing says comfortingly, "That was much better than last time."

I'm buzzing like a high-tension wire in a snowstorm. I need to cool off away from people. Even nice people. "Excuse me," I say faintly. "Bathroom break. Save me a seat?"

I'm halfway across the lobby when Craig calls, "Liz! Hey, Lewis!"

My heart fossilizes in my chest. There's only one reason he would chase me.

I was blocking it out, but I kind of knew. I hoped magic would get my ideas heard. But maybe my ideas were just as square and uninteresting as my spreadsheets.

I might as well take the bad news now, when everyone else is at lunch.

"What can I do for you, Craig?" My words echo off the chic concrete surfaces before vanishing into bright pops of chatter from the dining room.

"Just wanted to say, before you make any calls to Keller—"

"I'm not calling *anyone*, Craig," I say, weary to the bottom of my soul. "No one's recruiting me. Sharon is my friend, nothing more."

"Sure," he says, winking. "Got it. I wanted to say congratulations and welcome to the West by North exec."

I frown, hugging my arms across my chest to keep my armpits sealed. He's not making sense.

Craig spreads his hands, grinning big. "First place, Lewis. What can I say? Great pitches."

He means "pitch," singular. Or does he think the rebranding and the off-season tours are separate pitches? Doesn't matter; he could tell me he liked my taxidermy collection and I'd still be feeling this rising flutter in my chest.

Me. It's ME.

"I'm . . . I'm shaking," I say, when I trust myself to speak. "Oh my god, I can't . . ." I fan myself with my hands, blinking. Craig laughs—with me, I note.

I did it. All the work, all the sacrifice, all the struggle. I made it, with my own idea. My own voice. Alone.

I wish Tobin were here.

I wish he could see me win this job, right now, and it wouldn't mean he had to lose. He'd shout with happiness, and that would unlock the scream inside me. He'd pick me up and twirl me around and kiss me hard, hard.

This joy is so fierce, and so lonely. It's not the bursting pleasure of the first kiss with the person whose little glances leave you weak, or the soft sweetness of marrying your true love. It's molten steel, fiery and raw, and I can't temper it on my own.

"Thank you. Thank you so much! I can't—you mean it? I can't believe it. Oh, sorry, I'll keep my voice down," I say, looking over my shoulder. "I'm just so, so excited to be moving forward with the project. There are so many tours I'd love to discuss; I don't know where to start. Maybe you can tell me what part of my pitch resonated most?"

Fishing for compliments is a dangerous game, but apparently caution is for losers. I'm starving for praise. Salivating at the thought of Craig saying he can't believe he overlooked me all these years.

"I mean, I hope you loved all of it, but it seemed like Tobin and McHuge's—I mean, Tobin and Lyle's pitch caught everyone's attention."

"Well, yes, naturally. Theirs was a game changer. Original. Special. The exact pitch I've been looking for. Can't wait for you to develop it."

There's a bubble in my ears, and it's filled with the tinny static of snow and electricity. I shake my head, trying to dislodge the pressure. "So we're . . . developing Tobin's tour, too? I mean, that's great! So great. But you didn't say anything about mine and—did I really win?" This feels like a breakup speech that softens you up with "You're an amazing person" before hammering you with an obviously untrue "It's not you, it's me."

"You won, Lewis, never fear. I figured out what you want. You two were smart to coordinate that way, so I knew it was double or nothing."

No. Please, no. "That's not what we did."

"Sure you didn't." He winks. "Yours pushes opportunities for guides; his needs extra ops capacity? Classic. Love it. You've come a long way. With my mentorship, that is. Get ready to be very busy developing your husband's tour."

Dazed, I ask, "What about my tour?"

"You can do that on the side. We know you can handle the workload."

The sizzle of frozen vapor on hot wires is so loud, the only

thought I can hear is *I can't cry here.* "So . . . mine wasn't the winning pitch?"

"Here's some advice from your mentor, Lewis. The winning
pitch," Craig lectures, blithely smashing me to smithereens, "is the
one that snags both halves of Grey Tusk's hottest tourism super-
couple for West by North. If I don't promote you, you'll look elsewhere. If you go, he goes, and so does his pitch."

My sweat turns to ice. "I won because you want to keep *Tobin*?"

"You say it like it's a bad thing," Craig protests. "He's a guide.
Not head office material. He'll need assistance to develop this tour
the way it should be done. And he put ops support right in his
presentation—so, let's give him who he wants."

A disbelieving breath comes out of me, like I've reached over
my shoulder and found a knife in my back.

"I can't cry here," I mumble, looking for an escape route.

"No need to congratulate me! You're a chess master, Lewis.
Never saw you coming."

"*No!*" Too much volume, not enough control. "Not *congratulations.* I said I can't *cry* here, Craig." Too late; old tears, made hot by
fresh injustice, prickle behind my eyes.

"That's not what you wanted?" Craig's neck flushes a bricky
red. "We can do it the other way—him in first place, you in second.
You're the handler, he's the talent. You're still on the same team."

I dig my fingers into my hair, forehead in my palms. "Tobin
and I are not a *team,* Craig! When will you—no, when will *anyone*
look at me and see me?! Not him! *Me.* I'm not his handler. I'm not
his *anything*!"

The sole of a brand-new men's dress shoe makes a certain
kind of squeak when it stops short. It's loud enough to cut through
the rise and fall of lunchtime conversation, quiet enough to stop
my heart.

I don't want to turn my head. I don't want to know who came to an unexpected stop when they heard what I said.

As it turns out, it's McHuge.

He takes Tobin by the shoulder.

"Come on, buddy. Time to go."

Wordlessly, Tobin lets himself be piloted toward the front door.

"What the hell?" Craig blusters, his head cranking between me and Tobin like this is Wimbledon. "I'll see you at the awards ceremony in fifteen minutes, Lewis. Don't make me regret choosing you."

With that, he takes off after Tobin and McHuge.

Chapter Twenty-four

One way to end a scene is to return to the beginning of
that same scene. . . . All of life follows a cycle, and improv
is no different.

—*Truth in Comedy*

The West by North parking lot is in an alternate universe from the
one we left only yesterday, the uncomfortable quiet broken here
and there by whispers that stop when I look around.

Pretending Tobin and McHuge had been called away, Craig accepted second place on their behalf, but the tension between him
and me as we shook hands for the winner's photo made it clear
something big had gone down over lunch.

I should have gone after Tobin right away instead of standing
there, frozen, not knowing what to do. When I ran out to the parking lot after the awards ceremony, his truck was gone.

The buses didn't get back until three thirty, so I've had plenty
of time to agonize over how much he heard. Hours to craft an

explanation for what I said. An eternity to wrack my brain over what to do about the disaster at West by North.

There has to be a way to fix this.

At six, he's expecting me to move back in. I was supposed to come back to Amber's, pack up, then come home so we could grab dinner before driving to the improv showcase together.

I don't know if I should knock on his door right now and acknowledge that everything is fucked, or respect our schedule so he at least isn't ambushed by the wife who told his best friend and his boss she wasn't his partner.

Wasn't his anything.

I have my parents' house to myself for one precious hour. Very valuable for alternating between planting myself face-first into the couch in despair, and motoring around the house doing everything from vacuuming to pre-cutting Eleanor's cheese cubes and veggie sticks in a fruitless attempt to get away from myself.

I can't decide whether I'm relieved or not when Amber and Eleanor crash land at five fifteen. At least I'm not alone, but now it's the unhinged hour between work/school and dinner, with everyone hangry and losing it after a long week of holding themselves together.

I spend a good twenty minutes searching for my black leggings, which Eleanor took out of my bag and repurposed as a Jolly Roger before forgetting them under the living room couch. Eleanor melts down over losing the leggings, and because Aunt Liz is leaving. Amber gives warm hugs to her daughter and death looks to me, for the crime of agreeing to her request to move out while wearing my own clothes, I guess.

She doesn't ask about the pitch presentation, and I don't tell her.

At ten to six, I'm finishing a final sweep of my parents' bedroom. My phone rings: "Sharon Keller-Yakub," the screen flashes.

"You didn't text. You didn't call," she says, with no preamble. "So. You didn't win."

"No. I won."

"You don't sound like it." Sharon exhales a sympathetic mom breath. "You sound like you fell off your bike, then a car ran over it. Knowing Craig like I do, I highly, highly suspect he was behind the wheel. Hold on one second."

She mutes me while I try to zip my bag closed over a half-empty box of tampons.

"Sorry. I've got showcase gut grief like you wouldn't believe. Like race-day tummy, but so much worse. Kareem's at the drugstore buying me everything in the stomach aisle. Give me the thirty-second update."

"Craig didn't like my pitch, but I got the promotion so he wouldn't lose Tobin. I . . . said some things. Craig smoothed it over in front of the company, but . . ."

"Ah, what an ass—" There's an ominous hiccupy sound. "Can't talk now, but this is not your fault. We'll discuss after the showcase. See you at the theater, if I'm still alive." She hangs up without saying goodbye.

"What *things* did you say? Did you melt down at work?"

I whirl to find my sister at the bedroom door.

"I can handle it."

"If only someone had seen this coming," she says, going for the jugular in her Amber way.

Bright red anger spatters across the floor of my soul. "Goddammit, Amber! Would it kill you to take my side for once?"

"Language," she snaps, looking over her shoulder. "Eleanor, bunny, you can play Minecraft. Go find the iPad, okay?"

Eleanor drifts reluctantly down the hall, eyes big. She's not fooled by the grown-ups sending her away when things are getting exciting, but she's six. Illicit screen time beats forbidden eaves-dropping, hands down.

Amber sighs, massaging the bridge of her nose. "I hate to say this. But the best thing for you would be to stay at the job you have now."

"What? I *won,* Amber. Why would I say no to a promotion I worked years to earn?" I don't have to fight with her about this. But the compulsion to make my sister *see me* overrides common sense.

Her skin reddens under her eyes, just like mine does when I'm upset and struggling to be heard. How can we be so alike, yet she doesn't understand me at all?

"Remember when you followed me into debate club, and choir, and Model UN, and ended up hating them but you were too stubborn to quit? What if you chased this for the wrong reasons and you burn out doing a job you hate, but won't leave? And maybe . . ."

Whatever she's holding back, it's so much more awful than what she's already said that she has to steel herself before unleashing it.

"Don't say it, Amber." I'm back in that hotel bathroom on my wedding day, afraid to listen, afraid not to.

"Maybe you're not the best judge of what's good for y—"

"*Don't.* Not again."

"Stop avoiding the truth, Liz! Some jobs aren't right for au—"

She cuts herself off hard, her expression melting into guilty uncertainty: Did I hear what she didn't quite say?

I did.

Tumblers fall into place with a boom like thousand-pound doors blowing open. The sledgehammer beat of my heart is the only thing connecting me to my body. All I can hear is high, tinny ringing and the hundreds of times she's said, *You're so much like Eleanor.*

"For *autistic* people."

Everything about me pulls into painfully sharp focus through Amber's lens. The awkwardness. The sensitivity to rejection. The failure to pick up on unspoken cues.

And the loyalty, persistence, focus, and sense of justice. The ability to think in a way not everybody can, the talent for seeing things from a different perspective. A *valuable* perspective.

And now I have a word for it. Like what Stellar said at our movie night, about her coworker—I can use this knowledge to build bridges between me and people who might not otherwise understand how I work and what I need.

I'm the same person I was five minutes ago. Everything I believed about myself when I thought I was an anxious introvert is still true. In a way, this doesn't change anything.

And yet, it changes everything.

"*This* is why," I say, astonished. "You think I'm like Eleanor. You didn't want me to do hard things because *she* needs to minimize stress and disruption. You're Tobin's biggest fan because he'd never leave me the way Mark left you two."

"Yes!" she says, her eyes pinning me with a forceful kind of hope. "You don't need to put yourself in risky situations. You can be happy with what you have, with the people who understand you. You fit *here*, Liz. With your family."

Disappointment takes a couple of breaths to stop squeezing me too tightly to talk.

"That wouldn't be a bad life. *If* I wanted it. But Amber, I'm tired of making sensible progress toward my sensible targets. Fuck targets! I want to chase my dreams!"

"Can you get over your stubbornness *one* time, Liz? Once. For Eleanor. What will she learn, watching you beat yourself up with this endless trying?" She glances toward Eleanor's room, her fear radiating toward her daughter. Toward me.

"I hope she'll learn I'm brave," I say, my voice raw.

"And what if you burn out being brave? What if you keep melting down at work?"

A wild laugh bubbles up. "Everybody melts down. You've done it yourself. At my *wedding*."

"Yes!" Amber yells. "And you've never let me forget it!"

Breath eddies in and out of my chest. "It's not that you melted down, Amber. It's that you never said sorry for the damage you caused. That's why it still matters."

Silence falls, dense and dark.

Finally, "If I apologize, will you think about what I said? Will you not wreck yourself to prove a point?"

I don't know. I think I might enjoy proving a point—to Amber, to myself, to everyone.

"Amber, I'm sorry, but it's not up for discussion. I have to go."

I shoulder my bag and head for the foyer. It's past time to find Tobin. He deserves better, and so do I. I led myself into this mess, where I spend more time with the sister who thinks I'll fail than the husband who's always rooted for my success.

And now it's my job to get myself out of it.

"Liz, you—"

I turn back, halfway out the door. "Stop, okay? *Stop*. I don't need you to be my keeper. And one day, Eleanor won't need that, either."

From behind Amber comes a high, thready wail. "Stop! Fighting! *Please*."

"Eleanor! I told you to go watch the iPad!" Amber scoops up her daughter, dislodging Yeti from her arms.

Sensing freedom, the cat darts toward the open door. Kris Kristofferson and I lunge at the same moment; in a flash, I'm tangled up with the dog and landing hard across the doorstep, tampons scattering like confetti down the stairs.

Amber, soothing Eleanor, pins me with a knowing stare. "Fine. Maybe you'll listen to Tobin, if you won't listen to me. You got one of the good ones. Better than mine. I hope you can keep him." Turning away, she carries Eleanor up the stairs.

By the time I pick myself up, Yeti's gone.

But Amber's words still echo like an omen.

Chapter Twenty-five

Questions aren't forbidden in improv, but they're not usually helpful. Questioning your partner(s) without adding any of your own input unbalances the scene and forces your partner(s) to guess what you're thinking. Do your share of the work.

—*The Second Chances Handbook*

I scoot my car the ridiculously short distance home, knowing I don't have the words for what comes next, letting myself balance on the knife edge of hope anyway. I'll make a mess of it, no doubt, but when I ask him to forgive me, he'll say yes. He always does.

Halfway up the front stairs, I lose my nerve, turn around, turn back, get stuck.

"I really screwed up today, and I'm sorry," I whisper, practicing with the spruce tree he planted when we moved in. Three years ago, it was nothing but a sprout; now it's a gangly teenaged tree, taller every time I turn around, two shoots competing to be the main trunk.

"When I said we weren't a team . . . when I said you weren't my anything . . ." Just hearing it makes me crunch my shoulders to my ears, trying to block the awfulness. "I didn't mean it the way it came out."

The tree doesn't answer.

But Tobin does.

"Didn't you, though?"

The shock of his voice hits me between the shoulder blades, startling a squeaky "Oh!" from my throat.

He's leaning in the open doorway, eyes down, mouth twisted. Curse that silent, lubricated hinge. "I think you did. I think you've been trying to tell me that for . . . for a long time now."

It's worse because he's not angry. Or sad. Or even very surprised. He just looks so, so tired. Like it would be a relief to shut his eyes for the next hundred years.

My mouth opens and closes. I'm frozen in the most important improv of my life.

And the man I rely on to give me a "yes, and" . . . isn't doing it.

"I heard everything, by the way. After your presentation, you looked like you left it all on the field. I thought maybe you might need me, so I followed you out, and . . . yeah."

"I'm so sorry, Tobe. I never meant to hurt you. If I could take it back, I would. I didn't know how else to get Craig to see *me*. I can't only be your wife. I need to be myself, too."

"Okay," he says, leaning harder against the closed door, not sounding like he agrees with me at all.

"We should . . . we should talk about what happens next. What we're going to do about the whole pitch thing."

He shakes his head slowly, every turn a hammer on my heart. "*We* don't do anything, Liz." It's not even a little bit mean. It's only final, like a referendum. Yes or no.

"We have to! It's not fair for Craig to promote me to develop your pitch." I'm purposely not picking up what he's putting down. I have to turn this scenario. It can't go where it's going.

"I didn't mean I'm not planning to challenge Craig. I meant I'm not planning to challenge him *with you*." He lets that linger in the air, settle on my skin like soot. "Lyle and I pitched this project on the condition that we own the idea. It's not Craig's to run as he sees fit. We're free to leave and find people who want to work with us."

A thin streak of bitterness colors his words, and I know he isn't talking about Craig.

"I said I'm sorry, Tobin! Please believe this wasn't about you at all. You saw what happened—Craig literally used me to get to you! The pitch competition was supposed to be about me becoming someone in my own right. I never intended to steal your proposal or your promotion! Please don't be mad at me for that."

"Liz—" He presses his lips together. The rest of what he was going to say comes out in a sharp, almost inaudible growl. I've never seen him look like this, face drawn, chin tipped skyward. He must've been outside today; he smells like a summer storm, ozone and ice wind sweeping down the mountainside, surrounded with unstable charge.

"I didn't want the fucking promotion. *I* wanted to start my own business. Lyle wanted to have a venture ready to go when his book came out, so he could capitalize on his big moment to build his name. I'm not angry with you because Craig's being an asshat. I'm not angry at all!"

He squeezes his eyes closed, letting his head fall back against the door with a deliberate thud.

"Why did you marry me, Liz? Tell me why you said yes. I need to know."

I have to nail this. Everything McHuge ever told me about

bringing myself to a scene, letting people know me, taking risks—I need it all.

"I married you because I loved you. And because I thought, um."

Even in my head, this sounds small. Petty. Unworthy.

"The summer we met, I was . . . so miserable. Physically, I could do the job you did. I wasn't the best, but I was better than some. But there was something about me that made the company put me where nobody could see me. I wasn't the kind of guide they wanted."

Autistic, I think. I can't say for certain that's what happened, but I've read the research. And I've seen it with Eleanor—kids simply decide they don't like her. It's nothing she says or does; she's never unkind and she tries hard to fit in. But kids can tell she's different. And so can adults. Amber has a hit list a mile long of people who parentsplained to her that their kids shouldn't be "forced" to have Eleanor in their playgroups.

"It was like I didn't exist. Making breakfast before anyone woke up, packing up tents and food on my own, racing down the river to set up camp and have snacks ready and drinks chilled. Clients liked not seeing me, because if they had to acknowledge how much work went into their luxury, they'd feel bad. The guides mostly stopped talking to me, too.

"And then one night, I was washing up alone. You came down to the river, picked up a pot, and started scrubbing. You didn't even ask if I needed help. You saw how lonely I was when nobody else did. You saw *me,* a person, not just an invisible chore monkey. You had better, cooler things to do, with better, cooler people. And there you were, with me.

"I didn't think I could hold on to someone like you. But I loved you too much to say no."

He nods, fingers pressed across his lips, not looking at me. It's perilously close to too late, and we both know it.

His voice, when he speaks, is all wrong. The opposite of big and confident and joyful and loud.

"Part of why I fell in love with you was because you were so *real*. You never tried to sell anyone a version of yourself that wasn't true. You weren't afraid to go your own way."

A pang of guilt slices me. He thinks I did all that because I chose to, maybe, but the truth is I didn't know how to be like everyone else. The first time I intentionally drove a stake into the ground with a flag that said "This Is Me" was this morning—and look how that turned out.

"That's not why I asked you to marry me, though. I did that because I saw you keep trying when you failed. You had this map of your life in your head, and when your route was blocked, you kept searching for other paths. You never gave up when the road got hard. And I wanted that for us. I wanted us to stick with each other. I wanted us to be a *team,* Liz. Win or lose. Together."

A Tobin montage plays in my head, from the way he looked up through his gilded eyelashes as he scrubbed that pot, to the blank look of shock five seconds after I screamed, *I'm not his anything.* And I can't bear what's coming. I can't bear it, so I don't think it, and I don't feel it, and I don't know it.

"But somewhere on the map, both of us thought we saw a better way and decided to take it without telling each other. We don't support each other or tackle problems as a team. And I keep thinking about what you said on your birthday. When you left me. We're not together, are we? We're just . . . near each other. And that's not enough."

I've been so stupid. Only now do I realize everything that's at stake.

I spent all this time trying to be someone else. Wishing I knew how to lie, when the thing that could have saved me was the truth.

I told my husband not to let people hurt him, and didn't count myself among the people he might have to protect himself from.

"I didn't want to end up like my parents," he says, like the words are tearing out of his chest. "I didn't want to leave. Or be left. I tried so hard to make our marriage perfect, I made it into something two real people couldn't live inside. I admit I made you do too much of the hard stuff, like saying no. That's on me.

"But you own this, too. You talked about being your real self and saying yes. But I've been the 'yes' this whole time. I asked you to do the book, and I played whatever part you wanted me to, and I took whatever love you could give me while I was giving you all of mine. You let me do that. And I watched you say yes to improv and friends and work and even Amber, while you broke every rule you made for us except the one where you won't say you love me. While you rejected the job you dreamed of winning because I came with it. And I feel like . . ."

The stars in his eyes. They're out. Freezing blood courses through my body.

"I feel like you said yes to everyone but me. So now I'm saying no."

I'm frostbitten for real, face tingling, fingers stuck. "Tobin. Is this . . . What is this?"

Please let it not be the end.

"This is me figuring out what's important. Taking a hard look at what this relationship *is,* instead of what I wanted it to be. And deciding what to do about it. And you should, too."

He scrubs one rough, beautiful hand across his eyebrows before turning away. "I need time to think. I'll find someplace else to stay tonight."

"No. No, don't, I'll . . . you shouldn't have to move out. I'm already packed. I'll go." Where, I don't know.

"You sure?" So polite, like I'm a stranger.

"Yeah. It's, uh. Not a problem."

"Thank you. I appreciate it." The door closes as silently as it opened. I hear the lock slide firmly into place behind him.

This time, he lets me walk away without a fight.

Chapter Twenty-Six

Brilliant improvisers step willingly into the void of the future.

—*Impro for Storytellers*

I pull into the Little Theater's parking lot with no memory of how I got here. I shouldn't have driven anywhere in this state, but I couldn't think of anywhere else to go.

Or maybe there's nowhere else I *can* go.

My brain has powered down to essential life functions. I can't process anything—work, my maybe autistic self, Tobin.

Tobin.

Improv is the only thing I can control. So here I am.

With a capacity of just a hundred people, the Little Theater is supposed to be cozy. From the wings, however, the shadows in one hundred tipped-up red velvet seats scowl at me. Backstage looks complicated and technical, ropes and cords snaking everywhere. It looks like I should know what I'm doing, and I really, really don't.

Onstage, McHuge supervises warm-up activities. He does a double take when he spots me lurking, then jogs over with a light step.

He considers me for a moment, arms crossed. With classic McHuge understatement, he says, "A lot happened today."

"If you don't want me here, I'll go." I can't meet his eyes. "I'm sorry for today. And I understand if you'd rather not, um. Do anything at all with me ever again."

"Whoa, little bud. From what I saw, you got set up. We all did. You and my friend for sure have some shit to work out. But I did write a whole book about good people who have the same problem. And I know you're a good person, Liz. You're always welcome."

The rush of gratitude is so intense, I have to close my eyes and swallow. "Thanks, McHuge. For everything." After an awkward pause, I add, "Your book is great."

"I know," he says. "But thanks for saying so. Are you here for the showcase? It could be a lot, on top of . . . the other thing."

"I'm okay." *Breathe in. Breathe out.* I just want to get through this show, find someplace to sleep where not every adult in the house is furious with me, and wake up yesterday before any of this happened.

"Right on. I trust you to judge your own energy. But glue yourself to the wall if that's what you need."

I follow him onstage. A quick glance reveals our group is the loser group.

The ten members of the Tuesday Teals wear bright blue shirts with their name done in The Second City's font. They're hugging each other and throwing themselves into silly stunts with abandon.

Across the stage, the Saturday Night Specials do a group cheer based on a Nickelback cover, showing a scary amount of teeth while screaming, "Saturday! Saturday! Saturday night's all right!" They have custom T-shirts, too, in gunmetal with acid-green lettering.

The Friday Night No-Names didn't get the wardrobe memo. At least we agreed to wear black. Like mimes, now that I think of it. The stage is backed by a plain black wall where the players stand when they're not in the game. We're going to look like disembodied heads up there.

Time to lean into the suck, I guess. Fail joyfully.

Or just fail.

David doesn't look happy to see me, but Sharon and Béa open a place in the warm-up circle. We're playing Zoom, the improv equivalent of full-body exercise: engage your physicality, pay attention to your fellow players, stay in the moment.

"Youuuuu," Jason drawls, throwing an imaginary ball to Béa. She catches it, then chucks it to David with perfect form, repeating, "Yyyouuuuu," in the slow, exaggerated way of the game.

My heart pulls tight, fibers frayed to breaking. If Tobin and I had played this game, he would've thrown to me every time, and I would've dropped it at least half those times.

I thought I was so smart. I thought improv was the secret to becoming, or at least faking, the person I wanted to be.

Instead, I learned nothing that improv tried to teach me. I left my heart in the past, jammed my head into the future, and didn't see what I had in the present.

"Liz!" David snaps his fingers. "You!" He points to the imaginary ball, which has fallen at my feet.

I've abandoned the present yet again. "Oh! Uh . . . oh. Sorry. Yyyouuuu," I say, picking it up and serving a soft underhand to Sharon.

It's time to stop making excuses and start living right here, right now.

I've messed up my marriage, probably beyond repair. I got promoted by a boss who doesn't see me any more clearly now than he did eight weeks ago. I'm at the beginning of a long, difficult, expensive path to seeking a formal autism diagnosis.

I don't even know where I'm sleeping tonight.

If ever there was a time when the past is over and the future is a blank, it's now. There's no contest tonight, and no prizes. I'm not doing this so someone else will want me.

I'm doing it for me. Speaking up and taking social risks are harder for me than for some, but I can't let fear of failure run my life. Maybe I'll always want to go home early from the party, but for me the victory is wanting to be at the party.

It's a win if I want to be myself.

"All right, kids. Audience is here. Time to head backstage." McHuge has special fancy braids in his beard tonight, styled like Celtic knotwork and fastened with soft twine. This might be his professional performance look. If so, he's rocking it.

"Remember, these are your people and they love yo—" McHuge breaks off, a look of shock and longing transforming his easygoing demeanor. He clears his throat, his face flushing an adorable pink under the freckles. "We'd better go."

I look around McHuge's shoulders, curious to see whether Tina Fey has walked in or something.

It's ten times better than that. Stellar's marching down the aisle, right to the front row.

New friends are great. But when you've just flushed your entire life, you need someone who's loved you for a long time to catch you as you fling yourself off the stage.

"Stellar," I whisper. "You came. Thank you, thank you, thank you. You don't know how much I needed you."

She hugs me tight with her tiny ripped arms. "Jesus, you're shaking. Are you all right? We can pull the rip cord right now."

"No, I need to do it. I'll tell you everything after the show. Just, thank you. I can't believe you flew back for this."

She makes our squished-up face. "I would totally fly in for your show, babe, but I'm mostly here because I quit my job."

"Stellar! Your dream job. Oh no!"

"I should've told you. It just felt wrong to complain, when you would've given your left tit for that promotion."

I know the pain of not telling the person you want to pour your heart out to. "You can tell me anything. No matter what."

"I will. But Lyle's gonna combust if you don't get backstage."

"Wait. You call McHuge *Lyle*?" I thought the only person who did that was . . . I stomp that thought.

"Long story. *Go*."

In the Friday No-Names' dressing room, everyone's in various stages of breakdown. David pretends to be chill while checking his phone every twenty seconds. Jason hops, head down, eyes closed, humming; Béa watches him, fascinated. I'm toxically overdosing on every known stress hormone, second-guessing this decision every minute and a half.

Surprisingly, Sharon is worst off. She ducks out of sight of David and Jason, pulling a tailored black T-shirt from her Birkin bag before peeling off the one she's wearing and dropping it on the floor with a sodden thump.

"Hot flash," she mutters, wriggling into the new shirt. "Ah, who am I kidding. I considered crashing my car on the way here to have a reason not to show up. My husband and teenager are in the audience. Somebody sedate me."

McHuge knocks a cheery rhythm. "Good news, citizens of improv—the Fridays are up first!"

Sharon puts her head between her knees. Jason's humming turns to moaning. I'm floating in another galaxy as we troop toward the stage like we're going to our execution.

McHuge stops us in the wings. "You're all picking up nervous vibes right now. I've been where you are. I've felt what you're feeling."

"You have *not*," Sharon retorts.

"I have emotions, Sharon. I'm not a machine," McHuge says, straight-faced. We burst into fear-tinged giggles.

"It won't be as bad as you think. Remember, the past is ego. The future is pride. Stay humble; stay in the present."

McHuge is managing the audience for us tonight, since none of us have ever seen it done. He's as easy onstage as he is in class. Although maybe this is hard work, and he's skilled at making it look like nothing. The same way Tobin—no.

"The game is freeze tag. We need audience suggestions for a relationship between two people," he calls, eyes roving across the many empty seats.

A competition breaks out among the audience members as to who can be the most silent. McHuge told us they'd be shy—it's their first improv show, too.

"Friends," calls a woman's voice. Stellar, waving from front-row center.

"Friends," McHuge repeats, a funny catch in his voice.

"Enemies," comes a shout from the back.

"One-night stand!" Stellar retorts. McHuge's mouth goes weird.

"Couple getting divorced!" yells the heckler in the back. The word leaves a deep, ugly ache under my breastbone.

"Divorce it is," McHuge says.

The Fridays shuffle our feet, uncertain. Conflict makes bad improv. Why would McHuge pick such a loaded topic?

McHuge launches the scene as a man waiting for his turn in divorce court. The past starts yelling in my left ear, the future in my right.

Breathe in. Breathe out. Stay in the present.

David pushes off the wall first, joining the scene as McHuge's lawyer, contradicting McHuge's every bid. The cringe factor is off the charts.

The rest of us hug the wall. Make love to the wall. We live here now. We won't leave to join a sagging, flailing scene like this one. Even McHuge looks panicky, his gaze returning again and again to the front row.

"Freeze!" Béa steps forward, tagging David out of the scene to recruit McHuge into a slapstick search for her pet boa constrictor, who escaped into the ducts during a supervised transfer of custody. She gets the first laugh of the night when she hangs off a chair and pretends to fall headfirst into a vent, legs thrashing.

A surge of exhilaration grips me. Maybe this will—

"Freeze!" David tags out McHuge. Béa manages not to grimace. Mostly.

"What seems to be the problem, ma'am?" David swaggers toward Béa. He's excellent at playing himself. But he's broken one of improv's biggest rules: don't ask questions.

"Um . . . it seems my pet snake is missing."

"That's what she said!" David booms, exultant.

The crowd doesn't laugh. David went for the joke, instead of giving Béa a "yes, and." It's killing the scene and the trust, like McHuge warned us it would.

I'm betting everyone on the wall is thinking what I'm thinking: tag David out, and he'll tag himself right back in and push the scene off the same cliff. Tag Béa out, and end up locked in a scene with Dick Head.

"We should call Animal Control," Béa tries, smile faltering.

David bursts out laughing, violating the rule that to be funny, improv has to be played straight. "Like I told you, ma'am—that's what *she* said!"

The audience fidgets audibly. David's shoulders lose their

broad confidence. He's failing, and the audience understands he's not doing it joyfully. He's not okay, so they're not okay.

I don't *not* feel good, watching David realize the bro code he relies on at the office doesn't apply here.

This would be the perfect time to let him take himself down.

But if David falls, the Fridays go down with him. I'll doom myself to staying where I am, when what I want most is to get off this fucking wall I've been on my whole life.

As long as I'm on the wall, no one can reject me. But no one can see me for who I am, either.

Improv isn't the solution to all my problems. It wouldn't be right for every autistic person, or every neurotypical person, either. But it's pushing me out of my comfort zone in the best way.

Can I let myself have this? I think . . . yes. Because the person I need to say yes to, before everyone else, is me. If I fail, I'll go down joyfully, with everything I have.

"Freeze!" I'm stepping forward before I can think. Béa scampers to the wall when I tag her, practically kissing it in gratitude.

I shoulder through an invisible crowd to David, putting a beer into his outstretched hand. "So. He left you. Drinks are on me."

David seems relieved I turned the scene. He quaffs the beer in one go, wiping his lip and signaling for another. Sharon peels off the wall as a world-weary barkeep who pulls David another pint and examines the high counter pointedly for her missing tip.

A ripple stirs the audience. It's small, but a shot of warmth blooms in my heart.

The Fridays are doing it.

"I can't wait to forget about my marriage." David downs his second pint.

"Really?" I say, surprised. "I wish I could remember mine."

The audience guffaws, laughing even harder when I stare at them in slack-jawed surprise.

"Freeze!" Jason taps me out.

I wasn't trying to be funny. I was only sharing Marijke's truth, now my truth. So many of my memories happened with Tobin. I don't want to forget those years. I don't want to lose our love, even if I made mistakes. Even if we both did.

The truth is a funny thing.

At the end of our ten minutes, the Fridays gratefully accept luke-warm applause. The Saturdays don't clap as we tumble into the wings. Sharon's expression promises them we're more talented at violence than we are at improv.

There's a minute of ecstatic full-body hugging and muted squeals between Jason, Béa, Sharon, and me, while David tries to chuck everyone on the shoulder.

I was afraid to be seen, and I showed myself anyway. I'm exhausted to the point of dizziness, almost high on the amazement of not having died onstage. Wild.

We spy on the Saturdays from the wings. "They're better than us," Béa says.

"Nah, we warmed up the audience for them. And that horseback skiing bit was totally rehearsed," Jason scoffs.

"They better not be at the Kraken afterward. Or else." Sharon makes murder eyebrows. "Everyone's gonna be there, right?"

I join the chorus of yeses, even though it feels wrong not to be going home. It feels like my mistakes compound with every second I'm not knocking on Tobin's door.

But he asked for time. What can I do but say yes?

There's much more applause for the Saturdays than for us. I join in, but Sharon grabs my hand. "Shut it down, Liz. We're not here to clap for them when they didn't clap for us. Fuck being classy, I'm googling how to slash a tire."

Sharon's hardly proper, but her straight spine and excellent diction, combined with threats and profanity, make Béa scream.

The theater explodes into sound just as the Tuesdays take the stage, an eruption of unsilenceable shrillness. Every phone in the audience howls, lighting up as people pull them from pockets and purses.

In the front row, Stellar cries out.

"Liz," she screams, bolting out of her seat. "Liz Lewis! Does anyone know where Liz Lewis is?"

I push through the stunned Tuesdays to the front of the stage. "Stellar?"

She turns her phone. "AMBER ALERT" flashes at the top of the screen.

"It's Eleanor."

Chapter Twenty-Seven

The "group mind" happens when players pay such close attention to each other—hearing, remembering, and respecting everything—it feels like they share one brain. Brilliance is often the result, in partnership as in improv.

—*The Second Chances Handbook*

Nights are cold in the mountains, no matter what the season.

Knowing I need to feel useful, Jason lets me arrange silvery thermal blankets at the first aid station, which consists of a card table, some basic supplies, and thermoses of coffee donated by heartsick neighbors. He's here to patch up cuts and scratches sustained by searchers. Any serious injuries will go to the paramedic crew, whose rig is standing by behind the taped-off perimeter.

Standing by for Eleanor.

My insides drop like I'm trapped on an endless monster coaster ride whenever I think her name.

Mom and Dad booked the first flight tomorrow morning. They made me swear to text them every hour, whether we have news or not. Amber—I can't even imagine what she's going through. Her puffy, tear-reddened face presses against the uniformed chest of a search and rescue official.

It feels bad not to be someone Amber would turn to, but that's not a role I can take on without her permission.

Stellar pops over to give me a long, rocking embrace. "You sure you want me to go? I can stay, if you need someone."

"No, go. Eleanor needs you more than I do."

"Okay. I'll see you soon. With Eleanor."

She jogs toward the expanding mass of searchers. I swallow a painful amount of gratitude at the sight of all the locals suiting up, many of them guides from West by North.

McHuge clips a two-way radio to his waist next to a coil of rope; Stellar adjusts some borrowed, too-big gear on her petite frame. He tentatively reaches out to tighten her headlamp, fingers careful to touch only the straps. Nearby, Stéphane and Béa whisper in rapid French, showering each other with reassuring touches disguised as gear checks.

And Tobin. He's here, like I knew he would be.

He dips his chin my way, mouth tight, before joining the rough circle of climbers and skiers and trekkers in battered boots and weather-resistant layers. They all know the risks of this territory in the dark.

Eleanor, in the dark.

My stomach rolls over into another dead drop. Amber put her to bed at eight, then found the bed empty and her sandals and windbreaker gone at nine. It's ten thirty now, the temperature ten degrees above freezing and falling.

Because our street backs onto a wooded hillside, the search and rescue team thinks she's most likely lost in the trees, curled up somewhere to wait until morning.

It's going to be difficult work, covering the rocky, uneven

ground. There are countless hidey holes a kid could seek refuge in—hollow logs, shallow caves, cedars with low, sheltering branches. I try not to think about ravines and drop-offs and loose rocks.

Searchers pair off and head out, their calls of "Eleanor" growing fainter as they move farther afield. I pour coffee and hand out energy bars and don't scream as I think about the fresh bite to the air, and the mountain lion that stalked a jogger last summer, and mama grizzlies with curious cubs.

Tobin's the odd one out after everyone else pairs up, standing by to help another team.

I always loved watching him work—he's so focused and joyful. Wholly in the moment, no matter what he's doing. Tonight is different, because it's Eleanor, but also because he's careful not to look over here. He doesn't have a smile for anyone, not even the cute paramedic who asks me for two cups of coffee, then gives him one.

We've hurt each other so much, Tobin and I. Maybe too much. We're stuck in conflict, telling each other "no," not able to move ourselves forward.

It doesn't make good improv, and it doesn't make a good marriage.

"Liz." Jason tugs a silver foil packet from my hand. "You've rearranged the blankets six times. Take a break, yeah? I can handle things for a bit."

"Yeah, no, for sure." I'm twitchy, filled with destructive, fearful energy. There's no possible way I can rest.

I'll make sure the house is okay. Let the dog out.

Kris Kristofferson whines and shivers inside the front door. "Hey, girl," I whisper, even though there's no one I could wake up. Kris wiggles away when I try to hug her. It's for the best; if I'd been able to bury my face in her fur, there's no telling when I would've stopped crying. I need Yeti for cuddles.

A quick scan of the main floor turns up no evidence Yeti's made it home. Although if anyone would know where he is, it's Kris.

"Where's the cat? Find the cat. Find him," I tell Kris, hopeful. She prances in a circle, ears up. It's impossible to tell whether she knows the cat isn't here, or she's choosing to disregard commands from the least important member of her pack.

"Come on, girl." Defeated, I grab her leash from the hook by the door. A walk will do us good, away from the flashing lights and radio static.

The night would be beautiful under any other circumstances. The wind sighs through the treetops, stars showing off in the moonless sky. After a couple of blocks, Kris settles down and stops pulling, and I feel calm enough to type a list into my phone, Kris's leash looped precariously around one arm. I hope all the squirrels are safe in the treetops, because this arrangement won't last if the dog makes a break for it, but the list gives me a sense of purpose.

Get Mom and Dad's bedroom ready. Grocery shopping—vegetarian for Dad.

Find somewhere to board Kris.

On second thought, I delete that. Amber and Kris would rather be together.

Find reliable friend to walk Kris.

That's a tough one. Someone close to the family, good with dogs, who can be trusted not to ask painful questions.

Kris and I round the corner into the gauntlet of people and vehicles. Tobin's chatting to Jason, which, oof. Guess he waited until I was gone.

I try to give Tobin space, but the dog catches his familiar scent. One pull on my absurd leash configuration, and she's bounding toward him.

"Sorry. She got away, and I . . . Sorry."

Tobin looks up from giving the dog an energetic neck rub. "It's okay. You want me to take her around the block so you can stay near?"

"Thanks, I just took her. But . . ." I shouldn't ask Tobin for anything ever again. He should never have to say yes to me. Or no.

But if there's one thing he is, it's a reliable friend. "Could you take her out tomorrow?"

He doesn't hesitate. "Sure. Morning and evening, or add a nooner in there as well?"

"Twice would be great. Three times would be amazing, if you can."

"No prob. You want to bring Yeti back to the house for now?"

I don't deserve any of his kindness. I'm weak for letting myself have it anyway. "Thanks, but Eleanor will want Yeti when she gets home. She adores that old himb—"

I blink. The cat. Eleanor.

"Tobin," I say urgently. "Where does Yeti like to hide, outside?"

He blinks back, face pulling into alert lines, waiting for me to finish.

"Yeti got out earlier. What if Eleanor tried to find him?"

Tobin grimaces. "I don't know. He used to like sleeping outside, but lately, not so much. My guess is he's at someone's house, drinking warm milk and living the high life."

I shake my head. "Remember that cut on his chest? He was gone for two days, and we checked with every neighbor. So there's at least one place. A small space, that he has to squeeze in or out of."

Tobin's eyes meet mine. "We can look."

Tobin checks in with the search coordinator. Two minutes later, we're knocking on the first door, asking to search outbuildings, wood piles, porches—anywhere a cat might find a dry place to bed down.

There's a disturbing amount of scuttling under some of the

porches. Kris is having the time of her life, sniffing around a zillion places she's normally not allowed to explore. I shouldn't have brought her; she's got a well-documented history of pushing skunks' boundaries and finding out whether porcupines taste as spicy as they look.

Tobin searches steadily, but every empty tool bin and abandoned playhouse adds to my conviction that this is pointless. The police already went door to door. Surely neighbors have checked their own properties.

My voice, thin from fear and grief, gets hoarse from shouting questions no one answers.

"We aren't going to find her, are we? Eleanor!" I scream at a ramshackle chicken coop, pulling fruitlessly on the nailed-shut door. There were chickens here a few years ago. But the house changed hands, and neither the new owner nor their tenants ever bothered to get more birds or knock down the coop.

"Maybe we won't. But someone will. This is helping, Liz. You know Eleanor better than anyone except Amber. You know what might pull her to go somewhere. It's a good idea." He tugs at a window.

Kris bounds back and forth, eyes big, sniffing like crazy. The coop stinks, even years later. She pulls me partway around an airy part of the enclosure, barking at a spot where the flimsy wire is torn, sharp ends pointing inward like a funnel-shaped fish trap.

I wouldn't be surprised if a few wild things had squeezed in to check out the potential dinner situation. It's wide enough for a good-sized raccoon or even a determined cougar. The wire would cost a laceration or two on the way out, though. I play my flashlight across the opening. Sure enough, rusty streaks coat one particularly wicked point low down.

Right where a cat's chest would be, if that cat were old and stiff and not great at jumping.

My lungs fill and fill with surprise and wild hope. I intend to use all that air to call Tobin, but what comes out of my mouth instead is a primal scream. "*Eleanor!* Eleanor, are you in here?"

Tobin comes skidding around the corner. "Did you find something?"

"The smell! Yeti, when he came home with that cut—he smelled awful! He's been here. Eleanor!" I tear at the wire.

"Eleanor!" Tobin bellows, easing my fingers away from the stabby metal, then pulling his camping multi-tool from his pocket and flipping open the wire cutters. "Does she sleep any lighter these days?" *Snick snick* goes the tool, wire springing apart with each calm, deliberate cut.

"She could nap through an air-raid siren. Amber worries the smoke alarm won't wake her."

"Okay, then we have to go in. We'll also have to come out safely. Let's take our time and do it right." His calm is infectious. He's got the bottom and one side of a smallish doorway opened, and he moves across the top with steady competence while I point the light where he needs it.

In a flash, he's got three sides open. He bends the wire toward the outside of the cage, twisting the ends into the rest of the mesh so the door stays open.

"Clever," I say, tying Kris's leash to a corner post. "Eleanor! Eleanor, honey!"

The coop stinks of rotting wood and the ghosts of poultry past. I charge across the outer enclosure, fetching up against an inner door that won't budge no matter how hard I push. No way can I fit through the low chicken door. But Eleanor could. "Tobin!"

He's beside me in a second, shoving the door so hard the building sways, and then, humiliatingly, pulling it open with no effort at all and holding it while I run through.

The small room has roosting shelves at various heights, some still holding boxes with nest-shaped mounds inside. Moldy hay squishes under our feet, releasing a powdery miasma of rot. I whirl around, frantic, beaming my light into all the corners.

"Eleanor!"

Nothing. Nothing but manure-soaked wood and empty feed sacks and a tetanus shot in both our futures, based on the pain in my hands.

She's not here.

I lean forward, hands on my knees, sucking down damp, spore-filled air, trying to ease the crushing pain underneath my breastbone.

We stand there, me bent over, Tobin awkwardly turned away, not making a move to come any nearer. We've never worked together more closely, or been further apart. Neither of us speaks. There's only the wind and the trees, talking to each other.

Into the silence comes a rhythmic clicking sound, a rusty, clunky purr.

Yeti uncurls himself from the back of the highest corner shelf, picking his way delicately to the edge.

"Hey, buddy," Tobin murmurs. Testing his weight first, he steps on the bottom shelf, ducking to avoid bumping his head on the ceiling. He hands Yeti down to me, then reaches toward the half-hidden back of the shelf for a bundle that looks like crumpled burlap in the dim light.

". . . Uncle Tobin?" the bundle says sleepily. "Is it morning?"

I'm crying.

Tobin carries her out, and I call it in, and there's a big blur of flashing lights, and Amber sobbing, and the ambulance pulling out with my sister and niece aboard.

I guess it'd be all right for me to sleep at Amber's tonight. Considering. But Sharon said she's a night owl, and to text her if I need anything.

And I need a place to stay. Stellar, too, if I've guessed right and she was planning to crash with me.

Tobin walks me back to the house, leading a proud Kris Kristofferson. I carry Yeti, who's very content to snooze in my arms. He absolutely reeks, and now I do, too. I'm too tired to have the shampoo fight with him. Would it be so wrong to Febreze him, just till tomorrow?

"There's no possible way to thank you enough for tonight. Oh, Tobe, your hands." He's scratched and bleeding far worse than me. "I'll get Band-Aids."

This pause is so awkward, with him shifting from foot to foot, not meeting my eyes.

I step back, stumbling a little. "Sorry, I wasn't thinking. Jason can take a look."

He looks down for a moment, then up at me, eyes like blue lightning shocking my heart. "I'd appreciate it, actually. Jason's probably busy with takedown, if he hasn't left already."

Ah. Right. I tell the wild burst of hope in my chest to mind its own goddamn business. It isn't that Tobin wants me to touch him. He's being considerate of Jason.

I stick Yeti in his carrier for smell reasons while Tobin washes.

After scrubbing my very sketchy, post-chicken arms, I take his damp hands in mine, resisting the urge to dawdle over my inspection. I dab on antibiotic cream, then pick out Band-Aids to stretch over the deeper scratches.

"Liz."

"Yeah?" Peeling open the last bandage is a convenient way to keep my eyes off his face.

"You taking that promotion?"

I fumble the packaging. "Um, I haven't had time to think about it. Craig asked me to save face at the awards ceremony, and I did, but . . . I wish I'd told him no. That was a screwed-up stunt he pulled."

"You should take it." His fingers flex in mine.

"I . . . What?"

"I watched you tonight. And I was thinking, I'm glad you won. You think of things other people don't. The way you put facts together is totally unique. Craig made the right choice, even if it was for the wrong reasons. You're just what this industry needs."

He takes the last Band-Aid and sticks it over an ugly abrasion on my knuckle. "Anyway. I wanted to tell you, I'm, uh. I'm rooting for you."

His hands slide away.

He tries to smile. It's a heart-smashing six out of ten, his worst effort ever. But his eyes are on mine, and there's not a shred of doubt that he sees me.

He *sees* me.

And he's pushing me away.

I love him. And now—right now—is the only moment I'll hold him and my dream in my hands at the same time.

I want this to last forever, but it doesn't.

"I'm rooting for you, too. It's such an amazing thing you're doing with McHuge. Your company's going to be wildly successful. I would've given a lot to work at a place like that."

He makes a rueful face. "I know."

I want to throw something. How many times will my heart take another hit after I've told it to stay the hell down?

"I'm sorry, Tobe. For everything."

I'm so, so sorry. I did all the things I mentally accused him of doing. Clammed up when things went wrong, instead of trying to fix them. Failed to see who he was, and who he'd become.

Made him chase me, instead of working on a relationship where we chose to walk toward each other.

"Don't be. I shouldn't have talked you into the book. I'm learning I need to let people go if they want to leave. Let *you* go."

"No," I whisper. "We planned one more scenario. We're not finished."

"It's okay, Liz. We're sad, but it's okay. We'll be all right."

He's on his feet, and I'm flooded with panic.

"You don't have to go."

"We both know I do. I'll see you, Liz."

All I can think, as I watch him walk away, is that I failed. It isn't until well after the door closes behind him that it hits me.

I still have a chance to fail joyfully.

Chapter Twenty-eight

SCENARIO 7: THE GRAND GESTURE

Partner relationships are deeply affected by the people around us, for better and for worse.

At the most important moments in a relationship, partners need to focus on each other, without the distraction of other people.

For your final scenario, create an imaginary place where you can be alone together. Visualize yourselves walking away from the people who want to influence your characters' actions for their own purposes (actually do this, if you like—it could be fun to start the scenario in separate locations!). Then walk toward each other. When you've left all the outside voices behind and it's just the

two (or more) of you, what do you want to tell your part-
ner(s)? What do they need to hear from you?

—*The Second Chances Handbook*

It's not easy putting together a romantic costume at nine o'clock
on a Sunday morning.

Unless you're a guest of Sharon Keller-Yakub.

I'm rifling through my third Keller-Yakub closet, which is saying
a lot because these things are huge. From Sharon's: wide belt and
loose white shirt (which I hope fares better than the last one, because this one cost about a hundred times more). From Kareem's:
waxed canvas coat, big on me but *such* Regency-era greatcoat vibes.

Sharon's nineteen-year-old daughter (she of the yellow dress)
left early this morning for her job at a non-Keller workplace, which
vexes her mom to no end. But her hips and boobs are roughly the
same size as mine, and she's on board with today's fashion mission as long as she gets the photo rights for her socials.

From deep in the custom shelves, Stellar hands me pair after
pair of black pants.

"I can't tell the difference between any of these."

Stellar shrugs. "I'm no help; you've seen what I wear. Pick a
pair and go with it, I guess?"

I smooth a nervous hand over my hair, which I've styled a
bit puffy, tying it low at my neck in a reasonable approximation
of English style circa 1850. My brown ponytail, pulled over one
shoulder, shines warmly against the matte canvas lapels.

It won't be perfect—not like the costumes Tobin put together.
But I want to come as close as I can.

I want him to know I've thought about it, and worked on it,
and tried hard to give him as much magic, and as much *yes,* as I
could.

"These could win hearts," Stellar says dryly, handing me a pair of tan suede boots festooned with straps and hardware. They look like the love child of a one-night stand between an English saddle and a vat of glitter, which is a pretty reasonable compromise for boots I'm getting for free.

"I hope so. But there's a decent chance I'll come back single, dressed in period costume, not on Halloween."

Stellar emerges from the closet to flop onto the bed. "You're using your freak-out voice again."

"I am not."

"Let's take a minute anyway."

I throw myself facedown beside her. "This is unhinged. I'm terrified."

Stellar's voice is so full of love. "Did I tell you how proud I am of what you've done?"

My head comes up. "You are?"

"I am. I wasn't an early fan of your evil plan, but I've never seen you so full of *life,* Liz. You sort of . . . glowed, on that stage. You're afraid today will be a huge fail, and you're not backing down. I quit my job because of you."

I sit up fast. "Stellar. You didn't."

"I did. I saw you going ovaries-to-the-wall for what you wanted and I thought, how can I give my thirties to a job that's eating my soul? I want to be stronger than that. I want to believe I'll be okay, no matter what. Same way I believe you'll be okay."

I'm emotional, and I haven't even left the bedroom. "That's very improv of you."

She rolls her eyes. "I know. I'm surrounded by theater kids, and now I've got improv all over me. Get dressed; let's see how everything works together."

"Everybody decent?" Sharon peeks around the door.

"What do you think?" Stellar turns me toward Sharon and the mirror, smiling.

I look great. Not just the costume, but the look of uncertainty, and bravery, and hope.

But it's not enough. "Something's missing."

"Chest hair," Stellar suggests. "I have an eyeliner pencil you can use."

"I know." Sharon takes off her necklace and loops it around my neck. "Nope. You're too pale for silver. You need gold." She rummages in her daughter's hanging jewelry organizer, handing me a pair of abstract gold dangle earrings before fastening a delicate gold chain at my nape, arranging the quarter-sized medallion so it rests between my collarbones. "Perfect."

It's lovely, but it needs . . . more. This has to be big. The biggest. The prompt said I have to think about what he needs to hear from me, and if I mess up the words, I need my costume to do some talking.

My text alert goes off. "Ugh, Amber," I say before I can engage my filter.

> Can we talk? I'm outside.

> I told you where I am as a courtesy. I wasn't inviting you over.

"You want me to get rid of her?" Stellar asks, drawing a threatening finger across her neck.

"I'll be fine. Back in five."

I jingle up the stairs in my cowboy sparkle boots and duck out the front door. I don't have a ton of time, since I told Tobin I'd meet him at ten.

Well. I didn't exactly tell him. I sent him a text last night.

> I know you wanted time to think, and Friday night screwed that up already. Just wanted to say, if you want to do the scenario tomorrow, then I want to, too. You don't have to reply. I'll come over at ten. If you're not home, I'll take that as a no.

Amber cranes her neck as I close the door behind me. I'd be curious, too, if I were outside Sharon Keller-Yakub's spectacular home, a jewel box of light waterfalling down the side of a ravine. It's very California; Sharon said some famous architect designed it in the seventies. That's when this neighborhood was developed by investors who, hoping to win a bid for the Winter Olympics, turned Grey Tusk Mountain from a backcountry secret into what would become the top-rated ski resort on the continent.

There's a lot of money in Grey Tusk, but this street is where people live when they have the outrageous funds required to commission one-of-a-kind houses and maintain them as they age. It's Downton Abbey, mountain edition.

"Hi, Amber. This needs to be quick. I'm going out."

"Mom and Dad are asking why you haven't been over."

Amber's subdued. She uncharacteristically has said nothing about my outfit. Yesterday, she left a bunch of messages on my phone, at first ecstatic with relief and gratitude, then confused after my sole reply was a brief request for Eleanor updates. Then businesslike: Please call, we need to talk.

"I bet."

She blows out a breath. "Thank you. For Eleanor. You were the last person I expected to find her."

"Amber . . ." I turn to go, not up for any of her backhanded compliments.

"I wasn't a good sister to you, back then."

"What?" My rush of surprise feels like a dream where I'm looking up at the ocean's surface, running out of air, and suddenly I discover I can breathe underwater.

Her lips tremble, squeeze, tremble again. Amber's a nurse. She's seen it all, and she *never* cracks. "I hated Mark for bailing after Eleanor's diagnosis. But I was glad, too. El didn't need anyone who wouldn't love her and advocate for her unconditionally. So, we came home.

"One day, Mom dug out some old photo albums, and Eleanor got so excited about this one picture. *That me, that me,* over and over. It was you and me, outside the art classroom at the community center. You know how El smiles when she's stressed, but still trying to do what people expect? You were doing that, too."

I know the photo she means. We were five and eight, maybe. Amber's giving the camera a saucy smirk. I'm showing lots of teeth, less like a smile than an animal backed into a corner.

"That night, I looked through the albums. That time you were so into your book, you didn't notice Dad had built a fort of kitchen chairs around the couch. You on your first solo canoe, frowning until Mom told you to smile. Your first day of high school . . ." She takes a breath. "And I'm pretending I don't know you because I don't want to be seen with my weird little sister."

"Not helpful, Amber."

She spreads her hands wide. "What do you want, you were a weird little kid. But I didn't have to be a shit about it. There's all these pictures at my birthday parties, and you're hiding in the background, on the outside looking in. It's like a Lewis family *Where's Waldo,* except Waldo needs her sister to get her head out of her ass. You needed someone to love you unconditionally. I wish that would've been me, when we were kids. I wish that would've been me on your wedding day, too. I'm sorry it wasn't."

"Oh, Am-bam." I reach for her hand. I don't remember the last time I called her that nickname, but it feels right.

"After I figured it out, I way overcompensated. I had no right to think I knew better than you how to run your life. As you showed me," she says, rueful. "You have a way with solving problems. It's a gift." She pins me with a direct look. "And it's why you're going to kick ass at your new job."

Well. Maybe. I haven't answered Craig's emails yet.

"Can you make it for dinner tonight? Eleanor would love to see you." There's a note in her voice I haven't heard before. The respect grown siblings show each other, maybe?

"I'll come tonight. But after that, you and I need time and distance to make a fresh start, without the pressure of Mom and Dad's expectations. We both need to take responsibility for our share of the damage."

I should know. I only hope it's not too late to repair the damage I've done to the one I love. We're alike in that way, Amber and I—we both had to lose people to find out how much we needed them.

A subtle crease pops up between her eyebrows. "Not too much distance. Eleanor still needs you."

Somehow it's reassuring that Amber's still Amber, bossing me around—or trying. "I know. I need her, too. See you tonight."

I step back inside. My hand stings; when I unclench it, gold gleams from my palm. I'm going to lose these if I don't put them in right now.

The left one winks at me from the mahogany-framed foyer mirror as I slide the hook through my earlobe. The tangle of golden lines looks kind of like a horse.

I pause, the other earring halfway to my right ear.

That's it.

I clump down to the kitchen, jingling in double time. "Sharon— huge favor. Did you keep any of your kids' old toys?"

She laughs. "They're nineteen and twenty-one and they still flip when I threaten to throw out a single comic book. Bins are in the basement; it's all yours."

"Thank you. And also. I know you're not formally my mentor, and you work for the competition, and this is a big ask, so you can totally say no. . . ." I'm babbling. *Breathe in, breathe out.* "I need help finding another job."

Her smile is so evil, and so good. "I thought you'd never ask."

When I pull up to the house, Tobin's truck isn't there.

Maybe McHuge borrowed it again. Maybe Tobin's racing home from the farmers' market with unnecessary seedlings, worried he'll miss me.

Or maybe not. Panic swirls darkly, ink in water.

Next door, Marijke straightens up, holding a trowel and a crate of flowers. From the other side of the yard, Renata waves a dirt-smeared hand. Blooming annuals in shades of pink and peach dot the black earth, a stack of empty compostable plant containers leaning against the painted stairs.

If they're surprised to see me dressed like a hero in a historical romance, they're not more surprised than I am to see them together. Tor must have talked a good game to get out of that jam.

"Marijke. Renata." My boots jingle up the sidewalk like it's the O.K. Corral. "Nice day for gardening. Tobin didn't happen to tell you when he'd be back?"

Marijke's sporting a suspiciously wide grin. "Tobin's gone out, my dear."

My steps slow, then stop, but what I really want is to go backward. Put this whole sequence in reverse, like *Sliding Doors.* Back myself into my car, rewind all the way to April. I want a second chance at this timeline, so I can learn the hard, true lessons I needed, but faster. In time to save Tobin and me.

"He's at the high school."

Crass of her to be so cheerful. She knows what it means that I've showed up in costume.

"Strange place to go. He said it had the biggest field in town."

"He said what?"

"He said he needed a field. Something about space for walking."

Walk toward each other. That's McHuge's line, from *The Second Chances Handbook.*

It's a bad idea to let all this hope run roughshod over me. If this isn't what I think it is, I'm going to be so ruined. "Gotta go," I blurt.

"Liz! Wait." She produces a folded square of paper. "This is for you."

I unfold it in a hurry, trying to get the politeness over with so I can go.

I have to reread the word "Zwetschgenkuchen," written in Marijke's own tall, slanted handwriting, three times to believe it.

The precious family plum cake recipe. The wedding gift I wanted so badly from the mother-in-law who didn't consider me a friend and told me with towels I didn't qualify as family.

"Why . . . ?" *Why this? Why now?* I wouldn't expect her to pick up on anything unspoken coming from me, but surprise, surprise, she does.

"Tobin asked me to give you this, but I should have gifted it to you myself, a long time ago. I have made . . . many mistakes in my life." Her voice wavers before she cinches some invisible corset, making her already straight back impossibly straighter. "I told you marriage meant staying with your partner. But you and my son showed me it could be more. You had the courage to ask each other to do better. I see now that you were asking me to do better as your mother-in-law, for Tobin's sake. I'm hoping we'll have many years to become friends, as well as family."

Friends? With *Marijke*? I bark out an incredulous laugh, then clamp my hand over my mouth in horror.

Marijke cracks a ghost of a smile. "Perhaps I deserved that. I hope you enjoy the cake."

"Thanks. We should bake together sometime." It's polite, and maybe someday it could be true. "Say hi to Tor for me."

"I'm afraid Tor and I aren't in touch."

"Oh. But then . . ." I look over at Renata.

Marijke waves a hand in a sophisticated Euro-gesture. "Renata reached out a few days ago, and, well, one thing led to another. She's staying here until after the baby comes. Perhaps she'll even work for me part-time when she's back on her feet—did you know she was a digital sales expert at a Norwegian souvenir manufacturer?"

"Um, I didn't! Would love to know more about that. At another time. See you," I call, backing away. Back on the road, I put my boot all the way on the accelerator and pretend I have to lean into the curves. I pull up without a screech at Pendleton High, a square gray building with the functional, flat vibe of eighties-era public buildings. The Pendleton Pikas' mascot grimaces adorably from the scoreboards framing the soccer field. It's not possible to make a hamster-sized rock rabbit look scary, but kudos to the high school art department for the effort.

What's scary is the man leaning against the far goalpost, chin angled down, hands in his pockets.

Oh, my heart.

He's waiting for me, beautiful and hurt and daring to hope anyway. He's grand-gesturing right back at me.

I pull Sharon's portable speaker from the front seat. It's the size of a pop can, so the *Say Anything* effect isn't perfect when I raise it over my head. But it's loud and the sound is great and this song has been in more rom-coms than I can count, for good reason.

"Let My Love Open the Door."

Tobin's head comes up with the opening chords. The white-painted stands echo with music that's all synthesizer and optimism and reaching out with an open hand.

From the back seat, I pull out a battered gray hobbyhorse,

stick it between my legs, and start galloping toward him on my white horse.

I'm overloading just seeing him peel off the goalpost to come my way, striding across the manicured sports field that in no way resembles a dewy English hillside. He's a perfect moment come to life in denim and boots, his shoulders cocked at that hopeful, uncertain height. The crook of his elbows, the swing of his hips, even the drape of his fingers—every angle of him wrecks me with love and longing. He moves with an easy curl, not rushing, like a warm breeze.

Oh, help.

In the song, Pete Townshend offers a four-leaf clover. Damn, I should have thought of that. Tobin would've. One of those would be the best gift. Very meaningful. Argh.

I shove the speaker in my pocket so I can rip a handful of green strands from the cool ground. When I pop back up, he's stopped, uncertain.

"It's fine!" I call. "Clover! Keep going!" I think he's trying not to laugh. I don't care how ridiculous I'm being; if he's laughing, I'm doing it right.

He's dressed for the weather: soft, faded jeans, threadbare at the knees and the corners of the pockets. The high collar of his black wind shell caresses the sides of his neck.

I don't doubt he had a perfect outfit for this scenario, and I know why he didn't wear it.

As much as I have to show him I want to say yes to him and our marriage, he has to be able to say no, and trust me to hear it, and know I'll still love him.

Both of us have work to do. Today won't be the finish line of our journey back to each other.

But it can open a door.

It gets awkward as we get closer. My legs tremble from prancing. I have to fumble with my phone to turn off the music. The pocketed speaker pulls one side of my oversized coat almost to the ground.

Even after all that improv, putting myself out there doesn't come easily. I have to work hard for it. But I can do it. My successes buoy me, and my failures teach me how to get up when I fall.

I'm a mess. And I'm okay.

"Hi." I pull the coat back up my left shoulder, rolling my eyes at myself for the worst opening line of all time.

"Hey." His forelock shifts in the light breeze, an unreadable expression on the angular planes of his face.

I didn't want to practice this speech. I wanted to stay in the present and let the words come from my heart. But my heart can't talk right now, as it's busy drinking him in.

"This is for you." I thrust a handful of grass at him, stalling for time. "It's a four-leaf clover."

"I can see that," he says, accepting the uneven strands.

Delaying didn't help. When I try some *breathe in, breathe out,* I sound like I'm trying to blow out birthday candles instead of putting out the fire in my brain.

The perfect way this was going to go vaporizes like mist into dry mountain air. I don't think I can find any characters at all.

It's going to be him and me. Just a girl, standing in front of a guy.

Like it was when we split.

When we agreed to do McHuge's book.

When we drove home from Béa's wedding and burned rubber away from his dad.

Improv let us be who we needed to be, sometimes, but at all of our most important moments, we've been ourselves.

The words that finally come are "I've been so wrong." The ground is all I can look at right now, grass twitching in the wind. "I had it all backward. Taking for granted the people who loved me for who I am and knocking myself out trying to impress people who never bothered to look at me twice. And if I've gone too far, Tobe . . ."

Every breath saws like a knife in my chest. "If you don't love me anymore, I wanted to tell you it's okay to stop if you need to. You don't have to keep trying after I hurt you like that. You can say no."

He turns his face up to the sun, eyes closed against its fierce brightness. "Liz," he starts, his voice slow and careful. "It took two of us to get here. I'm not—"

"Please, Tobe. Before you say anything, just, please. Let me finish."

He breathes out long and soft, lips pressed together. When he's finished, he nods once.

Here I go. Step one. Establish trust by sharing myself. Not my strengths. My weaknesses.

"I've always felt like I was, um. Different. I liked weird stuff. I said the wrong things; I didn't have many friends. No one could pinpoint it, but I could tell I was . . . you know. A lot. Too much. So I tried to shrink myself to the right size, hoping that was the answer.

"And then I met you. You're so, so easy to love, Tobe. Not like me at all. I was afraid that one day you'd stop wanting a wife who couldn't get friends or jobs and never had good news to share, because she didn't have that magic that made people love you. No one thought someone like me deserved someone like you. People said it to my face."

He winces. "People say thoughtless shit sometimes."

I manage a small smile. "They said it to you, too, huh. At least when I'm rude, it's an accident. Anyway. I edited myself down to one square inch, and then couldn't figure out why I was so furious, trapped in this tiny box. Instead of waiting for you to leave, I pushed you away first, when all you wanted was to be on the same team. I told myself I couldn't let you save me, when it was me who was terrified I wasn't strong enough to save myself and our marriage, too.

"But you never stopped trying to save us. Even when I banned the word 'love' because I was convinced I didn't deserve yours."

He waits through my foot-shuffling, finger-rubbing pause, lips rolled between his teeth. He knows I'm not finished; he won't help me unless I ask, no matter how hard he has to hold his hands in his pockets.

"I didn't take the promotion."

"What!? Liz," he says, part surprised, part dismayed.

"But I didn't turn it down, either. I don't want to come to you with solutions I decided on alone. You were right when you said we'd gone down different paths. From now on, we need to choose our route together.

"Long-term, I don't want to work at West by North. It's never been a good fit for me. But if you want to go indie, I can tolerate Craig for another year, to give our family financial stability. Once you and McHuge get off the ground, I'll start job hunting.

"Or . . . you two can stay at West by North and develop your tour, and I can give notice. Don't worry about me," I say, heading off his objection. "I've already started asking around my network for potential openings. And it's a great opportunity for you. Built-in infrastructure and funding."

The silence is long yet fast, like I've jumped out of a plane and the earth is hurtling upward at great speed.

"Is that what you want?" Tobin asks, finally. "To give up your dream job, for me?"

I shake my head. "It's not about what *I* want. And I'm not giving up something for you, either. It's for *us,* together. For love. Because

I love you, Tobin. I never stopped. I should have told you that, every day. The truest thing about me is how I'm so in love with you."

The first little smile teases the corner of his mouth, lighting the edge of his eyes blue and gray and gold, like a snowfield at dusk. "You broke your rule."

"I broke them all. Should've known rules can't stop magic." I gesture to my clothes, and the field, and him. "You had a lot of misplaced confidence in me, thinking I'd find you here. I would never have guessed this location."

"I told my mom if you showed up dressed weird, she should tell you where I was."

"This better be weird enough. I mean, you can see the effort that went into it." My heart is doing something not right. The rest of my body isn't behaving that well, either. I wipe sweaty palms across the hobbyhorse's soft coat, remembering too late that it's borrowed.

He takes his time stepping closer. Bringing his hand to my face. "Oh, I see you, Diz."

Knockout punch. There wasn't a single thing he could say that would be hotter than telling me he *sees* me. From his satisfied look, he did it on purpose.

Tobin's other hand comes to my cheek. I close my eyes to feel it. This moment, no past, no future. Him and me, right now. I didn't realize I'd pushed hope away, afraid to give it space; now it pulses under my skin like a brand-new heart.

"You said I saved us. But you saved us, too." He's kissing me. Gently, tenderly, a brush of his heart against mine. When he pulls back, his eyes are full of stars. "You wouldn't settle for the illusion of love when we could have the real thing."

"Tobe, you don't have to say—"

He stops me with another quick kiss. He's killing me with his hands on my jaw and his mouth on my mouth. I want this conversation to never stop, and also to wrap up immediately, because I just remembered his truck is somewhere nearby.

"I do have to. I thought about your story. Why you married me." His hands leave my face, stroke my neck, slide under the coat to rest on my waist, fingers fiddling with my shirt.

"I stopped seeing you. Didn't I? I tried to distract us from what was wrong, when you needed me to look closer. I could've paid attention instead of letting you deal with our families, and your job, and everything that wasn't easy and fun. Everything I was afraid of.

"So obvious, right?" He passes a hand over his eyes with a laugh of disbelief. "Every time my dad came back, I killed myself trying to be an easy kid. The *best* son. No matter how hard I worked, I couldn't make him stay. But my tricks worked on everyone else. I'd learned people wouldn't stick around for the hard parts, so I was the most easygoing, the most fun, the most helpful.

"You were so different. In the best way." His lip trembles for the tiniest moment, his eyes sparkling with love and pain. "You wouldn't ask me for anything. You wouldn't take my help unless there was no other choice. Half the time, you opted out of the fun stuff and went off on your own. You don't even like sea shanties! But for some reason, you liked me."

"I like sea shanties," I protest.

"No, you don't." He sticks his tongue in his cheek.

"No, I don't. But I like when you sing." I kick at the dirt.

"I'll sing for you," he says, voice pitched low.

A shiver like a standing wave jolts down my spine. I glance around the field, suddenly aware of how exposed we are. "Maybe not now."

"Later, then," he agrees. "Anyhow. It was . . . I mean, it was terrifying, how much I wanted you to stay. So when things got hard, I tried to be the hero and didn't want to see how that forced you into being the sidekick, or the bad guy. I made it my mission to shine, and pushed you out of the spotlight.

"I held on so tight. Because if the person who never quit decided to quit me, then I'd know it was always me, all along." His arms clench around me, then deliberately relax.

"But you can't keep love that way. Love needs room to grow. And you, Diz—you need space to shine the way you were always meant to. I love being at the same company, but we can work in different places for a while. Or forever. I can work on the moon if you want, just as long as I get to come home to you. I love you, Diz. Enough to let you go, if that's what you need."

He kisses the tears from my cheeks, one, two.

"Don't let me go, Tobe. Never let me go, okay?" My love demands more than is possible in this world: more contact, more pressure, all of him, breaking the laws of physics. I wrap my arms around his midsection and squeeze. "Hold me tight. I want . . . I want your *molecules*."

Is it possible to love him more because of the way he laughs, like I'm delightful instead of strange? It is. Which reminds me.

"I should tell you, I'm pretty sure I'm autistic. Getting a formal diagnosis takes time, but I did some reputable screening tests, and . . . yeah. The results aren't subtle."

He strokes my hair, spreading a lock between his fingers so the strands pick up the sun. "If it makes sense to you, we'll go with it. You know that doesn't change how I feel. But if it changes what you do, or what you need from me, that's cool. Just tell me."

"I'm still figuring it out. For now, I only need you, Tobe."

He slips his shoulders under mine and lifts me up so I can push my face into his cheek, spread my hands wide across his back, wrap my legs around his hips. We stay and stay this way, while he rocks us back and forth.

Magic. It's the perfect word for everything Tobin and I thought we were doing, because it isn't real. You can't make problems disappear any easier than you can vanish a quarter; you can only hide them in your other hand.

Just like you can't pursue full-body contact in a public place, no matter how much you want to disrespect very expensive clothes by tearing them off and throwing them to the turf.

When I ease back on my attempts to burrow inside him, he lowers my feet to the ground.

"What should we do about work? Did you and McHuge discuss anything?"

"Lyle thinks Craig's a weasel and trust is more important than easy money. I agree. We have interest from a possible angel investor, though. If we close the deal, you could quit West by North with no reservations. And if we don't, follow your heart anyway. We'll find a way for you to go after your dreams, Diz."

"Meh. I think dreams might be things you make, instead of things you chase."

"Then I want to make mine with you. If you'll have me." His work-roughened hands strike against my skin like flint to tinder as he gathers my fingers and brings them to his lips.

It's midday, and my eyes are full of stars because he put them there. He's smiling, all sunshine and no shadows. I'm going to make a note: *Think of Tobin's smile.* I'll keep it at the top of all of my lists.

"Where's the truck?"

"In the teachers' parking lot. I thought you drove." His eyelids drop a fraction. He knows where I'm going with this.

"I did." I grab his hand, tugging so he'll follow me. "But my car doesn't work for what I'm planning."

"Oh, no?" He cocks one side of his mouth upward and I see now what he meant about crooked smiles and delightful secrets. It feels like the perfect moment to rise on my toes, lean in, and touch my crooked smile to his. Some people might think our smiles are too different to fit together. But they do.

We do.

Chapter Twenty-Nine

Players **establish** a relationship in the first beat. Since relationships are always in the process of changing and mutating, after the actors have discovered their relationship, it changes to its **potential** in the second, and comes to a **resolution** in the third.

—*Truth in Comedy*

One year later

The first thing I did after joining Keller was get pregnant.

"Ah, this is the worst, aaaaaaaagh, Tobin!" Liquid pain, liquid pain, liquid pain. I scream the four worst swears I know, back-to-back.

"I'm here, Diz. You're doing great, keep going."

"Noooooooooooo, I can't. No no no no no, I'm too tired." I'm not too tired to crush his hand, but he won't point that out if he knows what's good for him.

"Yes, you can. You're doing it. I see the head, we're almost there."

I melt into a sad, sweaty puddle as the contraction eases, flopping my head toward the labor and delivery nurse. "Are you sure it's too late for an epidural? I'll donate a four-night Quiet Raft tour to your holiday raffle. It's Keller's fastest-growing expedition. Very popular with people in high-stress jobs. Please."

She laughs and calls the doctors for delivery.

I plaster Tobin's hand across my damp, scarlet face. "The miracle of birth is a big, huge scam," I moan through his fingers.

Such a scam. First of all, it takes days. We embarrassed ourselves by coming to the hospital yesterday, right when my contractions decided to slow down. Then, scared of another false alarm, I stuck it out at home until it was almost too late, despite Tobin going bananas with Google and a stopwatch. My birth plan was a single word, "epidural," and like every birth plan, it went wrong from the drop.

"I love you so much." My husband smooths gross hair off my forehead to drop a kiss on my sweaty skin. Rude. How dare he imply I'm beautiful at a time like this.

The obstetrician blows into the room, opening a crackly package of gloves.

"A couple of pushes, Mom, and we'll have this baby out. Dad, can you give us an assist?"

Sharon told me this would happen—a roomful of people elbows deep in my hoo-ha, my beloved spouse hauling one leg practically up to my armpit.

She also said I wouldn't be embarrassed, which was a lie.

I turn to the nurse. "Promise you'll forget me. You don't know my name. You never saw my vagina. I wasn't here."

"What about me? Don't I get some threats?" The doctor settles herself on a rolling stool.

"You called me 'Mom.' I think we've established you don't know my name. Oooohhhhhhhhh, here it comes. Aaaaaaah, Tobin, your hand. On my face. HAND ON MY FACE NOW."

Maybe he puts it on. I think he must. I'm not here to feel it; I'm inside myself, a creature of muscles and knowing, and it's happening.

Yes, I think. Yes.

"Congratulations, it's a girl!"

Tobin sobs like we didn't already know the sex, his face transformed with surprise and joy. He kisses me with a new kiss, something I recognize as love and relief and a deep sense of pulling together, toward something bigger than ourselves.

"Go." I flap my hand at him. "Cut the cord. Guard the baby."

He takes a video with one hand, sawing at the cord with the other. Legendary under-eye shadows decorate his face, from forty-eight straight hours of staring at my belly.

I don't know if I've ever loved him more.

"Very small tear." The doctor cracks a pack of sutures. "We'll see you again in two years, Mrs. Renner-Lewis."

From the infant warmer, Tobin grins at me. I stick out my tongue. He would *love* to have another baby in two years. He'd be thrilled if we fielded an entire hockey team, but I'm holding him at two with the option for a third.

We'll see how he feels when he's changing half the diapers. Although last week I spied him practicing on a honeydew melon, callused fingers fumbling with the fastenings. As the stay-at-home parent he'll have plenty of chances to do the real thing.

And then she's on my chest, nude, a couple of those striped baby blankets across her frowny forehead. She's looking right at me, her eyes big pools of eternity.

Oh, no, I'm in love. Again.

I turn to Tobin accusingly. "She looks like *you.*"

When I wake up from my post-breastfeeding nap, Tobin's got his daughter cradled against one golden forearm, her tiny head cupped in his huge palm. She's wrinkled and red, with a heck of a conehead; he's looking at her like she's simultaneously the most beautiful human ever invented and the keeper of all the secrets of the universe.

My heart doesn't miss the chance to flip-flop in my chest at the piercing, exquisite tenderness between this man and our baby. And he was a goddamn rock during the delivery.

And during the pregnancy. About everything, and I mean *everything,* from insisting on a perfect attendance record at my prenatal visits to being my safe harbor in the hormonal and emotional storm of the last nine months.

"We should pick a name," I say, wanting to be part of his reverie.

He looks up, startled. His face is a study in unabashed adoration, softness joined by something fierce as he looks from the baby to me.

"Knock, knock," our nurse calls, bustling in. "Time for a temperature check." She scoops the bundled-up baby burrito away from Tobin. He trails after them with his phone to take another hundred pictures.

"Perfect. Dad, you're keeping this baby nice and warm. Does she have a pediatrician?"

We smile and say yes to all the standard questions. When the nurse gets to the part about using precautions to avoid unplanned second pregnancies, both of us smirk.

This was only a half-planned *first* pregnancy. It happened during the blur of leaving West by North, getting my autism diagnosis, starting my new job at Keller, and, yes, hanging out with my new work friends.

It was a strange feeling at first, moving through the same world, as the same person, with a whole different understanding of myself. I used to accommodate people by changing my face, editing my thoughts and words, dialing down my intensity. But my new colleagues insisted on accommodating *me*, instead of the other way around. They invited me to every party and networking event, because I told them I liked being asked to join even though I only sometimes wanted to go.

Although I said yes to enough late nights that I messed up my routine a couple of mornings in a row. Tobin found me clutching my pill pack, counting and recounting.

"Whoops. Missed a few?" His mild tone should've tipped me off.

"Yeah. Whoops. We're probably okay, but we need to use condoms for the rest of the month."

He passed me a cup of coffee and curled his hand around mine. "Yes, and . . . what if we didn't?"

Our daughter happened to us at the perfect moment. We didn't yet know we'd reached the place where we could ask each other for something that big. But both of us felt how right it was when we did.

We'll take it easy this summer. Tobin will hang around with McHuge part time, welcoming their first clients; Stellar's filling in at The Love Boat (honestly, McHuge) when Tobin's home, in between figuring out her next career move.

Tobin's back, nestling the baby between us. She smells irresistibly new, fluffs of pale hair sticking out under the hospital-issued tube sock of a hat. I could watch her making those sleep faces all day.

"Hold that thought." Tobin raises his phone for a selfie. He's cute, wanting a picture of me doing silly love eyes at a sleeping baby.

"Can I send it to the baby announcement list?" He flips the phone to me.

The baby's perfect. Tobin and I look wrecked. My smile is kind of pained, because the freezing in my stitches is wearing off. The harsh hospital light isn't doing anyone any favors.

It's the most beautiful photo ever.

"Send away."

Tobin's phone lights up with notifications. Stellar. McHuge. Béa and Stéphane send a pic of Béa's ginormous belly: We're right behind you!

Marijke and Renata send a video of Tobin's one-year-old half brother (the best-dressed baby in Pendleton, by far) clapping to squeals of encouragement. Six months ago, Marijke built a basement suite for Renata and little Aksel to entice them to stay, and now they have a shockingly functional multigenerational household, and Renata's working at Marijke's company. Can't say I saw it coming, but they're great neighbors and Renata and I bonded over the one million weird pregnancy questions I asked her.

Sharon emails a huge gift certificate for a fancy baby store, and threatens to pull her angel investment in The Love Boat if Tobin answers so much as a single one of her emails in the next two weeks. Although she funded their project outside of the Keller umbrella, she's been coaxing McHuge and Tobin to consider joining the company. If they do, I might think about transferring to their division. Tobin and I are ready to work together without losing sight of who we are individually. And I have a lot of ideas about where their tours can go next.

Another photo pops onto Tobin's screen—Amber must've given her phone to Eleanor so she could take this blurry, off-center shot of herself with a smear of orange fur in the foreground.

Tobin and I made the heart-wrenching decision to leave the cat with Eleanor. He was too old to move again. Besides, anyone could see Yeti and Eleanor were in love. He's thriving on a diet of cheese and pure adoration.

Welcome to the club!

Amber's next text is a voucher for a local meal delivery service.

Not because you can't do it all. Because you shouldn't have to.

Aww, that's nice. She didn't have to add that clarification—we're doing pretty well at respecting each other's boundaries—but I love how careful and considerate she is.

We get a bounce back from Tor's phone number. Not surprising; he hasn't shown his face since Renata moved in with Marijke. But Tobin's okay with that these days.

My husband levers himself out of bed, fixes up the blankets, then creeps under the covers beside me. His body is long and warm and safe, curling around the baby and me, telling me he'll protect us at this moment when my body is hurt and I'm vulnerable.

"We have to pick a name for this kid," I say, messing with her fingers, their nails purple-pink like the tiniest, most perfect shells on the beach.

"Okay. I'm thinking." Tobin's eyes are closed. His voice is soft, blurry.

He's not thinking.

"Lola." I'm messing with him.

He doesn't bite.

"Elsa. Redfern."

He tries not to smile, but I can tell he wants to.

"Tobin. Wake u—"

"Jess," he says, out of the blue.

"Jess wasn't on our short list—oh," I say, catching the echo.

Jess. It sounds like "yes." "Jess Andie," I say. *Yes, and.*

I tuck my head in the crook of his shoulder. Find his hand so I can stroke his knuckles with my thumb. Twirl his wedding ring.

Tell him everything.

Acknowledgments

Once upon a time, when I was an awkward, nerdy young bookworm who liked to read the acknowledgments section, I truly believed authors did all the work themselves and were more or less forced to thank a lot of people just to be polite. Having now written a book, all I can say to that is: hahahahahaha GOOD ONE, YOUNG MAGGIE. It's a pleasure and a privilege to be grateful to so many excellent people.

Claire Friedman, my incomparable agent, saved my life countless times with actual CPR—or at least that's what it felt like after every writerly heart attack, when my eyes fluttered open and she was the first person I saw.

Lisa Bonvissuto, my brilliant editor, never stopped working to make *Rules* the best book it could be in every way, all while fielding a cringeworthy number of incredibly overinclusive emails. Thank you to the amazing people at St. Martin's Griffin, including editor Christina Lopez; marketer Kejana Ayala; publicist Alyssa Gammello; production team Chrisinda Lynch, Kiffin Steurer, and Jeremy Haiting; and copy editor Sara Thwaite.

For making my book so beautiful, I owe my deepest, most emo thanks to cover artist Andrew Lyons, cover designer Olga Grlic, and interior designer Omar Chapa.

My devoted critique partners Alexandra Kiley and Sarah Brenton are my sisters in crime, my go-to companions and conspirators, and pretty much my cowriters at this point. No words can express what it means to be able to drape myself across the group chat in those moments when writing is too hard (which is all the moments).

My sister, Sarah, and her dog, Charlie, gently untangled many a plot problem on our pandemic walks, for which Sarah gets a flood of random emoji and all my love forever, and Charlie gets a lift into the hatchback anytime.

I would not be here without the support and encouragement of the writing communities I've had the good fortune to belong to. Much love to the RomDoms, Reapers, 2024 Debuts, Team Claire, Bananas, Friday Kiss, SF2.0, and The Kitchen Party.

To everyone who supported *Rules* along the way: Livy Hart and Jessica Joyce for reading more than once and cheering just as much the second time; Courtney Kae, Regina Black, Michelle Cruz, Sarah T. Dubb, Naina Kumar, Ella Sinclair, Nikki Payne, and Ingrid Pierce for their invaluable early feedback; and Amanda Ciancarelli, Anya Simha, Tania Lan, Dani Frank, Amanda Wilson, Laya Brusi, and Tobie Carter for beta reading and cheering. Very special thanks to Stephanie Archer, who won the Olympic Pentathlon of support: she was a primary source, an early reader, a late reader, a blurber, and generally a spectacular person and amazing friend.

To the rock-star authors who blurbed this book, in alphabetical order: Stephanie Archer, Ruby Barrett, Rosie Danan, Helena Hunting, Jessica Joyce, Chloe Liese, Annabel Monaghan, and Alicia Thompson. There's no proper way to repay this gift, unless you need help burying a body, in which case you know who to call.

A big "yes, and" to improv wise women Helen Camisa and Della Haddock of Hot Snack Comedy. Any improv inaccuracies are mine. Additional research came from classic texts *Truth in Comedy* and *Impro for Storytellers,* as well as scholarly publications of therapists and comedians who made the link between improv comedy, social anxiety, and couples' therapy long before I did.

I had the great good fortune to belong to both the Pitch Wars and RevPit communities. Editor Megan Records had the wisdom to help *Rules* grow into its strengths and let go of its pretensions. Rosie Danan and Ruby Barrett's mentorship and friendship have been a gift beyond price. Deepest appreciation to the Pitch Wars mentors, mentees, and liaisons of 2020, and to Jenny L. Howe and Susan Lee, whose advice made all the difference.

What I know about love, I learned from the very best. To K, who now has something of a cult following on my Instagram for his romance hero exploits: I'm your biggest fan, too. And to A, who generously gives her plot-whispering skills to her mama's books even though she isn't allowed to read them until she's thirty. You two started this book, you're ending it, and everything in between is for you, too.

About the Author

Lindsey Gibeau

Maggie North lives in Ottawa, Canada, with the man she met in ninth grade, their kid, and a rotating cast of hypoallergenic aquarium friends. Her hobbies include long-distance open-water swimming, saving the world, and being relentlessly Canadian. She enjoys being autistic a lot more since she received her diagnosis as an adult. *Rules for Second Chances* is her first novel.